''If you go any farther, we'll end up in your bed,''

Stewart said, glancing up the stairs, her next line of retreat. "Not that I object, you understand. The parlor's taken."

"No," Jane said. It was a "no," but it lacked conviction. She felt the need to explain. "You see, we were both surprised by the crash of the tree. Then there was the emotion of seeing that man possibly dead, then the relief of his narrow escape. It's not what you think—between us—you and me. We were awakened so suddenly and so violently from sleep—"

"I wasn't sleeping," he said.

"I was," she countered. "Fast asleep. Deep asleep. Dreamlessly asleep."

"You led me on this evening."

"You provoked me."

"You rose to the challenge...."

Dear Reader,

There is a lot to look for this month from Harlequin Historicals.

Sweet Seduction by Julie Tetel is the first of two intriguing stories set in Maryland during the early 1800s. Heroine Jane Shaw was raised as a Southern belle, but she is more than a match for the British soldiers who sequester her family's home. And don't miss the sequel, *Sweet Sensations,* coming in July.

Readers following the TAGGARTS OF TEXAS! series by Ruth Jean Dale will be delighted to discover the prequel to the earlier books in this month's lineup. *Legend!* is the story of Boone, the Taggart who started it all by turning the little town of Jones, Texas, on its ear.

Captured Moment by Coral Smith Saxe is set during the California mining days. Straight off the boat from the old country, the impish Rowen Trelarken stumbles into an immediate series of misadventures, dragging an unwilling Alec McKenzie along for the ride.

Frenchwoman Elise de Vire marries Sir Adam Saker as an act of revenge, but the force of the attraction between them places them both in mortal danger in *Beloved Deceiver,* a medieval tale from Laurie Grant.

Four new romances from Harlequin Historicals. We hope you enjoy them.

Sincerely,

Tracy Farrell
Senior Editor

Sweet Seduction

JULIE TETEL

Harlequin Books

TORONTO • NEW YORK • LONDON
AMSTERDAM • PARIS • SYDNEY • HAMBURG
STOCKHOLM • ATHENS • TOKYO • MILAN
MADRID • WARSAW • BUDAPEST • AUCKLAND

Harlequin Historicals first edition April 1993

ISBN 0-373-28767-4

SWEET SEDUCTION

Books by Julie Tetel

Harlequin Historicals

Sweet Suspicions #128
Sweet Seduction #167

JULIE TETEL

has always loved both history and romance, making it easy for her to love reading and writing historical romances. She is from a suburb of Chicago and currently lives in Durham, North Carolina. She has two sons, two careers, at least two points of view, and one husband.

For Francis and Gerard

Chapter One

North Point, Maryland
The Shaw Plantation
August 1814

With all the manner of a young woman about to make a grand entrance, Jane drew a deep breath, daintily lifted her skirts, and proceeded to climb out her bedroom window. Without looking at the ground some fifteen feet below, she grasped the thick oak branch that reached out to her, scrambled across it and shinnied down the trunk. She landed noiselessly, liking the feel of soft earth against her bare feet. Hardly pausing to dust the bark shags off her calico, she lifted her skirts again, less daintily, and dashed to the first outbuilding, fifty yards from the house.

Once behind the protective shelter of the tobacco shed, Jane stopped and peeked around the corner to make sure she had not been seen. She knew she had little cause to worry on that score, for the Chesapeake fog lay so thick that the house had dissolved into little more than an eerie outline. It was unlikely that any redcoat billeted in the barn some hundred yards away could have seen more than a spirit sprinting through a cloud.

It was also unlikely that any redcoat was up and about at this ghostly hour before dawn. Assured that she had, once again, made a safe escape, Jane struck out down the path behind the shed, her feet knowing the way. Although this was the coolest time of day, the fog was already lying hot and oppressive over her father's plantation. It held in its wet embrace all the familiar late-summer scents of white magnolia and moss rose and mimosa. Traveling quickly, Jane stopped only once to unbutton her bodice a ways and flap the two halves, creating a soft rush of air against her breasts. She plucked the damp fabric away from her back, knowing that it would be plastered there again within the minute. Then, hitching her skirts again, she ran on.

She reached a slope leading to the bank, slipped down it ungracefully, and came to a stop in front of a little rowboat tied to a weathered mooring. Releasing the rope, she launched the vessel, dappling her feet in the muddy waters, not caring much about soiling her skirts. She hopped into the boat and rowed across the wide backwater of the Patapsco River, which slumbered sluggishly in the heat.

On the other side of the river, she secured the boat, climbed the opposing bank and ran through an open field to the edge of thick trees. Checking her bearings, she entered the forest at a precise point and found her way to the first water oak, the second, and then, finally, the third. She slumped against the last tree, heart pounding, and as breathless as any woman who had ever awaited a lover.

She lifted the frizzing wisps of hair that had escaped her kerchief and let them fall. She flapped the two halves of her bodice. She shook out her skirts. She yawned. The protective mists had not yet begun to burn off, but her impatience was rapidly sliding toward anxiety. She could not afford to wait much longer.

Finally, the tall, lean figure of a man materialized some ten yards from her.

Jane pushed herself away from the tree. When she saw who it was, surprise crossed her face, but it was mild and without concern. "Mr. Skinner!" she hailed.

As he approached, his gaunt frame and wizened features came into focus. He was wearing dirty overalls and a torn shirt and was puffing badly from the heat and his haste. "Lucas couldn't make it, Miss Jane," he explained, mopping his brow with a wet rag of a handkerchief. "Some redcoats are suspicious of what he's been doing these past several mornings." He fought for breath. "We thought it best if I come today. I'm old, and the redcoats haven't yet paid me no mind. I slipped out early to milk the cows. Best be getting back, though. So, what's the news?"

"No maneuvers in the immediate offing, though I finally heard the total number of General Ross's troops. They are three thousand five hundred," she said, with the tiniest ray of hope.

Ben Skinner nodded. "Three thousand five hundred," he repeated. "I'll pass that on. The information should be in the hands of the Fifth Maryland—God love 'em—by nightfall."

Jane shrugged. "I wish I had more. Tell Mr. Lucas's contact that General Ross will not be moving out from Shaw Plantation to attack Baltimore tonight, or even, I would say, tomorrow. I would have heard the plans."

Ben Skinner frowned. "Does your father know what you are doing, Missy Shaw?"

Jane shook her head. "When Johnnie and I set up this chain, we decided that it was best that our father not be in on it. He's an honest man, and we love him dearly, but he has a face that can't hide a useful lie. It was out of the question, anyway, that he should do it, for if he were to be caught . . ."

"The British would do less harm to you than to either of your menfolk," the old farmer finished on a wheeze.

Jane looked up at him, half defiantly. "Am I wrong?"

"No, but—"

She cut in. "No buts! It's the least I can do, since the redcoats have chosen to make their headquarters in the dining room, just below my bedroom!"

"And you can hear them clear?"

"Every word," Jane replied with satisfaction, "every aside, every scrape of their—*our*—chairs."

He coughed, bringing up phlegm, and said irritably, "They've a gall, taking over the Shaw Plantation!"

"And then some!" Jane agreed. "It's been a week already, and they act as if we had invited them! The staff officers have taken possession of the lower floor—politely enough,'' she added with asperity. ''They ordered the family to retire upstairs. Yes, I would say they've a gall!''

Ben Skinner took in Jane's provocative dishevelment for the first time. ''Now, look here, Missy Shaw, with the redcoats sleeping under the same roof, I'd like to think you're well protected.'' He wheezed again. ''And that you're modest!''

Jane grinned. ''My father hardly lets me out of his sight. Oh, it's the diligent farmer he is at the henhouse, keeping the foxes at bay.''

The old farmer wagged a finger. ''And don't you go teasing, neither, Missy Shaw! Soldiers are soldiers, when all is said.''

Jane winked. ''There's none that tempt me!'' she replied. Before she could be reprimanded for this impudence, she continued, looking out beyond the forest to the ever-lightening sky. ''We'd both better go.'' She glanced back at the old man. He did not look as if he could keep up the pace of meeting her before dawn without doing harm to his health. ''Do you think Mr. Lucas could come again tomorrow?''

Ben Skinner shook his head. ''My son is being watched real close, miss.'' He added that the whole farm was under careful watch, it being so strategically located on the main road to Baltimore.

''His wife, then?''

''It's too close to her lying-in.''

Jane had forgotten the young Mrs. Skinner's pregnancy. That was the only reason Ben Skinner's son had been exempted from the draft. ''Well, if your farm is being watched so closely, you should not do this twice, either. Send Michael, then,'' she suggested. ''He's a good man, and he knows me.''

Ben Skinner promised that someone from the farm would be in the forest before sunrise tomorrow. He would not, he vowed, be the one to break the chain. No, sir, not at the first link.

They parted. Jane retraced her steps, though not as quickly as before, for the heat was heavier now. Her slowness served to double her fear, for in the rising sun the dense mists were quickly dissipating into a gauzy opal haze. She could be seen at a hundred yards now, she judged. She ran on, despite the stitch growing in her side, panting lightly with the effort.

The effort. The effort kept her going. If the Fifth Maryland could know, could absolutely *know*, that General Ross was not moving his Forty-fourth Foot out tonight or tomorrow, that piece of information could prove invaluable to the American militia, which was severely underfunded and in disarray. Jane knew that they needed all the help they could get. Although the Fifth Maryland was an elite volunteer militia under the command of Lieutenant Colonel Starrett, they had the ill luck to be fighting alongside Brigadier General Stansbury's sadly equipped militia brigade down from Baltimore. The two forces together numbered about four thousand, which was five hundred more men than Ross's Forty-fourth. However, the British were well trained, well equipped, and disciplined. Experienced, too, since most of them were veterans who had served Napoleon a defeat in April.

Jane knew better than most of her compatriots just how great a threat to American independence was the British occupation. During the past five nights, through the floorboards of her bedroom, she had heard the precise and appalling figures confirming British superiority in every arena. With her bedroom rug flipped up and her ear to the wood, she had heard the British general Robert Ross state, matter-of-factly, the number of men and guns he could move with ease over the salt marshes and wetlands. She had also heard that the British admiral Cochrane had swept into Chesapeake Bay unopposed, and that the American fleet was outnumbered by British ships one thousand to fifteen.

To distract herself from the pain in her side, Jane pinned her attention on all the numbers rattling ominously in her brain.

One thousand British ships to the Americans' fifteen!

Her next step fell more slowly.

Three thousand five hundred British in the region. Four thousand Americans in Washington alone.

Better, but not good enough, for she had heard the British assessment of those American troops. Since the Americans in the District of Columbia were under the command of the buffoon Winder—given the title of major general by the Americans—General Ross reckoned to encounter little more than an eggshell defense.

Jane stopped dead in her tracks, unable to continue.

But Johnnie is one of those troops!

One. That was the only number that mattered. One man. Johnnie. Yes, one was enough to keep her going. No, make that two, for she would count Bobby, as well. Two men, then, Johnnie and Bobby. One man would keep her feet going. Two men would make her feet fly.

Jane got her second wind, a rush of energy and emotion that pumped from her heart to her legs.

She knew now that she would make it back to the house before first light. She would keep alive the human chain of communication she had hastily rigged up with her younger brother, Johnnie, during his most recent leave, and keep the information flowing from Shaw Plantation through the chain that crisscrossed farms and settlements and villages and towns, leading to Baltimore and Washington. Most crucially, she would continue listening through the floorboards to hear the British devise their strategy, and learn whether their immediate objective would be Washington, the capital, or Baltimore, the thriving seaport.

Just as dawn was breaking, promising another day of blazing sun and torrid heat, she arrived back at the tobacco shed, panting in earnest. Peeking around it, she saw nothing in the yard, and no movement from the house. She waited and peeked again. The barn showed no signs of life from the soldiers billeted therein. She lifted her skirts and tore across the yard to the tree, scrambled up the trunk, slid across the thick branch, and nearly tumbled through the open window of her bedroom.

Safe! she thought, with profound relief, as she looked back into the empty yard below her. Then she turned hastily—too hastily—and knocked over a chair by the window. It clattered against the wall before falling to the floor with a dull thud.

She muttered a mild oath, ripped off her dress, kicked it under her bed, then jumped under the covers. When she put her head back, she remembered her kerchief. She snatched it from her hair and stuffed it under the pillows. Closing her eyes, she lay still.

She had moved none too quickly. Within the minute, her door was flung open, and in strode a British underofficer who had been sleeping in the dining room below. He was followed by General Ross, the commanding officer, and Jane's father. Mr. Shaw was still in his flowing nightshirt, and his wisping red hair was wild with the disorder of sleep. He was cursing the redcoats' "demmed impudence" and "severe lack of manners," all with no effect whatsoever on his "guests."

"I heard a noise, sir," the half-dressed young man explained to his superior. "I thought there might be an infiltrator come to the house by way of the upstairs."

At the commotion, Jane cracked her eyes and feebly raised herself on her elbows, then sank back, as if too weak to maintain the position.

"Now, look here—" Mr. Shaw began on an angry bluster, but he was cut off.

"Thank you, Richards," General Ross said calmly, striding to the foot of the bed and looking critically down at the young woman lying so still. Then he moved to the wall with the window. "It must have been the chair that fell," he added with a good deal of suspicion in his voice as he looked out the window at the big old tree extending a thick arm toward the house. He looked across at his host. "Hiding any spies, Mr. Shaw?"

"Now, look here, you demmed redcoats!" Mr. Shaw expostulated with force. He waved away Lieutenant Richards and marched round the side of the bed. "My daughter has been feeling poorly," he continued, looking down at the flushed Jane with concern, "which is why she had to retire early last night. She fell into a fit of coughing right after dinner, as you'll recall. Now, there is a logical explanation to why the chair fell, so you needn't go searching through her cupboard or beneath her bed!" Under his breath, he muttered indignantly, "Demmed redcoats in my daughter's bedchamber!"

General Ross returned to the bedside. He had not had time to shrug into his scarlet coat, yet he retained an air of calm authority. "Miss Shaw?" he inquired.

Jane cracked an eye and made as if it took her an effort to focus on the general. She uttered one word: "Cold."

Mr. Shaw glanced back at the window. "You wanted to close the window, child?" he asked.

She nodded.

He stretched out a hand and put it to her forehead. "Ye gods! She's burning hot!" he cried. He patted her cheeks. They were hot, too. "Jane. Can you hear me, child?" he demanded anxiously. When she nodded, he asked, "You feel cold? Were you trying to close the window, my dear, and fell against the chair?"

She nodded again.

In some alarm, Mr. Shaw grabbed one of his daughter's hands from beneath the covers. Her hands were hot, her fingers were hot. "She says she's cold, yet she's burning hot. She's delirious," he said, over his shoulder, looking as if he held General Ross personally responsible for his daughter's condition.

General Ross brushed aside his host, his expression changing dramatically when he, too, put his hand to Jane's forehead. He felt her neck, even pressed his fingers over her shoulder and down her back. She was drenched in sweat.

"Cold," she croaked again. She remembered to cough once or twice, with great, weary effort. Silently thanking her honest, innocent father for his beautiful interpretation, she managed, weakly, "Yes. Wanted to close the window. Fell over the chair."

General Ross took up her hand, which she made as limp as possible. He put it back down again and then patted it absently. He turned to Jacob Shaw and said, "I see. She is very hot. I'll call the medic."

Shaw turned a fierce eye on the general. "There'll not be another man in my daughter's bedchamber, by God! Not another man, do you hear? I'll tend to her myself! Myself and none other!"

General Ross mentally debated the matter briefly, then nodded. "Very well," he said, suddenly seeing this early-morning episode as a complete waste of his time. He turned to Lieutenant Richards, who was looking mulish that his alarm had not produced better results than evidence of a sickly female, and summarily dismissed him.

General Ross did not immediately leave, however. When Jane cracked her eyes again, she saw her father still hovering at her bedside, and the British general standing motionless and silent in the center of her room.

For one horrible moment, Jane wondered whether the general was listening for sounds coming from the dining room below her bedchamber. Now that the household had been roused, it was natural that the officers should congregate in the room they used as their headquarters. She was glad that her thick old carpet absorbed the sounds from below. The only clear sounds to be heard were those that drifted in through her window, the sounds of the soldiers in the barn rising for the day. Her panic passed, and General Ross left the room without another word to her father.

"Jane, Jane," Mr. Shaw said, worry leaping from his voice. "Are you delirious, child? Can you hear me?"

It would not do to show a change of face now, so Jane responded weakly and conveyed the idea that all she needed was a cool cloth on her head, a drink of water, and a good morning's sleep. When her father withdrew to find her a basin of water, Jane immediately flipped off the covers, for she was truly burning up under their weight and her sweat. She bit her lip to suppress her grin at having fooled the best of the British army. The only negative side of her feigned illness was that she would have to spend a long and boring day confined to her bedchamber.

* * *

When he left Jane Shaw's room, General Ross was satisfied. He descended the stairs and strode out onto the wide front porch. He was crossing the yard when he saw a soldier, still in shirtsleeves, whose alertness had caught his eye in the past several weeks.

"You there, Stewart," he said, recalling the man's name. "I want you to find Smyth for me."

"The medic, sir? Yes, sir." Stewart replied, saluting.

"And send him to the house," General Ross instructed with a nod to the old mansion.

"Someone sick, sir?" Stewart asked.

"Just the young woman. Fever."

"Should I send Smyth to her room?"

"God, no!" General Ross replied, almost on a laugh. "I'll have Shaw at my throat! I simply want Smyth to be in the house in case she takes a turn for the worse, and Shaw can't handle her alone. It's a precaution. Tell Smyth to wait in the parlor next to the dining room."

"Yes, sir. Right away, sir." Stewart turned to go.

"Oh, and Stewart," General Ross added as an afterthought, "since you're less susceptible to the heat than most, it seems, I'll have you join the reconnaissance party this afternoon. We'll be going at least as far as Sparrows Point to check on possible future anchorage positions on the Patapsco."

"Yes, sir. Pleased to, sir," Stewart replied promptly, and added, "but all men sweat."

General Ross smiled. "Wretched heat. You're one of the few not wilting. I did not mean to imply that you are not suffering." His eyes swept his soldier and took in the young man's medium build and light, though muscular, frame. "The beefier men aren't taking it as well as you. You're a good man, Stewart. Dismissed."

Stewart saluted and turned smartly on his heels to go in search of the medic. He executed this duty as happily as he would the reconnaissance mission later that afternoon. He was a man General Ross could count on to carry out all orders assigned him. However, Stewart had neglected to mention to his commanding officer that he had been up for a stroll well before dawn this morning and he had seen a young woman leave her bedroom by a branch outside her window and return over an hour later.

Good soldier Stewart kept this information to himself, for his private enjoyment. He had enjoyed, in particular, the view of her backside he had had as she climbed up the tree. It had left him with a lasting image of her petticoats and drawers, which had appeared to him as snowy white as a winter camellia.

Chapter Two

J ames Stewart squinted into the blue afternoon haze at the westering sun. His eyes were deep-set, and a color that was not quite green. His hair was as undecided as his eyes, being somewhere between brown and blond. There was nothing indeterminate about his features, however. His nose was straight and defined. His mouth was well shaped and mobile. His jaw was lean and rather long, and showed a scrabble of beard of about three days' growth. Beneath the stubble, his skin was tanned a deep bronze. His thick hair badly needed cutting. It was tied back at the nape and topped by a black leather shako.

The day had begun hot and muggy, and had only gotten worse. By midafternoon, at General Ross's command, Stewart had had to muffle himself in his uniform coat. The coat was regulation red, swallow-tailed and with a high choker collar; however, he was allowed to wear it unbuttoned, a small concession to the heat. His white shirt and trousers of white drill, along with the coat's facing, were better described now as gray, and he was slowly baking in the clothing, which took no account of comfort or climate.

Hot and scruffy though he was, Infantryman James Stewart was one of the better examples of Britain's finest to be found on the Shaw Plantation. This was to say that he was dressed and upright, not yet having succumbed to the heat. In his ability to withstand the heat, Stewart had the advantage of his fellow soldiers, in that he had grown up in such a climate. He had even known worse.

Stewart had not intended to distinguish himself in any way in the Forty-fourth, but if his habits of economical movement had caught the general's eye and won him a place in Ross's reconnaissance party this afternoon, he was not complaining. He welcomed the opportunity to size up the situation with his own eyes, and it felt good to be once again astride a horse, instead of plodding on foot.

So the party of ten men rode out from the Shaw Plantation to see what they could see of this bit of the strategic North Point. Stewart was near the rear, behind the four underofficers, who, in turn, followed General Ross. Stewart would have advised waiting another hour or two for the sun to complete more of its arc, but he had not been consulted on the timing of the sortie, and he had not volunteered his opinion. He was torn between an admiration of the general's flat refusal to adapt to the climate and a belief in his commanding officer's folly.

The party trotted down the drive from the plantation, then fanned out to wade through ripening fields that might never be harvested in this year of war. They fell in two by two when they crossed over to the scraggly Long Log Lane, which curved around this spit of land that thrust itself into the Chesapeake. Traveling five or six miles, they surveyed the creeks that poked their fingers into the North Point from the Patapsco River. Some fifteen miles upriver, at the head of the estuary, lay Baltimore.

They passed the Skinner farm and the local meeting house on Bread and Cheese Creek, encountering no one. Then, two miles later, they sighted a pair of men walking, shouldering muskets. The reconnaissance party cantered ahead, kicking up clouds of dust from the dry lane, and caught up with the two just as they were attempting to dive into a thicket of trees.

"You there!" General Ross bellowed. "Halt!"

The men on foot were quickly surrounded by ten on horses. "Trying to escape?" General Ross demanded.

"Why, no, sir, why should we, sir?" the one answered. His tone was respectful enough, but there was something cheeky in his smile.

General Ross peered down at the men, who were unshaven and on the thin side. They were poorly dressed, one in a gray coat and one in a brown coat.

"American army?" the general demanded.

They shook their heads solemnly. "No, sir," and "Never think it, sir," they said, one after the other.

The general nodded to their firearms. "And those, my boys?"

"For shooting quail, sir," one said.

"For our dinner, sir," the other added.

General Ross considered the two ill-kempt men at length. Then, surprising the rest of his company, he looked back over his shoulder and called, "Stewart! Come forward!"

Stewart felt the eyes of the soldiers in the rear of the party slide toward him curiously. Keeping his expression bland and his gaze straight ahead, he wheeled his horse out from the others and walked it up to General Ross. "Sir?" he said, when he had drawn next to the general's black stallion.

"What's your opinion, soldier?" the general asked.

"Of the men, sir?" Stewart replied, casting impersonal eyes over the two ruffians. "They look to be civilians, sir."

"Most American militia look to be civilians," was the general's rather arrogant rejoinder.

Stewart smiled appreciatively. "True." He added, "The Americans wear blue."

Stewart had merely stated the obvious, and yet he knew his statement was only partially true. He knew, for instance, that the British blockade of Americans shores had contributed, during the two years of the war, to shocking shortages of cloth in the United States Army's supply department. On the other hand, he did not know whether General Ross had guessed that the traditional blue of the American uniform was frequently eked out by brown or gray cloth. The British general had not yet engaged in combat since his arrival on American shores the month before, and he had not seen American infantrymen at first hand. Stewart had, and he had seen American volunteers who still looked well enough. The drafted militia were lucky to wear clothing of any sort.

It was not clear to Stewart whether the two men before him were in the military, but they might well belong to the Tenth or the Thirty-sixth. Their hungry look suggested they had, indeed, been out hunting for quail or woodcock or pheasant which hid in great numbers in the tidewater marshes. Their ragged demeanor did not bode well for the American cause.

The general nodded, considering the implications of taking prisoners at this early date. He wondered whether these two were worth the trouble. "And their firearms, soldier?"

Stewart turned a well-trained eye on the two muskets. "They look like the Brown Bess," he answered, "though heavier than eleven pounds, at a guess." By way of comparison, he shrugged the shoulder where lay his own eleven-pound Brown Bess musket. Regarding the American pieces more closely, he could see they were frontier products, for shooting game. "No bayonet," he added.

The lack of bayonets was the first thing about the men and their weapons that the general had noticed. In his experience, the principal function of the firearm was to carry the bayonet that, in the last resort, decided an infantry action. He looked with approval at his soldier. "Very well, Stewart. Thank you," he said, by way of dismissal. He had determined that the Americans were not worth taking prisoner and feeding, militiamen or not. They might be worth some information, though, and so the general asked them for the number of men defending Baltimore.

As Stewart was turning his horse away from the head of the line and returning to his place at the rear, he saw the men scratch their heads and puzzle over the question, frowning. He heard one of them answer, with loyal exaggeration, "About twenty thousand, sir." The second one quickly confirmed, "Oh, aye, twenty thousand, I'd say."

General Ross smiled. He had ridden a dozen times against Napoleon's best troops, who had far exceeded twenty thousand. He was not worried about American forces, even double the number, if the two men before him were at all representative. He observed, unperturbed, that he did not care "if it rains militia. Go to your quail, men."

The party rode on. Finding nothing farther ahead, the general decided to head back, including on their return an inspection of the contours of Bear Creek and of Sparrows Point. An hour later, they arrived back at the Shaw Plantation at just about the time Stewart would have chosen to start out, tired, thirsty, and very dirty.

General Ross and his officers dismounted, handed the reins over to the accompanying soldiers, and disappeared into the house to clean up and to eat. The soldiers took the horses around to the stables, brushed them down and gave them to feed before seeking to satisfy their own bodily needs.

Three of the soldiers returned almost immediately to the barn, where they would find their evening rations. They would most likely spend the evening with their cohorts, dicing and playing cards until the light became weak enough to make cheating inevitable. Stewart felt no inclination to join that group, and had other business to tend to first. Before he left the stables to walk in a direction opposite the barn, the fifth soldier clipped Stewart's shoulder with one hand and thrust a thumb of the other in the direction of the three soldiers.

"Not eating with us tonight, Stewart?" he asked, a hint of belligerence in his voice.

"I'm eating, Lawler," Stewart replied, working his shoulder to release it of Lawler's hand, "but not just yet."

The bigger man let go his hold. "So. What was that all about this afternoon?"

Stewart did not pretend to misunderstand. "The general's taken a liking to me," he replied tranquilly. "You had similar treatment last week, as I recall." He addressed the man's real question. "Don't worry. If Ross has any promotions in mind, he won't be advancing me ahead of you."

Lawler did not like having his motives so easily exposed. He looked down at Stewart malevolently. "You're too quiet. I don't like a man who's too quiet," he said, his voice and stance a threat.

Stewart did not flinch in the face of the deliberate provocation. "When a man is quiet, he'll never be done wrong by a too-active tongue."

Lawler frowned, trying to make out whether he had just been insulted. He had taken an instant dislike of Infantryman Stewart who had received a transfer and joined the Forty-fourth at Benedict, on the American side of the Atlantic. He had never liked Stewart's air of self-containment, his slow but efficient manner, or his way of talking, which sounded uppity. Lawler could not have described what irritated him about the quality of Stewart's speech, and his inability to articulate his thoughts frustrated him. His frustration made him pugnacious.

Stewart saw that they could easily come to blows, and held the heat and the timing of the sortie responsible for Lawler's temper and jealousy. "And to prove my point," he said, "I will decline further talk." He then took a step outside the circle of Lawler's arm reach, turned deliberately, and presented his back as he walked away.

His gamble worked. Even with his back turned, Stewart knew he would not be attacked. He was sorry to have made an enemy, but not surprised. He had imagined difficulties of this sort along the way, and he was glad that the hostility was open. Lawler's hostility came from the fact that he simply did not like him, and not because Lawler was suspicious of him in any way.

Lawler was taller by a head, and more muscular, but Stewart knew his own strength, and he had long ago learned to deal with the bullies. He knew he could best Lawler in a physical contest, if it ever came to one.

It might come to one yet, Stewart thought. Since he did not like Lawler any more than Lawler liked him, he was not disposed to becoming a more comradely comrade simply to suit Lawler's tastes. Stewart had been bred to the niceties of social conversation, but he did not consider the present circumstances social. He treated them for what they were: a military expedition.

Stewart veered away from the barn and headed into the woods, where he relieved himself. He found his way out again, but did not go back in the direction of the barn. Rather, he angled toward the main house, approaching from the side, with the intention of cutting across to the backyard. He passed close enough to the wide-open windows to catch the smell of fried ham and fresh-cooked greens, and the sounds of soft chinking of cutlery against china and low voices enjoying a good meal. Although he felt a sharp pang of hunger, he did not feel envy for the officers seated within, who were benefiting from what he guessed was the very reluctant hospitality of Master Shaw. He walked on to the kitchen garden that lay at the back-door step, past the neat rows of vegetables and beyond the fragrant herbs. The far end of the garden was bordered by a tall flowering hedge. He sought the narrow passageway in the middle of the sheltering bushes.

Brushing through the branches to the other side, Stewart stepped into a grassy, private little clearing. In one corner of the clearing, he saw what he had come for. On one of his predawn ambles through the Shaw property, he had happened upon this little clearing and discovered three rain barrels, a low, wide trough, and several buckets, all full. The water was his objective, and so ardently did he crave a good wash that he imagined it swishing and gurgling and beckoning to him.

While he crossed the grass, he stripped off his coat and peeled off his shirt, which was stuck to his skin with dirt and dried sweat. He threw his uniform down on the ground in front of the line of barrels. Then, in one fluid movement, he kicked off his black regulation shoes, unhitched his trousers, picked up the bucket closest to hand and poured the water over his head, relishing the initial *swoosh*. He savored the momentary glow of cool, clean trickles against his skin. However, even before the first water could run out of his pant legs, he heard an angry splutter and a lapping of water from behind the barrels. In that moment, he realized that he was not alone.

He looked across the top of the barrels and down into the angry, upturned face of the young woman whose petticoats he had seen that morning. She was wet, and she was naked, and she was seated in a copper tub. She had nothing to cover her but her arms, which were folded across her breasts, and the iridescent bubbles of soap rising to her waist. Her hair was dark with water, and slicked back. From her coloring, he judged that her hair might be red when dry. His immediate, whimsical thought was *A pretty peach!* But then he amended it to *An angry peach!* Her brown eyes were flashing fire. Her delicate features were transformed by her evident fury. Her mouth was open and speechless.

She was not speechless for long. "Have you no decency, redcoat?" she snapped. "Have you no manners? Know you no bounds? This is *my* house and *my* land and *my* water! Now, get you gone, and leave me in peace!"

Stewart leaned leisurely over a barrel, propping up his weight with a forearm across the rim. "Do I have the honor of addressing Miss Shaw?" he hazarded. She did not look the least bit sick. In fact, she looked like an extremely healthy young woman, from what he could see. And he could see a lot.

He met her fierce eye with a slow smile that apparently only added fuel to her flames. "This is not a social occasion, redcoat, and introductions are quite beside the point!" she told him with a huff. "Now, if you please..." she continued, with an impressive ring of indignant authority.

Stewart watched her evidently struggling to maintain whatever composure could be maintained by a woman at such a severe disadvantage. Did she truly hope to face him down? He was charmed by the possibility, and hardly motivated to behave as he ought and leave her to her privacy.

He shook his head. "This was not wise, Miss Shaw. The land and house you claim as your own are now crawling with soldiers. It was too great a risk for you to take a bath outside."

"All the officers in the house are eating just now, and the rest of you are—*or should be*—behind the barn," she said defensively. "This clearing is strictly forbidden to you!"

Stewart was in no hurry to end the encounter, for he was enjoying his advantage. "I did not know that, you see, and I, too, desired a bath." At that, he scooped his hand into the water in the barrel and began rubbing his face and his neck and his chest with it.

"You have the run of our house and our food already," she said, her voice low and angry. "You cannot have our rainwater, too! For bathing, you can go in the creek through the forest behind the barn. I'll tell you how to get to the path."

So she was trying to be helpful, was she? He slapped his face with water and replied, "I've been there, and it's too muddy for me. I prefer the barrels."

"I do not care what you prefer, redcoat, but you've had just about all you're going to get from me!"

He did not respond to that unfortunate phrasing, and he saw her pretty peach skin ripen several shades. Her flush of awareness produced a reaction in him, and he was suddenly glad that the barrel shielded him from the waist down. Very deliberately, he resumed his washing, his eyes resting appreciatively on her as she sat, trapped and exposed, in the tub.

He soon discovered that she was not completely defenseless. Her voice and eyes were fierce when she stated, "I am finished with my bath. I am going to get up. If you do not leave before I get up, I am going to use this knife on you. Whether I am dressed or not." With a glance, she directed his attention to the kitchen knife on the ground beside the tub. Her voice was menacing.

He was charmed. "Very fierce!" he commented lightly, then offered his professional opinion. "However, a kitchen knife is too tame a weapon for the circumstances, I think. The best you could hope is to stab me once before I overpowered you."

"Too tame, you think? Next time I'll bring my tomahawk," she shot back, "for scalping purposes! You redcoats think you have come to chastise the savages!" She flung at him the infamous phrase the *Times* of London had used as their rationale for war. "And savages you'll find us!" She made a minimal motion as if to rise up from her slowly disappearing protective cover of soap bubbles and toward her knife.

Stewart realized, with regret, that his enjoyment had now gone far enough. He forestalled her with an upheld hand. "That won't be necessary, miss," he said. "I'm almost finished myself. Now, if you'd be so kind to hand me the soap?" he asked, glancing away from the knife toward the white square bobbing on the surface of the water in front of her.

He had put her at something of a loss, of course. She had been prepared to uncover herself in order to clutch the knife and to lunge at him in an aggressive action. She was not quite prepared to uncover herself in order to politely hand him a bar of soap. He saw her dilemma chase across her features.

He resolved it for her. "Never mind. I can reach it myself," he assured her. With that, he leaned over the barrel and stretched an arm out to grasp the soap. She slid back in the tub, as far away from him as possible. He did not touch her, but he glimpsed the provocative curve of a thigh and a hip beneath the water through the ever-dissolving bubbles. Then he was back to his original position on his side of the barrel and vigorously soaping his hair, neck and chest.

Under her very amazed and wide eyes, he picked up the second full bucket of water and dumped it over him, rinsing off the soap. He scooped another bucketful to rinse again, and yet a third, making sure that most of this last bucketful of cool, fresh water reached the place where he now needed it the most, namely down the front of his unhitched trousers.

When he was done, he tossed the soap back into her tub, where it fell in front of her navel with a little splash, against which she blinked. He fastened his trousers and bent to retrieve his discarded shirt and jacket. Tossing the garments over his clean, muscled shoulder, he bid Miss Shaw an agreeable "Good evening" and left the clearing by the way he had entered.

When Jane saw the last of him swallowed by the hedge, she let out a long-held breath, leaned back against the tub and closed her eyes. She hung her head back, flung her arms wide so that her breasts bobbed on the surface of the water and uncurled her legs so that they hung out of the other end of the tub, thus exposing in full all that she had tried to hide moments before. She realized that she had just had a narrow escape, and her relief tasted as sweet and tangy as a lemon drop.

A narrow escape? She sat up, causing a swirl of water. No! This was her house, as she had said, and her land, and her rainwater, to do with as she pleased. She had no cause to feel sweet relief that the redcoat had not taken greater advantage of the situation. She had more cause to feel hot outrage. The sweetness vanished, and an acrid fire sprang up on her tongue. She tasted the outrage that he had dared enter her private clearing, dared set his eyes on her nakedness, and wash himself in front of her. Arrogant, insufferable, presumptuous redcoat! Just an infantryman, too—not an officer, for they were all in the house—and he'd acted as if he owned the place!

The outrage flared out and quickly burned down to ashes. The most galling part was that the redcoat had been right: She should never have taken the risk of slipping out her bedroom window again, soap and towel in hand, to take a bath in the open, with her land crawling with soldiers. But she had been so hot and restless and *bored* after her day of enforced inactivity.

So much for her impulses!

Impulses. She closed her eyes and had a sudden vision of Bobby Harlan as he had been on their last night together. She opened her eyes abruptly. It had been a long time since she had thought about him in *that* way, without the grief. She resolutely pushed away the vision.

Firing up her indignation, she rose from the tub, thinking instead of the exchange with the redcoat. It was strange to hear them speak with intonations that were oddly familiar and alienating at the same time. Lucky for her that their accents were so similar, for tonight she would listen, once again, to the strategies planned in the room below her bedroom. With the information she gathered, she would help to bring the redcoats down, even the bold soldier with the hazel eyes.

Chapter Three

Jane was not the least bit tired, running over field and forest at this hour before the dawn. In fact, she felt relieved. She felt exhilarated. Soon she would be climbing back into her bedchamber by way of the trusty tree branch. Everything was going according to plan—even better, for the plan, such as it was, had been wild and risky from the start. As promised, Mr. Skinner had sent a replacement to the meeting place to receive Jane's news, and her news this morning was extraordinarily important, the kind she had been waiting for. The night before, she had heard that the British intended striking first at the capital. It was almost unthinkable, but Washington was soon to be attacked.

Not directly from the North Point, however. Jane had heard that General Ross was sending troops southward, down Chesapeake Bay to the Potomac. From there, Ross projected a five-day campaign back up the Patuxent River. He figured he could move his troops over both ground and water at the speed of ten miles a day if he had to, and he was prepared to fight anywhere along the way that was necessary. Yet he imagined the first real engagement would be at Bladensburg, up the road and to the east of George Town. He intended to begin the descent down Chesapeake Bay the day after the morrow.

Jane could hardly believe her luck in having heard such details. She had not closed her eyes during the night in her excited anticipation of relaying such news, and in fear that Mr. Skinner would not be able to make it or find a replacement. Her fears had not been realized, and she had found in Mr. Skinner's stead Michael Shiner, a freed slave. Michael had arrived early at the meeting place and faithfully repeated her valuable information, committing it to memory. He had assured her that he would have the information passed along to the next person in the chain by midmorning.

As Jane sprinted ever nearer to the Shaw property, she was looking forward to falling gratefully into her own safe, comfortable bed. She wanted to sleep the sleep of the just and the carefree. She wanted to sleep the sleep of one who had done her duty and done it well. If she harbored one remote, one tiny, niggling doubt about the success of her morning's mission, it concerned Michael's loyalty to the American cause. However, the doubt had only to occur to her to be pushed aside summarily. She believed she could trust Michael Shiner. She knew she could trust him. And yet . . .

And yet she did not know for sure whether she could trust him or not. He was a freed slave, after all. It was possible, even probable, that he would want to help the American cause, but his loyalty was not as certain. She had known Michael Shiner a long time. However, she could not see into his heart, nor could she properly weigh the variety of his experiences as a freed slave that would determine the balance between his sympathies and antipathies for the American cause. She had heard that the British were shamelessly stirring up trouble among the slaves, trying to create a union between the black man and the English "liberator." But Michael Shiner was not stupid. Nor was he any longer a slave. He was too free now, and too smart, to trust the British ruse, was he not? And yet— What if—?

No. She trusted him. She *had* to trust him. She had no other choice.

From the twists and turns on the pathway, she determined that the tobacco shed was within a couple dozen swift paces of her, although still shrouded in a ghostly fog and invisible to her. She was puffing with the uphill slope from the river. On one side of her was a forest, on the other a ripening tobacco field rolling away, cutting a large rectangular swath across the Shaw property. Her breath was flagging. She called on her reserves to carry her through, for her goal was so near. Just as she was about to round the tobacco shed, she felt a second wind coming. She had never before felt so good, so satisfied, so useful, so effective—

"Heavens!"

Or so frightened, or so *trapped!* A large form had stepped out from the mists swirling around the shed, and she was stopped dead in her tracks by a firm arm clamped around her waist. Caught in midrun, her body was whipped by the force of its sudden halt, the surprise and the sudden stop causing her to gasp.

Before she had time to catch her wits or her breath, her captor uttered one dry word: "Heavens?"

Jane momentarily sagged against the masculine arm that held her. Now that she had been forced to stop, she felt her lungs burning with her exertion and her muscles' singing pain. She summoned all her last forces and raised herself up. Her diaphragm rose and fell against his arm as she tried to regain her breath. With creditable composure, though still winded, she retorted. "Would you ... have preferred ... if I ... had said ... 'Eek'?"

She turned to the man to whom the arm belonged. It was exactly as she thought. Holding her was the bold soldier of the day before who had interrupted her bath. She had been caught by him twice now. He looked different, yet the same. His hair was not wet, but tied neatly at the neck. He was dressed, too, and wearing trousers and a loose, light cotton shirt, open at the neck, with the sleeves rolled up above the elbow.

"I had no particular expectations about what you might say," he replied.

His voice was familiar, yet foreign. It was also enticing. She resisted its pull and concentrated on his words. "You were waiting for me?" she asked suspiciously.

"It was too hot to sleep," he explained. "So I got up for a walk. I was resting against the shed and heard some noises of movement coming from down the path. I thought, at first, that it was an animal.''

"Which you tried to stop with an outstretched arm?" she demanded, her suspicion hardly abating at such an explanation.

"As you came closer," he said smoothly, "I could discern by the sounds that it must be a human running."

"Good hearing," she observed, knowing that her step was light on the dirt and that she had broken few branches underfoot.

"Better vision," he replied. "I could also see a human outline as you came within ten feet or so. I was naturally curious to find out who it was."

Should she believe him? She certainly wanted to. The alternative would be that he knew of her predawn activities and had been lying in wait for her. If that was the case, he was now in a position to stop her from meeting Michael tomorrow. She groped for an explanation of her movements and discovered that he had given her one, ready-made.

"I can understand," she said, "why you were up and about at this hour. I, too, found it too hot to sleep this morning and decided to get up for a walk." She looked him straight in the eye. She saw the hazel gleam was drained of color and had paled to mere luminescence. "I needed to cool off."

He returned her regard unwaveringly. "It didn't work in your case, then."

She was aware that he was still holding her at the waist. Her body was steamy from running. Where his bare arm stretched against her middle, the cloth of her gown was sticky and wet. By contrast, he was cool and clean. She caught the scent of her soap on him; it did not smell the way it did as it radiated off her skin, but had taken on a particular masculine personality all its own. Her sweat and his scent met the perfumes of heavy late-summer blossoms and mingled with the memory of him bare-chested with fresh water running down his hair and chest. She strained away from his arm. He released her, and she deliberately took a step away from him and the distracting fragrance that had risen up between them when they stood close together.

"I tarried too long in the forest and had to hurry to get back before the dawn," she answered.

"Which defeated your purpose in cooling off," he persisted.

She shrugged and admitted, "Yes, and now I have learned my lesson."

"Which means you won't be getting up early again?" he asked. "Or that you won't tarry so long the next time?"

She answered his questions with one of her own. "What business is it of yours, redcoat, what I do on my own property?"

"No business at all," he replied, "but I don't think you were up early just because you were restless and could not sleep." He paused, then said, with one mobile brow quirked, "I can't help asking you why you were running through the forest at such an hour."

She could either refuse to answer or divert suspicion from her real activities by providing him with a plausible explanation. Only one such explanation came to mind. She hated to have to use it, but she had no alternative.

"I hardly care to answer you," she said, as provocatively as she was able, "for that would be telling."

His regard became instantly more penetrating. Jane could feel him assessing and evaluating the dishevelment of her appearance. She saw his eyes, just a glitter of hazel in the ever-dark dawn, take in the skew to her kerchief, the damp curls that escaped therefrom, the opened buttons on her bodice, and the ragged hem of her skirts.

"And you don't kiss and tell?" he said.

She made a pouty gesture with her mouth. "Surprised, redcoat, that savages have manners?"

He did not answer that. She felt, rather than saw, his glance, a glance that stripped her naked and placed her back in her bathing tub, the curves of her breasts and hips exposed to his view, her skin wet and glistening with soap bubbles. "Well, now," he said slowly, "that explains why you were so determined to have your bath yesterday evening. You were freshening up for your love, despite the dangers of being discovered by any passing soldier.''

Jane flushed up to the roots of her hair and down to the tips of her breasts. He had gotten the point that she had tried to convey to him, of course, but he had added the reminder of having seen her naked. An insult had been implied, as well, that she was loose enough not to mind risking the gaze of any passing soldier. She did not resist the impulse to insult him in turn.

''Indeed, 'any passing soldier' is entirely right, redcoat,'' she replied sweetly, ''and the riffraff showed up.''

Appreciation flashed momentarily in his eyes. ''Pretty fine talking for a savage,'' he murmured.

Jane did not deign to reply. With a haughty lift of her chin and a swish of her skirts, she turned to go. She had explained herself to him, for better or worse. Since there was no profit in bandying words further, she left him behind at the shed. Although she did not look back, she did not think he was following her.

She made her way steadily down the dark path, deflated and disturbed. She still had plenty of time to climb up to her room before the household would awaken, but that thought hardly comforted her. All the bold soldier had to do was to tell General Ross that he had met her in the woods that morning for her room to be put under strict surveillance. She would know, from her next encounter with the general, whether or not she now stood under suspicion from the British.

After a restorative sleep that took until midmorning, Jane emerged from her bedchamber, respectably dressed. She met the general at the bottom of the staircase as she was to go about her daily chores. He bowed and asked, considerately, after her health.

Jane thanked the general for his concern and explained that she must have had a one-day fever, ''for I was burning hot when I awoke yesterday morning, as you know, but by nightfall my fever had dropped considerably.'' She added brightly, ''All I needed was a good sleep last night, and I feel fine as a shiny new dollar today!''

"I am very pleased to hear it, Miss Shaw," the general replied to this, with a blandly polite eye and only the smallest grimace at her quaint American turn of phrase. "Very pleased, indeed."

"Thank you, sir," she said, searching his face for signs that something hidden and menacing lay behind his civil veneer. She found nothing beyond perfunctory interest and determined that he had been told nothing of her predawn activities. "I am sorry to have caused you trouble."

"No trouble at all, miss," he replied, still polite, with a faint hint of boredom with the topic and a slightly discernible desire to get on to the more important business of the day.

Jane curtsied to his bow, and she continued on her own business for the day, which would, under the circumstances—a plantation full of idle soldiers—keep her within calling distance of her father and the house. This included the morning duties of sweeping the downstairs and the porch that ran around three sides of the old mansion, helping Mamie in the kitchen, and tending her garden. Wearing a wide-brimmed straw hat, she waded into the garden that stretched away from the back-door step. The day was hot, and getting hotter by the minute, despite the occasional breeze that gusted over the field and through the forest, whirling small columns of dust up and down the straight rows of her vegetables.

Her bodice was sticking wetly to her back, and perspiration was trickling down her forehead and into her eyes. She had learned long ago not to resist the heat, but to give herself over to it entirely. Every now and then, she would look up and over to the far hedge, beyond which lay the clearing. Her eye traveled to the thick green shade under the old trees ringing her house and garden, to the glare of the sun on the hard-packed dirt of the carriage circle that swung out from the house and was visible on one side of the garden. She saw the old well at one corner of the garden, with its border of petunias, pink and white and lavender, that she had planted herself. They were drooping in the heat.

She experienced the heavy, hot stillness of late morning. It held a silence that overrode the sounds of the bustle of an occupying army. Of course, she heard the sounds of horses and bridles and equipment coming from the barn that lay on the opposite side of the house. She heard the occasional calls of men, and the answering voices. She heard the regular clatter of a tin dipper in the buckets set up under the eaves as men bent to drink. She heard the hateful voices of the British officers drift out, indistinct, from the dining room window, as they planned the American defeat. Yet nothing seemed louder than the stillness and the silence, not even the buzz of bees or the pulse of crickets or the sizzle of mosquitoes or Mamie's quiet humming drifting through the open kitchen door at her back.

There would be green beans, yellow squash, beaten biscuits and golden fried chicken for the midday meal. She would eat with her father in the kitchen, served by Mamie, while the British officers ate off the best china in the dining room. At least they had assigned several of their own men to serve them and not reduced her to the status of their menial. Even without that indignity, however, the situation was hateful enough. She hated the war. She hated *them*. She hated how they lived so carelessly, so arrogantly, off her father's bounty and hard work. She weeded, watered and picked with renewed energy.

After the meal, she was working in a small flower garden that was placed at some distance away from the main garden and gave her full view of the carriage drive and the space between the front of the house and the barn. Surrounded by the fragrant blooms of heartsease, meadowsweet and feverfew, she looked up to see General Ross emerge from the house and pace with stern boots across the porch. He called to a soldier who was lounging at the side of the barn, just beyond her line of vision. She heard the general call out the soldier's name. It was Stewart.

The soldier Stewart came around the side of the barn. He approached, saluted smartly, and exchanged a few words with his commanding officer. When Jane saw the face of soldier Stewart, she watched the fleeting episode with interest. The general was clearly giving orders, and the soldier was clearly accepting them, judging by their very correct postures and the directness of their speech. Jane had no way of knowing, of course, whether this encounter between General Ross and the bold soldier Stewart was the first of the day. Yet she would have bet that Stewart had not just then been telling his commanding officer of his meeting with her. Jane considered this piece of information and foresaw the possibility of escaping from the house once again, the next morning before dawn. She continued her gardening.

Later, when the sun was no longer beating directly down on man and beast but it was still far from cool, Jane was hauling water from the well. The shade from the trees slanting across the garden and the back of the house allowed her to feel her own tiredness, a sort of heavy limpness that spread slowly up from her hands to ache across her shoulders and down her back. Since midmorning, she had been working steadily, with only the break for the midday meal. She had slept little the night before, or any of the four nights before that, and she had little prospect of sleeping this night if she was to carry out her mission.

She returned to the well to fill her buckets and watered the ring of petunias at the same time. When she felt the cool water trickle between her fingers, she gave in to an impulse to splash her face and bodice. She bunched her sleeves above her elbows and smoothed water over her wrists and forearms and elbows, sighing with contentment.

She turned to carry on and found herself confronted by the large frame of a soldier she had seen a few times. He was big, and he had black hair, black eyes, swarthy skin, and the stubble of a coarse black beard. He was sweating and dirty. He had never before been so close to the house, and she did not like it. She quickly looked around to see if anybody were there to protect her. From the menacing look on the man's face, she thought she might need protection from him. He must have chosen his moment with care, for she knew that no house officers were on hand to whom she could call.

"Well, missy," he said, following with great interest a trickle of water dripping down her cheek and collarbone to disappear between her breasts. "It's a hot day, ain't it?"

Jane said nothing, but preserved a stony silence. Her heart was jerking painfully. She willed herself to still it.

His hand reached out for one of hers. She snatched it away, and put both hands out of his reach behind her back. Then the soldier grabbed Jane's woven hat off her head. "Red," he pronounced with satisfaction, looking at her hair. "Just as I thought."

The retort *My hair is not red!* sprang to mind from force of girlish habit at having had to endure this taunt from all the boys in the region. Again, Jane said nothing. Then, with a movement quicker than his, she reached out and grabbed her hat back. Her face was set and unfriendly.

The soldier's heavy brow lowered. "Dick Lawler's the name, missy," he said. "I guess you've not heard of me, else you wouldn't be acting so uppity." He smiled a thick smile. His lips were fleshy. "It's but a first meeting," he commented, "and there's time yet."

Jane was about to say that his accosting her in this fashion hardly counted as a meeting, but chose to preserve her silence. She was sorry a moment later that she had held her tongue, for he said with blatant suggestion, "Meet me again tonight, and you'll see what I mean."

At that moment, Stewart came close enough to the well on the side of the carriage drive to hear his words. At his arrival on the scene, Jane's gaze drifted over to him, and she saw the speculative look that crossed his features.

Stewart checked his step only briefly before he said, curtly, to his fellow soldier, "You're wanted in the barn." A jerk of his head indicated the direction.

"I'm conversing with the lady, don't you know," was Lawler's equally curt response.

"Now," Stewart said. "It's the lieutenant who wants you, not me." Stewart flicked a last glance at Jane, and at her hair in particular, and walked off.

Lawler took a last, lingering look at Jane. He debated whether to retreat without having so much as touched the pretty little American, but then he remembered that the lieutenant had asked him to redo an assignment that he had done wrong in the morning. He had no choice. He took himself off, with a swagger for the little lady, mightily displeased with the turn of events and with Stewart's part in it.

He's caught me twice and saved me once! was Jane's thought concerning Stewart as she watched the ridiculous roll of Lawler's hips while he crossed the carriage drive. *And so what if he thinks this lump of a man is the one I met this morning in the woods?* It was a purely rhetorical question, of course, one she did not intend to answer. Nevertheless, before Jane carried on with her chores, she uttered a single word under her breath, a heartfelt, "Damn!"

Chapter Four

Jane looked into the large almond eyes, eyes that were set in a face as dark as a riverbed. "The troops begin to pull out this afternoon," she said. "They should be gone by tomorrow."

"Gone by tomorrow," Michael Shiner repeated, holding her gaze steady, the shadows cast by his features in the dark of dawn betraying nothing. "It's confirmed, then, what you told me yesterday."

Jane nodded. "It's confirmed. I don't think I could have misheard the same information twice."

"And the plans remain as you heard them yesterday?"

"Exactly as I heard them. The troops are to move south, down the Chesapeake to the Potomac. It's Washington they're headed for first. It's to be a five-day campaign."

"Washington, first. In five days."

"Washington." Jane shifted from one foot to the other. "Washington," she repeated. The name of the capital made her uneasy, for more than one reason. She shifted feet again. "The attack on Baltimore will presumably come later. September, maybe, depending on what happens in Washington." She paused. "You'll pass it on?"

"Yes'm, Missy Shaw," Michael Shiner replied. "I'll pass it on. Just as I did yesterday."

"Good, Michael." She nodded her approval. She continued to watch him intently, her doubts damming up and swamping her thoughts. "You'll pass it on to the widow Johnson, then?"

"To the widow Johnson," Michael affirmed.

"Right."

"Just as I did yesterday, Missy Shaw," he added.

"I know." Her uneasiness increased.

"I'll be at the widow's just after sunup, Miss Shaw," Michael Shiner volunteered, not lowering his eyes from her penetrating gaze. "I know the cricks. Mr. Skinner lent me his rowboat."

They continued to regard one another. The moment stretched. At the point when it became embarrassingly long, Michael Shiner asked, "Is there anything else, Missy Shaw?"

Jane's little dam of doubts broke. "Yes. Yes there is," she said in a rush. "I have to know...I *truly* have to know what you think of the rumors coming from Washington."

"Rumors, missy?" Michael Shiner was a cautious man.

"The rumors of a slave uprising," she said, not mincing words. She poured her discomfort into words. "The British are stirring up trouble there. I've heard General Ross speak of it. It's deliberate, you know, the attempt by the British to turn the slaves against their masters. With the British attack coming within the week, it could be chaos in earnest in the capital."

She let out her breath in a whoosh. A small silence fell.

Michael Shiner broke it. "I heard the rumors," he said levelly, without a flicker of emotion in his face.

"How judge you the sentiment among the Washington slaves?"

"Like the driest of kindling, ma'am," Michael Shiner acknowledged. "It needs only a spark to set the rebellion off."

"And you, Michael?" Jane demanded anxiously. The matter was too important to be hampered by manners or delicacy. "Where stand you with respect to the British lies for a better life for African slaves?"

Michael Shiner had two thoughts on the matter. "I'm a free man, Missy Shaw," he said first. His second thought was a question. "And what do I reckon the British would want with such a nigger as me?"

Jane vaguely intuited that this was the best she was going to get from Michael Shiner. He was not going to avow allegiance to the American cause. He had nothing to call his own beyond the frayed shirt on his back, his patched trousers, the hands that he worked with and the strength of his back. He had no property, no political convictions, no country, no vote, no flag. He was not going to wrap himself in the Stars and Stripes, even for show, and shake a militant fist against the Union Jack. He was not going to demean himself by espousing doctrines he did not believe. It was a white man's war, this Second War for Independence, and the white man owned the word *independence*. He had determined which side suited him best on practical grounds, not moral ones, and he was acting accordingly. His actions spoke for themselves.

Jane said, "Good," and touched his arm in acceptance. But with this gesture of understanding and fellow feeling, she had miscalculated.

Jane saw a trace of several emotions cross Michael Shiner's blunt-sculpted features, but they vanished quickly, like cinders in the breeze; and although his body did not move an inch, Jane sensed that he had stepped back from her. He had withdrawn, shuttered himself against her, from displeasure at her overfamiliar touching, in a silent reproach to her for having questioned his loyalty.

He stood not an arm's length away from her, but he was as remote from her, in thoughts and emotions, as a man fifty feet away. She found it extraordinary that such a strapping man could so effectively diminish his presence. Without looking at him, Jane made some noises about having to leave before the light of day should expose them. She gestured vaguely in the direction from which she had come.

Michael Shiner responded to this with a measured, "Yes'm."

She glanced up at him quickly and asked, "Tomorrow?"

He repeated, obediently, "Yes'm."

"I can count on you?"

He confined himself to a third, deliberate, "Yes'm."

"Tomorrow, then," Jane said. "It will be the last day I come, to signal that the troops have begun the pullout. After tomorrow, there should be no more need for these meetings."

The two departed, Jane to hurry across the open field covered by shreds of scattering fog, Michael Shiner to blend into the shadows of the woods.

Jane felt awkward and relieved to have the meeting ended. However, she could not have guessed that Michael Shiner's withdrawal from her touch was not from disapproval, but from fear. A fear from which he would never be free. No good could come from white skin touching you. If the touch came from the skin of a white man, it was because he had raised his hand against you. If the touch came from the skin of a white woman... White skin on yours, either way, meant harm or death. When you had no country, no property, you also had no rules to guide you, no ways of interpreting, no knowledge of where the lines were drawn.

While Michael Shiner made his way to the widow Johnson's, Jane was rowing across the backwater of the Patapsco River. On the other side, she made a detour from her usual path back to the house. She could not risk being caught again by soldier Stewart, so she had planned an alternate route to the Shaw house by way of her favorite, most private spot on the plantation. There she intended, simply and sensibly, to take a long morning nap.

This morning was the seventh in a row that she had left her bed before dawn. The day that stretched before her would be the seventh in a row crowded with chores performed without sleep. Late the day before, she had had the foresight to leave a yard broom and a chicken pail at her favorite spot, so that when she awakened from her nap and returned to the house it would look as if she had been early at her chores. She had even left some food for herself there, wrapped in a cloth and tied to a tree branch, high off the ground. And before leaving her bedchamber this morning, she had carefully made her bed.

Having left the path, she had to pass through underbrush that was thick and unwieldy. It scrabbled at her clothes and bare ankles as she traveled along a twisting ravine overgrown with vines. She tucked her skirt into her drawers in order to slosh across some moist, marshy runnels where trees dipped their branches in the surface water and ran great slimy roots across the muddy bottom. As the day lightened, she walked along the edge of some trees, staying in the tunnel of their shadows. Finally she came to a small, silent meadow, where the scarf of fog had tattered enough to expose Venus, sailing high overhead, on the point of fading from sight.

She freed her skirts and ran across the meadow to a bank of trees that hid her favorite spot. Beyond those trees, private from all eyes on land, lay a tiny, woman-sized spit of grassy earth that thrust itself down between two thin, useless legs of sandy coastline straddling Chesapeake Bay. The nub of land was the accident of a crisscrossing of channel creeks and coves that did not quite meet. It was hers to share with duck and snipe, wild goose and reed bird. Upon arriving there, she was witness to the flush of a rose-and-gold sunrise. She sank, exhausted, down on her knees in the grass.

As the sun was hoisting itself over the horizon, General Ross had already saddled his horse and was riding out from Shaw Plantation. Ross had not chosen this hour for a ride because he had benefitted from any sudden insights into how best to support the sultry summer heat. He had chosen this hour because he was beginning to move his troops toward Washington this day rather than the next, and he wanted to check the route to Baltimore once again in order to plan his eventual attack on the port city. He would return to North Point within the next ten days, once Washington had been conquered.

General Ross rode out, heading west toward Baltimore, in company of Lieutenant Richards and two underofficers. They went a ways down Long Log Lane, passing the Skinner farm. Ross intended to go as far as the local meeting house on Bread and Cheese Creek, but before he got to that point, he came to a crossroads and decided to try an as-yet-unexplored turning to the left. He imagined that this new lane would lead to the Patapsco and one of the many interesting Chesapeake bays, and thought it strategic to discover whether the bay might be suitable to serve in the near future as the British anchorage for the naval defeat of Baltimore.

What General Ross discovered before coming to the water was another little farm, far off, tucked out of the way down a dusty, dual-rutted trail not indicated on his field map. He did not like surprises or details overlooked. He decided to investigate. Just as he motioned his men to follow him, he saw a tiny dot of a wagon pull away from the homestead. It seemed to be heading toward them and the main road.

Ross held up a hand to halt his men. Then he cantered off down the trail to meet the wagon alone. When he was within a hundred yards of the vehicle, he perceived that it was occupied by a lone driver. Coming closer, he saw that the driver was female, and soon enough he was within sight of the most alluring woman he had ever seen.

Ross reined in his horse when he was next to her. He looked down at her a moment, considering her, without speaking. She was not classically beautiful, but there was a mature beauty about her that appealed to the subtle requirements of his mature taste. The blond tresses that escaped her bonnet were burnished like old gold. Her eyes were as deep as had been the blue sky over the heads of the ancient Greeks. There were faint lines at the corners of her eyes, and the beginnings of a parentheses around her full mouth. The curves of her breasts under her thin cotton dress were round and heavy. His eye lingered on the cameo brooch at her white throat. He could not have guessed it, but this woman was more beautiful now, at thirty-one, than she had been at twenty.

She looked up at him steadily, meeting his frank appraisal. She saw a strong, fit, broad-shouldered man who sat straight upon his stallion. His dark hair was pulled back at the nape with a ribbon. Silver winged his temples. His eyes were gray, and his nose was thin and aristocratic. His mouth was hard, his chin firm. He was handsome, distinguished. And he wore a scarlet coat gloried with gold braid.

He did not introduce himself, nor did he need to. He demanded, "Where are you going, ma'am? It is hardly seven o'clock."

She glanced down at the basket at her side. "To deliver fresh eggs," she answered, calmly enough, "which accounts for the earliness of the hour."

"Where?"

She nodded her head and gestured. "To the meeting house."

He looked and gestured in the other direction. "And what is down that way?"

She did not follow his gaze. She knew that Michael Shiner was long gone down that road, and hoped he was well out of sight. "The water," she said.

"The Patapsco River?"

She shrugged. "Old Roads Bay. It opens to the river, yes."

"So you are off to the meeting house?" It was a question.

"To deliver my eggs," she repeated.

"You go alone?"

"It's my job to deliver the eggs every day." She added, "Everyone on the farm has a job." She wanted to make it seem as if she were not the sole occupant of this land.

"May I ask your name, ma'am?"

She hesitated, minimally. "Mrs. Johnson."

He looked down at the wedding band on her finger, then back at her face, with its mature beauty framed in curls of old gold. "We will accompany you to the meeting house."

"I'm used to going alone," she replied.

"We will accompany you."

Thus it was that General Ross, Lieutenant Richards and two British underofficers accompanied Mrs. Johnson and her eggs to the meeting house. The short trip allowed the general to engage in desultory conversation with Mrs. Johnson, who knew to answer a direct question directly, but initiated no conversation herself.

At the meeting house, General Ross kept his eye on Mrs. Johnson. He thought nothing of it when she distanced herself in order to engage in a short private conversation with a very old man seated at one side of the building. Ross was, rather, contemplating how long it would take him to ruin the capital and to return to North Point. He felt inspired now to accomplish the task in a week, instead of the projected ten days.

Jane awoke after several hours' sleep. She rose, feeling remarkably rested and refreshed, grabbed the broom and the pail she had stashed and made her way back to the house by way of the chicken coop.

There, behind one of the outbuildings, as ill luck would have it, Jane encountered soldier Stewart.

He had been tending to some riding tackle and was just then shouldering a saddle. In the act of straightening, he looked up and at her. His eyes took in the broom and pail in her hand, then critically surveyed her clothing, which was in proper order.

"Miss Shaw," he said. "Good morning."

His voice held no insinuation, but she read the drift of his thoughts in the hard gleam in his eye. She bit her tongue to stop from defending herself. She was not going to cry innocent. It was a good ten o'clock in the morning, after all, and it should be obvious that she was engaged in chores.

She looked beyond Stewart to the yard and the drive which were alive with men and equipment and activity. "It *is* a good morning," she said with a deliberate touch of surprise in her voice, "if I am correct in thinking that the troops are departing."

He shifted the heavy saddle across his shoulders. "We're to be gone by noon," he confirmed, "but hadn't you already seen our movements this morning and guessed the cause?"

She regarded him levelly, unblushing. "Of course I knew it, redcoat. I made a remark, merely." She brushed past him. "Good morning to you, then. A *very* good morning."

To her back he called out, low, "You may be interested to know that there's talk that we'll be returning to North Point."

At the curious note of warning in his voice, she stopped and turned to face him again. She asked, cautiously, "When?"

"A week, maybe. Ten days."

She regarded him a moment longer, then humphed noncommittally. She turned away and walked around the bustle of the departing troops. Although she knew the troops' departure meant danger to the capital, she nevertheless felt her heart soar in happiness that the British soldiers would soon be off her property—and a day earlier than anticipated. She would have to warn Michael Shiner of the acceleration in the British plans.

The next person she met was her father, whose anxious brow smoothed in relief upon sight of her.

He hailed her, saying, "There you are, Jane, and already about your chores like the good girl I know you are!"

She smiled guilelessly. "What else would I have been doing, Father?"

"Well, I don't know, and that was what worried me!" Jacob Shaw confessed. "What with the redcoats on their way to Baltimore!"

"Baltimore, is it?"

"Where else would they be headed?" Jacob Shaw wanted to know, his eye fixed on the hubbub in the yard.

Jane declined to inform him. "Is that what the general told you?"

"The general did not confide in me his plans," her father replied irritably, "but he did ask me about Barbara Johnson."

Jane asked quickly, "What about her?"

Master Shaw drew his eye to his daughter. "Why, nothing! I told him she was a widow and lived alone."

"Anything else?"

"Well, I told him she never looked at men, if that's what you're asking, impertinent girl!" her father told her reprovingly. "Remember how she turned me down? Not a thing wrong with me, she said. Just not interested in remarrying. Who would have thought it? It was not as if I was in the same position as your Bobby Harlan, trying to marry above me!''

"Father..." Jane began warningly at the mention of her lost love.

"Not that I am wishing to speak ill of the dead," he said. "Bobby was a brave boy who gave his life for his country!"

Jane quickly suppressed her pain at this subject. "Did the general ask anything else about Mrs. Johnson?"

"No, for he was eager to be on his way, and it'll be good riddance to the lot of them."

Jane had to be satisfied that Mrs. Johnson had done nothing to raise the general's suspicion. "At least we'll have the house to ourselves once again," Jane said.

"That is just what you won't have, Jane, my girl," her father said. "It's a poor father I've been these past days to have allowed you to sleep under the same roof as the redcoats. Not that I *invited* the redcoats to make camp on Shaw Plantation! And it was all I could do to keep from planting my fist on the general's British jaw the other morning when he and that scallywag of a lieutenant marched into your bedchamber. Looking for spies, they called it, and you burning up from a fever!'' Jacob Shaw's face was suffused with a color that swore violently with the red of his hair. "So I've decided to send you to your aunt Patty's."

"Send me away?" Jane echoed, much struck by this development. "To Aunt Patty's?"

Jacob Shaw held up a hand, anticipating his daughter's objections. "Now, I know you're thinking your aunt Patty is too straitlaced and proper, but I can't be letting you stay on here with these . . . these *men* making free with the house and your room."

Jane thought this turn of events almost too good to be true. Her Aunt Patty lived in Riverdale, just outside the capital. Her father was sending her to the heart of the war. "When do I go?" she asked, subduing her excitement.

"I'd do it today, if I could, but the general's forbidden us to leave the property—as if we were going to follow them and report on their movements!'' he grumbled. "I'll be taking you to your aunt Patty's tomorrow morning.''

Time enough to alert Michael Shiner, she thought.

"Now, don't say a word against my plan, Jane!''

She didn't.

By noon the house and yard were miraculously empty of soldiers and movement, and the very house seemed to breathe a sigh of relief. Jacob Shaw went to the north fields to oversee what he could of the work of the white field hands. Mamie was inside, removing the traces of redcoat occupation. Hot and contented, Jane was in her gardens, savoring the first solitude in a week. She rose up, peeled off her cotton gloves, and arched her back to stretch the crick out of her muscles. She looked up away from the house and surveyed the western horizon. Far off she saw drowsy, swollen thunderclouds moving lethargically toward her. She turned back around, and her eyes stopped at the stone well, shielded by the shade of thick elms at the other end of the garden.

Blissfully aware that she was alone in the yard, she felt a joyous sense of newfound freedom overtake her. Happy as a spaniel, she went to the house and darted into the kitchen long enough to grab a cloth and a bar of soap from the sink stone. She sang out to Mamie on a note of liberated defiance, "I'm going to wash my hair, and I'm going to do it at the well!''

She bounded across the garden, tossed her straw bonnet from her matted hair and sent it sailing toward the well. In grand gestures of bravado, she stripped off blouse and chemise. Next came her skirt and her drawers, leaving only her petticoat, a modest afterthought. Then she scooped up a bucketful of water and bent with gusto to the task of washing out dirt and dust and memories of the week of enemy occupation.

Chapter Five

A battalion of goddamn shrimp dipped in boiling water, James Stewart thought as he looked over the troops in their regulation red, simmering in the torpor of the August afternoon.

To him had fallen the task of harrying straggling infantrymen back into formation, which made him only slightly more popular than a tax collector or an undertaker. At least he got to perform that task on horseback. He had been traveling restlessly back and forth along the column of heat-exhausted soldiers and lumbering artillery since they had left Shaw Plantation hours before, spending most of that time mentally cursing his superior officer for having chosen, once again, the exact wrong moment of the day to start a forced march. The general had obviously learned nothing since his arrival on this side of the Atlantic, at least as far as adjusting to the weather was concerned.

Having come to the end of the column, Stewart turned his horse around to return to his place at the head. Through the waves of heat and dust that rose up regularly from the earth, he cast his eye over the nearly perfect rows of soldiers.

Stewart had been surprised, then impressed, this morning when he learned that General Ross had chosen to lead his men north along the Chesapeake. That was to say that they were not traveling west along the Patapsco to Baltimore, as anyone following the movements of the British would have predicted from the selection of North Point as army headquarters. They were heading to the ships waiting for them in an inlet, ships that would sweep them south, down the Chesapeake and then up the Potomac to the unprepared and unsuspecting capital.

Stewart dragged an already sodden sleeve across his brow, smearing the grainy dust that clung to his perspiration. He ambled his horse a hundred feet or so before his ear was caught by the conversation between General Ross and Lieutenant Richards.

In response to some remark by the lieutenant, the general turned to his underofficer, so that he was in profile to Stewart. "She did not breakfast this morning with her father, you say?" he queried.

"No, sir. She did not."

"How do you know?"

"I was able to keep my eye on the kitchen throughout the early morning. Shaw ate alone. Only his Negro woman was there to serve him."

"I gather you do not mean to inform me merely that Miss Shaw was late in rising."

"No, sir. When she did not come down and her father had left the house, I went up to her room—" At the general's sharply raised brow, Richards coughed into his fist and added quickly, "Only to see if perhaps she was feverish again, sir!"

"A relapse, you thought? I think not, for she recovered so thoroughly and so speedily," the general remarked mildly.

"Yes, a little too thoroughly and speedily, I would say, sir!" Richards returned immediately.

Stewart heard a hurt, defensive note in the lieutenant's voice. He could not know for certain whether Richards chafed under the embarrassment of the false alarm he had called that morning by bolting into Miss Shaw's bedchamber at the sound of the overturned chair. However, Stewart knew enough to have guessed, at Richards's feelings about the incident. Stewart had been positioned below Miss Shaw's window that morning, and had heard the subsequent scene in her bedchamber.

"She was most definitely feverish, Richards, if that is what you are doubting. Burning hot, in fact." The general smiled thinly. "Nevertheless, you went to her bedchamber this morning, and..." he prompted.

Richards drew a breath. "This morning, after knocking on her door and receiving no response, I opened it and looked in. She was not there, and what's more, her bed was made!"

"Suggesting that she is an early riser, and neat in her habits."

"She may be both, for all I know, but you see, that was all before seven o'clock," Richards confided, "and *I* rose well before five this morning. To prepare for our early start."

The delicate, inquiring lift of the general's well-shaped brow did not alter. "Which is to say, Richards—?"

"Which is to say, sir, that she must have left the house *before* five o'clock, for I did not hear anyone descend the stairs after that time, or before Shaw came down around six o'clock. Even if she had been very quiet, I would have seen her, because once I was dressed I had the door open. The dining room, as you know, has a clear view of the staircase."

The general did not immediately reply to that intelligence. His handsome profile was impassive, and his gaze was fixed on Richards's troubled features. Stewart could almost see the gears in Ross's mind turning over the questions: Was there, possibly, a back stairwell at the Shaw house? Was Miss Shaw capable of climbing out her bedchamber window and descending by way of the sturdy tree? Was it possible that Miss Shaw had not spent the night in her chamber at all, but had been out adventuring all night? Were Miss Shaw's movements of any concern whatsoever regarding the British attack on Washington?

"Do you suspect the little American of something?" the general asked at last.

When pushed on the subject, Richards answered with a cautious "Possibly."

The general paused. Then: "Yes. Possibly."

For his part, Stewart suspected Miss Shaw quite definitely of something, but it was not spying. He imagined that
Richards and Ross had not fully considered the possibility
of an amorous adventure—only because they had not seen
her in her bath, or caught her returning from a tryst with her
lover, or seen her obvious surprise this morning at the signs
of the army's departure.

Stewart had no experience with Maryland women, but he
had no reason to think them particularly virtuous—and
certainly not Miss Shaw, who evidently liked her body and
its possibilities. It was easy for him to believe that Maryland men were not so doltish to let Miss Shaw's ripe beauty
go to waste, war or no war. Surely there was one man in the
vicinity resourceful enough to have won Jane Shaw's favors.

"I'm thinking that her father might have put her up to
something," Richards suggested. He obviously thought
women incapable of acting on their own.

Stewart privately doubted it.

The general nodded and asked reflectively, "What think
you of our Jacob Shaw, Lieutenant?"

"I thought at first that he couldn't see beyond the end of
his nose, sir," Richards said, bluntly enough.

"Yes, a naive inconsequent," the general translated
smoothly. "My initial sentiments, as well." He paused. "Or
perhaps he is a consummate actor. As for his daughter...what can a mere girl do, after all?" After handily
dismissing thoughts about the mere girl he continued,
"However, I am beginning to be able to imagine our Jacob
Shaw has *not* been in his fields the day long as he has been
claiming these days past! He has made quite a fuss over the
harvesting of his tobacco." The general frowned. "Of
course, I did forbid him to leave his property today, so that
he would not follow us. The man seemed so blustering and
cowed by my orders that I did not think it necessary to have
anyone remain behind to contain his movements! Perhaps
he *did* put his daughter up to some mischief against us this
morning, if he were worried about us suspecting him. And
what is more—"

Here the general broke off suddenly. Stewart saw his back stiffen into perfect rigidity. The general slowed his horse. Richards followed suit. After a moment's charged silence, Richards ventured a probing "Sir?"

The general drew in his reins, thereby bringing Stewart and the rows of wilting red soldiers behind him to a successive, wavelike halt. The heat rose around them like a solid thing, the clouds of dust rising to remain suspended in air sticky with moisture. The general's response came slow and measured. "It seems that we may have underestimated our Jacob Shaw."

"Sir?" Richards replied cautiously.

The general smiled again. "Did I tell you that Shaw asked my permission to have his daughter removed to her aunt's home? I granted it, naturally, after that scene in her bed-chamber the other morning." The general held up his hand in a staying gesture. "No, Richards, I am not blaming you. I am now blaming myself for not having asked the simple question of where this aunt might live." The general came to a rapid decision. "I think it only right now that a small party of men return to the Shaw house and provide safe escort for Miss Shaw to her aunt's home—wherever it may be."

"Yes, sir! Excellent idea, sir!" Richards seconded promptly.

The general turned in his saddle to consider which of his men he would part with for this mission, and his eye fell first and directly on Infantryman Stewart. The general's face lightened perceptibly. "Stewart!" he said. "You are a man who seems to be always in the right place at the right time. I commend you! I have new plans for you. Did you perhaps hear what Lieutenant Richards and I were discussing?"

Stewart said that he had gotten the gist.

"Well, then," the general said, "I am informing you that Lieutenant Richards is now in charge of the escort party for Miss Shaw, of which you are a member." At the slightly strangled sound coming from his lieutenant's throat, the general said, "Yes, Richards, you shall be in charge. Call it your reward for having alerted me to the possibility of a leak in our plans. Let me see, now, for the third man in the escort party..."

The general's eyes scanned the mounted soldiers, and Stewart followed the direction of the general's gaze. Stewart saw that Lawler's eyes were on him, hot and hateful, for Lawler was close enough to have heard the developing plans. The general's gaze stopped on Lawler, and he called to him.

While Lawler was bringing his horse forward, the general turned to Stewart again. "Go on, soldier, and head back to the Shaw house alone. We have little time to lose, and I'll want to brief Lieutenant Richards before he and Lawler follow you. Be quick about it, man. If you don't find Shaw or his daughter anywhere on the property, wait for Richards and Lawler. I'll detail a plan for that contingency. Richards will have a map, and I'll expect to see the three of you again in five days at our camp outside the capital."

Stewart saluted and turned his horse. When he had passed the point where his horse's hooves would kick up an unnecessary insult of dust upon his fellow soldiers, he broke his horse into a trot. Then he unbuttoned his coat, worked his arms out of it and laid that innocent instrument of torture across his saddle. He unhooked the chin strap of his black leather shako, removed it, and slung it over the pommel. He trotted along until he reached a shady stretch in the road where he felt he could urge his horse to a run without overworking the animal. The movement of the air in his hair and against his face felt good.

The thick-forested lowlands of the Chesapeake were becoming hazier by the hour. Through the trees he could see the shallow fingers of the bay spreading into the land, rock-flecked ribbons of silver flashing in and out of sight as he rode. He found that he much better appreciated the view on this unexpected return to Shaw Plantation than he had traversing these same miles in the opposite direction. Perhaps it was the rare enjoyment of his own company that sharpened his senses and made him more aware of his surroundings. Or perhaps it was the fact that General Ross, in one easy, fortuitous stroke, had made possible what he, Stewart, would have needed precious days to engineer. His mind was suddenly alive and alert to the possibilities. Not even Lawler's inclusion in the plans dimmed his prospects.

Without the cumbersome weight of an army trailing him, he returned to Shaw Plantation in half the time it had taken to travel from it. Soon he was turning his horse down the main drive to the plantation and rounding the Shaw house. He stopped his horse at the front porch.

He was aware, first, of an atmosphere of deep, restful quiet, whose calm surface was hardly rippled by the occasional clucking of a lazy chicken or the feathery flare of a bird's wings as it took flight. Before dismounting and presenting himself at the front door of a possibly empty house, he decided to look around. He urged his horse forward. The sounds of the horse's hooves were pillowed and absorbed silently by the deep, dry dust of the yard. Even the creak of the leather of his saddle seemed to melt and disappear into the surrounding silence. His horse moved beyond the house, giving him a full view of the area around the outbuildings and the back garden.

When he turned his head to the right, he was witness to a sight of arresting and luminous beauty.

He beheld a singular landscape of perfect proportion between central subject and surrounding composition. The balance of the design was provided by a cluster of towering trees, spreading in dense patterns of complicated greens, and the sky, which receded to a deep horizon of thunderclouds. The sun was in retreat before the storm, but still determined to impart its light upon the earth. Stewart caught the sun at the moment it was spending its last magical, transfiguring rays.

Under the dark parasol of the trees, in the center of the tableau, was an old stone well. Next to it stood the young woman of the house, naked, her body turned three-quarters toward him. She had raised her elbows above her head so that her hands were at her nape, fussing with a ribbon that would bring to order the cascade of auburn curls turned redgold in the westering sun glowing orange beyond the shadows of the spreading elms. The naked skin to her waist was petal-beautiful and soft to the eye, and carried just a hint of sunlight across her shoulders and collarbone.

Her breasts held the focus of his attention as his eyes skimmed the gentle slopes to the ends, where pink buds flowered. Those tender roses were tipped upward, held aloft by lush, bulbous nests of softer flesh and by the lift of her arms. The muscles of her left side and back were exposed, and tapered down in slender definition to the top of her petticoat. His eyes met the cloth and slipped in under it. They traveled downward, beneath the thin cotton, which was clinging to her, transparent in places from trickles of water. With his eyes he touched the curves of her hip and thighs, the bend in her knee, the swell of her calf, the arch of her bare foot.

The whole tableau was bathed in haze and humidity, awash in the peculiar hues of a coral reef, hues that heralded the arrival of a distant thunderstorm. His eyes grazed on the beauty of the picture; for a split second he had a distant memory of sitting on the hard bench of his Eton College classroom, with the emerald English lawns rolling away outside the window, tempting his thoughts away from the tedium of art history.

He remembered the moment when the sober, black-robed don had shown the students such a landscape, that of a naked woman performing her toilette at an ancient well, and suddenly the youg men in the classroom were no longer bored. Now, with the very real picture of Jane Shaw before him, he was neither bored, nor inappropriately aroused. Instead, he had a sense of why the artist had painted the picture, and it was a moment of exquisite sensuality.

The moment passed. She dropped her hands. He knew he must retreat. Fortunately, she turned toward the well, away from him. He took the opportunity to back his horse several silent steps, so that the house shielded him. He smiled a smile of sublime aesthetic satisfaction. He sent a silent double thanks to Ross and decided what to do next.

He maneuvered his horse back out of the main drive and jingled the bridle. He dismounted and lashed the reins to a porch post. Then he walked solidly up the few steps and across the wooden planks of the porch, making his spurs ring. He knocked loudly on the front door, and for good measure called out a strong "Hello!" He waited a moment, and then, because he expected no answer, walked back across the porch, down the steps, and around the side of the house. Before emerging in full view of the well, he called out another "Hello!" He supposed he had made enough noise and given her enough time to arrange herself.

Then he stepped out from the house, looking first, deliberately, in the direction of the barn. Walking slowly, he cast his eyes toward the tobacco shed, the chicken coop and then, finally, the well. He paused, midstride, affecting surprise to see someone. She was there at the well, fully dressed, with an anything-but-welcoming look set on her pretty little features.

He walked straight toward her and stopped a respectful five feet away. He looked regretfully at her clothes, which cruelly covered her beauty, and noted an errant middle button on her blouse that she had not fastened in her haste. The gape revealed nothing to him other than her chemise underneath.

"I thought I'd seen the last of you this morning, redcoat," she said with barely suppressed anger.

"And good afternoon to you, too, Miss Shaw," he replied affably.

She cocked her head at this spurious politeness. "You'll understand that I thought I would have some time to work up a desire to see any of you again."

"There's been a change in plans," he explained.

"Forget something, redcoat?" she demanded.

"Only my manners," he replied, with a fluid bow and the tones of a true gentleman. His heightened awareness of her did not flow from his cruder self, for it was, in origin, visual and cerebral. As he bent, this awareness sent a fizz of gentle sensibility to his shoulders and down his arms to tingle in his fingertips. It coursed down his spine and the back of his legs to keep him rooted before her.

When he straightened, he saw that her mouth had vanished to a thin horizon of displeasure. She was, apparently, in no mood to be attuned to his gentle sensibility. He was not surprised when she shot back, "The most mannerly act you redcoats performed was to *leave* this land!"

"Well, ma'am," he said, "it occurred to us only after we had departed that you had been left vulnerable and that our manners had been at fault. And after all you had done for us! We've returned to provide you escort."

"*We?*" she echoed, craning her neck so that she could look around him.

"Lieutenant Richards and Infantryman Lawler," he said.

The face she made at the mention of Dick Lawler told him all he needed to know about what she thought of that man. She quickly recovered and asked, with mordant irony, "Who distinguish themselves by being invisible?"

He smiled, bemused, besotted. "They're coming along later, with instructions from General Ross."

"Instructions to escort me *where,* precisely?" she wanted to know.

"To your aunt's home, I believe."

"To Aunt Patty's?" she echoed, incredulous. "*You* are to escort me to Aunt Patty's?"

"I did not, of course, know her name."

"But how did you know I was to go there?"

"Your father apparently told the general his plans."

Jane scowled in disgust. Could her father keep *nothing* to himself? she wondered. He would be the ruin of her plans yet.

"He neglected to mention her address, however," Stewart continued, to her obvious displeasure. "Where, exactly, does Aunt Patty live?"

"South of Baltimore," Jane hedged. She hardly wanted to advertise Riverdale's proximity to the capital just yet, and so swiftly changed the subject. "And who came up with this...this mannerly plan? General Ross?"

In contrast to the high poetry of his recent experience, he had the rather prosaic thought that she was beautiful when angry. He smiled. "You'll be wanting to thank Lieutenant Richards for the idea, I believe," he answered smoothly. Taking advantage of her strangled silence at the thought of having to thank a redcoat for anything, he followed this comment by asking the whereabouts of her father.

"He's in his fields, where he said he'd be!" she snapped. "I'll be happy to direct you to the path that will take you there, if you care to confirm it for yourself!"

"That won't be necessary," he declined politely. "It's been a hot day on the road, and I'd rather see to washing up." He cast his eye over the well, as if judging its bathing potential. Then he looked at her and smiled. She gave herself away by glancing furtively at something behind the well. He paused a delicate moment before saying, "On second thought, I think I'll go to the clearing for my bath, as I did the other day. What say you, Miss Shaw?"

She successfully fought down a blush at the reference to that episode, and covered her embarrassment with a gruff "I can't stop you."

"Perhaps not," he agreed cordially. "I'll be about it, then. When Richards and Lawler come—" He broke off.

"When they come?" she prompted.

"Tell them I've gone to the fields to locate your father."

"And when they ask for a bath?"

"Tell them to go to the creek behind the barn," he answered, "as you once suggested to me."

From the look on her face, it did not seem that she would give him any credit for keeping the clearing with the rain barrels a secret. Neither could she stop him from using that water. She merely inclined her head briefly, turned her back, and flounced into the house.

He considered her shapely backside a moment before making his way around the well and heading in the direction of the concealed clearing. He had not gone two paces before something on the ground on the other side of the well caught his eye. He looked down at the white cotton heap, and his eyes traced the twists of the disfigured legs to their lace cuffs. So that was what she had glanced at behind the well. It was, apparently, the one item of clothing she had not had time to don. He walked on.

He was smiling. The sight of her naked beauty might have appealed to the refined sensibilities of his sublime, aesthetic self. However, his baser, masculine self most certainly enjoyed learning that he had just been speaking to a woman who was not wearing drawers.

Chapter Six

Without looking back, Jane marched back to the kitchen, feeling the hot prickle of anger and embarrassment. By the time she had reached the open back door, she had sorted through her feelings enough to know that anger was there, yes, but embarrassment, no. It was a heightened awareness she had felt just now with his green-flecked eyes resting on her, as if he could see through her clothes.

As long as she was being honest with herself, she had to admit that the sensation was not unlike what she had felt when he had first caught her at her bath in the clearing. This time, however, she could find no healthy outrage. And why had she been so aware of his hazel eyes, the clean planes of his face, the set of his shoulders? Why had she been so aware of his awareness? More to the point, why did she have to react to him at all? Why couldn't she be, simply, indifferent?

Blasted redcoats!

All these thoughts made her remember her drawers. Now a touch of true embarrassment crept across her skin. She peered out the kitchen window and saw that dratted man disappear behind the hedge beyond the garden that ringed the clearing. Safe for the moment, she ran back out to the well, grabbed her drawers and ran back to the house.

Once again in the kitchen, she confronted Mamie. At the knock on the door, Mamie had bustled down from upstairs to see who was there. Finding no one, she had gone out into the yard and across to the barn to see if she could see the rider who belonged to the horse that was lashed to the porch post. Again finding no one, she had puffed back to the house.

"The redcoats have come back," Jane announced.

"Lord, chile!" Mamie exclaimed, her licorice-black eyes widening. She seized on what she considered the fundamentals of the situation. "And you carryin' you drawers in you hands!"

"That is not important," Jane informed her majestically. "They've returned, and they mean to spoil everything—again!"

"But, chile, they's only one horse in the drive. You can't bring back no army on one horse."

"There are three of them returning," Jane explained. Then, feeling the dramatic force of her announcement diminishing, she clarified, "Only one has already arrived. The other two are on their way."

Mamie was difficult to disconcert in the general way of things. Her response to these disclosures was practical. "Then get you out in the garden and pick me a basket of beans and fetch me two ripe melons." At Jane's look of surprise, she said, "We're to be feedin' three more at supper, and Amos is down helpin' Massa Shaw today." Satisfied, she wiped her hands on the vast cloth swathing her middle. Looking down at the bundle Jane held in her hands, Mamie added, "But only once you're decent, Miss Jane."

In a characteristic act of defiance, Jane dropped the drawers on the nearest chopping block, causing Mamie to shake her head and mutter dire prognostications concerning Miss Jane's future. The ill-fated Miss Jane grabbed the nearest basket and headed out to her garden to execute at least one of her Mamie's requests. When her basket was full and she cradled two melons in the crook of one arm, she returned to the kitchen, where the atmosphere had already begun to change from clear to agreeably overcast, with little clouds of flour dust billowing in the herb-laden air.

Tall and wide and solid, Mamie was at work. She was humming melodiously, fussing at the fire in the fireplace and dredging her chicken parts—all at once, it seemed, and all without great effort.

When Jane heard more sounds of arrival in the front drive, she left Mamie in her element and passed straight through the house by way of the hall running from front door to back door. The hall was a passage at all times, but in summer it served as the assembly room because of the current of fresh air it produced, and for the escape for hot air given by the stairwell that rose out of it.

Jane loved the Shaw house for its stairway, with its low tread that gave climbing an easy grace devoid of effort. The stairway was broken midflight and across the back end of the hall by a deep balcony above the entrance to the kitchen, where musicians had once played for dancers in the hall and the other rooms below—though never in Jane's lifetime.

The title "plantation" given to the Shaw house and its property was little more than a remnant of its grander days. The house was big, too big, and it was run-down now, from lack of funds and hands to keep it up. It remained a lovely structure of wood, with graduating clapboards from earth to eaves, a wide porch wrapping three sides of the rectangular building, and brick chimneys bristling from the roof, but the wood was weather-scarred, a number of boards needed replacing, and several neglected chimneys smoked badly in winter. The rooms were notable for their noble proportions and their carved mantels, chair rails, cornices and fine paneling, but like the exterior, these interiors were better evidence of glory days gone by than of present comfort.

The Shaw Plantation's run of ill luck had started well before this Second War for Independence, and even before the First. Once it had been a plantation of a thousand acres. However, during the time of the current Master Shaw's father, the plantation had dwindled to several hundred acres through successive seasons of bad weather combined with a variety of astonishingly bad agricultural decisions.

In the time of Master Shaw's grandfather, the plantation had been in full flower and operated on the economic model of a town. Around the main house had stood a variety of domestic buildings for horses and cattle, coaches and farm implements, cooking, living quarters of the servants, and for the essential domestic arts, as well: the blacksmith, the wheelwright, the painter, the joiner, the carders, the weavers and the shoemakers. Now, only a few of the outbuildings remained standing. Distributed over the remaining acres were the "quarters" for the field hands, crude log cabins at the edges of the clearings.

When Jane arrived at the front door, she found, sure enough, Lieutenant Richards on her porch, in the act of raising his hand to knock at the frame of the open front door.

"You just couldn't stay away from the charms of Maryland hospitality, could you?" she greeted him, without a trace of hospitality in her voice.

"Good day, ma'am. No, ma'am," Richards answered, first with a salute, then with a belated bow. Flustered, he clarified, "That is to say that hospitality is not what is at issue."

She put a hand on one hip. "Oh? I heard that you're repaying our hospitality by providing me with an escort to my aunt Patty's." At the lieutenant's look of mild bewilderment, she explained, "At least, that was what your friend Stewart told me."

Richards's brow cleared. "Well, as to that, ma'am, yes, I suppose you could put it that way. He's come, then, Stewart?"

She looked around him and pointed at the horse that was munching on a weed sprouting out from behind a large flowering bush at the porch edge. "You recognize his horse, surely?" At the same time, she saw the third redcoat, the hateful Dick Lawler, caught in the uncomfortable chemistry of hot sun and dusty drive. He had the audacity to leer at her. She hoped he fried in his own juices.

Richards was hot and tired, and no match anyway for a testy American beauty. "Where do you think I can find him, ma'am?" he asked, as polite as he could.

"I have no idea," she said. "Perhaps he's gone off to check on my father in the north tobacco field." Then she turned her back to him, saying, "I'd ask you in, redcoat, but I don't think that's necessary. You'll be doing what you want."

She crossed the hall and mounted the stately staircase. When she had gained the door to her bedchamber, she heard with satisfaction that the redcoats had not yet entered the house, but had headed toward the barn. Entering her chamber and plopping unceremoniously upon her bed, she could just imagine her father's face and fury upon returning from the fields, as he was soon to do, and discovering that the redcoats had returned.

Jane lay stretched out for a moment, contemplating this turn of events. Then she rose and decided it was time to make herself decent for the evening. It was with some dismay that she turned and saw her reflection in the pier glass. She looked like a wild strawberry, with her hair tumbling down her back and her skin fresh-scrubbed and shining clean. *Savage* was the word that came to mind to describe how she looked in her old, rumpled clothing. She thought it perversely fitting that she was wearing no drawers.

However, for the evening ahead, she was determined to dress as properly as she could. Once that was done, she descended to help Mamie in the kitchen. She was heartened by the smell of food and care that had begun to permeate the house, a smell that intensified with every step she took toward Mamie's comforting retreat.

The Shaw Plantation's kitchen was a kind of sanctuary, and Mamie its dark priestess. The dogmas of her cult were not written down, since she could not read or write, but she carried on with such vague oracular hints as "a pinch of this," "a taste of that," "turn when ready," and Jane's personal favorite, "cook until done." Jane had long since given up being puzzled over why it was she had never learned to cook from her extraordinary Mamie.

Mamie was little disturbed to be practicing her superior arts on the enemy. The British presence had reminded her of the "old days" on the plantation, when she was a very little girl, when her ma'am had been alive and there had been hustle and bustle and many mouths to feed.

This week past, Mamie had provided creations only for the house officers, of course. Even so, she had liked the feel of the yard alive with men and work, and she had produced meals in accord with the abundance she felt in their presence: a half chicken with wing and leg unsevered was a mere first helping, ducks came in braces, vegetables followed and were accompanied by hot breads, gravies, sauces, puddings and pies. This evening was to be no different.

However, Jane drew the line at one of the delicacies Mamie had intending serving up. "I refuse to allow the redcoats to eat our terrapins," she stated flatly when she saw the diamondback shells on the long working table.

"Amos, he got them this morning, Miss Jane," Mamie explained. "Oh! Such a time he had! Oh! So pleased he was to find such in this season! Nooo, Miss Jane. It's a sign, sure, and a gentleman's dish." Mamie thought to clinch her arguments for serving the terrapins with the observation that "A good meal makes the character better."

Still, Jane refused. "These are no gentlemen," she argued, "these are redcoats. And their character will have to be improved on the strength of the rest of your meal. You've spoiled them, as it is."

The fresh unseasonal diamondback terrapins were not served to the three soldiers that evening. Neither did Master nor Miss Shaw enjoy them, for it happened that the master of the house and his daughter sat at the table in the dining room with the British; and thus it was Mamie and Amos who feasted on the turtle flesh later that night, on the back steps outside the kitchen.

When Jacob Shaw returned to the house and entered the kitchen to greet his daughter, he had already spoken with the three redcoats. He did not seem as angry as she would have expected him to be, and his relative good humor derived from an even more extraordinary occurrence.

"We are to *what?*" she demanded, when her father informed her of the evening plans.

"We're to dine with them," he said. He corrected himself. "That is, they are to dine with us."

"In the dining room?"

"Of course."

"Where we haven't eaten in a week," she retorted. So this explained her father's equanimity: he was to dine again in his own dining room. "But how does it happen that they are eating with us—or that," she said, putting the matter in its true light, *"we* are eating with *them?"*

"That soldier Stewart speaks a lot of sense."

Jane blinked in disbelief. She could only imagine the charm soldier Stewart must have exerted to persuade her father to sit with the enemy at his own table. She would have been even more surprised to discover the reason for Stewart's machinations.

Stewart returned to the barn from his bath in the clearing to find Lawler stabling the horses.

The two men eyed one another measuringly.

Lawler took several steps forward so that he could look down at Stewart. "The girl's mine," he stated.

Stewart gazed up at him tranquilly. "I thought Miss Shaw did not welcome your advances."

"And you think she'd welcome yours?" Lawler asked aggressively and derisively.

Stewart smiled. "That remains to be seen."

Lawler hated Stewart's smile. He hated Stewart's tone. In his hatred, he was reduced to crudity. He rudely described what it was that women welcomed in men, and how the little American was going to like it.

The idea came to Stewart as an inspiration: *A civilized dinner table will cut this boor down to size. And I won't even have to lift a finger against him!*

The supper began pleasantly enough, and Jane would have accounted it almost agreeable, if it had been a true social occasion, and if Dick Lawler had not been seated across from her. However—as Stewart had so shrewdly guessed—the disgusting Lawler's usual swaggering demeanor was completely subdued, and he had lapsed into a sullen awkwardness.

As it was, Jane was happy for the opportunity to impress the redcoats. She was proud of the succulent soft-shell crabs that opened the meal Mamie served them. She was proud, too, that even in their relative indigence the Shaw family had not been forced to sell their china or their silver or pewter or their linen napery. She enjoyed the soft dazzle of the well-appointed table, with the spoons and knives and salvers winking in the light of mellow tallow candles. She savored the welcome cooler breezes wafting in through the tall windows, carrying with them the gentle grumble of distant thunder and lifting the old Holland curtains. She was even glad to be appropriately dressed and shod, although, once seated, she had slipped off her shoes.

Her father was at one end of the table, Lieutenant Richards at the other. Jane was seated alone on her side, across from Lawler and Stewart. In response to Mamie's shadowy presence in the dining room, Lieutenant Richards treated Mamie much as he would a piece of furniture, by putting it to its proper use, then ignoring it. Soldier Lawler, on the other hand, was clearly amazed by the black Juno's height and girth and color. He tended to gape silently at her, as if he had never seen a Negress up close—which he had not.

Soldier Stewart, on the other hand, knew to a nicety how to treat Mamie. He looked at her as a person when she served him. He spoke to her and complimented her on her dishes. He actually smiled at her. He had second helpings of almost everything, and Jane noted that Mamie selected the tenderest bits for him.

As the meal proceeded, Jane observed that, whereas soldier Lawler was in acute discomfort, soldier Stewart was at his ease at the supper table. At one point, when the conversation threatened to turn to politics, Stewart deftly raised the question of the sleeping arrangements for the night. He announced his decision to sleep again in the barn, being now used to the straw, he claimed. Richards stated his desire to sleep downstairs in the parlor, and Lawler was chosen to pull a mattress out on the porch, where he would keep watch.

Thereafter, the talk settled safely on the topic of farming, and Stewart drew Master Shaw out on the topic of his tobacco. At first Jane was surprised by the soldier's knowledge of this most American of agricultural products, but then she realized that he was only asking intelligent questions.

"Country boy?" Jane asked him when the occasion presented itself.

"In part," he answered.

"And the other part?" she queried.

"City boy," he responded, easily enough.

"And you, sir?" Jane asked Lieutenant Richards.

"I'm from the city, ma'am. Birmingham," he replied.

"Ah. And you, Mr. Lawler? Are you from the city, as well?"

"Yes, ma'am."

"Which city?" she pursued, when he did not look up from his plate, obviously embarrassed at being addressed a question.

"York, ma'am," he answered, finding articulation possible only in monosyllables.

"Indeed," Jane said. Then back to Stewart, she asked, "And what part of the country are you from?"

He smiled a sleepy green smile with his eyes and said, "The south."

Jane caught her breath, but was able to remark, blandly, "Which has prepared you to talk tobacco with an American."

He responded slowly. "I could talk cotton, if you prefer."

Master Shaw broke into this. "Now, I don't hold with cotton. Not at all. We haven't the soil for it. Tobacco is what began Maryland, and tobacco is what will end it—" He cleared his throat uncomfortably. "Not that Maryland is coming to an end, mind you! No! But it's tobacco I'm loyal to! Why, in my granddaddy's day, there was that Charles Carroll who began with wheat. Bad idea, my granddaddy called it. Worse, my daddy called it, and he would have been right, too, if Carroll hadn't had all that money behind him to build dams and mills and whole blamed towns! Wouldn't you know that someone or another would want to turn Maryland into a grain field!"

A round ball of thunder rolled through the window just then, giving Jacob Shaw's thoughts a further unhappy turn. "But we won't be having a tobacco crop—or any crop!—this year, either," he continued morosely, "if honest American farmers aren't allowed to work their fields without an enemy army camping out on them! I've lost a week now, and the rains are coming!"

Lieutenant Richards had little knowledge of, and less patience for, the agricultural discussions of the evening thus far. However, he did know the North Point operation, and he observed that the British had in no way hampered Master Shaw's daily movements, and that the tobacco fields themselves had not been trampled or otherwise harmed by the British encampment.

"But you're here, aren't you?" Master Shaw growled, glaring across the table at this proxy for General Ross. "And my son's had to go away to fight you devils and isn't home to work with me. That's disruption enough!"

Perhaps the good food had softened Lieutenant Richards enough to say, unwisely, "We wouldn't be here, if your President Madison hadn't asked your Congress for a declaration of war on Britain." He pronounced the name of the American president with a decided lack of respect.

"And a good hawk our President James Madison is, too!" Shaw answered. "I voted for him!"

"Voted," Richards echoed on a scornful chuckle.

That was all Jacob Shaw needed for the slender ties of civility to snap. He jerked the napkin from his collar, swatted it down on the table, and happily resorted to name-calling. "Yes, you monarchist bully, voted! And we're going to keep it that way. We hold dear our system and our freedom, and we would not have had to declare war in the first place if the British hadn't been illegally impressing American seamen into their navy."

Richards indulged in a little name-calling himself. "You *colonists* should not have been trading with France this decade past, and if you're wanting to speak of bullies, you certainly consorted with one in Napoleon."

"The French came to our aid when we needed it in '76," was Shaw's answer to that. "Besides which, we had nothing to do with your recent quarrel with Napoleon."

"Playing both sides of the street, you mean," Richards replied. "You thought to make financial hay through trading with both. Well, it didn't work—and it led to this."

Shaw knew that President Madison had stated four major grounds for the declaration of war on Britain, impressment being merely the first. "It was not just that American seamen have been impressed into the Royal Navy—that is but one grievance!" He counted on blunt fingers. "You monarchist bullies have, secondly, violated American neutral rights and territorial waters. Thirdly, you've blockaded American ports."

At the escalation of this most volatile of topics, Stewart did not seem inclined to step into the breach. He was rather more interested just then to gaze idly across the table at Miss Shaw. He thought she looked absurdly fetching in her outdated dress, with its little puffed sleeves that ended in a flounce at the dimples in the elbows. He reflected that this was the first time he had seen her with her hair coiffed, and in real clothing. He vastly preferred her without her clothes, but he was content to see her in this dainty moss-green dress that gave her skin a rich peach glow.

As he thought of the expanse of that skin hidden below the dress, his mind's eye traveled down her body and ended at her toes. On an inspiration, he imagined that her feet, at least, were naked. He dropped his napkin to decide the issue and found, as he bent his head and lifted the table cloth, that he was right. It was titillating to think of the curve of the bare arch of her foot but the table's width away.

A pause fell when Master Shaw could not remember the fourth reason the Americans had so foolishly entered a war they could neither afford nor win. Stewart roused himself and said, "Yes, and then there were the orders in council, don't forget."

"That's it!" Shaw exclaimed, striking hand to forehead in an act of recollection. He seemed inclined to thank the redcoat, but irritation overcame any sense of gratitude.

"The British had no business issuing the orders in '07. *That's* what started it all!"

"Five years later," Richards said. "You're slow to cast down the gauntlet."

Shaw uttered angrily and with slight exaggeration, "It took those five years to accomplish the strangling of a dozen sovereign American ports, the ruination of hundreds of our agricultural markets—"

"Not to mention the crippling of certain American industries and trading companies," Stewart interpolated.

Shaw rounded on him. "Proud of it, aren't you, redcoat?"

Stewart declined to reply.

Shaw finished his recital of the damage the British had done. "And the impressment of thousands of honest American seamen! For an American to be captured and suddenly find himself in the British navy—! It's illegal, I say!"

Stewart glanced over at his host and added on a point of information, "But no. From the British point of view, the orders in council made the impressment of American seamen entirely legal. The force of the Orders is to bar all neutral trade with France and her colonies. The Americans who choose to trade with France and who are caught are impressed into service of the Royal Navy."

"The British should have revoked the demmed orders! That's what Madison wanted, and that's what he didn't get. It's British stubbornness, I tell you, and we've had enough of it!"

"Speaking of stubborn..." Richards was provoked into saying.

Shaw cut him off by rising from his chair and uttering a choked curse. Richards rose in turn. Two pairs of fists were raised, and two pairs of eyes bulged murderously.

Just then Mamie entered the dining room, carrying a fragrant platter.

"It's pie!" Stewart said. He inhaled deeply. "Blueberry. My favorite!"

Chapter Seven

Until that moment, Mamie's contention that "A good meal makes the character better" had been generally disproved. However, the presentation of the pie did serve to maintain the appearances of decorum, at least. Jacob Shaw was certainly not one to forgo the fitting end to an excellent meal simply because he felt like punching some rag-mannered redcoat in the nose; and Lieutenant Richards, as the ranking officer, could hardly stomp out of the room and cede the territory to the man whose house he was occupying. Thus, the two men sat back down and applied themselves to consuming their dessert. It might even have been the case that the flakiness of the crust and the excellence of the filling insensibly soothed some of their more ruffled feathers.

It had been too much to expect that British and Americans at war with one another could set to table together without coming to verbal blows, at least. The two erstwhile combatants were completely absorbed in rather violent consumption of an innocent blueberry pie. Lawler had been reduced to humiliated silence in his inexperience of what passed for dinner-table conversation.

That left the conversational field open to Stewart, instigator and self-appointed mediator of this ill-assorted supper party. During the final course, he maintained a flow of innocuous remarks directed entirely at Miss Shaw, and got up what he considered to be an agreeable flirtation with her, right under Lawler's nose. When they all rose from the table, not too many minutes later, Stewart, for one, felt himself to be well satisfied with the evening, although he knew that Lawler would be aching to meet him on some terrain other than the polite field of the dining room.

Jane walked out of the dining room on her father's arm. In the shadowy hallway, she took her leave of the soldiers, nodding rather coldly at the three of them. She made a stately exit up the staircase, treading the shallow steps with grace, a slight womanly swing to her hips. She could feel Stewart's eyes following her eloquent progress, and hoped that the effect was not totally lost in the relative darkness of the ill-lit hallway. Below her, the men thrashed out their activities for the morrow.

Jacob Shaw flatly refused to leave the next day for his sister Patty's home in Riverdale, which was Lieutenant Richards's preferred plan. When a roll of thunder rambled into the hall, he pronounced, "The rain will hold off for another day, and I'll not be setting off when I should be out in my fields, tending to my business!" Then, adamantly, he added, "It'll be ruination for certain if I'm not out there overseeing the workers. And I'll have to pay them, in any case! I'll not leave for Riverdale tomorrow!"

"Then we'll be starting out in the rain if we delay a day," Richards countered.

"You won't melt" was Jacob Shaw's answer to that.

"But your daughter—"

Shaw fired back, "My Jane—Miss Shaw, to you!—is a hearty American woman who can take a little bit of hardship. American women don't complain, and they know how to run a plantation, which is more than sewing samplers and dipping candles, I can tell you! Yes, it's women like her and my poor departed wife who have helped make this country what it is! Not like those overbred English excuses for women who break in the breeze, and let me tell you—"

Master Shaw was prevented from launching into an impassioned comparative analysis of American and English womanhood by the lieutenant's quick concession. "Have it your way, sir! We'll stay the morrow. But I warn you—I'll be down in the fields with you the entire day—"

"I can use an extra pair of hands, God knows!"

"Watching you the whole time!" Richards finished, restraining himself with effort.

Jacob Shaw was determined to have the last word. "And as for my Jane," he added, "*she* knows how to behave like a lady at the table, which is more than I can say for *your* manners!"

At this second mention of her, Jane, who had reached the door to her bedroom, crept back to the banister and peered down over the railing. She feared that it was going to come in the end to a physical contest between her father and Lieutenant Richards. In the half second that she inched her head over the railing, Stewart looked up and caught her glance. Even in the shadows, she read the look that leapt from his green eyes. It was bold and challenging and knowing. She quickly ducked out of the line of his vision, bracing herself for the scuffle that was sure to ensue between her father and the lieutenant.

Instead, what she heard was Stewart's pleasant voice saying congenially, "Yes, Master Shaw. Miss Shaw is a charming woman who makes a well-behaved addition to any dinner table. Why, I hardly noticed it when she slipped her shoes off under the table. I was tempted to do so myself, but it's these boots, you know. Couldn't manage it!"

Jane's head shot over the edge of the banister. The confounded *nerve* of the man!

Evidently taking advantage of the moment of stunned silence he had created, Stewart put a restraining arm around Richards's shoulder and continued affably, "It's time to turn in, don't you think, Lieutenant? Let's help Lawler set up his sleeping quarters. Me, I'm for the barn." He yawned capaciously. "Sleep's the only thing after a good meal." He turned toward his host who was regarding him, mouth agape. "And thank you, Master Shaw, for an excellent meal!" Then he shot another glance up at the red head peeping up from the banister.

Jane ducked back down, fuming, and went to bed in a quandary. Was it too much of a risk to make contact as usual with Michael Shiner on the morrow? Or had soldier

Stewart just given her the message that he was watching her more closely than she had suspected?

As Jane drifted off to sleep, she mused with satisfaction that Lieutenant Richards was more suspicious of her father, bless his guileless heart, than of her. When she awoke at her habitual hour before the dawn, she decided that she must, at least, risk the meeting with Michael Shiner, in view of the new developments she had to pass along to him. With Richards somewhere downstairs and Lawler camped out on the front porch, she could still use the trusty tree to come and go. She rose and dressed in her climbing clothes. With practiced ease, she stepped out her bedroom window and grasped the branch, along with a thought: *What if Stewart was lurking about?*

Shinnying down the tree, she decided she could embroider the story of her imaginary lover and take the consequences.

And what if Stewart was lurking about to catch her on her return?

Landing nimbly on the ground, she decided she could embroider the story of her imaginary lover and take the consequences—and still derive satisfaction from the fact that she had accomplished her mission.

Her worries concerning Stewart's possible interest in her early-morning escapades seemed to have been misplaced. She went to her meeting unseen and unstopped. She relayed the important news that the British had already accomplished the full pullout from Shaw Plantation the day before. Thus she was able to state confidently that General Ross would be at Bladensburg by way of the Patuxent River by the twenty-fourth, and that the attack on the capital would come from the north. She also informed Michael Shiner that she herself would be outside Washington within the next two days. She was pleased to have persuaded him to follow her into the heat of the action in order to keep the chain of communication alive.

After Jane had outlined the plans to reverse the order of the chain from Riverdale to Baltimore, she returned home in her usual haste. She was tired from the running, and she was perspiring from the cocoon of heat and humidity that wrapped the plantation, made even denser than usual by the coming storm. By the time she passed the tobacco barn un-hindered, she decided that it had been a safe and wise deci-sion to risk this meeting with Michael Shiner.

She suddenly liked the feel of her cheeks beating with blood and her legs aching and her bodice sticking wetly to her breasts, for these were signs that she had been doing her job. She sprinted the last few yards toward the tree. At the trunk, she paused only to grasp the limb above her head. Then she swung gently so that one leg could reach the low-est branch, by which maneuver she would hoist herself up. One leg was a good four feet above the ground when, with disbelieving ears, she heard a very familiar voice.

"I'd rather watch you climb a tree than anything so or-dinary as the stairs."

Stewart appeared before her, as if he had been waiting behind the tree. With her leg raised, exposing a great ex-panse of petticoat, calf and thigh, Jane had the fleeting thought of just why he might like seeing her thus. How-ever, in this same moment, she lost her grip and her foot-ing.

She swallowed a rather breathless "Oh, good heavens!" which served as a response to both his remark and her slip.

"Not that you did not make an effective exit last night up the stairs," he continued, amused and enchanted by the comical combination of surprise, indignation and wom-anly awareness that crossed her features. "Elegant. Grace-ful. Even provocative."

All this was too much for Jane. She had brought her leg down, but she could not keep her footing on the ground. Her surprise kept her off balance, and her indignation prompted her to jump back from him. Her body could not reasonably respond to the various messages it was receiv-ing, and she stumbled. In an awkward attempt to remain upright, she began to windmill her arms.

Stewart stepped forward to catch her before she fell. One of her circling arms caught him on the side of his face. Thus, instead of grasping her smoothly behind the back, he caught her at her waist, rather heavily, further jeopardizing her already precarious balance. Her leg went up, and she accidentally kicked him in the shin. This action knocked him off balance in turn, and sent the two of them tumbling backward. Stewart had no other choice than to twist his body so that he would bear the brunt of the fall.

With a swirl of petticoats and a tangle of legs, the two hit the ground with a thud. Stewart was flat on his back. Jane was sitting smack on top of him, her knees touching the ground on either side of his hips. The tops of her feet were facing down, and her legs were in the dirt from the length of her shins to the tips of her toes. Her first impulse was *not* to spring off him. Rather, she was initially very happy with the way their bodies had "fallen out," for it gave her the advantage, and the opportunity to treat him in the manner that he sorely deserved.

"This is the worst you've done yet! How dare you lurk outside *my* house and hide behind *my* tree and scare me like that!" she said angrily. She sat on him as she had done as a girl, scuffling with her younger brother. She grasped the collar of his shirt, raising his head slightly off the ground. "Now see what you've gone and done, redcoat!" Then she began pommeling his chest with her free fist.

Upon impact, Stewart had momentarily had the breath knocked out of him. His arms lay useless at his sides. By the time she had begun hitting him, he had recovered. In an act of self-defense, he shot both hands up and grasped her wrists. In an economical movement that proved he could be quick when necessary, Stewart rolled out from under her.

She had been prepared for his eventual resistance and was ready to counter it. She had not been prepared for his rapid mastery of her. He was only a head taller than she was, and he was of a medium build that looked more wiry than muscular. However, when she suddenly found herself pinned beneath him, Jane had the occasion to revise her estimation of his speed and strength.

"What *I've* gone and done?" he echoed. "You've a gall, my girl, beating me like that, when I tried to save you!"

She attempted to free her arms, which he held down at her sides, but she was unsuccessful. He was raised above her by the length of his arms, which were straightened, with elbows locked. His shirt was partly opened, and his shirt-sleeves were rolled up, giving her a fair view of the muscles of his forearms and shoulders and neck. She had a vivid memory now of the expanse of his muscular torso as he had taken his bath in the clearing, the first time she had met him.

Clearly defeated, but unwilling to concede, she looked up at him and said, "*Save* me? That's rich, redcoat! After what you said to me? You knew it would throw me off balance. You just *knew* it!"

"I only said that it seemed more fitting for you to climb a tree than the stairs."

She squirmed beneath him, but did not thereby obtain her release. "As you would expect of a savage? Isn't that it, redcoat?"

"Which I am not wearing."

"It hardly matters. A redcoat is a redcoat whether he's wearing his uniform or not." She fairly spit her words at him in her anger. "And a redcoat expects us poor Americans to behave like savages."

He smiled slowly. "Not necessarily. I also noted that your ascent of the stairs last night was most befitting a haughty young lady. Elegant and graceful, I think I said. Most effective." She squirmed again as he looked momentarily away from her. "Even provocative." He cast her a shadowed glance from the corner of his eyes and said deliberately, "However, perhaps not more provocative than the present encounter," adding slyly, "my savage little American."

Jane immediately ceased her movements. It was only then that she fully realized that their positions had been exactly reversed. Embarrassingly reversed. She was stretched out beneath him as he had been beneath her moments before. This time she was flat on her back, and her feet were on the ground, soles down in the dirt. From her previous position on top of him, her skirts had been caught up around her waist, and her petticoats now foamed around his crotch.

There was no denying that the position was a provocative one, and from her point of view, as well. She was shocked at her response to him. To cover it, even from herself, she tossed back defiantly, "That's right! Insult me now, when I can do nothing to retaliate! It's a lesson in manners you need! You and every other redcoat!" But her courage was false, and her voice betrayed her by wavering in fear.

"If there's a lesson to be learned," he replied evenly, "it's not to beat on someone who's stronger than you."

Her brown eyes flashed fear. Still, she maintained her defiance. "Which applies to the present war, I suppose you would say."

"I did not say it."

"But you meant it!"

"I meant only that you could not have hoped that I would not defend myself against your attack."

"And how," she asked in her still defiant yet wavery voice, "am I now to defend myself against you?"

He had wondered, at first, how far this encounter might go. From the look on her face now, he understood that it would fall far short of his initial surge of expectation when he had found himself on his back beneath her.

"No defense will be necessary," he said with regret. He released her and rose, allowing her to arrange her skirts. Then he bent and stretched out his hand to her. "And to show you I need no lesson in manners, I will offer to help you up."

Jane had made it to a sitting position, and she looked up at him warily. Then she took his hand and was raised to her feet. "Thank you," she said primly, and it nearly choked her to utter the civility.

"You are welcome," he said, bowing politely. He began to brush himself off, just as she was brushing off the dirt and dust.

Her head came up, and she looked at him in the barely lightening dawn. His breath was coming rapidly. In being aware of his heightened breathing, she became aware of her own. "Spare me your redcoat gallantry," she snapped, "and tell me instead what you think you are doing out here. I don't suppose it was to learn a lesson in manners."

He had come out to see her, of course, and why not? She was a dewy, delicious young woman in the delicacy of her sensual flowering, and visions of her beautiful nakedness had filled his waking dreams the night long. He had already assumed her unmaidenly morals, and with the unconscious condescension of his well-bred youth, he had factored in the dilapidation of Shaw Plantation and Master Shaw's blustery ineffectiveness to arrive at the sum that Miss Jane Shaw—a beauty without a grand dowry to keep the local gentlemen respectful or a strong father to protect and control her—was fair game.

He folded his arms and leaned against the tree, considering the answer to her question. Then he said, boldly, "Knowing your habits as I do now, I was hoping to run into you. Not literally, of course, but—"

She broke in. "How did you know about the tree? Have you been following me?"

He assumed the mien of an innocent. "No, ma'am," he said politely, "but I figured the tree was merely your likeliest point of entry and exit in and out of the house."

Jane did not believe him for a second. "You *have* been following me—as if you had the run of our property! First it was the clearing and my bath—" She broke off, vexed to have brought up that unfortunate incident.

He smiled at the pleasurable memory. Then he admonished her, "You should never have taken the risk of that bath, you know."

She did know it, but she hated being wrong, and she hated even worse admitting it. It was her worst fault, and it was a bad one to beset an impulsive nature like her own. In bristling defense, she fired back, "I suppose that *you've* never been in the wrong?"

He considered the question. "No, that's not my particular fault."

"What, never being in the *wrong?*" she said, incredulous.

He laughed. "No, never being unable to admit it," he replied slyly. "If you're going to take risks—"

She held up her hand, "I know! But let us make this tit for tat on the subject of character faults. Your besetting sin is clearly arrogance."

"I've been called arrogant," he admitted, as if the characteristic were more of a quality than a fault.

Since she was not going to get the better of him on this score, she returned to a more pertinent subject. She smiled prettily. "And in your arrogance you have not yet explained what you were doing, waiting for me behind the tree."

His smile matched hers. He decided to disarm her. "I thought you would appreciate the opportunity to continue our stimulating conversation of last night."

It worked. Jane was momentarily speechless.

"And I timed it to accommodate your busy schedule," he continued smoothly. "I guessed that you would have gone out again this morning to kiss and not tell. Did I guess wrong?"

Jane gasped, flushed vividly at the implication, then recovered. "I wouldn't be telling, of course," she retorted, adding swiftly, "and you thought I would appreciate *what?*"

"The opportunity to continue our conversation from supper."

"What made you think that?"

"Because you were flirting with me last night."

"I was not!"

"But you were!"

She could only shake her head and roll her eyes heavenward.

"Take, for example, your response to my question about local social engagements. Now, never minding the obvious fact that there has not been much socializing around North Point for the last year or two, you were quite expansive on the subject of church socials and house parties."

"And how can that be interpreted as flirting with you?"

"Because you were responding in kind to all of my gambits."

"Perhaps I was simply too well mannered not to respond under the circumstances."

"Ah, but you did it so beautifully, I thought you liked me. I did not guess it was because you were too well mannered."

She put her hands on her hips. "Is there no limit to your good opinion of me? You may as well have said that I have been hard up for male company these many months past!"

The comment surprised him. She would hardly think that he imagined she had been hard up for male company, since she had given him the opposite impression of her adventurings; and this little slip gave him a fleeting new perspective on her early-morning activities. Armed now with knowledge of the floor plan of the house, he suddenly realized that her bedroom stood directly over army headquarters in the dining room. He also recalled that the row of windows gave onto the side of the house, not onto the back, thus making the tree the perfect means of escape.

He dismissed the possibility of her spying as easily as it had come to him, for he did not want to call into doubt his casual assumption of her easy sexuality. Nor did he comment on the implication of her reference to lack of male company. Instead, he remarked, "You've had a regiment of men on your property for over a week. If you were truly that hard up for male company, I assure you, you could have had your pick."

"Dick Lawler, for instance?" she said, her tone falsely sweet.

"I've never thought you had bad taste."

She opened her mouth to retort. She closed it. She had to laugh at the very backhanded compliment. "Are you always this irritating?"

He grinned. "Oh, no, I can be more irritating, if I set my mind to it. For example . . ."

She did not need to search far for a fitting example. "Yes, your comment about my shoes being off under the table."

He smiled innocently. "I spared your father a bloody nose and saved several of his teeth, no doubt! You should be thanking me for having created such an effective diversion!"

"*Extremely* irritating," she remarked pointedly.

"Does that mean you won't be thanking me?"

She bit back her pert response. She was enjoying this a little too much. It was bad enough of her to have given him the impression that she was a woman eager for early-morning adventure. It was even worse of her to realize that if she lingered any longer he would try to charm her out of her clothes—which was his obvious intention—and that he would credit her with good taste if he succeeded!

"It means, redcoat," she said, "that I'll be leaving you now."

She glanced up the tree, and his eyes followed hers. When he lowered his eyes again, they fell on her feet. Her bare toes peeped out from under her skirt.

"*Much* better without the shoes," he murmured.

"Much better for climbing," she answered. "Now go, do!" She shooed him away with an impatient gesture. "I can't climb back up with you here." When she made as if to grasp the branch above her and he did not move, she repeated, "Go away! And don't look!"

He declined to say that he had already had that view of her backside, and a delightful view it had been. Instead, he confined himself to saying, "See you at breakfast." Then, like a ghost, he disappeared into the swirling white morning mists.

Chapter Eight

The sun slipped up over the eastern horizon an hour later, searing an earth turned sultry. In the west, the clouds were steaming and angry. The sky was pied, haze-blue and thunder-black.

With the appealing prospect of spending the day in his fields before him, Jacob Shaw arose in an excellent humor. He rounded up his companions of the night before and ushered them into the dining room, where they breakfasted on salty red ham, china-white eggs with canary centers, powder-light biscuits and brown gravy. Master Shaw's bluff good humor carried him through the meal, heedless of the currents swirling through the room.

Master Shaw did not seem to notice, for instance, that his daughter had little appetite and was toying with her food. Jane's spirits had sunk in glum acknowledgment that Stewart had been right: She *had* been flirting with him the evening before. She was determined not to do so again, but was not given much opportunity to show that she was not interested in him, for Stewart was directing few comments toward her. However, she did look up once to see his speculative hazel gaze resting on her. Their eyes met for a moment before he turned and said something inconsequential to Lieutenant Richards.

Jane could have sworn that, whatever else Stewart had told his superior officer this morning, he had not mentioned the predawn encounter below the tree outside her bedroom window. She tried to be happy that Stewart had believed her story. For his part, Lieutenant Richards was as determined as ever to spend the day by Master Shaw's side, still suspecting him as the possible spy in the house, and not her.

Despite his blunt sensibilities, Jacob Shaw was not completely unmindful of his duties toward his pretty young unmarried daughter. When finished with his meal, he shoved his chair back and rose. Very congenially inviting Lieutenant Richards to "be quick about it," he stated his desire to get his hands dirty in honest labor. He added jovially, but with a significant look at Stewart and Lawler, "Now, boys, don't think you'll be lying around the house today, getting under my Jane's feet as she goes about her business!"

Stewart announced his intention to go fishing for the evening supper. This suggestion was met with approval, particularly from Master Shaw, who liked the thought of at least one of the males far away from the house.

"And you, sir?" Shaw continued, eyeing Lawler.

"I don't like fishing," he said with angry challenge.

Jane had been busying herself by helping Mamie clear the table of dirty dishes. At the moment her father addressed Lawler, she was removing his plate. The note in the redcoat's voice, and the darkling, predatory look he shot her, filled her with fear. An amorphous but palpable anger radiated from him. She drew back, anxious to hear how his day was to be apportioned.

"Well, then," Shaw continued, "you can bear us company in the fields." There was a charged moment in the room before Shaw looked over at Richards. "What say you, Lieutenant?"

The lieutenant must have sensed the charge, for he said, authoritatively, "Yes, Lawler, you can accompany us to the fields."

Lawler's assent was a growl.

Soon the four men were out on the drive, ready to depart in their respective directions. Shaw wished Stewart good fishing, to which the latter replied, "It'll be easy today. With the storm coming, some of the fish will be swimming higher in the water, making them easier to catch."

Master Shaw looked out to the west and pronounced confidently, "The storm won't be arriving today. The clouds behind us are a good day away. They're big and fat and can't move any faster in this heat."

So Shaw and Lawler drove out into the fields in the rickety wagon, with Richards next to them on his horse. Stewart ambled down to the river. Jane stayed close by the house with Mamie. The clouds moved in swiftly, defying the drag of the heat and proving Jacob Shaw dead wrong as the rains came.

In midafternoon, spatters of rain began to sizzle onto the dusty drive. The air was crunchy with bugs, and Jane was working in the garden, alternately swatting at the bugs, wiping the sweat from her brow and plucking the weeds. When the first drops came, she closed her eyes and held her face up to receive the welcome water. It felt wonderful and was all the more delightful in that it had come upon her so sudden. When she opened her eyes, she saw that the sun was blotted out from the sky and that the storm clouds had gathered straight above her into a rumbling, malevolent mass of dark violence.

She rose and ran into the house, and none too soon, for without further warning, the heavens opened up and poured out their fury. In less than a minute, the rain had gone from a few soft drops to a drenching. Leaning against the open back door of the kitchen, she watched the dirty curtain of wet gauze descend on the earth. She thought of her father, out in the fields, and hoped he had had the sense to return home.

She heard a noise on the porch and hurried out, expecting to see her father. Instead, she saw Dick Lawler, stomping his boots to free them of water and mud.

Jane came as far as the front door. She looked at Lawler, then out beyond him into the drive, then back at him. She asked, "Where are my father and the lieutenant?"

Lawler took a step toward her. This was just the way he liked it. He had been seething since last night, wanting to get this little piece away from the table and all that polite conversation. He hated words. Action, that was what he knew about. That was what counted. He wanted the action of her under him, where she belonged. Where he could prove to her he was a man. He'd let the man in his trousers do all the talking. He'd show her. He'd show Stewart. He'd have his way.

He took another step toward her. "They're still out in the fields."

"What are you doing here?" She did not disguise her distaste at his presence, but she tried to disguise her fear.

He took another step. "I was sent back for some equipment. It hadn't started raining when I left."

Jane stood her ground in the doorway. Her heart was pounding painfully. She was alone with this man. In the middle of the day. With no one around to protect her.

"Won't this be fun, missy, just you and me and the rain?" he said, taking yet another step, so that he was before her.

His hand came out to touch her. Jane was imagining how best she could defend herself when a series of whoops and hoots came across the drive, diverting Lawler's attention from Jane.

Stewart bounded onto the porch. He bent over and shook spangles of rainwater from his hair and shoulders. When he stood upright, Jane saw that he was laughing, his hazel eyes dancing with green. He was obviously delighted with his run across the yard and the wetting he'd had. When his gaze fell on her, as she stood framed in the shadowy doorway, his eyes glinted and lingered a moment. His gaze shifted to Lawler, whose hands had balled into fists.

In a flash, Stewart had taken in the complexities of the situation. However, as if unaware, he gestured with his heavy catch of fish. "Dinner," he announced with boyish satisfaction, extending for inspection a string of shad, bonito and perch, shiny, finny creatures fresh from the water. "I'll take them to the kitchen. My guess is that cook knows to a turn how to fry a fish."

"I'll follow you," Jane said quickly. She moved slightly to allow Stewart to pass by her. He did not physically brush her as he strode through the doorway, but it felt as if he had, for her senses filled with the scent of the river, of the rain, and of a man pleased with himself. She told herself that this response to him was only in reaction to the relief she felt at his very timely arrival.

As she followed him down the hallway, she asked, "How did you happen to come back just at the moment the storm blew in? Was it luck?"

"No," he said. "I saw the storm coming about half an hour ago. I had my catch by then, so I hastened back."

"You caught so many fish in so little time?" she asked, impressed.

He grinned back at her over his shoulder. "I blocked the creek this morning by building a dam, so that I could catch them with my hands."

"A dam?"

"I never outgrew liking to play in the dirt," he answered.

Lawler was left speechless on the front porch, but hardly abashed. He had no intention of returning to the fields and leaving the pretty little piece for Stewart's personal amusement. And he had the perfect excuse: There'd be no returning, given this rain. He followed them down the hallway. He felt his swagger return. He'd be running the show now.

In the appetizing sanctuary of the kitchen, Mamie was at the far end of the room, conjuring a low fire in the fireplace. She was heating up her cast-iron spider in the glowing coals between the andirons. Outside the open back door, the rain was falling in torrential sheets. Through the windows, the drain chutes at the sides of the house could be seen spouting water like large open taps.

Stewart went to the sink stone, explaining that he needed to gut his catch.

"Why, yas, Massa James," was Mamie's easy response, and she supplied him with one of her precious kitchen knives.

So his name is James, then, Jane thought. *And Mamie already knows it!*

To Jane he explained, with a devastatingly attractive smile, "The sooner I eat, the better. The bread and cheese I brought down to the river this morning was not enough to sustain me during a hard day's fishing.''

"A hard day's fishing?" she echoed skeptically, putting up a strong guard against the effects of that smile.

"Strenuous, in fact," he returned complacently. He wielded the knife deftly. Then, again over his shoulder, he asked, "How goes the fire, Cook? Are we ready to fry 'em? Let's eat here in the kitchen. What say you, Lawler?"

Lawler had arrived at the door to the kitchen, but he hung back, as if something were preventing him from actually entering the room.

Sensing the new presence, Mamie looked up and gave Lawler the eye. "Come in, boy," she said. "Come into my kitchen."

Her words had the form of an invitation, but to Jane's ears, they sounded more like one of her Mamie's commands. Lawler obeyed. Mamie sent the "big strong boy" to fetch the two long benches stacked in the adjacent pantry and to set them on either side of the trestle table. Again, Lawler obeyed, if only because he did not know how to refuse a black giantess as big as himself who had reduced him to a "boy."

Thus was Stewart's question answered: They were to eat in the kitchen. Stewart finished his preparations. He crossed the kitchen, bringing the fish to the fiery altar in his upturned palms. The dark priestess was ready with a bowl of batter to dip the offerings in. Soon enough the smell of fried fish would billow throughout the expansive kitchen and chase away the pervasive damp and the sharp smell of newly wet earth.

Jane watched these proceedings with some astonishment. Stewart had all but taken over Mamie's retreat. To Jane's further amazement, he seemed to be at home in this environment, fiddling at the fire and chatting frivolously with Mamie. When Lawler had done with the benches, he turned and said, "You'll join me?"

Lawler had hardly nodded yes before Mamie again enlisted the aid of "the big strong boy" in helping her to fetch and set the heavy iron grille athwart the andirons so that she could lay two skillets at once.

While Lawler was occupied in this cumbersome, lumbering task, Stewart asked Jane if she would join them in the afternoon fare. She declined, saying she had eaten at midday. For lack of anything better to do, she motivated herself to wipe up the table. She went about setting two places for the men, then paused and asked aloud, of no one in particular, "Or should I set the table for four, anticipating my father's return with the lieutenant?"

Stewart gazed out the windows lining the back of the house and asked, "What's your father's custom in bad weather?"

She glanced at him and answered, a little ruefully, "He's usually a better predictor of the weather than he was today. I haven't known him to get caught before." She added, defensively, "He's been uncommon disturbed this past week, and he wanted to make up today for some lost time."

Stewart did not respond to that. Instead, he asked, "How far away is the field he was working today?"

"Under half an hour on foot, if you walk straight through the property," she said, "but he took the wagon, as you'll recall, with the intention of driving around, and the lieutenant no longer has his horse. By wagon, it's a slow drive of upwards of an hour the long way around."

Stewart judged that the rain had already been falling for half an hour. "In that case, then, they might be halfway home."

"Perhaps Father had the sense to leave the wagon there and to return on foot," Jane said, "in which case, they should be here any moment now." At that, she left the kitchen to return to the front porch. There she hoped to see signs of her father's return.

Stewart followed her out of the kitchen. "That depends on whether he realized soon enough that the storm was upon them, and whether he and Richards could subsequently agree to return on foot together."

Jane was hurrying, but she slowed enough to swerve her head around. "Is your Lieutenant Richards truly idiotic enough to insist on a return by wagon?"

"He is," Stewart answered gravely. "He prides himself on his cavalry status and doesn't like to walk." To Jane's smirk, Stewart added, "And your father isn't likely to have acknowledged the strength of the storm until *after* it had started."

Jane's smirk vanished, and she hurried down the hallway. She stepped onto the porch and surveyed the front drive. It was awash in puddle-wide streams. The muted roar of the deluge was louder and more insistent out here, where the buckets of water fell directly on the porch roof. Jane's eyes suddenly widened at the thought of her father and Lieutenant Richards attempting to negotiate their return.

"Imagine the two of them agreeing on *anything,* even a plan of action in the rain," Jane said with a little gasp.

"I can't," Stewart replied.

"The wheels will be mired in mud by now if they took the wagon," she said in a voice of doom.

"Could they make it back by walking?" Stewart asked.

Jane ran her mind's eyes around her father's fields and access routes. She looked down at the deepening mud in the drive. She peered into the rain for any distant sign of returning men. She could hardly see twenty feet in front of her. "Not by the main drive," she answered at last.

"How about straight across the fields?"

She looked up to see Stewart gazing down at her. "I'm afraid it will be hardly possible now. Our property is all lowlands, and the fields must be five feet deep in muck by now."

"And if they cannot return to the house in this weather—?" Stewart asked.

Without turning her eyes from his, Jane struggled to assimilate the implications of the possibility that her father would not be returning home this day. "There are workers' cabins on the edge of the fields," she answered slowly. "If Lieutenant Richards has the sense to agree to seek them out, they'll be able to spend the night in dry shelter with food."

"Then you needn't worry," Stewart said. Their gazes remained locked, and then he dropped his eyes to her lips.

I needn't worry? she said to herself. She dropped her eyes to his lips, as well. She suddenly thought of plenty to worry about.

The aroma of frying fish drifted out to the porch and curled around them.

"I'm ravenous," he said.

"Then you'll want to eat it while it's hot."

He smiled and said, "Mmm-hmm," rather dreamily.

"It's ready now."

"Is it?"

"I think so. Can't you tell by the smell?"

He looked back up at her eyes. His nostrils flared delicately. "Usually."

Something electric and compelling in his regard caused Jane to break eye contact. She turned away and walked, a little unsteadily at first, down the hallway. "If you're wanting to eat, you'll have to do it in the kitchen."

He seemed to consider that. "I don't object to satisfying my hunger in the kitchen," he said, following her.

She did not dare counter that statement. It was playful enough. On the surface. In its way. But then again . . .

She felt that danger had slipped into the house. It had not taken so obvious a form as that of the hateful Dick Lawler. The danger she sensed was subtle, elusive, insidious. It seemed to hover about this man, who was not at all hateful, who had seen her naked in the bath, who had caught her one dawn, thinking she was running back from her lover, who had flirted with her the evening before, who had had her stretched out beneath him only this morning, who had impossibly beautiful lips, who wore a red coat.

She had a shivery prospect of the hours ahead, and of how she was going to fill them without the protection of her father and without Lieutenant Richards to keep his soldiers in line. Perhaps Mamie could be counted on to lend propriety to this highly improper situation.

Jane returned to the kitchen. She was not initially reassured by Mamie's unconcern over her father's and the lieutenant's absence. The proposition that Master Shaw might not be returning this night drew from Mamie the chuckling observation that he would be in sorry spirits on the morrow, after a night in a field hand's cabin, for "Masser Shaw, he like only my food and his mattress!" Nor was Jane heartened by the sight of Mamie fussing over James Stewart as if she had dandled him as a baby on her knee. However, Jane noticed that Mamie exerted a strange influence on Lawler's behavior. Mamie seemed to have taken Lawler's strutting maleness and balled it like biscuit dough so that she could shape it to her will.

For all the strangeness of the present situation, Jane had no desire to leave the cheery atmosphere of the kitchen. The two men had tucked into their pan-fried fish and cold green beans and ripe summer melons. Lawler, oddly cowed and obedient, was almost cordial to Stewart, who teased and talked when the spirit moved him. Mamie was happy and humming. Jane stirred the fire on the hearth with the poker, encouraging the flickery flames to keep the damp at bay. The steady thrum of the rain on the roof two floors above lulled the whole and cut this cozy contentment off from the rest of the world. It was as if the house had broken its moorings and was floating, isolated, in an ocean of mud and water.

The afternoon drifted on, formlessly, since the usual rhythms of the day had been rendered irrelevant by the rain. The men consumed their belated dinner, but somehow the eating slowed and stretched and eventually became the evening meal. Hungry, Jane sat down across from the two men to eat, but not Mamie, of course, for no human being alive other than Amos had ever seen a morsel of food pass her lips. By Mamie's magic, there appeared on the table more vegetables and more fruit, and griddle cakes and pitchers of water. By the same magic, Stewart and Lawler found more appetite.

The day, dimmed since the onset of rain, had thoroughly drained to dusk. Candles were lit, and two lanterns hung.

The thick curtain of rain was still falling. Streams of water continually drizzled down the irregular panes of the kitchen window glass, etching weird, melting faces in silver filigree against the wet bat's wing of the night. With the unpredictable upcurrents from so much heat and steam rising from the rain-swollen earth, the candles flickered and smoked, smoked and flickered. Even the flames in the lanterns sucked and coughed within their glass globes. At one moment, all the flames flattened and died. The next moment they blazed unnaturally bright.

It was in the interval of those two moments that Mamie had begun to speak. Her voice was thick and dark as the licorice of her eyes, and she was telling a story about a girl, a Negro girl. It seemed that the story had been begun in the middle, or else it had started before the lights had died and sprung, bedeviled, to life again. But not one of the three white faces listening to the story remembered Mamie speaking before the lights had died and been reborn. They could not have stated the beginning of the story, or when Mamie had begun to tell it, or how that Negro girl got into the forest, or where she was going, or what was in the basket she was carrying, or why she had an irresistible attraction to that tree.

There that Negro girl was, though, amid a circle of trees, holding the basket, and surrounded by bushes that looked like rhododendrons. One tree stood tall and proud in the center of the circle. She took a step toward that tree and stepped onto a mossy floor. She took another step and sank to her ankles. She dropped her basket and grabbed the waist of the tree, which shivered in her arms and swayed as though it wished to dance with her. She struggled to lift her feet and sank a foot farther down into the moss-covered jelly. She tightened her arms around the tree and swayed with it, accepting the dance. Hang on, she thought, hang on and dance. That is what it wants. There was murmuring and music from above. She looked up to identify the source of the sounds, but saw nothing, for they were coming from hidden places high in the tree. She had erred in wanting to find the source, for as she raised her head, she sank farther into the jelly. Now she was knee-deep.

Hang on, just hang on. She wanted to put her legs around the tree, encircle it with her legs as she had encircled it with her arms. She wanted to edge up the tree to save herself. She agreed to dance. She thought, no point in looking down at the slime, it would make her think of worms or snakes or crocodiles. Don't sweat, or you'll lose your partner, the tree. Cleave to it. Cling to it. Creep up on it like an inchworm, a fraction at a time, slower than the slime. Cover it like the moss. Caress its bark and finger its ridges. Leave tender skin behind. Sway when it sways, and shiver with it, too. Love it and trust it with your life, because you are now up to the tops of your thighs in jelly.

The tree sighed and swayed. The murmuring and music stopped. The women hidden in the branches looked down at her. They were delighted by the girl. The girl was fighting to get away from them, but the women hanging in the tree knew that the black girl was theirs. They wondered at the girl's desperate struggle to separate herself from the tree, to free herself from the mire into which she had sunk to the tops of her thighs but would sink no further.

The story ended as raggedly as it had begun. The silence in the kitchen was, at once, eerie and enticing.

Lawler, who had bent his ear effortfully to the tuneful contours of Mamie's voice, had blanched. It fell to Stewart to gamely ask the question, "And what happened to the girl?"

"Gone."

"She died?"

"Gone."

"Where?"

Mamie did not answer.

"How?"

"The womans."

"Were they tree spirits?"

Mamie exhaled softly. "Zombies."

Jane had heard many of Mamie's stories about the zombies, but not this one. She wanted proof. "How does anyone know about this?"

"From the basket on the ground, and from the skin on the tree. Black skin."

"Where did you hear it?" Jane persisted.

"Tonight. Now."

"Mamie!"

"From the zombies. They tol' me. They come."

"Tonight?"

"On the air. They cut the flames. They lit them again." She added, as a point of information, "They come tonight as womans."

Lawler was spooked. He had never heard of the zombies before, and did not want to hear of them again. He stood, and in standing encountered a weird, skittering shadow. He jumped, prepared to wrestle with it. He shook himself. He cleared his head. He told himself that he no longer wanted the pretty American chit, but the truth was that, deep down, he feared the power of Mamie's zombies. Something in that story had made him want to clutch the cowering man in his trousers, to hang on to him, to make sure the little man was still attached to him when he awoke the next morning.

What he said aloud was "I'm setting up my bed on the porch again." He did not add that that was the place on the first floor of the house at the farthest remove from the kitchens. Without another word, he helped himself to one of the lanterns and abruptly left the room.

Mamie vanished into the shadowy recesses of the kitchen. She moved soundlessly from fireplace to sink stone and back again.

Jane looked into the hazel pool of Stewart's eyes, and their gazes held. She decided to rise and bid him good-night, but found that her legs could not support her.

"So," he said, crossing his hands on the table in front of him, "tell me about this lover of yours."

Chapter Nine

As if there were some good reason I should respond to that! Jane mentally huffed, torn between surprise and indignation.

"Unless, of course, there is nothing to tell," he continued. "Unless you were doing something else these past mornings."

And here just might be that good reason! she mused, less indignantly, more warily. She turned his words over in her mind, using her best intuition to determine what he knew about her and what he did not.

But what her intuition told her was not what she wanted to hear. What she heard was of this moment. She caught the faint whisper of soft, flickering flames, the strange, sensual echo of Mamie's story, his smooth, seductive voice asking smooth, seductive questions, and the steady beating of the rain, like the pounding of a racing heart, reminding her that the two of them existed in the here and now of the kitchen, cut off from the world by the muffle of a wet curtain. That was what she heard, the sounds of isolated intimacy, and these sounds conspired to heighten Jane's awareness of that intimacy, and of him.

The contained, unformed danger she had felt before supper, which had been suspended during Mamie's story, had now been set loose. It had a body and was sitting two feet away. It had a velvety voice and a lazy green gaze. She did not look away from him. His well-cut features were sharply defined in the light. His well-set shoulders cast a large shadow projected onto the wall behind him. The sleeves of his shirt were rolled up to his elbows, revealing the sinews of his forearms sprinkled with hairs bleached blond in the candlelight.

And his statement still demanded a response. She swallowed. She stalled for time. "It's difficult to know where to begin."

He was helpful. "Did he touch you first with his hands or with his lips?" He paused. When she did not immediately respond, he suggested, "Or did you touch *him* first?"

"No," she managed.

"So, then," he said, "he touched you. Where?"

Jane wanted to look around for Mamie, but she could not be so craven as to do so. She knew that Mamie's body was present in the kitchen, but she imagined that Mamie's mind was absorbed in communication with the zombies who were swirling around her head. Still, nothing could happen to Jane with Mamie's body present, no matter where Mamie's mind was.

"I need some details," he said, softly, persuasively, "to be convinced."

"He kissed me," Jane said.

One of his brows quirked with interest. "On the lips?"

"Yes."

"Did you kiss him back?"

"Not at first."

"But eventually?"

She felt herself sink ankle-deep in moss jelly. She could, she *should* stop this conversation right now. However, if she did, she might be forced to explain what she had really been doing these past mornings, running, hot and sweaty, through the plantation. "Yes, I kissed him back."

"Was it a long kiss?" he asked. His eyes lingered on her lips.

He might as well have been kissing her himself, for the sensation she felt. "Long enough."

"Long enough for what?"

Now she was knee-deep in the mire. She could see that he was not going to let her wriggle off the hook he had so deftly caught her with. He was intent on hearing the details. All of them. To be convinced. But there weren't any. Yet she did not quite have to make up a love scene, either. She remembered her last meeting with Bobby Harlan, almost two years ago. Strong, quiet Bobby Harlan. The man she had meant to marry. Bobby Harlan, now gone, never to come back. She did not regret for a moment how they had spent their last evening together. If she had a regret, it was that she had held him off too long.

"Long enough to make the next step possible," she said, "even necessary."

"Ah."

Warming to her story, Jane sank deeper in the jelly. It aroused old grief, and even older lust. She had not felt that lust in months and months, and it had been bottled up all this time, strong and unspent. It felt good to let a little of it out, to feel it spreading around her ankles and knees and thighs. She felt it now in tribute to Bobby Harlan. However, it was not just a lust for his kiss and his touch, but for his life, as well, and his life was gone.

"After the kiss," she said quietly, "we touched."

"Where?"

"Everywhere."

He prompted her to continue with just the lazy, leading look in his eyes as they swept her face and touched her shoulders and her bodice. Her remembered lust for Bobby Harlan's kiss and touch and life intertwined with her heightened awareness of the danger seated across from her. She felt light, feathery fingers graze the inside of her legs, above her knees. They were not human fingers, but zombie fingers, arousing her. She pressed her legs together to ward them off. She was not sure that movement helped.

Why had the zombies come this night to tell Mamie such a story? Jane was a pure—or almost pure—white girl. She was not in some forest. Nor was she carrying a basket. So why did she feel the moss jelly coming up around her? To straighten her confused thoughts, she brought back to life the long-buried words Bobby Harlan had said to her during that last, lovely evening they were together.

"He touched me everywhere," she said, her voice still quiet, but more confident now, "but mostly here." She placed her hand on her breast and let it rest over her heart.

His eyes followed her gesture and watched the rise and fall of her bodice with her quickened breathing. "With his hands, then," he said boldly, "he unbuttoned your bodice."

She shook her head slowly and favored him with a chiding glance that held just enough sultry reproach to cause his lazy eyes to widen a bit. "You are too literal, redcoat," she said.

"But not, ultimately, wrong, I think," he commented, unchastened.

"No, not ultimately wrong," she agreed with a provocative look and inflection of her own, "but not quite right, either."

"And the rest of your clothes?"

If he intended to have her squirm on his hook, she could set him to dangling, too. "What clothes?" She took her hand from her breast and drew up her shoulders, teasing him, tantalizing him, by giving them a little shake. Then she leaned forward, looking straight at him. "But there is so much more to feel when kissing and touching—" here she looked away, then back at him "—than, well, just lips and hands." She dropped her lashes, then swept them up again. "Even if you are kissing and touching everywhere. With no clothes."

He was willing to take the bait. "More to feel? Such as?"

"It's a lesson in love you need now, redcoat."

"Is that what we're talking about?"

"Yes, love," she said. "You see, he'd known me most of my life, and—"

He seized on her error. "Had known?"

"Has known," she corrected swiftly. "He's known me most of my life, and so he knows what I like. And I know him and what he likes."

"Which is—?"

"Love, redcoat." She relaxed further, leaning forward, into her hands, which were crossed on top of the table. His eyes were fixed on her, and on the curve of her bodice, which gaped slightly. She told him, her voice low, "What he likes is love and affection and honesty. What I like is constancy and good faith and respect." Now that her love and lust had been reawakened in the presence of this man, she realized that she was, indeed, in a forest whose floor was covered with moss jelly. However, she had found the strong tree that would save her from sinking past the tops of her thighs. She grasped its thick trunk. Her voice had dropped almost to a whisper when she added, breathlessly, "And commitment to the American victory."

She saw from the expression on his face that she had succeeded in hooking him and pulling him right out of the water to dangle. She smiled with satisfaction. "And then, when he reached my heart and I reached his, we kissed and touched some more and did everything to make the next step, then the next step... and then the very next step... possible... even necessary."

She straightened and dropped all pretense of provocation. The expression on her face and in her voice were like a cold shower. "Now I've kissed and told, redcoat, as you wanted me to do. Are you convinced by my details?"

Stewart made an effort to pull himself together, but the light of desire in his eye was not entirely quenched. "Almost," he said. "You give him love, affection, and honesty, while he gives you constancy..."

"Good faith and respect," she said when his voice trailed off. "And we're both committed to the American victory."

He slanted her a meaningful glance. "I'll remember that."

"See that you do." Jane stood up. Stewart did likewise. She looked at him. "I am ready to retire. Good night, redcoat."

Mamie emerged out of the shadows, saying over her shoulder to her spirits, "Hush, now, womans! Shoo!" To the two human bodies, she said, "Yes'm. Time for goodnight. The zombies they tell me remind you, Missy Jane, about the girl in the forest. Now it's off to bed with you. Massa James, you can bed in the parlor."

Jane rolled her eyes at the familiar form of respect, and in so doing caught Stewart's impudent wink. It was as if he were signaling to her that she had not entirely gotten the better of him in their steamy little tête-à-tête. Each bearing a candle, the three of them left the kitchen together, Jane to mount the stairs, and Mamie to fuss over her newly adopted white son.

Later, Stewart lay stretched out in the dark on the parlor sofa, covered by a soft, well-worn linen sheet, listening to the rain. His hands were clasped behind his head, which rested on a pillow. One leg lay across the opposite arm of the sofa. The other leg was bent at the knee. He was naked and breathing slowly and deeply. He had known since childhood how to relax into the moist heat of the night in order to sleep in such a climate.

Unfortunately, his regulated breathing could not counteract the arousing effects to his body of his conversation in the kitchen with Miss Jane Shaw. He was completely filled with the vision of her kissing and touching her man, moving through all the possible and necessary steps of grasping liquid fire and giving it. That scene blended easily with the sight he had had the day before of her petal-beautiful pink-and-ivory nakedness and perfect curves, and this composite bled, like colors running in the rain, into the memory of having her fully beneath him this morning under the tree outside her bedroom window. In his mind's eye, the pastel pinks and soft yellows of that composition suddenly flared orange and red. When the heat fanned through him and threatened to become white-hot, he groaned aloud.

Now, James Stewart knew that he had brought on his own discomfort by insisting that she give him the details of her early-morning lovemaking. He had had two motives for invoking her supposed lover. He had been half expecting—and half hoping—that she would fall into maidenly confusion, that she would admit to a few indiscreet kisses and caresses, that she would disavow any suggestion of the completion of physical passion. From her response, however, it was clear that she stood by her story and frankly admitted to her desire. Should he condemn her for her lack of virtue or applaud her honesty? He did not know. She had also intimated satisfaction with her lover. Lucky man. But 'had known'? Who was this man, and when, exactly, had he satisfied her?

She was comfortable with her body and listened to its needs—that much he knew. Although he felt a careless superiority that no lady of his class would display such comfort or acknowledge such need, he felt a kind of grudging respect for the simple nobility with which she had invested her lovemaking. Nevertheless, he still considered her fair game, and perhaps even more so now.

Which brought him to the other half of his expectations and hopes for the conversation he had initiated in the kitchen. It was simple. He wanted her. He had seen too much of her not to want her. And she was ripe for the plucking. So ripe and dewy that it made his mouth water. It seemed a sin and a shame not to taste her fruit, especially now that he apparently need not fear bedding a virgin. If, with talk of kisses and caresses, he could have stirred her embers, nudged her into offering herself, prodded her into giving him the smallest opening, he would have known what to do.... But it kept slipping his mind that she detested red-coats.

That, and something else, deep down, told him that possibly, just possibly, these mornings past she had been—desirable, desiring, beautiful, luscious, ripe woman that she was—*spying* on the British. When he turned that interesting possibility over and over in his mind, he still did not imagine her anywhere but next to him, on top of him, under him, her skin next to his, surrounding his, now.

He did not know how long he lay awake, indulging this exquisite torture of his imaginings, but almost at once he became aware of two contradictory sounds. The first was the absence of the pounding of rain. He shifted his head slightly to glance out a window and saw a sword of silver moonlight cutting a slanting path across the floorboards, signaling that the clouds had parted and the heavens had cleared. The next moment, he heard an ominous creaking, as of branches, and a strange, sloppy shifting of the earth.

This was followed by a terrifying crash, perilously near the parlor.

He shot off the sofa, automatically grabbed his trousers and put them on in one movement, then ran out into the hallway. The sound of the crash had come from the porch, so he dashed out the front door. Aided by the bright light of the moon, he saw that a large tree had become uprooted and had fallen across one side of the porch. Under the trunk and the crazily broken boards of the porch roof, he saw Lawler's head and shoulders and one outflung arm, fixed under a beam, frozen in his sleeping position.

He waded into the tangle of splintered wood to see what, if anything, he could do for the man. He had almost reached Lawler's inert body when he heard a gasp behind him and turned to see Miss Shaw on the porch, wide-eyed, her hand covering her mouth. Her hair was tangled from sleep and tumbling down her back.

"Good God," she breathed, her eyes surveying the damage. She looked across at Stewart, then peered into the wreckage at Lawler's head. "Good God," she said again. She came forward, saying, "Is he alive?"

"I don't know," Stewart answered, applying himself to his task and breaking off the broken boards that blocked his way. He reached Lawler's body, bent down, thrust a hand under the boards covering the body and placed his palm on the man's chest. After a moment, he announced, "He's still breathing, and his heart is steady."

"Good. But how badly is he hurt?" Jane asked, picking her way through the wood, stepping gingerly.

Stewart felt for broken ribs or bones, but found none. He crouched down and stuck his head under what he could of the broken canopy of wood atop which lay the tree trunk. The shadows were dark where the moonlight could not penetrate. He saw little, but he felt a thick beam running just a few inches above Lawler's body. He followed the beam with his hand and discovered that one end of it was resting on the porch railing. He followed the beam back and, in the process, touched Lawler's forehead. The beam seemed to have merely grazed his skin.

Stewart stood up and turned to Jane, who was next to him now. "It seems nearly a miracle, but I think the beam saved him from being crushed by the tree trunk. I think he escaped unscathed. At a guess, the beam tapped his forehead and knocked him out—or, at least, put him in a deeper sleep."

As if to affirm Stewart's assessment, just then Lawler snored loudly, snorted once. He attempted to shift on his cot, but was, of course, unable to move.

Jane breathed a deep sigh of relief. "Awful man. As much as I dislike him, I do not wish him dead." She considered his unconscious form. "However, I must admit to preferring him this way to his being awake. What's to do?"

Stewart smiled wryly at her comments. He looked around him. "Do any other trees threaten the house?"

Jane shook her head. "No. We've known for some years that this one was dead in the center and had weak roots. Because it's so old and big, we wanted it one more summer to shade the house. We had planned to cut it down in another month or two. It was the heavy rains that uprooted it, I suppose."

"The tree is down now, but all in all, I'd say you—we all—were lucky tonight."

"I'd never heard such a noise!" Jane shuddered at the memory of the crash shattering her sleep. "Father will blow his top when he sees this mess in the morning." She shook her head and turned once again to practical matters. "Well, all right. I don't suppose we can leave him here all night. Let's get him out from under and put him in the house."

Stewart agreed. They worried at first that removing him would cause the heavy wooden canopy to collapse on top of him, but with a little experimentation they found that the beam would hold the whole, even when they shifted a few boards to completely dislodge the body. Fortunately, the cot on which he lay had removable legs, so it was easiest to dismantle the wood pegs supporting the canvas and pull him out, as if on a stretcher.

When Lawler was free and clear, they struggled together to get the large, limp man through the front door and the hallway and then to place him on the parlor sofa. When he was stretched out where Stewart had lately lain, Jane suggested lighting a candle, in order to attend to any wounds, so that he would not bleed all over everything during the night.

Stewart found the flint and lit the candle he had earlier taken from the kitchen. Jane motioned for him to put it on a table next to the foot of the sofa so that it would spill its light across the inert's man face. Stewart obeyed, and when he stepped back around Jane so that the candle was behind her he had to suppress a sharp intake of breath.

Jane had evidently flown from her bed at the crash, as he had from his. She was wearing only a thin, sleeveless night shift, rendered more or less transparent by the light shining behind her. He saw unmistakably that she was wearing nothing else, and she might as well have been naked, for he saw every shadow, every swell, every seam, every detail, of her body. He saw the round shadows under her breasts, the slope of her narrow waist, the curve of her hips and the precise outline of her thighs. It was his nighttime fantasy in petal-beautiful flesh and hot blood before him. He remembered how perfectly she had fit beneath him that morning. He would have her. Now.

"Well, it appears that he did get a scrape on his head," Jane said matter-of-factly, bending over to touch a raw spot at Lawler's temple where the skin was torn. She looked up at Stewart and asked, "What do you think? Do we need to bind it?"

She was taken aback by the look of undisguised desire in his eyes. Absorbed by the emotion of the fallen tree and the sight of Lawler under the wreckage coupled with the exertions of removing him to the parlor, she had not yet noticed the state of undress they were both in. She saw the expanse of his bare chest, the muscles cording his shoulders and arms and torso and gut. She saw his trousers, half buttoned, fitting his legs snugly, seemingly supported by nothing but his hipbones. She drew a now-familiar breath of awareness, of him, of her own equally undisguised attraction to him, of the unfair balance of power between them. She took a step back.

Her movement seemed only to intensify his gaze. She did not realize at first that, in stepping closer to the candle, she had made the outline of her naked body beneath her thin shift come into finer display. From the look in his eyes as they roamed her body, however, she understood and stepped out of the circle of the revealing light.

Intent and determined, he took a step toward her. She took a step back. Dissolving under his gaze and in the closeness of his desire, she backed out of the parlor, trying to put distance between her and the dark, massive cloud that rose between them. He followed her, step for step, keeping alive the sparks dancing on her skin, keeping her heart pounding, fueling the electricity that shot out and tantalized her shoulder, the back of her waist, the nape of her neck, the inside of her thigh, the underside of her breasts, the tip of her nipples, the tip of her tongue. Her gaze never broke his.

When she was at the foot of the staircase, she stopped. He stopped a breath away from her. She raised her hand to the knob of the banister post. She palmed its bulbous surface, slid her hand around it. She swayed and grasped the knob tighter for support. She felt weak in the knees and strongly desirous, drenched in moss jelly, as if the zombie's thick forest had sprung up around her. For the life of her, she could not remember a single feature of Bobby Harlan's face. But she remembered clearly the shape and feel of desire for another man, a man who had deep-set eyes of hazel green, light brown hair rumpled from sleep, a straight nose, a well-shaped, mobile mouth, a lean jaw, and a wide, muscular chest, tanned a deep bronze.

"If you go any farther," he said, glancing up the stairs, her next line of retreat, "we'll end up in your bed." He let those words sink in. "Not that I object, you understand. The parlor's taken."

"No," she said. It was a no, but it lacked conviction. She felt the need to explain. "You see, we were both surprised by the crash of the tree. Then there was the emotion of seeing that man possibly dead, then the relief of his narrow escape. It's not what you think…between us…you and me. We were awakened so suddenly and so violently from sleep…"

"I wasn't sleeping," he said.

"I was," she countered. "Fast asleep. Deep asleep. Dreamlessly asleep."

"You led me on this evening."

"You provoked me."

"You rose to the challenge."

"It's my house, and I'll not be bested by a redcoat."

"Which I am not wearing."

"I'll repeat what I said to you this morning."

He put a finger to her lips. She felt the shock of his touch to the tips of her toes. "I remember what you said to me this morning on the subject of redcoats and the wearing of their uniforms, and perhaps now is the perfect time to tell you—"

She never learned what he was going to tell her, for at that moment Mamie appeared at the head of the staircase, having come down from her third-floor chamber, breaking the spell between them. She was dressed in a voluminous white night shift.

"The zombie womans is gone," she announced. "Oh, and such a fuss they made! I never heard such a fuss! Jane, come back to bed now. They gone! You can sleep peaceful now."

Jane snapped back to her senses. The zombie forest disappeared. She was free of the moss jelly, or almost, enough to separate herself from the danger standing in front of her. She turned to mount the staircase under Mamie's watchful eye.

"And you, Massa James," Mamie continued, "you go see to that other soldier fella. The zombies wanted fun with him tonight. Go outside and see if he all right." When Stewart did not immediately move, she said, "Shoo, now. See to the soldier fella, and get some sleep you'self. You be needin' it in the morning! Ooh, the zombie womans gone now. Had fun this night!"

Chapter Ten

The zombies had spent the night wreaking their mischief on Shaw Plantation. Come morning, they had retreated to the branches of their tree in order to laugh gleefully down on the aftermath of their fun. In truth, when the sun rose, no one on Shaw Plantation could be said to be in a good mood, save Mamie, who had had a nightlong communion with her familiars.

James Stewart greeted the morning with little sleep, as sore as a bear, and wondering what to do next about satisfying his lust for the lust-inducing Miss Jane Shaw. He knew one sure way to have her, but that might possibly require putting his life in jeopardy. Still, to have her might be worth the risk—and yet . . . Caught between the competing imperatives of lust and life, he stumbled into the kitchen, hoping to fulfill part of his very visceral hunger with Mamie's edible sorcery.

Dick Lawler awoke disoriented and with a monumental headache. Rising from the parlor sofa, he discovered that he could not stay on his feet for more than a minute or two without becoming dizzy. With great effort, he made it into the kitchen, where he heard the story of the previous night's work. He was diagnosed by Stewart to have a slight concussion, but his vision was good, and he was pronounced to have been "extraordinarily lucky." Lawler, who had heard of zombies for the first time the night before, was today a true believer. There was little more for Mamie to do than bind his forehead.

When Master Shaw returned at the crack of dawn to gawk at the large tree lying drunkenly across his front porch, the choler that had been mounting since the onset of the downpour the afternoon before overflowed. He blasted and blustered and blamed an astonishing variety of persons and things for the uprooted tree—everything and everyone except, of course, himself. He fussed, fumed, figured the cost of the damage, then fussed and fumed some more.

Lieutenant Richards, for his part, was fit to be tied. To be drenched and stranded in a poor white field hand's cabin with only corn and beans to eat and a floor to sleep on was bad enough. To be condemned to that misery in the company of Jacob Shaw was worse than even he might have imagined. He would have preferred to be on the battlefield. Not only that, but the detour back to Shaw Plantation had been a complete waste of time. Jacob Shaw was clearly not engaged in espionage.

So Richards returned with Shaw, damp and dirty and silent with anger. It was only that angry silence that prevented him from voicing his opinion that the uprooted tree would have done better to destroy the whole house—thus avoiding a situation that would have led to the certain death by strangulation of either himself or Master Shaw.

Jane was up and about before her father's return. By the time she had dressed and descended the stairs, she had convinced herself that her strong desire for James Stewart was a bald sign that she had been too long without a beau. It was nothing more. And it was nothing she could not control. However, when she arrived at the kitchen and saw him standing there, speaking with Mamie, she revised her opinion about her control.

Stewart glanced over his shoulder at the sound of her entrance. She was struck by the angle of his hip as he stood at ease, the cut of his shoulder under his cotton shirt, the shadow of beard along his unshaven jaw, and one glance of his green gaze nearly melted her on the spot. It was broad daylight, too, with no flickering flames and shadows to tease and provoke, no black-velvet rain to moisten air and skin, no stories of girls sunk thigh-deep in moss jelly clinging to tree trunks, no zombies to stir up trouble and desire.

This morning it was the smell of frying eggs and ham and strong coffee, a clean sky above, a cleansed earth below and a journey ahead. Even these innocent elements seemed to swamp her with anticipation of his touch, his lips against hers, his hands entwined with hers, his legs pressed to hers.

Mamie turned, as well, smiling seraphically on her charge, and asked, "Hungry, chile?"

Jane answered, too quickly, on a lovely moan, "Mmm, yes, Mamie, I need food!"

At that, Stewart smiled and Lawler groaned. It was only then that Jane noticed the other redcoat, his head swaddled in a white linen cloth. She crossed to the table and asked the kinds of questions one would ask of a man who had narrowly escaped death from a fallen tree trunk. Then she helped Mamie set the places for eating and sat down opposite Lawler when it seemed that Mamie was ready to serve the three of them.

She was disturbed by Stewart's presence next to Lawler, and was determined not to look at him. He, in turn, was determined to disturb her. The inevitable topic of conversation centered on the events of the previous night. Jane looked up at Stewart when he mentioned having examined Lawler for broken bones on the parlor sofa in the light of a single candle. She met his eyes, and his glance stripped her naked.

Jane was aroused by that look, but she felt something else, too. In the blatant light of day, she felt a sadness and regret that had been obscured from her at night. The night before, in her evocation of the height of her passion for Bobby Harlan, she had stressed her love's constancy, good faith and respect for her. She realized now that constancy and good faith were out of the question in any dealings with James Stewart. And, worse, he plainly did not respect her.

Stewart held up the coffeepot. "More coffee?" he offered.

"No, thank you."

"More bread?" he said with a gesture to the cutting board.

"No, thank you."

"More of anything, Miss Shaw?" he asked—rather impudently, Jane thought.

"A no is a no, soldier," she replied, and this time it was a no with force behind it.

Stewart did not mistake her meaning. He understood her words and the look on her face. He also understood, from her use of the term *soldier* instead of *redcoat,* that it would be unwise of him to risk exposing his cover in an attempt to win her willing submission. She was likely to reject him now in any case. He nodded his understanding and withdrew from the field, but only partially. He was not going to deny his attraction to her, or the force of the currents that flowed between them.

Just then, the heated eloquence of Jacob Shaw's voice penetrated the kitchen. The master of the house had evidently returned, and was just as evidently commenting on the state of his front porch. Jane was happy that everyone's thoughts were given a new direction.

Master Shaw's attentions were so thoroughly engaged by the state of disrepair of his plantation home that it did not even occur to him to ask how Jane had fared in the company of two soldiers, with only Mamie to chaperone them. In fact, the effects of the torrential rains and the general state of his fields, now compounded by the broken porch, so irritated Jacob Shaw that he was ready to send Jane off on her journey without him. He was also prepared to trust Lieutenant Richards and two redcoats with the safe delivery of his only daughter to Riverdale, a point some forty miles distant. But of course, he could not send her off unaccompanied.

Within an hour of the return of Shaw and Richards to the big house, Jane, her father and the three British soldiers were packed and ready to head out on the journey to Aunt Patty's on horseback. Lawler was the least ready of the lot. Although the lieutenant was certainly glad that Lawler had not been crushed to death, he was hardly cheered that Lawler could not sit astride a horse. So, after a less-than-diplomatic exchange with Master Shaw, Lieutenant Richards decided that Lawler would ride, stretched out on a pallet, in the back of the wagon that Shaw had not wanted to use, as it would slow their progress down. Once the wagon became part of the journey and Shaw had to drive it, he insisted that Jane ride next to him. Then Richards decided to unload a variety of supplies on the wagon bed, making use of the empty space.

So, in the still early morning, heading out from Shaw Plantation was a traveling party of two riders and three in a wagon. It was, indeed, slow going due to the mud and the muck. Soon enough, though, they had traveled down Long Log Lane, past the Skinner farm, then turned south at the crossroads that would lead to Old Roads Bay. Shaw had decided to cross the Patapsco at that point and angle inland toward Riverdale in order to avoid the fighting that he imagined would be raging around Baltimore.

When they turned the corner, Lawler rolled off his pallet, bumped his head, and began moaning and writhing. Jane turned her head and frowned. She could see that the only way for Lawler to regain a comfortable position would be for her to clamber to the back of the wagon and to set him straight again herself.

Once at his side, she adjusted Lawler's body and the makeshift canopy that had been devised to keep the sun off his face and neck during the blazing day ahead. She imagined that the jolting of the wagon had increased his headache, so she fished in the large duffel of supplies for the flask of whiskey she had seen Richards toss in at the last minute. She had to cradle the large man and hold the flask to his mouth, since he had become too weak to drink for himself. She thought it just as well for Lawler to sleep the day off in an alcoholic stupor.

Observing her awkward ministrations, Stewart let his horse fall back in step beside her. His shadow fell across her.

"Need help?" he asked, with no hint of insinuation.

She looked up at him. She shook her head. "No." She gestured with the flask. "An aching head on the morrow can be no worse than his present condition."

Stewart agreed.

"And I had to find a way to stop the poor man's moaning! It was likely to give me a headache, as well, hearing his distress the day long."

Stewart nodded and said, "Let me know if you need my assistance," before trotting off again to catch up with Richards.

The sound of Stewart's voice momentarily roused Lawler. The whiskey had loosened his tongue. "Never liked that man," he said.

Jane paused, her ears pricked with interest at Lawler's tone. "Oh?" she said. "What don't you like about him."

"Uppity."

"An infantryman like yourself?" she queried. "Uppity?"

"It's his voice," Lawler explained. "Don't like it. It's uppity."

Jane had noticed that Stewart spoke with a slightly different accent than Lawler and then again Richards, but they were all British accents to her ear, and she did not have enough experience with them to distinguish them by class. As for province of origin, she knew that Lawler was from Yorkshire, Richards from Birmingham, and Stewart from the south.

"What's more," Lawler continued, "it's suspicious, an uppity infantryman. Acts like an officer sometimes. But he's not, and doesn't want to be one, by my reckoning."

"What do you mean he acts like an officer?" she asked, trying to hide her avid curiosity.

Lawler could hardly articulate his suspicions, for he had never been able to pick out his thoughts clearly or express them in words. His headache and the whiskey were, strangely, helpful in formulating his ideas. It was not one thing about Stewart, not even the way he talked, but everything about him. The way he walked, so slow and efficient in the heat. The way he held himself, sweating but upright,

not wilting like the others. And more: the way Stewart knew
how to behave at the dinner table when Lawler's tongue had
been tied past unknotting, the way he knew how to treat the
black giantess, the way he listened to her story of the zombies without batting an eye. Lawler had watched him.
Stewart had seemed to enjoy the story, had even seemed to
understand it. That Stewart did not fit his rank seemed
blindingly clear to Lawler now, as blinding as his headache.

All these impressions and suspicions added up to one
thing in Lawler's mind, and that was "book-learning. The
man has too much book-learning for a soldier."

Jane did not think that Lawler was suggesting that Stewart had ever quoted literature to his fellow soldiers. She
imagined that Lawler was saying something else about
James Stewart, that he was referring to something in Stewart to which she herself had instinctively responded.

She looked up at Stewart, who was riding straight, his ri-
fle shouldered easily. Both he and the lieutenant were in
shirtsleeves, for they were not disposed to advertising their
enemy identity on their backs. Stewart turned to say something to the lieutenant, and Jane saw his air of quiet authority, his lack of submission to his superior, his
assumption of equality. His profile was sharp and clean,
masculine and compelling.

As if feeling her gaze on him, he turned back and met
Jane's eye, directly. The message in his was equally direct.

For the first time in his presence, Jane blushed red. She
did not know if he could discern her heightened color at this
distance, but she quickly lowered her eyes and turned her
attention back to Lawler, who was ready to fall, mercifully,
into a drunken doze. She crawled back to the head of the
wagon and the perch where her father sat, her mind and
body consumed with a case of divided loyalties. From the
waist up, her heart and head were committed to an American victory; from the waist down, she could surrender on the
instant to a handsome British soldier. And he could have
had her in the back of this wagon, now, with only the sun
canopy for privacy.

As the traveling party arrived at the drive to the Johnson farm, it happened that Mrs. Johnson was in her buggy, waiting to turn out to the road. Richards and Stewart greeted the woman briefly and rode on by. Jacob Shaw pulled up his wagon beside the beautiful widow. The little twinge he always felt upon seeing her and remembering her rejection of him several years before was, this morning, swept aside in a mental movement of purest inspiration.

"Barbara!" he greeted her jovially. "You're up early!"

"I am up early every day, Jacob," Mrs. Johnson said. It was not a reproach, only a statement. "Give you good day."

"And a good day to you," he said. "That is, it hasn't been a good day so far! But I am hoping it will get better!" He lowered his brow and said grumpily, "I'm taking my Jane to her aunt Patty's today."

"Riverdale, isn't it?" Mrs. Johnson said, not unfamiliar with the extensions of the Shaw family. "You're benefiting from an escort, I perceive."

"Military," Shaw grumbled, "but it's a necessity with the trouble around Baltimore."

"Baltimore, is it?" the widow asked.

"Did you not see the troops moving out down the lane yesterday?"

"No, I did not."

Shaw scratched his head. "But...then...where'd the scallywags go if it wasn't west to Baltimore?"

"Why don't you ask them?" Barbara Johnson said, nodding in the direction of the two riders, for she recognized Lieutenant Richards from the morning before, even without his coat.

When the two riders halted and turned around to look back, Shaw perceived that he would have to make quick work here. "There's no talking sense to *them*," he replied. "But, listen here, Barbara. It's under a woman's care that Jane needs to be, what with the British occupation of my house and lands! But the devil of a rainstorm—begging your pardon, ma'am—near blighted my tobacco yesterday, and I can't spare the two days to Riverdale and back that it would take me to deliver her safely." Jacob Shaw's voice became as friendly as had ever been heard. "Now, I'm thinking it would be neighborly of you—as a woman, a grown woman, that is, and a respectable widow—if *you'd* accompany my Jane to Riverdale. I'll send over two hands to your farm for everyone you need for every day you're gone, so you'll be getting twice the work done in half the time!"

While Barbara Johnson considered the deal in a moment of silence, she touched the cameo brooch at her throat. She said, finally, "Yes, I'll do it, Jacob."

After a little friendly haggling and a generous deal for Mrs. Johnson, Jacob Shaw called to Lieutenant Richards and explained the change in plans. Since Richards could find no objection to seeing the back of Jacob Shaw, the latter heartily kissed his daughter goodbye, climbed out of his wagon, exchanged places with Mrs. Johnson and took up the reins to the Johnson buggy. On the recommendation that Jane ask her aunt Patty to bake her brother, Johnnie, a pie, the happy farmer began his way back to the Shaw Plantation.

Jane, now in company of Mrs. Johnson, headed down to the ferry that would take them across the Patapsco. Jane could hardly have been happier than to be seated beside Mrs. Barbara Johnson on the way to Washington.

At first, the two women exchanged no conversation. Jane was bursting with things to say, but because of Lawler in the rear, she had to suppress all talk in order to keep from saying anything indiscreet. After a mile or so, however, she could contain herself no longer. She said conversationally, "Did you notice that we have a fellow passenger in the back of the wagon?"

"I did," Mrs. Johnson replied. "What's his condition?"

Jane briefly recounted the story.

Barbara Johnson smiled gently and said softly, "No wonder Jacob was so anxious to return to his land!"

"Yes, that fallen tree served me in several ways. Half-conscious is the way I like this particular redcoat best," Jane remarked, her voice low.

"All redcoats," Mrs. Johnson murmured in return.

"Speaking of which...," Jane began cautiously. She swiveled her head to see Lawler's present condition, but could not determine whether his eyes were open or shut, given the canopy shielding his face. Although she heard him snore slightly, she did not want to take chances. She whispered, "I'm going to check on him. He's drunk a lot of whiskey, and he's pretty dim to begin with, but let's be sure he's truly asleep before we discuss what's near killing me to hold in!"

Jane crawled to the back of the wagon and did everything she could to be sure that Lawler was not feigning sleep. Satisfied, she returned to Barbara and, making sure not to raise her voice, said, "Now, tell me—what happened the other day with General Ross?"

"Nothing," Barbara assured her. "I don't think he suspected a thing."

"I knew you'd not give anything away, but you nevertheless managed to pass on the information at the meeting house, under the general's very nose?"

Barbara was smiling. "It seems I did," she replied serenely. "And I received information, as well. You'll be happy to know that your reports have helped our troops to reposition themselves. Instead of expecting an attack from the North Point, we have concentrated our forces on the south end of Baltimore, in case the redcoats come north from Washington."

Jane was smiling now, too. "Excellent. But I don't think the redcoats will be attacking Baltimore directly after Washington. I have the feeling Ross intends to return to North Point before."

"So do I," Barbara said noncommittally.

"There's time enough to get that information where it needs to be," Jane said confidently. "For now, is it not a piece of good luck that you and I are headed to the capital together?"

"A piece of extraordinary good luck," Barbara agreed. She chuckled softly. "And so eager was I to jump at the chance that I did not even make the usual noises about returning to my house and packing my clothing and hair-brush. Fortunately, your father did not notice the lapse.''

''Not when his rain-soaked fields were uppermost on his mind,'' Jane replied. ''But there are clothes enough for you at my aunt Patty's.''

They fell to discussing, quietly, their plans for Washington, their eventual meeting with Michael Shiner, and the extent of their contacts from Washington to Baltimore in the human chain of communication that began at Shaw Plantation and crossed the Johnson farm.

At one point, Stewart chanced to look back at the wagon, straggling some twenty feet behind them. He saw that the brims of the two ladies' bonnets were nearly touching, so close were their faces as they spoke to one another. It was an intimate tableau, that of feminine friendship. There was also a certain intensity to the set of their profiles as they spoke. Stewart did not think anything in particular of the picture of the two women. He merely filed it in the back of his mind, for future reference.

They came to the ferry dock and crossed the bay, with horses, wagon and supplies, in good time. They stopped for a light midday meal, and then again, briefly in the height of the searing afternoon sun, to rest and restore their forces.

These occasions gave Barbara the opportunity to take the two redcoats' measures. Lieutenant Richards she was able to write off after one conversational exchange. He plainly thought little of the effectiveness of women—as little as did his commanding general. Richards spoke loosely in front of her of the British plans. Because she already knew all of them anyway, she merely smiled inwardly.

Of James Stewart's character she was less sure. However, she had witnessed one interaction between him and Jane that was all she needed to know how things stood between the two of them.

It was hot, as usual, and muggy, as usual, but Jane felt unusually energized the closer they trudged to the capital. At Bladensburg they crossed the bridge over the eastern branch of the Potomac. As the sun was sinking, they arrived at Riverdale. Jane directed the traveling party to her aunt's home. With the promise of a warm, sweet twilight upon them, they turned onto Aunt Patty's drive, which seemed to lead into the heart of England.

The drive was two hundred yards long and planted on either side with double rows of tulip trees. At the end of the drive, upon a slight eminence, stood a snug two-story house, built of brick, nicely balanced by wings and scarved with ivy. At the point where the drive became a circle to curve around the entrance to the house, the two soldiers halted.

The women descended from the wagon. Jane withdrew her tapestry bag. Mrs. Johnson handed the reins over to the lieutenant, who had promised Jacob Shaw to drive the wagon back to the plantation upon General Ross's return to the North Point.

Stewart tied the lieutenant's horse to the back of the wagon. He turned to Mrs. Johnson and bid her goodbye. He turned to Jane. They exchanged a regard that could only be brief. "You shall be all right, Miss Shaw?" he asked.

"Yes, sir," she responded, "very well."

He held her eyes with his. "So, you see, we have done our proper duty and escorted you to Riverdale."

"And now we are safe," she said.

There was nothing more to be said. He nodded his goodbye. She lowered her eyes. He mounted his horse and left the property, with instruction to ride ahead immediately to Upper Marlboro, where they were eventually to meet Ross's Forty-fourth.

Richards waited behind in the wagon until the two women had reached the front door on foot and pulled the doorbell. Then, he turned the wagon around and left the property.

On the doorstep, Barbara slanted Jane a glance and said, pointedly, "That's an attractive man, your redcoat."

Jane gasped slightly and said, in an undertone, "Is it so obvious?"

"My dear!" Mrs. Johnson replied lightly. "The look he gave you upon parting, why, it must have melted you." She laughed softly. "It nearly undid me! What do you mean to do?"

"I don't know," Jane cried, a little plaintively. "What's your advice?"

Barbara paused. She said, "I don't give advice. Not on these matters. And you'll do what you want—or can't help—anyway." The sound of footsteps approaching the other side of the door could be heard just as Barbara formulated her thought. "You can lose your virtue, Jane. You can even lose your heart," she said. "But you must never lose your resolution. Remember that he's a redcoat."

Chapter Eleven

The door was swung open by an aging Black Thomas. Behind him appeared the surprised face of Patty McClelland, a feminine version of Jacob Shaw. She wore a hint of matronly stoutness and had red curls turned to rust and sprinkled with iron grey, and her brown eyes were lively, like her niece Jane's. She was as voluble as her brother, but with none of his irascibility. As a result, she had made a very good marriage that had been lived out in relative contentment for more than twenty-five years.

"Jane!" she exclaimed. "I was hardly expecting you, my dear! But glad I am that you are come!" She peered out the door into the dusk. "Surely you did not come on foot?" Not pausing for breath or a response, she turned to Jane's traveling companion. "Mrs. Johnson, is it? Yes! Well, come in and explain to me the reason for this delightful surprise. And won't your uncle George be pleased? Why, no need to answer *that* question! He will be delighted, and the sight of you will make him forget his attack of the gout! But you have so little baggage. I hope you do not mean to make this a *short* visit!"

On a continuing gentle flow of exclamations, remarks and rhetorical questions, Jane and Barbara were led into the finely appointed house. Black Thomas withdrew to the shadows, leaving his mistress to send for him when next he was needed.

"Not a short visit, Aunt Patty," Jane said finally, "but perhaps not a long one, either. The fact is, we don't know how long we're staying."

With Aunt Patty widening her eyes and emitting little gasps of "Upon my word!" and "I never!" Jane described how General Ross's Forty-fourth had seen fit to occupy the Shaw Plantation. She explained how her father had not wanted her there with all the redcoats swarming over the property. Although the British had now pulled out, Jane said that they planned to return to North Point. Since Jane had no clear idea of the British timetable, she could not predict precisely when her father would be sending for her to return home.

"It's a terrible time, to be sure," Aunt Patty said to these disclosures, "and my brother did right to remove you from the plantation! Now, come, and kiss your Uncle George hello. Don't expect him to get up for you, for he's confined to his chair in the parlor!"

The evening proceeded cozily enough, with a tasty cold supper and a warm family atmosphere, disturbed only by the consciousness that war on Maryland soil was inevitable. George McClelland, a kind man with hair as red as his wife's, had many questions to ask Jane about the size of the British Forty-fourth and their readiness. Jane replied honestly, and her answers were not the kind that boded well for the American future. When it came to the question of the immediate whereabouts of General Ross and his men, Jane thought her aunt and uncle should know the truth.

"They're on their way to Washington," Jane said.

"Not Baltimore?" Uncle George queried, surprised. He frowned, as much at a twinge of pain as at the information. "How do you know, lass?"

Mrs. Johnson chose to answer. Her voice was melodious and matter-of-fact. "I live near the road the redcoats would have taken day before yesterday, and I would have seen them if they were headed for Baltimore. There was no sign of them. There's no other way from North Point to Baltimore, save by water, and not one foreign vessel has been sighted there in the last couple of days. We've scouts posted at various points along the Patapsco." She paused, then added, "Of course, before we had already set off for Riverdale, we did not realize it—Jacob Shaw, Jane and I—that the British might be headed toward Washington. Now, however, it seems certain."

"Do our boys in Washington know?" Uncle George wanted to know. "General Winder?"

"I'm proposing to get word of it to Johnnie soon," Jane announced. "He's with the Fifth Maryland, as you'll be knowing, and they're stationed down at the Arsenal."

She did not add that Johnnie already knew this information, or mention that he was at the receiving end of the human chain of communication. Fortunately, neither her aunt nor uncle thought to ask her how she had come to know where the Maryland regiment was stationed.

In any case, Aunt Patty was more preoccupied by propriety than by the details of war. She was shaking her head. "I'm afraid that won't be possible, my dear. You mustn't be going alone into the soldiers' camp, and your uncle cannot accompany you these days with his inflammations."

"But I have Mrs. Johnson to make me respectable," Jane said, nodding at her friend, "and she's agreed to help."

The look Aunt Patty exchanged with Mrs. Johnson did not suggest that she thought the company of such a young and beautiful widow in a military camp would make Jane at all respectable. However, there was something both seductive and steely in the depths of Mrs. Johnson's heavenly blue gaze that prevented her from contradicting her niece.

Sensing her aunt's hesitation, Jane added with a bright smile, "Father specifically requested me to ask you to provide Johnnie with one of your pies that he so loves. Please say you'll give me one to offer him on the morrow."

In the end, Aunt Patty was persuaded to offer two pies, several loaves of bread, a roast beef and a salted ham for her nephew and the other brave boys from Maryland. The evening wound down, and since Jane and Mrs. Johnson had been on the road since the bright morning, they were excused early from the table and counseled to seek their rest. The beds in the guest rooms were made up, and Mrs. Johnson was provided with the bedclothes and toiletries that she was lacking.

When Jane had changed into her light, sleeveless night shift, she slipped into Barbara's room. The widow was brushing out her hair. The curls lay around her shoulders soft and full, as soft and full as her breasts and hips under her borrowed shift. In the light of the single candle, Jane thought Barbara Johnson looked very beautiful and very wise.

"Tomorrow we'll see if our chain of information has helped our troops prepare for the attack on Washington," Jane said.

"Yes," Barbara replied, not stopping the movement of the brush through her hair, "but don't expect too much."

Jane clung to a shred of optimism. "Our information may just make the decisive difference."

"Perhaps," Barbara was willing to allow, "but from the look of General Ross and his officers, and the two redcoats today, I can tell you that the British are better equipped and better fed than our men."

"Better fed, to be sure!" Jane piped up.

Barbara's lips curved into a wry smile. It might have been at thought of Jacob Shaw being forced to expend his hospitality on the enemy. "At least you'll not have to witness again the redcoats eating off the Shaw property produce." At the quick flash of emotion that crossed Jane's face, Barbara set down her brush. "How are you feeling about that, Jane?"

Jane replied honestly. "If I don't return before the British leave the second time, I won't be seeing him again."

Barbara did not need to be told the referent for 'him.' "Somehow, I think," she replied serenely, "that he won't let that happen."

Jane was to see James Stewart again in Washington, several times, in fact, but it was not through any effort on his part.

The next day, Jane and Barbara were given the McClelland buggy for the day, along with one of the black ser-

vants to ride tiger on the platform at the rear of the vehicle.
With Barbara at the reins, the two women traveled into
Washington from the northeast on the dusty, deeply rutted
Bladensburg Turnpike, which was liberally hazarded with
rocks and stumps.

Although the capital was little more than a town, with
some five thousand inhabitants, and the broad streets were
shaded by the leafy green of maples, poplars, elms and lin-
dens, the feel of the city was one of urban heat and conges-
tion. Barbara did not know her way around, and had to
depend on Jane, who had spent time here over the years
visiting her aunt and uncle, for directions. However, Jane
was not a frequent visitor, because Jacob Shaw often complained that Washington was not for him and had made it a
point to avoid the place.

Traveling the rather pompously named avenues, not all of
which were yet paved, the two women made their slow progress toward the Center Market on Pennsylvania Avenue,
not far from the President's house. At the market they encountered the usual bawling and bargaining, and only the
faintest stirrings of excitement among the citizens of a city
who had not yet realized their fate. A sense of ominous
foreboding was forestalled by the fact that many of the lux-
uries of life could still be found in the market house.

Barbara was eyeing, intently, a colorful display of exotic
fruits when Jane caught sight of a figure and profile that
made her heart leap. She touched Barbara's arm lightly and
said quickly, "I'll be right back." Barbara glanced up,
nodded, and returned her gaze to the luscious fruit.

Jane threaded her way through the throng of people,
staying on the trail of the man she could have sworn was
James Stewart. He was not a tall man, so she could not keep
track of his head just by scanning the tops of the crowd.
Nevertheless, by bobbing up and down, she was able to follow his rather erratic path through the market. At one moment, in a particularly dense crowd of people, she lost him
for a moment, but then she caught sight of him again. Or,
at least, she caught sight of a man who was of his height and
wearing the same kind of plain blue coat. She hurried her

step to approach this man and stumbled into him, causing him to turn.

Jane looked up and into the face of a man she had never seen before. She murmured her excuses and returned, dejected and puzzled, to the stall where she had left Barbara.

They left the market and continued through town, down the Mall, over Tiber Creek and past the Capitol, which was surrounded by grazing fields and shabby country houses. At that point they angled down an avenue that led straight to the Arsenal at Greenleaf's Point, situated at the place where the eastern branch forked off from the Potomac.

Miss Jane Shaw and Mrs. Barbara Johnson were halted at the arch of the main gate, but gained easy access to the Arsenal by displaying two beautiful smiles and a large wicker basket containing pies and the meats for the Fifth Maryland. The scene of chaos and confusion within the walls did not encourage them to believe that the human chain of communication that had worked so miraculously well had produced any similarly miraculous benefit to the American armed forces. Judging from the readiness of the various American regiments, Jane imagined that if the British were to attack Washington on the morrow, they would be able to enter the city at any point, unopposed.

Johnnie confirmed Jane's worst fears. She found him, with great difficulty, lounging out of uniform beside his pitched tent, playing cards. At sight of his older sister, Private Shaw sputtered a happy greeting, jumped up and hugged and kissed first Jane and then Barbara, with whom he was on easy terms. He introduced his card-playing opponent as "Alpha Wright, down from Baltimore." Private Wright politely excused himself from what he rightly perceived would be a family conversation.

Aunt Patty's food was produced. For a Maryland gentleman accustomed to luxurious food, the idea of an army supper of fat pork and hard biscuit was viewed as a pleasant absurdity. However, a month of it had been long enough for Johnnie Shaw's sense of humor, and he wanted nothing more than for the war to be over, to return to the plantation, and to eat real food.

When Johnnie had properly appreciated what he could of Aunt Patty's package, Jane gestured to the disorder reigning around her. "Have you not passed along to Lieutenant Colonel Starrett the news of the British invasion?"

Johnnie's smile of pleasure at his sister's visit vanished, and his open face fell. He shook his mop of Shaw-red hair. "I've passed your information along to Starrett, all right, and he's inclined to believe me! It's the secretary of war who's having difficulty believing it. Starrett told me that upon reporting to the secretary, Armstrong replied that he acknowledged that *if* the British were to come up the Patuxent, it would be for the purpose of striking somewhere, but he did not believe they'd come to Washington. 'What the devil would Ross do here?' were Armstrong's exact words!"

Jane uttered a cry of dismay, and Barbara looked far from satisfied at having been proved right.

"Armstrong is convinced that the British target is not Washington," Johnnie continued, "and thinks the trip up the Patuxent is a feint to mask a real design on Baltimore."

"Do you mean to say that all my—*our*—work these past days has been for nothing?" Jane asked, incredulous.

"Not for absolutely nothing," Johnnie sighed. "Major General Van Ness, who commands the District of Columbia Militia, has been persuaded to take some action on the capital's defenses. So has Bridagier General Stansbury."

"That is very fine," Barbara said, in her quiet way, "when you consider that the British fleet has been in full command of the Chesapeake for nearly a year and a half."

Johnnie flushed and the color washed over the splay of freckles across his nose and cheeks. "Well, Starrett thinks that if Van Ness can persuade President Madison to remove Secretary Armstrong from office, we may just have a chance at winning the engagement here in Washington."

"And if you don't—?" Jane asked.

"Well, we've already determined that the American line of retreat will be to George Town."

So the three of them spoke on: Jane openly angry at the futility of all her early-morning adventures; Barbara quiet and determined to find a way to defeat the hated redcoats; Johnnie recklessly cheerful about the chances for an American victory in what looked to be increasingly desperate circumstances.

After that first trip to town, Jane and Barbara spent few of their daylight hours at Riverdale. Because their visit to the Arsenal had yielded much to discuss at dinner, Uncle George had encouraged the two young women, over Aunt Patty's frowns and clucks, to circulate in the capital.

Jane and Barbara had been circulating less than a week when they finally heard in town what they had known before leaving North Point. The British were on the Patuxent. They were at Nottingham. They had arrived at Upper Marlboro. They had crossed to Long Old Fields. Where would they move next? Jane knew for a certainty that it would be the capital.

The day of August 23 began as hot and humid as every other day before it. The effect of the heat seemed cumulative, with each day slower to dawn and to die, each day longer and more drawn out. Over Aunt Patty's most strenuous objections, Barbara managed to talk their way out of Riverdale with the McClelland buggy.

The city of Washington was now alert and alive to the danger that lay only a few miles to the east. Excitement was in air, and rumors were flying like the rockets that would soon be seen to flare outside the city. By now everyone had heard about the slave revolt forty miles to the west, and about the Tories in southern Maryland who had treated the British to food and information. Rumors of slave insurrection were always frightening, and never more terrifying than in times of crisis. The slaves one could almost understand, but those Tories—! To the Washingtonians, it felt like a stab in the back, pure and simple.

The American ranks mobilized to defend the city and chose to leave town through a circuitous route. They left the Arsenal and headed first north, to Capitol Hill. From the hill, they marched the mile west down Pennsylvania Avenue to the President's house. There, at the Treasury, they turned north and headed back east toward the Maryland countryside. The purpose of this indirect route was two-fold: as a display to reassure the apprehensive citizens, and as a way of gathering courage from the cheering of the apprehensive citizens lining the streets, waving flags, pressing bread and fruit on the hungry troops.

Jane and Barbara were on Pennsylvania Avenue that day at two o'clock in the afternoon. With the crowd around them, they cheered the ranks that passed in review, motley in their blue, gray and brown. The soldiers did not look very professional, but there was a quality about them nevertheless that was reassuring. Jane saw Captain John Davidson's Union Light Infantry with its cheerful band and Captain Benjamin Burch and his Irish artillerymen. She saw Captain Stull's riflemen—still without rifles—and Lieutenant Colonel Joseph Starrett's Fifth Maryland Militia. She saw Private John Shaw and waved and sang out as he passed by.

Then she saw James Stewart standing in the crowd on the opposite side of the street.

"Barbara, look!" She nudged her friend. "Isn't that *him*?"

Barbara looked over and in the direction of Jane's gaze. The crowd across the street was shifting, and Barbara caught a glimpse of the man. It was enough for her to say, slowly, "Why, yes, I think you're right. It looks like our soldier Stewart of General Ross's Forty-fourth. But, no—Oh! I wish that tall man would move so that I could get a better look!"

"So do I," Jane said, craning her neck, still trying to ascertain the identity of the man across the street, "but I'm nearly certain that it's him."

"I don't know," Barbara said, trying to get another glimpse of the man, as well. "What do you suppose he is doing here, in a plain cloth jacket, no less?"

"Spying, I suppose," Jane answered.

Barbara cocked her head. "He doesn't strike me as a British spy," she said, considering.

"He wouldn't look like one and still be a spy, would he?" Jane snapped back. "When the parade is finished, let's go across the street and trap him."

However, when the parade was finished and the crowds began to disperse, the man who looked like James Stewart was nowhere to be seen. Jane had no time to spare to look for the man, for she had arranged to have a meeting with Michael Shiner that afternoon on the steps of the building that housed the *National Intelligencer*, the city's only newspaper. Jane agreed to meet Barbara after that meeting at Center Market.

Jane made her way to the newspaper offices. When she arrived at the two-story brick building, Michael Shiner was already there, standing the shadows of a side doorstep. He was a shadow himself, out of the way and out of sight.

Jane greeted him briefly and asked, first, for news of the slave revolt in Frederick. When Michael Shiner reported that the leaders had all been arrested, she heaved a sigh of relief and asked, fearfully, "What of the sentiments among the free Negroes?"

Michael Shiner reassured her. "From what I hear, the free Negroes don't have much to say to the British admiral, Cochrane. He tried to stir some up, after the landings in the Chesapeake, but all he got was a sorry lot of slaves, and not many at that."

"Do your contacts in Washington know this?" Jane asked. He nodded, and she came to her point. "Johnnie told me yesterday that entrenchments have begun to be dug to protect the city from the east. You are to rally your Negroes and help with the digging. North of George Town. Can you do it?"

Michael Shiner could do it.

"Good," Jane approved. "Now, here's what you're to do. Take your Negroes to the Navy Yard and ask for Mansfield. He'll be expecting you. Mansfield is the chief engineer of the Corps of Engineers that comes from—" here Jane frowned, attempting to recall the detail "—West Point. Yes, that's it. West Point. Well, anyway," she continued, "it seems we're to have help from the military academy there.

Johnnie said something about several engineer officers having built some military obstacle that helped in the Lake Erie victory recently. It happens that several West Point engineers are stationed in Washington, so they're going to try the same thing here—whatever that is." Jane waved these cumbersome details away. "They'll be digging through the night, so you can present yourselves as soon as possible. And Michael," she added, "you all will be fed."

Michael Shiner repeated the instructions and left her side to slip into the lengthening shadows of the afternoon. He was off to obey her orders. It was difficult for him not to obey, for the habit of obedience was long ingrained. You could earn your freedom, but freeing yourself was one thing, while claiming ownership of that freed self was another. Time of war was not the moment to choose what to do or to have an opinion. If digging trenches is what you were ordered to do, digging trenches is what you and your fellow niggers would do.

When Michael Shiner had gone, Jane leaned back a moment against the brick wall of the building. She was attempting to recruit her forces for her walk to Center Market, when the sight of that familiar-looking man crossing the street away from her caused the hairs on the back of her neck to bristle.

All her senses were instantly electrified. She stood up straight and stared at the man. It was not just any man. It was James Stewart. She was sure of it. Even from the back, as he strode away from her, she knew unmistakably who he was, and that her eyes had not deceived her earlier in the day.

He was dressed as a civilian, and he was walking down the street, in the general direction away from the President's house and toward the Capitol. She did not once consider not going after him. Neither did she consider what she would do when she caught up with him. She hastened forward, calling out "Redcoat Stewart!" but he did not turn. Nor did he quicken his footsteps. At ten feet away, she called out "Redcoat!" and again, "Redcoat Stewart!"

Chapter Twelve

James Stewart was walking down Ninth Street, heading east. Latin phrases were jangling in his brain. A first fragment—*Ave, Caesar*—was put into place next to *Morituri*. Something came next, but what? And why should he think of those words now? He translated: *Hail, Caesar. Those who are about to die...* Right. So much for the *Ave, Caesar. Morituri...* After that, the next bit fell easily into place: *te salutant*. That was it. *Those who are about to die salute you.* The thought had a nice ring to it in Latin: *Ave, Caesar. Morituri te salutant.* The phrase brought to mind gladiators who were to be sacrificed in the arena to the claws of hungry lions for the amusement of the Romans.

With a grim turn of humor, he realized the ultimate value of his exclusive British education: He could quote classical Latin in the face of death. He reflected in a general way on that education as he continued to walk down the street, oblivious to the sights and sound around him. He cast further back to his youth and remembered his upbringing, which had made possible his privileged entry to Eton College, then to Cambridge. In reviving memories of his religious education, it struck him that a biblical passage would be more to the point under the circumstances than a salute to Caesar.

Yea, though I walk through the valley of the shadow of death...

The Twenty-third Psalm—the very thing. David walking through the valley of the shadow of death for his meeting with Goliath. Carrying a slingshot. Perfect. This, then, was the appropriate image: the foolish war as the confrontation of David and Goliath.

. . . I will fear no evil . . .

But he did fear stupidity, in particular that of the secretary of war, and even, if truth be told, that of President Madison, with whom he had just had a meeting.

. . . thy rod and thy staff they comfort me.

Rod and staff? That was about it, but he found no comfort there. David had for defense fifteen ships, seven thousand ill-equipped regulars, and a half-developed idea to dig trenches. Goliath had one thousand ships, many more thousands of Wellington's Invincibles, and several tons of firepower.

Thou preparest a table before me in the presence of my enemies . . .

He felt an inward mental movement between a smile and a grimace. This verse was really good: to sit at a table in the presence of enemies. He had done just that, not too many evenings ago at the Shaw Plantation, and he could name one desirable young lady, at least, who would be mighty surprised if she ever learned that his enemy was Goliath and that he was working on the side of David.

So absorbed was he in his thoughts that he did not at first perceive a feminine voice calling out behind him, "Redcoat Stewart!" His disjointed musings had turned, inevitably, to his most recent education, to his study of engineering, and to the academy in which those studies had taken place. This academy had none of the stately age and assurance that permeated the British colleges and universities, with their well-groomed, civilized lawns rippling the surface of the earth. This academy had no history and lay between abrupt and lofty mountains on a bold shelving plateau. It sat admid an untamed river whose prospect was touched only by the creative hand of natural beauty. It was a young, untried academy—the United States Military Academy at West Point.

He thought he heard, penetrating the mists of his reflections, the word "Redcoat," but it did not fully register.

Then he heard his name called out: "Redcoat Stewart!" And then he felt a small, feminine hand grab his arm.

Initially puzzled, and hardly pleased to have been recognized as a redcoat on the streets of Washington, he stopped abruptly, causing the woman who had called him to collide with his chest.

The woman jumped back at the contact, but did not release his arm. She huffed, "You have a habit of turning up in places where you're least welcome. Lose your way again, redcoat?"

Stewart was looking down at the flushed, upturned face of Miss Jane Shaw. From under her bonnet, a riot of curls glinting red-gold from the sun behind her framed her face. Her pretty features were set in lines of anger and indignation, and he noted involuntarily that he had seen that expression on her twice before: once when she was taking her bath in the clearing; and the second time just after she had washed her hair at the well. After that second encounter, he had discovered that she had not been wearing her drawers. He recalled that moment with delight. At the present moment, since she was standing so close to him, holding his arm, he caught the scent of her skin. That impression reinforced the pleasurable visual memories he had of her nakedness, of the petal-beautiful expanses of her skin and curves.

Her presence, coupled with his awareness of danger and death, instantly dispelled his dreamy musing on his education and the privilege of his family and birth that had made it possible. All his attention was focused on the small hand that was clamped around his forearm. He did not try to shake it off. His gaze traveled from her hand, up her arm, to her shoulder. There it lingered on the sheen of warm peach skin visible above the circle of her bodice, which was rising and falling rapidly. His eyes moved back to her face. She was not looking as fierce as when she had first stopped him.

He realized that something in his expression must have altered, too. After the second it took for him to recognize her, he saw a trace of apprehension cross her features. Her lustrous brown eyes grew shadowed, and she snatched her hand back from his arm. Perhaps his scrutiny had made too transparent his thoughts. It was strange that he had just been thinking of her—and Miss Jane Shaw had had a way of intruding into his thoughts at various odd moments during the past week—and here she was before him in the flesh. And what attractive flesh it was, too!

Stewart smiled slowly. His initial displeasure at having been recognized on the streets of Washington had slid into enjoyment. It was a diverting encounter, he decided, given all the other difficulties of life at the moment. But it was also, decidedly, a tricky encounter. The trickiness increased his enjoyment.

"Miss Shaw," he said, bowing slightly. "A pleasure."

He rather admired the way she stood her ground and demanded, again, "Lose your way, redcoat?"

"No, I did not," he replied amiably. "I believe that I am on—" he glanced up at a street sign "—Ninth Street, heading east. So, you need not concern yourself that I've lost my way."

"You've a nerve, redcoat," she said low and angry. "Do you think that I am stupid?"

"No, Miss Shaw," he answered. "I think you are incredibly foolhardy."

"I? *I* am foolhardy?" she echoed, aghast. "You come into town. You saunter down the street. You are recognized by someone who knows you for the enemy that you are. And you call *me* foolhardy?"

He had not reckoned on encountering Miss Shaw in the streets of Washington. He had not imagined seeing her again on the Shaw Plantation, for it was unlikely that he would be returning to North Point with Ross's Forty-fourth. He had not yet determined what he was going to do about satisfying his attraction for the pretty tobacco farmer's daughter, nor even if he would be alive long enough to satisfy it. However, one thing he did know: He was not prepared to explain to her who he was and what he was doing, strolling the streets of Washington as a common American civilian, when she had known him as a British soldier.

"I do call you foolhardy," he said. "That, and more."
The word that came to mind as he looked down at her was
adorable. However, because the pert, pretty, angry face he
was looking at seemed to bring out his deepest teasing self,
what he said was, "Impetuous, unthinking, and unwise."

She was about to sputter an indignant retort when he
continued, "And this encounter reminds me vividly of that
day in the clearing behind your house, when you were so
impetuous, unthinking and unwise as to take a bath when
your land was crawling with soldiers."

Her flush was as vivid as his recollection. "We have already been over that one!" she retorted hotly. "And I've
owned myself at fault."

"Oh? I did not know that you had seen the error of your
ways, Miss—"

"Do you think," she broke in testily, "that I am going to
stand here on the streets of Washington and listen to you
berate my actions on my own land? And do you think, redcoat Stewart, that I am going to allow you to leave town as
easily as you have, apparently, entered it?"

Stewart was charmed. She was just what he needed today. His voice was mixed with patience and amusement.
"Miss Shaw, please consider—you are alone and, from
what I can see, unarmed." His eyes roamed her very attractive person. "And we are on a completely deserted street.
You have identified me as a redcoat. What is it, exactly, that
you propose to do?"

She opened her mouth to retort, then shut it angrily, unable to think of a pertinent response.

He continued instructively, "Now, that is what I meant
when I said you were impetuous, unthinking, and unwise.
Attributes of yours that you have amply displayed before."

He recognized the moment when she was going to turn
and shout for help. He did not want to have to explain himself, or his presence in the city. Not now. Not to her. It
would be different if he were not so attracted to her. It would
be different if he could trust her. Trust her absolutely. Trust
her with the explanation of his presence in General Ross's
Forty-fourth. Trust her with his life. But since first seeing

her climb that tree into her bedroom one fog-ghostly dawn, he had been swept along by his initial interpretation of her early-morning amorous adventures, and he could not change course.

Although he had guessed by now that she was not consorting with any British officers, he was not about to trust a woman like her with the secret of his mission on Shaw Plantation. For if he trusted her, he would have to respect her, and if he respected her, he could not act on his most basic desires for her. It was as if there were a wall inside him, a barrier built of his fine British education and the righteousness of his riches, which kept dammed up behind it all the indications that she was a brave, resourceful young woman, worthy of his respect and more. However, with death so close at hand and her sensuality surrounding him, and with the wall so firmly in place, he had no wish to regard her as a woman to be respected. He preferred by far to regard her as a woman to be ravished.

And this woman to be ravished was about to turn away from him and denounce him as the enemy.

"However," he continued smoothly, taking one of her hands in his and covering her mouth with the other, "before you do something even more impetuous, unthinking and unwise, I suggest you walk with me a ways down the street."

His touch was light, but firm, and adjusted in strength to her reaction. When she tried to jerk her hand out of his and wrench her face away from him, he pulled her slightly toward him and held her there until he felt her struggles subside. With a questioning lift to his brow, he watched her features shade from anger to indignation to wariness to acceptance. As he withdrew his hand from her mouth, he said, "That's right, now. Yes. Put your hand on my arm, there. Like any strolling couple. Should you like to head toward that park over there?"

"Only if you mean to tell me what you are doing here in Washington today," she said, her voice low and throbbing, indicating that she was far from pleased to accept his suggestion, although she was constrained to do so.

"I don't mean to do that, Miss Shaw," he replied. He placed his fingers over her hand, which he had laid on the crook of his arm, and began to lead her down the street.

"You don't mean to say what you were doing at the parade of the troops earlier this afternoon on Pennsylvania Avenue?" she demanded, necessarily following his lead.

He had no reason to be ruffled that she had seen him there. "You were there, too?" he asked pleasantly, as if this were a social conversation.

"Yes, I was, and it is easy enough to guess what *you* were doing there."

"That's the spirit, Miss Shaw!" he approved. "You tell me what I was doing there!"

Jane was not amused, and she realized, belatedly, that she had indeed been too impetuous in having accosted James Stewart just now without first having devised a plan to have him captured. She was not, however, going to back down or cower now that she had put herself in such a disadvantageous position.

"I think," she said, "that you were checking on the American troops so that you could report on their condition to General Ross."

He looked down at her. "And do you think I discovered something that even the lowest British foot soldier does not know?"

She returned his gaze and thought she might have seen a hint of sadness in the depths of his hazel-green eyes. Doubts about his reasons for being in Washington, alone and unconcerned, assailed her. Nevertheless, he had provided her with no reason to think of him other than as a redcoat, and so she continued to think of him as such. It was also much, much safer to regard him as the enemy, for the feeling of enmity seemed to temper the strong attraction she felt toward him, even now, as they were walking down the street. Although the steamy heat and earthy sensuality of her encounters with him on the plantation were far away in space, they seemed very close in memory and in emotion.

"No," she admitted.

"Neither do I," he said.

She frowned. "And what would have been your reason for being at Center Market the other day?"

He paused in his step, still arm in arm with Miss Jane Shaw. He caught a strange, whimsical mood, and was aware of the pleasure that came from having a flirtatious conversation at hand and death just over the horizon. He answered, truthfully, "I was interested in seeing the products and the prices on the Washington market. I noticed that pineapples were much in evidence."

Jane blinked and asked suspiciously, "You were interested in pineapples?"

"I was initially surprised by the quantity," he continued, "because I know they are imported from the West Indies."

"Making them subject to British naval blockades, for instance?" Jane queried, her tone falsely sweet.

"For instance," he agreed. "But I thought the price remained within reason."

Jane remembered from the conversation during the dinner she had shared with her father and the redcoats that Stewart knew something of the effects on the war on American trading companies. Although she was still concerned to determine a way to expose Stewart without causing harm to herself, she caught his whimsy and realized that, since the street was deserted, she had no better plan at the moment than to walk with him and talk with him.

"If you call twenty-five cents apiece reasonable," she answered.

"More reasonable than the ice I saw," he said, "which was being sold at half a dollar per bushel, with the price rising daily, no doubt!"

"Well, it *is* a lot," she admitted.

"It's a scandal!" he replied.

Jane laughed. She had thought the price scandalous, too. They continued to walk, arm in arm, down the street, speaking of fruits and vegetables and the prices of goods. Neither quite understood the mood of whimsy and gravity that was balanced between them; neither wished to alter the strange terms of their temporary truce.

Looking up at him, she found it hard to remember that he was a redcoat. Looking around them, walking down a peaceful street, she found it hard to remember that war surrounded them.

Looking down at her, he found it hard to forget the sight of her naked skin, the feel of her against him, the swamp of heat that rose between them whenever they were together. Looking around them, he found it hard to forget that tonight he would be back in the heart of the enemy camp, posing as a British soldier, subject to swift and terrible justice if he was exposed as an American spy.

They had come upon a park, thick and shady with green trees. The secrets of the dappled green shadows beckoned to him. With a surge of life-affirming desire flowing through his veins, he knew what he wanted now, had known it, really, from the moment he recognized her, when she put her hand on his arm to stop him. As if it were the most natural thing in the world, he drew her down a path, and before she could protest had maneuvered her so that the thick trunk of an elm tree shielded them from the view of any chance passersby on Ninth Street.

Suddenly Jane found that he had taken her hand from the crook of his arm and turned her so that her back was against the tree trunk. He was not touching her, but one arm was raised, and his hand was placed against the trunk, above her shoulder, effectively trapping her.

Surprised, she looked at him and read what was in his hazel-green eyes. She shook her head. "No."

"Yes."

"No," she breathed again. "It's not right."

He smiled. "It's perfect." He leaned in toward her, but not yet quite touching her.

"No," she repeated, feeling confused and angry and fearful and desirous all at once. She grasped at her anger and felt it well up within her. "You're a redcoat," she spit out before she sprang into action.

Her efforts gained her nothing. At her most minimal movement to slip under his arm and away from him, he took both her wrists with one hand in a strong grip and pulled her against him. With the other hand, he clamped her mouth, as he had before, to prevent the scream that he knew was about to rise from the bottom of her lungs. In the next movement, he moved with her, against the tree trunk, and pressed her with his length in order to halt her struggles against him.

Their gazes met and locked. In that moment, the chemistry of the moment changed, and her struggles ceased. He saw the look in her eyes shift quickly and kaleidoscopically from anger to confusion to fear to desire. Her beauty and her body and the look in her eyes were irresistible to him, and he hit upon the idea—chivalrous thought—that if he did not tell her that he was an American, she would not have to mourn him if he did not survive the coming days. The barrier inside him, the genteel and durable wall that served to separate the rich and privileged southern gentleman from the rest of the world, remained firmly intact.

He slowly removed his hand from her mouth and heard the feathery sound of her released gasp. He felt it, too, in the momentary increase in the pressure of her breasts against his chest.

She felt helpless, in several conflicting ways. "What are you going to do now, redcoat?" she asked.

He heard the half fearful, half hopeful note in the question that trembled sweetly on her lips. Gone was her earlier indignant taunting, and in its place—and no doubt against her will—was an invitation.

He accepted the sweet, trembling, reluctant invitation. "Something I should have done a long time ago, when last I had you in my arms," he said, "under your bedroom window. Or, perhaps, after we had rescued Lawler from the fallen tree." His voice held a groan of remembered desire.

She looked up at him and realized that her gaze had fixed on the line of his jaw and his impossibly beautiful lips. She had often wondered what his lips would feel like.

He frowned, minimally, as if puzzled. "I wonder how I came to forget it?" He smiled slightly at the lapse. "It seems an odd oversight, but I have never kissed you, you know."

She knew.

Chapter Thirteen

Then his head blocked out the rest of the world, and Jane felt him place his beautiful lips on hers. Slowly. Delicately. Efficiently. The way he seemed to do everything in the muffling heat of this climate. And the day was hot, but never so hot as when he leaned into her, against her, put his lips to hers, his chest against her breast, his hands on her shoulders.

His kiss was dizzying, for he gave himself to it so thoroughly and transmitted so much a part of him. She drank deeply of the slow taste of his lips and tongue and mouth. She thought of tastes complex and cultivated, like the sweet, melting crunch of pralines, or something intoxicating, like bourbon pie. She was surrounded by his kiss, which seemed to draw her with him into an untamed southern garden that grew thick with cypress and live oak, palmetto and oleander. The luxuriant garden of this kiss was overgrown with flowers with improbably hued petals whose centers were spiked with nodding pistils dusted with orange whose names she neither knew nor cared about. She felt she was traveling deep, deep, into a wide-leafed, waxy-leafed, hot and humid garden, and she was surprised by the exotic familiarity of his lips to hers, his body to hers, his hands upon her.

He seemed to know how to make love in this heat, and she did not question it, for he was blending her into the kiss. He let her curves mold into his angles. He let his angles settle into her curves. He moved a little this way, moved a little that way, searching to find where she could give, where he could take, where he could give, where she could take, so that the fit would be the more perfect.

She felt his hands seeing her body. His palms traced the skin at her cheek, at the nape of her neck, at her collarbone, at her breast under her bodice. The tips of his fingers examined the soft peaks of her breasts, then the softer valleys, then the peaks again. She wanted him to explore this territory with her, to have him see her world through his fingertips. She opened herself to this exploration and felt the delicious geographical change, for when his fingertips came to her breast tips she felt her fleshly peaks harden like smooth pebbles rippling atop the liquid-silk swells of a creek, or like little nugget-treasures lying on ore-laden mountains. She wanted him to find the treasures, to claim them, to caress them.

He did so, and boldly. He let his hands observe her body the way she wanted it seen. He beheld it, cherished with his hands those places he had previously touched only with his eyes. She reveled in his revelation of her as he moved his hands down her breasts to her ribs, to her hips. He smoothed his hands around her and grasped the rich curves that arched from the small of her back to the tops of her legs. He moved his hands to increase his tactile witnessing, and suddenly she seemed to be revealed to him. Everywhere. Or almost everywhere. Everywhere but where she must protect herself from his sight, from his hands, from him. Everywhere but where the revelation would be complete and the embrace could be completed.

His grasp was intimate, and she pulled away. Not fully away, but enough to turn her face, to break the kiss, so that she could breathe. Enough to shift her legs so that she could stand more fully on her own. But she was no less aroused by the slide of his thighs against hers and by the glide of his lips from her mouth down to the shallow pool of skin stretching across her collarbone. She felt his tongue on her neck, absorbing the pearls of sweat beading her breastbone. She felt the hot shiver of his tongue down to her toes.

She found her voice with effort. "I'll repeat my question," she managed. It took her a moment and another breath to compose her next words. "What are you going to do now?"

Her question was a mistake, for it brought his head up, and then she was looking into green-flecked eyes gone black with desire. The look in his eyes undid her more thoroughly than had his hands. "Whatever I can think of," he said.

"Soldier Stewart," she breathed. "We're in a public park. It's broad daylight."

"Yes, and our clothes are on," he said, acknowledging the full sum of the inconveniences. "So we must be inventive."

His eyes fell first on her bonnet, and he raised his fingers to untie the strings, which had already been loosened under her chin. Her curls tumbled down, and his eyes followed the downward course of one limp red-gold wisp that drooped to her breast. His eyes continued their downward course until they fell, with disapproval, on the buttons of her disheveled bodice. Only one had popped open at his handling.

"Now, if we were to—"

When he raised his hands to work at her buttons, she pushed him away, for as much as she wanted him to explore her, she had not yet completely lost her senses. However, her freedom was only temporary. She quickly found herself pinned between his outstretched arms. His elbows were locked, his palms were flat on either side of her shoulders, and the tree trunk was at her back. He was leaning into her and regarding her with eyes stained irresistibly with desire. They held not a question, but a demand. A powerful demand. She felt a powerful response.

"No," she breathed, raising her arm to shield her eyes, to fend off the power of his demand, and of her response. "This is surely crazy! Whatever are you thinking?"

He circled the wrist of her raised arm with his fingers and held it back from her face, above her head. The stretch of her body from her armpit to her waist invited him to knead, with his other hand, the fine flesh and musculature straining under the cloth of her bodice.

"I'm thinking," he said slowly, as if her question demanded a serious answer, "that I'm alive today."

Her heart skipped a beat. She tried to stop his wandering hand with her free one. She could stop neither his hand nor the tremors touched off by his pressureful touch, tremors that rippled down to the pit of her stomach. Her senses had become disordered. The war was far away, and she was vaguely puzzled. "That you're alive today?"

He smiled, almost wistfully. "And I might not be tomorrow," he finished. "But I'm alive today," he repeated, with meaning. "Never more so."

Bobby Harlan! was her immediate thought. Such had been the meaning behind the words, or near enough, that Bobby Harlan had spoken to her on the night before he rode off to his death. But Bobby Harlan had not demanded, he had begged. He had not stated his desire so well, nor had he aroused hers to this degree. She had granted Bobby's humble request, of her own free will. Seduction, and the soft yet systematic destruction of her defenses had not been part of it. Bobby Harlan had taken what he received, and had been grateful for it. James Stewart had her where he wanted her, and he wanted her where he had her. She felt open and exposed and already conquered, save for the final deed.

There were many differences between this secretive, attractive man and the amiable, affectionate Bobby Harlan, who had been big and strong and had made up for his lack of skill with true love and devotion. Not the least of the differences was the crystal-clear memory that she had not wanted Bobby Harlan to die.

And this man? Her feelings for this man were less clear and, in fact, very cloudy.

"When you're dead," she said, recruiting her crumbled defenses for a valiant rally, "I'll rejoice."

He shook his head admonishingly. He brought down the hand that was above her head and caught her other wrist with the hand that had been roaming her breasts. Their two hands were now clasped, arms at full length and crossed, caught between them. It was an innocent, intimate stance. He made it less innocent and more intimate by nestling their crossed, clasped hands into the wedge of her thighs. He pressed his lower body against hers to create a hard knot of hands and legs and heat and desire.

"Miss Shaw, so cruel!" he murmured. "You wound me."

With her arms crossed tightly in front of her, her breasts were pressed together. Their swells crested just above her bodice, which was open at the top button, inviting him. He bent to place several kisses on the peach skin, nudging aside the flap of fabric with a movement of his cheek. Liking the unexpected feel of his nose grazing her breasts, he applied himself to this new movement, breathing in deeply, experimenting with the touch of face to breast, the taste of feminine sweat, the sound of lips against skin.

Jane closed her eyes, loving the sensation, hating her submission. "It's not possible to wound your vanity, redcoat."

He looked up. His dreamy eyes focused momentarily, registering her words. "It's just been wounded," he said cryptically. He went back to her breast, roaming the full range through her bodice. He considered ripping her buttons off with his teeth. Not for the world would he dislodge the clasp of their hands from her thighs.

She did not ask for an explanation. Instead, and in spite of herself, she stretched a little, providing him a greater expanse of bare breast to explore with his nose and his cheek and his chin and his tongue. Her light cotton dress had never felt so thick and cumbersome.

His touch was exquisite. He found the flap of her bodice, and a second button fell open, like a lovely gate parting and allowing entry to delight. He bent to reach the pebbled tip of her breast with his tongue. In his effort to reach this desirable nugget-goal, the shadow of afternoon beard along the sharp, masculine planes of his face rasped a full curve of her breast. A strong, lovely desiring sensation coursed through her. It spread everywhere, radiating from her breasts down her arms and legs, but the strength of the sensation grew weaker the farther away it was from the source.

She nearly cried out in frustration that the sensation had served only to pique, not to satisfy, the knot of hands and legs and heat and desire.

At her moan, he moved his lips back to hers. They sought. They fought. They indulged. They tasted. They feasted. They resolved their differences. They created new ones. Lips entwined, he slowly unlaced their hands, trapped gloriously between her thighs. He edged his fingers around her lower curves and grabbed her skirt on either side, bunching it into his hands.

Her eyes suddenly shot open. She turned her face away abruptly, surprising him, and thereby winning her release from his lips. "What do you mean by that?" she asked.

"You know exactly what I mean," he said, without hesitation. He lifted her skirt higher, by way of further answering her question. He did, indeed, mean to take her here, against the tree, in a lovely, deserted park, in the shadowed heat of the dying afternoon. He had never done such a thing before, but it seemed the easiest, most obvious, most natural thing in the world.

"No," she said, pushing his hands down, and her skirt with it. "I mean about my having just wounded your vanity."

He stopped and looked up at her. His eyes narrowed. He did not intend to answer her.

At his silence, she tried to recall Barbara Johnson's words to her about losing her heart and her virtue and her resolution. She could only remember the part about not losing her resolution. "Remember that he's a redcoat," Barbara had said, but Jane was having a hard time remembering that.

She shook her head, in an attempt to clear it. The movement helped, minimally. She was still awash in desire, but her skirt was her last shred of defense, and she intended to keep it protecting her. She retained the most ancient bit of feminine knowledge, that if he should touch her bare thigh, it would not matter who he was or what side he was on. It would only matter that he was the most attractive man she had ever met and that he had brought her to the brink of desire.

"Who are you?" she demanded. "And what are you doing here?"

The question caught him up short on the edge of sexual desire. While tottering precariously on a cliff and looking down into an abyss of violence and invasion, he moved his hands up from her thighs to frame her hips with his palms, like parentheses. He caressed her. This new touch did not decrease his desire for her. It was more a saving, cradling gesture than a seductive one. Yet he wanted her. He would take her with great delight, and even greater satisfaction, but he was not going to hurt her to get it, or force her physically.

He knew what she was asking, but he was not prepared to give her the answers. If he was prepared to give her the answers, it would be so easy now to have her—or would it? Would she believe him? Would his admission entail other commitments? Or would it incur her wrath? He wanted her, but only on his own terms. And on his terms, she would not take him. He leaned into her, suddenly weakened by conflicting imperatives.

"Are you who you say you are?" she asked, a second time, holding him slightly away from her with her palms against his chest.

She was unashamed of her response to him, which she still felt strongly, but her resolution was strengthening and not entirely related to the fact that she still thought him a redcoat. With this most intimate engagement of their bodies and their desires, but not quite of their hearts, they were simply a man and a woman, stripped of all politics. The word *resolution* was all that she could remember now of Barbara Johnson's advice, and a wall of resolution and pride rose up in her to defend her against the wall that she intuited within him, that wall that kept his heart from her, but not his body.

He looked into her eyes and saw the resolution. After a moment, he straightened slightly and answered her question. "More or less," he said. Then, slowly with a curious mixture of regret and humor, he added, "But nothing I could tell you now about myself would improve your opinion of my manners."

With that she agreed.

"Or win me what I want."

She shook her head, again in agreement. She still wore her desire in her eyes and in the willing posture of her body against the tree, open to him, but despite how much she wanted him, she was able now to say no.

It gave her a perverse satisfaction to see him make the damnably difficult, awkward, painful effort to draw himself back from the precipice of his desire and potential for violence. He slowly roused himself and became aware, again, of the park grass beneath his feet and the muted sounds of a city preparing for a siege. When he had a measure of control, he put a finger under her chin, lifting it slightly. If he could not have her, he would not stay near her, but he still wanted one more token, before leaving.

"Then kiss me, Miss Jane," he said, "and promise me that you will think of me tonight."

"Promise me you won't come back to town," she answered.

"I can't promise you that," he said, and put his lips to hers.

This time the kiss was sweet and lingering. It was a kiss not broken, but unfulfilled. She was nearly undone when he ended it and lifted his lips from hers and moved away, for his kiss still spoke of forceful desire. She sagged against the trunk for support.

"No need to alert the American authorities," he said, turning on an afterthought and speaking over his shoulder. "They know I'm here."

Good! she thought, as she watched him walk away. *Someone will surely catch him!* Then: *No! He's tricked me, for there is no one on his trail.* Then, a second time: *Good!*

It would take her a full ten minutes to recover and to think of making her way to Center Market to meet Barbara.

Ten minutes later, James Stewart had entered into the near vicinity of the Navy Yard, his thoughts reeling, his body roused to violence and confusion. Another ten minutes

ed him down, and yet another ten minutes brought him
ugh the Navy Yard gate where he was permitted to en-
in sight. By the time he arrived at Brigadier General
sbury's tent, he had thrust Jane Shaw and his desire for
o the back of his mind so that he could focus instead on
usiness that concerned his life.

e was saluted and announced as "Lieutenant Colonel
art." He ducked under the flap and entered the tent.

bias Stansbury rose from his field chair, saluted first
greeted him. "James! I hope you bring good news."

bring news, Toby," Stewart replied.

t's not good?" Stansbury inquired.

t's from the President's house."

You've just come from there?"

ewart stifled a groan and said, "Indirectly, yes."

Which means?"

That we can expect, in the next day or two, a stupid se-
ce of conflicting orders, of marching and counter-
ching, and general disarray."

ansbury seemed taken aback by the bluntness, but not
ided by it, and certainly not disbelieving of it. When he
poured Stewart something to drink and gestured him to
only other chair in the tent besides his own, the briga-
general asked, "And the precise news?"

The *good* news is that President Madison finally real-
the gravity of the situation."

ansbury choked on the draught of whiskey he had been
e point of swallowing. When he had regained the abil-
o speak, he commented, "You are an amusing fellow,
art."

t is our president who is the comedian," Stewart re-
, not mincing words. "Or, perhaps, one of the grand
emen who decided that the president of the United
s should also act as commander in chief." Stewart
ed, "If we get out of this with an independent govern-
, I think I will apply to Congress to amend the consti-
n and relieve the president of this particular duty."

We may thank God that Madison does not intend to
the field with us."

"He does not intend to do so for the moment, at any rate. Who knows but what that idiot Armstrong—or, God forbid, Winder—will convince him otherwise." He cursed inventively. "It does not bear thinking on!"

"What, the thought of Madison taking the field?"

"No, that of Armstrong as our secretary of war and Winder as a major general. Where I see clear disaster on the horizon, they see a muddle, which deludes them that victory is possible. And I'm not a military man, merely an engineer!"

Stansbury said, "Yes, but your clear vision of disaster has benefitted from firsthand experience with the British."

Stewart leveled his commanding officer an unwavering gaze. "Then what was the point of my infiltration of Ross's troops, if no one was going to listen to my report?"

"I, for one, am listening to you," Stansbury pointed out, "and so is Starrett, and the earthworks have begun to be dug between the roads to Washington and George Town, as you recommended."

"They are being dug by civilian volunteers," Stewart complained, "not by the Army Corps of Engineers."

"Better them than no one," Stansbury said, "for, as you well know, your fellow academy lads have been valiantly holding off the redcoats in the Niagara."

Stewart would have far preferred a commission at Niagara. He said with light irony, "Lucky me to have been the one with the British education and long experience with the British accent."

"We've had so few southerners at West Point," Stansbury pointed out, "and it's hardly *my* fault that all our northern lads, being of good Puritan stock, have been barred all these years from English education."

"And rightly so," Stewart remarked, displaying his own prejudices. "However, I've never thought the bar was on account of your wrong-headed religious convictions, but on account of your bad taste. You northern Puritans have no style."

To that Stansbury said, in a tone of disgusted invective, "Southern Anglicans! And you a high-toned Georgian, to

" Then: "Listen here, Mr. Stewart, I'll have you know
ur Harvard is equal to your Cambridge any day!"
wart merely laughed at that, not deigning reply.

nd for the good American that I know you are,"
bury continued, "you've retained a deal of British ar-
ce!"

wart thanked him kindly. He said that his easy as-
tion of arrogance had served him well, particularly in
st few weeks, during which time he had put his life at
ual risk in having joined Ross's Forty-fourth.

this remark, of course, Stansbury had no retort. Since
urpose of this meeting was not to trade insults, but to
ss strategy and Stewart's latest information from the
camp, they thrust aside their regional differences. To
bury's first question, Stewart explained how he had
ged to free himself from the British camp in order to
ate this day, and how he would return to the enemy
this evening. He described the precise British posi-
t Upper Marlboro, the probable movement of the
-fourth on the morrow to Long Old Fields, and then,
likely, to Bladensburg.

en Stewart had finished, Stansbury rubbed his chin
htfully. He said, "That is the second time in the past
ys that your information has confirmed news that has
y reached my ears." He paused. "Interesting."

ou've already heard of the camp at Upper Marl-
"

nsbury nodded. "I heard, oh, three or four days ago
y, that the redcoats were going to camp there."

ery interesting," Stewart agreed, "because we did not
there until yesterday. From what quarters did the in-
tion come?"

et me think.... It came from one of the units sta-
d at the Arsenal." Stansbury hazarded, "The Mary-
Militia, was it?" He made an equivocal gesture. "The
perhaps."

arrett's?"

lost likely. In fact, yes! I recall now that it came from
me source as did the news over a week ago that Ross

was bound for Washington and not Baltimore," Stansbury said, "which you confirmed several days later."

Stewart had a sudden vision of Miss Shaw and Mrs. Johnson riding in the wagon, bonnet brims touching, discussing some important matter intently. He had another vision of the tree outside Miss Shaw's window, of the position of her bedroom above the British headquarters. That image was lost when it collided with the memory of having fallen to the ground with her below that tree with her beautiful body trapped beneath his. He was suddenly back in the park with her, under another tree, a shady one. He was in her arms and kissing her, with her skirts in his hands, and ready to—

Stansbury broke into his lieutenant colonel's obvious reverie with a sharp "Stewart! We're discussing why, if the British are now south of Washington and their objective is indeed the capital, they would go so far north to Bladensburg before turning back south to invade?"

Stewart tamed his thoughts and said, "Because Bladensburg has a strong bridge across the eastern branch."

Stansbury observed, "Yet there are two bridges that Ross will pass before Bladensburg that lead more directly into the city."

"Yes, but the eastern branch is fordable immediately to the north of Bladensburg," Stewart replied, "and will allow for the swift passage of large numbers of men at that point."

"I begin to perceive the usefulness of engineers in time of war," Stansbury observed.

"I am glad you do!" Stewart retorted. Then, swiftly: "But I still want to know how all this information came to you by way of the Maryland Militia."

Stansbury shrugged. "Your guess is as good as mine."

Stewart's guess was probably far better than Stansbury's. He had finally admitted to himself what Miss Jane Shaw had been doing all those mornings when she claimed to have been meeting a lover. He had admitted it, but the admission was odd and uncomfortable, for it caused some

y acknowledged structure inside him to shift. Its solid
ations seemed to crack and split, but the edifice was
t ready to crumble.

Chapter Fourteen

his meeting with Stansbury, and before returning to
camp that evening, Stewart stopped at the place in the
where he had hidden his enemy uniform. He also
there until one of the two reconnaissance parties that
lden out from Upper Marlboro that morning were
ng, so that his reappearance in camp would coincide
eirs.

n the large encampment came into view, Stewart was
ing along behind a group of returning soldiers. He
epared for the possibility that his unaccounted-for
bouts for the day had been noticed, but they had not.
er, now came the hard part, for they were on the eve
le, and he had no plan for how to proceed. However
ful his subterfuges might have been thus far—and he
de it twice in the past week into Washington for per-
onversations with his superiors—he could not rea-
y expect to maintain the guise of British soldier after
t engagement, since he had no intention of firing on
ntrymen from behind British lines.

use his role as American spy in Ross's camp was
ifficult than ever, he had considered "deserting" his
ssion in the British army for good and not returning
er Marlboro this night. However, because he had
the attention of General Ross, he imagined that the
general just might notice his absence from the camp
ght. If Ross made the correct calculations to explain
Stewart's absence, Ross just might, as a result, alter

the plans that Stewart—and Miss Jane Shaw, apparently—had passed along to the American officers.

So Stewart returned to Upper Marlboro. The smell of victory was in the air, and that smell had produced a saliva in the common soldier's mouth that was mixed with the foretaste of blood. The soldiers in the Forty-fourth were hungry for it, too, hungry for the victory, hungry for the blood.

That hunger had brought out the worst in Dick Lawler, but then, so had the deep wound to his masculine pride caused by the fallen tree. Lawler did not like Stewart any better this week than last; and he had not quite forgiven Stewart for having been the one to rescue him from the wreckage of the Shaw house porch, for that meant that Lawler owed Stewart some gratitude, which Lawler grudgingly withheld. And the episode had occurred in the presence of that pretty American piece, too, which had not improved Lawler's feelings toward Stewart.

Not that Stewart cared, for he did not value Lawler's opinion or want Lawler's gratitude any more than Lawler wished to grant it to him. When Stewart returned to camp that evening, he was in no mood to interact with the brash, brutish British infantryman—nor with anyone else. Unfortunately, Lawler was feeling fine and feisty and felt like rubbing off a raw edge or two on Stewart. When dusk was falling, Lawler sauntered over to the edge of camp, where he saw a compact figure, standing apart from the rest, looking out of camp into the dense Maryland forests.

Lawler approached this zone between two worlds, where the clatter of camp and the occasional explosion of male laughter faded into the call and chatter of forest animals, where the fatty afteraroma of an army supper drifted into the heavy pine scent of tidewater overgrowth. Lawler was oblivious of the subtleties. Instead, he tried for a clever remark. "Saying your prayers, Stewart?"

Lawler was startled when Stewart turned, slowly, to face him. Stewart's eyes were little more than a glitter in the twilight, but the hard look in their depths was unmistakable.

," Stewart said, with the accent that so insensibly
ed Lawler's ears, "I'm enjoying my own company."
ling with his chin, Lawler said with a swaggering
ge, "How am I supposed to take that, Stewart?"

y way you please."

d what I please is to punch you on the nose, you
ng excuse for a soldier."

art regarded Lawler for a long moment, with a kind
ached interest. He had no need to prove his man-
not to this man, and although he had no particular
to make peace with him, neither did he want this en-
r to take the course Lawler seemed determined to
. Stewart had other thoughts on his mind this eve-
nd he wanted the peace to think them through.

uppose that you do," Stewart said indifferently, and
shrug. He turned back to contemplate the green-black
vs of the forest.

d what makes you think that?"

n the abrasive tone of Lawler's voice, Stewart knew
than to keep his back turned. Just as Lawler was
to grab him by the shoulder, he turned and stepped a
ace to the side, keeping Lawler off balance. He said,
er, I don't want to fight you."

ared, sniveling soldier Stewart?"

course I'm scared of you," Stewart lied. "You're
than I am."

ler's thick lips spread into a smile of satisfaction.
's what I thought."

u were right."

t tomorrow, sniveling soldier Stewart?" Lawler
l. "Are you going to be scared tomorrow?"

art smiled, with a nice touch of scorn. "What's to be
of in meeting the Americans?"

ler laughed heartily. "That's the spirit, man!" he
d, and slapped Stewart on the back. "We'll have the
cans for breakfast tomorrow!" He lowered his voice
nd of sleazy intimacy. "So tell me, little man—as a
f payment for not bloodying your nose, don't you
-where it was that we dropped off that nice little

American filly the other day." Lawler hitched up his pants and thrust out his chest. "I was under the weather and don't rightly recall the name of the place."

Stewart's smile became fixed when he thought of Lawler going after Jane Shaw. "It was at Bel Air," he lied again, with a kind of sincerity that suggested that he was grateful for the opportunity to avoid being punched in the nose by a big man like Lawler.

"Bel Air," Lawler repeated. "Right. That was it. Bel Air." He grinned and poked Stewart in the ribs with his elbow. "I'll be making my way to Bel Air after we wet the ground with American blood and wipe it up with their carcasses. Now don't you go getting in my way, little man. You'll like the results less tomorrow than you would have today." He paused. "And I like my women willing."

Stewart would have liked nothing better than to choke the brute where he stood. Instead, he kept his eyes carefully shuttered. "You'll not be seeing me anywhere near Bel Air come tomorrow night, Lawler," he stated with complete truth.

"Good, little man," Lawler said.

In the locked corners of his heart, Lawler was grateful that he had not had to challenge Stewart to a bout of fisticuffs to get the name of Bel Air out of him—which had been his whole purpose for talking to Stewart in the first place. Lawler wanted Jane Shaw, and he wanted her as soon as possible, to vent himself, to prove himself, to be a man.

"You're not half-bad, Stewart," Lawler said, with more relief than he was willing to admit to himself.

"And the other half?" Stewart asked.

Lawler laughed. "Don't push it, little man," he warned, slapping him on the back again. With his male pride assuaged and strutting around inside him again, he swaggered away.

Stewart regarded him a moment longer before laughing, once. David had beat Goliath, this time, with less even than a slingshot. It had been ridiculously easy to dupe Lawler about Miss Shaw's whereabouts.

rtunately, neither Lieutenant Richards nor General
as as stupid as Dick Lawler.

r that night, Stewart was roaming aimlessly through
Although he was not making obvious passes by the
's tent, he did cross in front of it or in back of it or
side of it with certain regularity. On one such occa-
e caught a snatch of a particularly interesting con-
on.

the discussion of battle strategy apparently at an
tewart heard General Ross ask, "Now, Richards, did
t tell me that Mrs. Johnson was lodged at the Mc-
d residence in . . . Riverdale, was it?"
s, sir," came the loyal lieutenant's answer. "River-

next morning, after a long discussion with Barbara
outright lie to her aunt, Jane hitched a ride with a
or and arrived at George Town before noon. She re-
ered that this busy little port, lying to the west of
ngton, had been designated as the Fifth Maryland's
ed line of retreat—God forbid that such would be
ry!—for its ferries could whisk away the troops to
safety, and she wanted to be on hand, if worse came
worst, to reassure herself that Johnnie was still alive
one piece.

was amazed and dismayed when, shortly after her
rrival in George Town, she saw a lone soldier—to
from the musket he carried, and his look of terror—
rough the neat, well-paved streets, toward the river.
ame another, and another. Then by threes and fours,
hem fleeing and shouting to the people who had gone
e streets to hear the news of the glorious American
y at Bladensburg.

news of a humiliating American defeat spread
y. At first, Jane did not believe it, for, by her reck-
, the engagement had not begun but the hour before,
could not conceivably be already finished. Follow-
crowd, she went to the brick church at the corner of
nsin Avenue and Volta Place where was gathering the

rest of the George Town citizenry to hear the real report from the battlefield.

Soon enough, a company of soldiers in disarray ran by, warning of "Redcoats and rape!" In an instant, the efforts of the town crier, who had arrived at the church panting and full of news, were rendered superfluous. The crowd dispersed, some to shut themselves in their houses, some to cross the bridges over Rock Creek that led into Washington, some to follow the soldiers to the steep embankments of the Potomac, where they, too, wished to take the ferries to Alexandria.

Jane kept in the vicinity of the centrally located church and carefully scanned the soldiers streaming by for signs of Johnnie. She grabbed one soldier, hard, by the arm, and asked anxiously, "Starrett's Fifth?"

His eyes round with terror, the soldier paused just long enough to shake his head and say, "No, ma'am. They stayed on the field longer than most. But they'll be coming!"

With the scene in George Town becoming more confused by the minute, Jane's anxiety rose. She moved with difficulty through the streets, threading her way between terrified civilians and terrified soldiers, her basket of provisions jostled and knocked at every turn. Suddenly, her heart leaping with joy, she saw Johnnie. He was running with the rest, glancing over his shoulder at every opportunity, as they all were, each American soldier convinced that a redcoat was personally following him.

She yelled to him, but could hardly be heard over the din. She ran after him, and finally caught up with him near Travers Tavern.

Johnnie's face, when he saw his older sister, was a comical mixture of reproof and shame and relief. "Jane!" he admonished her sharply, expressing first the reproof. "You shouldn't be here! Good God, get back to Riverdale!"

"We'll go back to Riverdale, eventually," Jane said, pulling him to her and hugging him fiercely. She stood away from him and stated, looking into his terror-stricken face, "It was bad."

"It was worse!" Johnnie admitted, for there was no point in covering up the ignominious rout with a brave front or talk of heroism on the parade ground. The shame of defeat was great. "The British regulars—" he choked on the words "—they were...unnerving!" He pulled his sister out of the stream of people running this way and that. They took shelter against the tavern wall. "Their pace," Johnnie breathed, still awestruck by the military domination he had just witnessed, "their precision... their teamwork..." He swallowed hard. "Their bayonets, so thick and evenly spaced, glittering in the sun!" He summed it up succinctly: "Outmanned, outmaneuvered, and outflanked."

"Did you have orders to run?" Jane asked.

Johnnie laughed. It was a cracked sound. "Most of us needed no orders to run." He bethought himself of the most extraordinary terror. "And the rockets! Oh, Lord! I hope never to see such again!"

"You're not hurt, thank God," Jane said, surveying him and feeling his arms and torso for wounds.

Johnnie laughed again. The sound was more human. "We were too swift!" He shrugged. "Those of us in the Fifth tried to mount a stand, but there was no hope." He looked around him at the general confusion. He smiled a brotherly smile. At last he could express his relief. "All right, I admit it! I'm glad to see you, Jane!" He nodded his head in the direction of the river and took her arm. "Let's go!"

She pulled him back. "We can't!"

Johnnie said seriously, "We've got to get out now. It's either Alexandria or Riverdale. Your choice. But we can't stay in George Town. It's a certainty the redcoats will follow us here."

"Michael Shiner," she said to that. "We've sent him to dig the earthworks to the north, and we can't just abandon him and his men there to face the redcoats unarmed."

Johnnie wavered.

"It's not fair to leave him, Johnnie," Jane argued, "and you know it."

ohnnie did, and his internal struggle manifested itself in
ransparent expressions on his open face. At last he said,
u're right—and after all he's done for us. To the earth-
ks, then, but *I'm* going—alone!"

ne shook her head and put her basket of provisions be-
her back. "But I've got the food, which you won't be
ng unless I accompany you."

gainst his better judgment, Johnnie gave in. They
bed the hill, heading north against the current of peo-
lowing down to the river. They made their way slowly,
wishing to be foolishly visible when the British swept
town, as they surely would any moment now. The
ts had become deserted. An occasional soldier strag-
by, shouting at them to find shelter, but other than that,
saw no signs of life. Nothing. No inhabitants.

nd, strangely enough, no redcoats.

hen they had scaled the heights, Jane and Johnnie
ed down over the town. Jane put her hand to the brim
er bonnet to shield her eyes against the westering sun.
saw that the frantic activity below had died down. Ev-
ne seeking flight or shelter had found it. From their
age point, Jane and Johnnie saw and felt the eerie calm
had fallen over George Town and the neighboring cap-
The battle had been over for two hours or more. The
sh should have been on the heels of the Americans, but
were nowhere to be seen.

ey walked a good mile or more to the earthworks and
d no one, just a few scattered shovels left behind, as if
rea had been left in haste. A sinking kind of premoni-
overtook Jane, as if something horrible had happened
ichael Shiner and his crew of men. She looked out east
north to scan for signs of the approaching British. She
nothing more than insignificant clouds of dust on the
zon. So where were the redcoats? On their way to Bal-
re already?

st then Johnnie's stomach grumbled, helping them to
le what to do first. While they ate the food that Jane
brought along, they discussed the problem of what to
bout Michael Shiner. Johnnie argued caution and pa-

tience. Jane wanted action, and knew just where Michael Shiner was staying in the capital.

In the end, Jane's plan was to prevail. For one, Johnnie was too emotionally exhausted to put up much resistance, and for another, he had never yet succeeded in thwarting one of his older sister's risky schemes.

Stewart endured a day of magnificent frustration. Although he had not lived the terror on the battlefield of his countrymen, he had fully experienced American ineptitude behind the lines.

After his desertion from the British ranks on the march at midmorning, just before they reached the eastern branch of Bladensburg, Stewart had sought out Major General Winder on the American side of the river. Stewart had wanted to wring the general's neck when he learned that the idiot-in-command had ordered the town of Bladensburg to be abandoned. That early piece of ineptitude seemed to have settled matters before they began, and the list of subsequent American failures was nearly endless: the failure to use the houses in Bladensburg to shoot at the British; the failure to chop down the bridge over the eastern branch; the failure to fix a rallying point in case of retreat. Most of all, Stewart saw that it was a failure of judgment to have risked so much on a single, formal battle between raw militia and polished professionals.

The crowning folly was, of course, the decision of the American leadership—President Madison and his cabinet, including Secretary of War Armstrong and Major General Winder—to retreat with the shambled militia to the capital. Stewart had argued vigorously that the British intended to storm Washington, but somehow Winder refused to believe it yet. President Madison, more inclined to believe the West Point engineer, had seemed concerned to return to the city and to save the portrait of George Washington from the president's house.

Stewart washed his hands of the American leadership and chose, instead, to invest his energies in helping those who were helping to protect the city against the coming assault.

ad gone to the trenches north and east of George Town,
for several hours had bent into the task of digging next
hite man and black man alike. He knew that they had
a few hours left, for he had learned the night before
Ross had allowed for a five-hour battle at Bladens-
, if necessary. Stewart also knew that Ross had ared to meet Admiral Cochrane in Washington, and that
hrane's fleet would be sweeping into the Potomac
nd six o'clock.

e day had been crystal-clear, blistering hot and bone-
Three o'clock had come and gone. Pausing in his la-
, Stewart climbed out of his trench and looked up at the
It would sink too rapidly now, especially with the storm
ds gathering on the western front. He looked briefly
h and east, to the Bladensburg Turnpike, curving
ugh the rolling countryside, its end feeding the street
led directly to the Capitol building.

en he saw it: a tiny, ominous cloud of dust trailing
g the horizon, traveling slowly south toward the city.
could only have been produced by superbly regulated
nns of British infantry. They had cooled their heels for
fternoon, and were now on their way to the capital.

ewart did not climb back down into his ditch. Instead,
ught the Negro who seemed to be the leader of the
 men. Stewart's breeding had taught him to learn the
 man's name, to provide him with a coin to turn, if
be.

ed was. "You, man," Stewart called down into one
h. "Michael Shiner."

deep charcoal face looked up from the pit. Sweat was
ing down his face and visible on the nap of his hair. The
chucked the tip of his shovel into the dirt and leaned
st it. "Yassir?" he replied.

Organize your men and get ready to leave the area."
chael Shiner continued to look up at the white massa,
mond eyes unblinking, his face closed tight as a tomb.
ewart sized up the situation. "You a free Negro?"
ry slowly: "Yassir."

Stewart surveyed the man's progress in the trenches, and that of the man's fellows. He commented, "Nice work."

Michael Shiner wiped the dripping sweat from his brow with his sleeve. He blinked, once, slowly. "I like to dig," he said, in a neutral tone.

Stewart heard the even tone, but also knew not to take it at face value. He replied, "So do I." He repeated, "If you want to be alive on the morrow to dig again, you can organize your men to leave the area."

"Yassir," he said, yet again, but this time there was a touch of compliance. He turned, and in strange words, called out for the men around him to stop. Voices babbled back at him. Michael Shiner looked up again at the white man. "Where are we to go?"

Stewart had no idea. He knew only that they should not remain here, unarmed. "Go to the parade ground at Bladensburg and clean up what the British might have overlooked—guns and muskets, principally."

Michael Shiner's face shuttered closed again.

"The British have left the battlefield," Stewart said, by way of explaining that he was not sending the Negroes to certain death. "They're on their way to Washington now."

That information required no translation on Michael Shiner's part. It also nearly overset his ability to lead his men. The Negroes scrambled out of the trenches. The white men, knowing a similar fear, followed suit, and Stewart had to yell some hasty instructions to the white man he had appointed leader. The ragged band of whites and blacks disappeared into the nearest thicket of trees, and Stewart mentally consigned the lot of them to the devil. For his part, he knew he needed to get to the Navy Yard before the British did, to help mount the last American stand to save the city.

Stewart went to a trench to retrieve his backpack and his British-issued musket. He slipped the pack straps across his shoulders, slung the bayoneted Brown Bess over the pack on his back, then ran across the tops of the trench until he reached the embankment along Rock Creek. He descended the ragged slope sliding on his boots and tore a nasty gash

is forearm on an outcrop of sharp stone. He ignored the
a and the blood, so intent he was on making his way
kly from Rock Creek toward Tiber Creek, by way of the
omac, in order to arrive at the yard without having to
ace on city streets.

scant five minutes later, Jane and Johnnie Shaw ar-
d at the abandoned trenches north of George Town.
en they looked out over the northeastern horizon and
the tiny clouds of dust rising from the Bladensburg
npike, they had no idea the British were coming.

everal hours later, darkness was descending, and the
ish troops were arriving at the city's doorstep. Stewart
stepping his way along the banks of the Tiber Creek past
Capitol building when, suddenly, deep explosions shook
ground. He climbed out of the river bed in time to see
ows of flame and smoke gush upward from the direc-
of the Navy Yard, to the south. Embers shot like com-
hrough the night sky.

e was too late; the yard had been set ablaze. He guessed
it had been done by the Americans, who knew they
d not defend it. He feared now for the fate of the rest of
city.

he streets were in an uproar, crowded with citizens ter-
d by the blast and the approaching British. Suddenly
ure of what to do next, Stewart waded into the crowds
ing in the streets. By sheerest chance, he caught sight of
ung woman, threading her way, as if looking for some-

e felt two contradictory emotions: one of happiness to
her again and to be able to help her; one of anger that
had, once again, been impetuous, unthinking and un-

Miss Shaw!'' he called. He ran after her and quickly
ht up with her. He stretched out a hand to grasp her
lder. He called again, ''Jane Shaw!''

t the sound of her name, Jane whirled, hoping to see
nnie, from whom she had been separated by the stam-
in the streets at the moment of the explosion. She was,
ace, afraid and reassured to be looking up into the face

er Stewart. She flinched away from his touch. He
ately dropped his hand from her shoulder, vexed that
nissed his opportunity to tell her who he was the day
n the park.

time to explain," he said. He shook his head slightly,
 deny her need to fear him. He reached out to her
This time, he grasped her hand. His fingers closed,
nd comforting, over hers.

s get out of here!"

Chapter Fifteen

The crowd was surging around her, and Johnnie was no-where to be seen. Jane had no choice but to cast her lot with Stewart.

"Where to?" she asked, tentatively accepting the grasp of his hand. She felt a surge of reassurance at his touch, and remembered that the last time they had been together on the street in Washington, she had been anything but reassured by him.

He looked straight ahead at the pyrotechnical display lighting the sky. "We can't go in the direction of the Navy Yard, for the whole south end of Washington will soon be in flames." He nodded over his shoulder in the direction of Tiber Creek, to the west. He thought they might be able to leave the city by the way he had come. He figured that the water of the river would protect them from the fire, should the southwesterly breezes catch sparks from the Navy Yard and carry them over the city. "Can you make it down the side of an embankment?"

"As well as you can," she replied matter-of-factly.

He quirked his brows at that, but confined himself to saying, "Right. Let's go, then."

Fingers intertwined, they started in the direction Stewart had indicated with his head. They were in the most volatile part of town, between the Capitol and the Navy Yard, with British soldiers soon to be surrounding them. Even more dangerous were the crowds in the street. The poor citizens of Washington had been left the afternoon long in a state of

nxiety for lack of information from their leaders as
they should do. Now, when it was too late and the
s surely to be torched, there was a mad crush to leave

art had a dozen things to say to Jane, but it was dif-
o carry on a conversation with the din and confu-
the street. Explanations could wait. For now, it was
of settling first things first.

n they had negotiated the first clot of bodies block-
r way, he bent down to speak to her. Her bonnet had
ushed back off her head, and it was dangling down
k, held only by the string still tied about her neck. He
ect access to her ear. "And what, may I ask, Miss
re you doing in Washington *now?*"

half angry, half teasing tone of his voice dispelled her
d roused her irritation. "I am not sure you may ask,"
d, meeting his eye with a glint in hers, "for when I
ou that question yesterday, you refused to answer!"

then, a man rushing past her knocked her flat into
t's chest. She was steadied by Stewart's arm, which
round her waist.

, but this is different," he pointed out, not releasing
t holding her to him.

, it's not—" she began, but she was not allowed to
e.

sterday," he said sternly, "the city was not under
Today it is. Yesterday my life was not in direct dan-
the streets of Washington. Today yours is. I can
think of anything more...more *impetuous*..." he

d unthinking and unwise?" she interpolated.

thinking and unwise," he agreed. "And so, Miss
whatever are you doing, here, now, in the midst of

eems pointless to argue about it like this," she said,
nding within the circle of his strong arm, "and if you
now, I came looking for someone."

d you chose to do your looking alone?"

," she said, "I was with my brother."

"You were *with* your brother and not looking for him?"

"That's right, *with* my brother. I lost him not more than a couple of minutes ago, for we were separated at the moment of the explosion." She craned her neck to scan the passing crowds to catch a glimpse of Johnnie.

A person running blindly came between them, momentarily separating their bodies. With a stab of panic, Jane reached into the darkness and was immediately calmed when she found Stewart's hand again, her only anchor in the sea of chaos.

"Your brother persuaded you to enter Washington tonight?" he asked, highly skeptical of this explanation.

"It was rather that he was unable to talk me out of it."

That much Stewart believed. He would have liked to know who she had come looking for, but they were wasting a deal of a time as it was, and his attention was momentarily diverted by the glare of another big fire creeping across the sky. This new blaze lit the dark horizon to the north and west, from the vicinity of the President's house. He knew that General Ross was entering Washington by the north and east. The new fire meant that the British navy had arrived as scheduled. Stewart reckoned Tiber Creek a risky escape route now, for it was likely to be filled with British seamen flowing in from the Potomac.

"Admiral Cochrane and his flotilla have arrived, it seems," Stewart remarked, somewhat absently, as he mentally remapped their path out of the city.

"With his six ships of the line, twenty-one frigates, ten brigs," Jane recited with some asperity, "and seventeen transports bearing more troops, making his command fifty-four sail in all."

Stewart looked down at her and smiled approvingly. "That's correct."

Before he could comment further, she added, almost unthinkingly, "My brother was at Bladensburg, you know." She added, unnecessarily, "On the American side."

The words *So was I* were on the tip of his tongue, but they never left his mouth. Instead, he muttered a curse at sight of a column of red-coated men entering the street to their

ot forty feet away. The passage was blocked by the
g Navy Yard; the passage ahead was barred by the
of the President's house; Tiber Creek, on the left,
ely dotted with sloops and dinghies and the British
edcoats were coming on the right. Stewart had but
urse of action available to keep himself and Miss
afe. Without wasting time with words of explana-
: stopped dead in his tracks, loosened the straps of his
om under the musket flung atop it, and slipped the
ff his shoulders. Opening it, he shook out the mili-
at folded inside and shrugged into his blaze-red badge
ish identity.
ook Jane by the shoulders and turned her to face him.
gan, "There's something I've been meaning to tell

aused, composing his thoughts, savoring the strange
nt. She was looking up at him, her lustrous brown
rst registering shock at the sight of his coat, then be-
g wide and expectant, willing to hear, willing to be-
hat he was going to tell her.
wisps of her hair formed a golden aureole around her
and her skin glowed peach in the reflection of a city
consumed in fiery destruction. Still, a tender trust
from her eyes. He had the flash of a memory that the
ae he had seen her she had kissed him as he had never
issed before. He doubted, for a fleeting moment, that
erved the trust he read in her eyes.
as a hot summer's night. Despite the breezes, it was
ome hotter still before it was over, with the heat from
ghtening conflagration licking the sky and spreading
waves through the tinder-arid gulleys of the streets.
g her shoulders, thus, and in turn held straight by the
ering light of her steady gaze, he was curiously
led in the intense reality of the moment.
opened his mouth to continue. He could no longer
til they were free and clear of the city and its danger
ain. "I should have told you yesterday, but I didn't."
he had to say felt like a confession. "You see, Miss
" he said earnestly, "I'm—"

"*Stewart!*" The gust of a deep voice came from behind him, and then a hearty slap on his back, pushing him against Jane's body.

"We'd given you up for dead!" boomed a second.

"And you're *what*, we're wanting to know! Randy?" a third chimed in. "And when you're done, man, we want a piece of the action."

A column of redcoats had filed into the street from the south. Stewart and Jane were now surrounded, red ahead and red behind, and circled by fire. It was a damnable position to be in, and he cursed Jane for her impulsive actions. More importantly, he realized that he had left his explanations to her too late. He did not dare look back at Jane, in case some expression on his face should give him away in front of his comrades from the Forty-fourth. Instead, he turned slowly and greeted the lads by name. He knew that the only way to protect Jane was to treat her rudely. He drew her to him, her backside to his front so that they were both facing the soldiers. He draped one of his arms over her shoulder, so that it hung down across her breasts, possessively, insolently, insultingly.

Jane was instantly on her guard, for she had felt every fiber in Stewart's body change. Her heart was racing, in fear, in uncertainty, in blinding disappointment at not having heard what he had to say to her. She lowered her eyes and wisely kept silent.

"No, I'm saving this one for Dick Lawler," Stewart said in an offhand way, thereby countering the comment of the third soldier. "But, randy, Randolph? Why would you think I'd have cause to be randy?" He boldly fondled Jane's curves, almost dismissively, as if he had considered her but found her wanting. "This one's for Lawler, as he and I agreed last night. He was to trade me the blondes he found for any redheads I ran across." Stewart fondled a red curl that had fallen from Jane's disordered coiffure. "I've already had my first blonde, so Lawler'll owe me."

"So that's where you've been!"

"We didn't think we'd seen you after Bladensburg."

"Or before, now I think on it."

"I was out on an exploratory mission for the general," Stewart replied, evasively, "and now our efforts have paid off with the capture of the enemy's capital." Fortunately, no one took issue with Stewart's account of his activities. "I didn't think Ross would begrudge me a moment or two to myself, with the city and its women at our feet."

"Where'd you find her?" one of them wanted to know.

Stewart jerked a thumb in a random direction. "That way, lads, if you're looking for the prettiest women. The other way, if you're looking for the most experienced."

"But I like the one you have," the second one protested.

"Are you willing to fight Lawler for her?" he asked.

In Lawler's absence, all three readily accepted the challenge.

Stewart dropped a nuzzling kiss on Jane's neck. The heat and salt on her skin seared his lips. He raised his head and said, lazily, "Are you willing to fight me for her?" There was just enough of a firm, desirous edge to his voice to make his challenge serious.

After a moment's hesitation, one stepped forward. "You've had your blonde," he complained. "Now it's our turn, Lawler or no Lawler. She's a pretty one, too."

"I know," Stewart replied, "and that's why she's making me change my mind about having Lawler owe me one. He can find his own, don't you think, lads?"

With the one arm draped over her shoulder, Stewart pulled her back against him, hard. With his other hand, he grazed Jane's neck and jaw. Then he caressed her nape and pulled her face toward him, so that it was tucked under his chin. His hand was splayed against her cheek. Two fingers toyed and nipped at her earlobe. Like his previous gesture, this handling was possessive, insolent, and insulting, but it was also, oddly, protective, for his hand shielded the side of her face from the hot gaze of the soldiers. The arm across her front held her safe.

He felt the whisper of her shallow breath against his neck. He felt the irregular rise and fall of her breasts under his arm. He shifted the weight on his feet and became aware that they were beginning to stick together, with the perspiration that moistened the back of her dress cleaving to the sweat that soaked the front of his shirt. Blood seemed to be rushing everywhere in his body. It flowed to the wound in his arm, making it throb.

She was maintaining a brave front so far, but he wanted to avoid stretching her limits. He also did not want to press his luck with the troops of the Forty-fourth roaming the streets. These three had not been close enough to Shaw House to recognize the mistress of Shaw Plantation, but there was no telling when he and Miss Shaw would come face-to-face with soldiers who would recognize her.

"You, too, lads. Find your own women," Stewart coaxed with a directive toss of his head. His eyes narrowed. His lips curled in smiling menace. His voice was soft and persuasive. "There'll surely be three American beauties in the next street willing to receive the favors of conquering soldiers."

The three men saw that they would have to fight their comrade in earnest and wrest the pretty one from his grip if they were to have her. There was also the problem of how to divide her, and of what to say to Dick Lawler, should Stewart tell him of his loss. And all three of them had the vague idea that it would be better to stay out of the antagonistic rivalry that always rasped between Dick Lawler and James Stewart.

The trio was not going to leave without salvaging their pride. Their parting vollies suggested, in the crudest terms, that the pretty one was going to miss the ride of her life.

Stewart followed their departure with his eyes. Not altering his bold, possessive hold on Jane, he nudged her forward, slowly, down the street, saying tersely, "Trust me." He needed to assume a careless disregard for the woman he held, and he did not deem it wise to attempt any open conversation with her. Nor did he dare lower his guard, even for a moment, to drop a word in her ear. He kept his head high, on the alert. His eyes, despite their lazy gaze, were ready to establish contact with any of the passing soldiers, to stare down any unspoken challenge for her favors. To all verbal challenges, he responded with curt, strutting comments, threats, or insults, as the case demanded. He was sorry that she had to hear such things.

Holding her close, negotiating the street with dangers on all sides, he felt her fear. He could not prevent her from hearing the coarse talk, and he could not completely protect her from receiving the looks and leers directed at her. He hoped, however, that she knew he would shield her from what he could. And she would just have to trust that he had no intentions of turning her over to Dick Lawler. There would be time enough to explain everything later, when they had safely escaped this basket of crabs. Less than five minutes had elapsed since he had first grabbed her hand, and everything was happening so fast that there was no time to think, only to act.

At one moment, he grabbed the bonnet hanging down her back and slipped it back on to her head. At first, she did not seem to understand what he was doing, but then she began to fumble with the strings. She retied them, securing the bonnet around her face. With his fingers, he tipped her head down so that the brim would hide her face as much as possible. She initially resisted the pressure. He realized that she would not want to lose the control of seeing where they were going, but he insisted, lightly, with this fingers. She eventually yielded by bowing her head, thus letting him direct their path alone.

They approached an intersection. Stewart was hoping to find a quiet sidestreet clear of redcoats. He was praying that they could either make a run for it or find a sympathetic civilian willing to hide them. He prodded her to the right. He let go of her in case they could make a fast break. They rounded the corner—

And came face-to-face with an underofficer from the Forty-fourth, in the company of two infantrymen.

"Stewart! What a piece of good luck!" Corporal Thomas remarked, apparently pleased by the encounter, which ranked, for Stewart, as the worst luck imaginable. "The lieutenant sent me to look for you."

Stewart greeted the corporal and asked noncommittally, "Richards sent you to find me?" He shifted slightly to move

in front of Jane, who had received a quick glance and a
frown from Thomas, as if the corporal were trying to place
her.

"Yes, he's sending you on an errand with the general and
said he hadn't seen you since Bladensburg. Because he knew
the Forty-fourth had fanned out in this neighborhood, he
sent me here to look. He was wondering what had become
of you." Corporal Thomas grinned. With a nod to the
woman partially shielded by Stewart, he added, "I know
now what you've been doing since we reached the capital,
but how was it that the lieutenant hadn't seen you since
Bladensburg?"

Stewart's arm had begun to throb painfully again, and
that wound gave him an idea. "I took a bullet early on in the
action." He grasped the lapel of his coat and peeled it away
from his shoulder and down his arm, revealing the tear and
the ugly mass of dried blood on the white sleeve of his shirt.
"I fell out of formation to tend to it, and by the time I was
back in business, the battle was over."

Thomas and the two infantrymen smirked at the mention of the swift engagement earlier in the day. The child's
play of the battle was briefly commented upon, thereby diverting attention from what Stewart had possibly been doing for the *rest* of the afternoon, once the battle had ended.

"True enough," Thomas said, obviously accepting the
explanation of Stewart's absence from his regular column.
He ran his eye over Stewart's coat when Stewart had hitched
it back in place. "Your coat is of a piece, however. In excellent condition, in fact."

Stewart inwardly cursed his disastrous oversight. He had
no explanation, of course, for why the sleeve of his coat was
not in shreds, and so said nothing.

Thomas's expression became a little grim. "How did he
die," he asked, "the soldier whose coat you picked off?"

Stewart felt a sharp stab of relief to be handed an explanation ready-made. However, his voice was cool enough
when he said, without hesitation, "Bullet in the temple."

"It's common practice," one infantryman consoled, imagining Stewart's bad feelings at having been caught taking a dead man's coat.

"You needed it more than him," the second agreed.

Stewart acknowledged their comradely remarks with a nod.

"Well, let's go," Corporal Thomas said, motioning for Stewart to follow him.

"Where are we headed?" Stewart asked.

"To the Capitol," the corporal answering, gesturing with his head in the direction he had just come from. "The general's determined to burn that building, if no other."

Trying to bargain for a fraction of free time and space, Stewart told the men to go ahead. He assured them that he would catch up.

"The general wants you now" was Thomas's answer to that, as he began to walk away. "Come on, then."

Stewart saw that to protest further would only raise suspicion, and he could not hope either to outrun or overpower all three men. Although he had necessarily to join Corporal Thomas now, he hesitated.

Thomas looked back over his shoulder and glanced at the figure half-hidden behind Stewart. He pursed his lips. "All right, bring her with you," he said. "You might have time for her later."

Although Stewart did not like to abandon Jane alone in the streets, he thought she would do better on her own than delivered straight into the general's hands. "Don't worry about it," he said with a shrug, as if he did not care whether or not he would have time for her later. "I can find another one."

Corporal Thomas thought it over, squinted thoughtfully at the woman whose face was hidden from his scrutiny, then shook his head. "Bring her," he said decisively. It was an order. "We'll let the general or the lieutenant decide what to do with her. They established a policy for prisoners taken at Bladensburg. I'm sure they'll have something to say about the capture of enemy women."

That was precisely what Stewart feared.

* * *

In the event, neither General Ross nor Lieutenant Richards had anything to say about Miss Jane Shaw or her presence in James Stewart's company, for General Ross was already riding out of Washington at the moment Corporal Thomas was leading Stewart and Jane to the Capitol. With the Treasury burning, the offices of the *National Intelligencer* ablaze, and flames racing through the War Department, Ross and his men had an easy time making their way in the light of the fires. Leaving the torched city behind, they encountered fleeing citizens, prostitutes eager for their business, and a very few American soldiers, still armed and ready to surrender their weapons.

Knowing that the general was impatient of any delay, Lieutenant Richards had, at the last moment, replaced the errant James Stewart with the nearer-to-hand Dick Lawler as the second aide. Eventually, General Ross noticed the replacement.

"And Stewart?" he inquired of his lieutenant.

"Gone, sir," Lieutenant Richards answered.

The general's brow lowered. "Was he among the casualties?"

"It's rather that he's unaccounted for," Richards replied. "When we were approaching the capital this evening, I searched for him and discovered that he had not been seen since the battle." Richards paused. "Since before the battle, in fact."

The general's brow raised. "And you think to tell me of this most extraordinary occurrence only now?"

Lieutenant Richards waited, stolid and silent, for a severe reprimand. He was surprised when the general said merely, "It is very odd."

Ross paused to puzzle the matter out, but came up with nothing. Stewart had been an exemplary soldier. "I trust nothing untoward has happened to him," he said, and left it at that.

Lawler had been listening to the exchange and, seeing his chance to bring himself to the general's notice, urged his horse forward. He saluted crisply. "Infantryman Lawler at your service, sir."

The general favored the large, beefy man with a haughty regard that had reduced many a soldier to pudding. "Indeed."

A while later, the general and his men turned down the long drive, lined with a double row of tulip trees, that led to the McClelland house. The orange glow of the burning city was behind them, and it lit the sky. Along the way, they had passed the occasional cluster of homes, whose owners were on their roofs, watching the conflagration. The McClelland house was no different. When the people on its roof sighted a party of six men on horseback trotting up the drive, looking fit, well-armed and confident, they did not need the light of day to know that the color of their coats was red.

Barbara Johnson was seated at the dormer window of her front corner bedroom, looking out expressionlessly over the brilliant destruction of Washington. She spied the men riding up the drive. She peered into the darkness. She was puzzled, then wary, when she recognized the commanding presence of General Ross by the set of his shoulders as he drew near the house. She shook her head minimally, trying to imagine what trick of fate should have brought him to this very house. Then she saw Lieutenant Richards and realized that it was not a trick of fate at all, but part of a deliberate plan.

She stood up abruptly, hastened to the window that gave out onto the side of the house, and called up, as loudly as she dared, to the people on the roof. "Get down and inside the house, now! We've redcoats on our doorstep!"

By the movement that had already begun on the roof, she realized that they had seen the men. She heard a scrambling down the ladder, and her heart began to pound unpleasantly, worried that there would be no one below stairs, save Mrs. McClelland and her husband, who was confined to his chair, to fend off the well-armed redcoats. She dared not leave the room herself, and she could only hope that the McClellands would know enough to deny her presence in their home. She felt cornered now. She thought, for the very first time this day, that Jane had been right to leave the house. Jane, who had wanted to go to the action, to do what she could, to help her brother if he needed it.

Barbara Johnson paced the room, feeling cornered. She heard the pounding at the front door. The redcoats would not be denied. She heard them in the front hallway. She heard them take command of the downstairs. She felt sick. She took a deep breath. Her courage could not fail her now. She went back to her seat at the window. She drew a deep breath and put a hand to her throat. The feel of the smooth cameo soothed her somewhat. She gazed out over the great flaming scar in the sky.

She heard the sound of boots, a single pair of boots, mount the stairs. She heard the boots stop on the landing at the top of the stairs. She heard the first door in the hallway open and close. Then the boots walked a few paces. The second door, the one next to hers, was opened and closed. Then the boots walked a few more significant steps.

Her door was opened.

At the sound, she turned slowly from her contemplation of the destruction of the capital. She saw him standing here. Handsome, proud, aristocratic. General Ross. In a beautiful red coat, hardly the worse for wear, hair neat, boots polished. General Ross. Who had won the day at Bladensburg. Who had put Washington to the torch.

He bowed politely, observing the proprieties.

She greeted him with the words "Get out."

He did not move. He just stood there a moment, framed in the doorway, looking at her sitting erect at the window, her blond hair alive with lights in the glow of the fire for which he deserved credit. She was beautiful. No, more than beautiful. She was inspiring, with her tarnished gold hair, and eyes the color of the sky of ancient Greece.

"Get out," she repeated.

He moved into the room. He tapped the door closed with his boot. It shut with a soft click.

When he walked toward her, she rose from her seat. She drew a breath. "You cannot believe that I want you here."

"I can believe that you do not know what you want," he returned confidently.

"It is not your presence in my bedroom."

At that he nodded slowly and smiled. "Yes," he said. "No."

He took a step closer. He could touch her if he wanted. Her curves were perfect, and perfectly ripe. She turned her head and upper body away. "I'll have you," he stated.

She turned back and slanted him a glance from her heavenly blue eyes. The look took his breath away. "Not willingly," she said.

He drank in the details of her beauty, heightened by the glow in the rectangle of the window. His fire, his victory, his woman. He raised his hand to her. She did not move a muscle at his touch. Her face was set against him.

A very slow, predatory smile curved his handsome lips. "This is the first real resistance I've encountered today," he said softly, capturing her chin in a light touch and lifting it. Her eyes shone with quiet defiance. "How delightful that it should be from you, Mrs. Johnson."

Chapter Sixteen

Jane was finding it increasingly difficult to keep her head down as she followed the redcoats heading toward the Capitol. Without Stewart's firm hand to guide her, she felt a fluttery fear of the unknown. To allay that feeling, she would sneak an occasional peek around her from below the brim of her bonnet. She reckoned the risk of exposing her face worth the relative calm produced by being able to see where she was going.

For, indeed, every nerve was jumping erratically inside her skin, and it was all she could do to hold fast to her wits and her composure. In the past minutes, which might well have been a lifetime, her emotions had been buffeted about by many contrary winds. First there was the sense that the world had come to an end when the Navy Yard exploded, and, hard upon the heels of that, the panic at losing track of Johnnie. Next had come the double miracle of Stewart's presence before her, and the unmistakable impression that she was safe with him. Then, when it seemed that, together, they might slip out from under the redcoat net that surrounded them, they had been trapped.

Jane was aware that Stewart had given two very different accounts of his activities for the day—one to the trio of soldiers, and another to Corporal Thomas. Although this meant that he had lied at least once, she still had no idea, really, why he was here, what he was doing, or which side he was on. It was simply too much for her just then to continue to believe in Stewart's sympathies, or in his ability to help her. And there he was, hardly two feet ahead of her, speaking to Corporal Thomas as would any cocky conquering soldier. Her confidence in him plummeted.

With the city burning around her, Jane felt her stomach weighted down with a sickening feeling of unreality. She was acutely aware of the interest taken in her by the two infantrymen on either side of her, and she did not like the way they would "accidentally" bump into her and touch her. She realized that it was not her life she feared for this night, but her virtue, and she did not know whether General Ross would save her or hand her over to the highest-ranking man who wanted her. The thought of being soiled by one of them caused her stomach to heave wildly, and she had ample opportunity to regret the impulsive folly of trying to find Michael Shiner in this chaos.

She had the hazy feeling that she was walking the plank, or ascending the gallows. She had the more distinct feeling of a lamb going to slaughter. Desperation gripped her.

She looked up and at the back of Stewart's head. He must have sensed something of her turmoil, for he turned just then and saw the way the two infantrymen were jostling for position on either side of her. He favored each of them with a cool look that read *Keep out!* Then he winked audaciously at Jane, for the infantrymen to see. It was a bold promise to her of future adventure with him alone. However, before his eyes left hers, a warmer, more complex message lit their depths, something like *I'll try and get you out of this!* He turned around again.

He had given her a moment of reassurance. She hung on to it and felt her lurching stomach find a precarious equilibrium. Her spirts rose.

Her spirits rose further when they arrived on Capitol Hill to see the Capitol whole and unharmed, although the British had officially taken possession of it in the name of His Majesty the king. Her spirits lifted another notch when they heard the news that General Ross and Lieutenant Richards had just left the area. She felt as if she had been handed a reprieve as she and her escort were absorbed into a group of men—from the Forty-fourth, she guessed, by the way they greeted one another.

"The general's already left?" Corporal Thomas echoed, clearly disgusted that this ultimately successful effort to track down James Stewart had been to no avail. "What was the hurry?"

"Ross spent an hour here and discovered that the Capitol was difficult to burn," said the spokesman of the group. "He left the task of destruction to Admiral Cochrane, so that he and a few of his men could be off to . . . Riverdale, I think it is."

Riverdale! Jane's heart leapt painfully. The implications of that message were clear to her. She could not just stand here, helpless. She felt she had to *do* something. She kept her head studiously down, looked left and right, and saw other groups of people around her, with women scattered among them. She peeked up at Corporal Thomas and saw that his attention was fully engaged by immediate events. Was there, possibly, a way for her to get to Riverdale? First, she must begin to inch away from the group, without anyone noticing. . . .

Corporal Thomas was scanning the various groups of soldiers and sailors. "The admiral's here? Yes, I see him. What's his plan?"

"He has the idea to blow the place up," came the cheerful response.

Stewart stepped forward. He knew all about explosives. "But that method will wreck the private homes in the immediate neighborhood."

"And so?"

Stewart stated what he knew to be common knowledge among the soldiers. "So Ross gave us strict orders not to destroy private property. The government buildings, yes, but no homes, unless the citizens show resistance."

"As if you care!" one man challenged.

"I don't," Stewart replied, indifferently.

"What's more, the general's gone," a second man said.

"But he'll learn of the surrounding destruction one way or the other," a third one countered. "He always does."

Corporal Thomas, who liked explosives, argued eagerly, "True enough, but the destruction will be on Cochrane's shoulders. It's his idea."

Stewart chuckled. "You're the ranking officer now, Thomas. I'm thinking the blame might rather fall on *your* shoulders, if you don't do something to stop Cochrane."

After that, the discussion became lively and rather heated. While the men were thrashing out the proper method of destroying the Capitol and deciding where lay the responsibility, Jane took another step away from the group. She glanced up at Stewart, who was keeping half an eye on her. He nodded, minimally, as if agreeing that she should break away.

Just as she was to make her decisive step, a hand clamped down on her arm. It belonged to one of the two infantrymen who had accompanied her to the Capitol. He had sensed her movements, and he was not about to let her get away.

"Our lady friend is thinking we've lost interest in her," he said, "and that's not polite now, is it?" He jerked Jane's chin upward and looked into her face. "Michael Garfield at your service, ma'am. I say let's have some fun and watch the damned building blow up."

Jane was afraid that she would attract Corporal Thomas's attention—and his recognition. Fortunately, Stewart's diversionary tactic had worked. The corporal was more concerned about the means of destruction of the Capitol than about the fate of the woman among them.

"I think we'd better advise Cochrane of Ross's order," the corporal said, fixing his eyes on the admiral and ignoring the byplay between Jane and the infantryman. "You, Stewart," he continued. "It was your idea. You go and tell him about Ross's orders."

Jane's chin was still in the infantryman's grip. She held his hot, lustful eyes with a steady, hateful glare from her own. Would Stewart have to leave her to this man's desires? Her heart lurched, once, against her ribs before she heard Stewart's response.

Stewart laughed again, easily, and directly flouted the corporal's authority. "Let the Capitol explode," he said cavalierly, "as Garfield over here wants, and why not?"

Stewart was not going to abandon her, then, and Thomas did not have enough authority to make him do as he had asked. However, the corporal did want to appear to be taking some kind of decisive action, and so he snapped, "Leave that woman alone, Garfield, and let's go talk some army sense into the admiral!"

Thomas put force into his words by grabbing Garfield by the scruff of his neck. Jane found herself abruptly released, and she turned her head away from the corporal, although she was sure by then that he was not paying her any attention.

Garfield was pulled away from the group, complaining bitterly, and received only unsympathetic jeers from his cohorts as he left the scene. The others, including Stewart, stayed where they were, and all of them seemed to be keeping a private eye on Jane. She was aware of it, and did not move. She exchanged a brief regard with Stewart. He seemed watchful. Again, she felt in his gaze the reasssuring message that he would find a way to take care of her.

Excitement was mounting to see the Capitol destroyed. The several hundred British soldiers and sailors milling about were becoming restless. Some soldiers joined Jane's group. Others left. Stewart stayed. His buddies invited him here and there. No matter what the talk, no matter what the reason, he had a glib answer ready to refuse.

Word finally spread that fire, not explosives, would destroy this citadel of American republicanism. It was reported that the absurdly solid limestone outer walls might only crumble and crack, but there was plenty to burn inside.

All eyes turned toward the Capitol. Jane saw fifty-odd men, a motley crew of sailors and soldiers, marched by an officer up the steps, each carrying a long pole to which was tied a ball about the circumference of a large plate. Each man was stationed at a window, with his pole and its machine of wildfire against it. At the word of command, the windows were simultaneously broken and this wildfire thrown in, so that an instantaneous conflagration took place.

At the sight, Jane felt her heart wince, then wither. There was no question now of her trying to escape. She was going to remain at the scene, a witness to the fiery death of American independence, her presence a tribute to her failed nation. She would watch, proud in defeat.

She turned her eyes toward Stewart and found his green gaze already resting on her.

His face was impassive, but his eyes were grave, even sad. Their gazes held, and they risked this long regard, knowing that the rest of the spectators stood transfixed in silence, watching as the building was wrapped in flames and smoke, the heavens reddening with the blaze.

She saw the burning of the Capitol reflected in Stewart's grave eyes and wondered what she knew of this man, after all? She did not know his age or anything about his family, not even if he was married. She did not know where he came from. She did not know what he was doing here this night in Washington, seemingly on his own. She did not know where he would go when the war was over. She did not know if his real name was James Stewart.

And yet she felt she knew him well. She knew that he liked early-morning strolls, fresh-water baths, and blueberry pie. She knew that he flirted and touched and kissed with passion and promise. She knew that he claimed the ability to admit a mistake when he was wrong. She knew that he liked to fish and to build dams. And she knew from the look in the depths of his eyes reflecting fire that he did not like to destroy things.

She saw that the color of his coat was red, but she also knew that, somehow, he was not a redcoat.

The realization teased her and tantalized her and made her reflect on the times she had taunted him for his red coat. She remembered their encounter below the tree outside her bedroom window, when she had been lying on the ground beneath him. She had assaulted him and insulted him and called him a redcoat, to which he had replied, merely,

"Which I am not wearing." Stretched out beneath him, with his strong arms and shoulders holding her down, she had been angry and aroused, hot and humiliated, but she had not been afraid of him. And he had released her.

She remembered the night of the zombie magic, when she had been in the kitchen, sinking in desire for him. She had pulled herself out of it only by remembering the color of his coat. And later, after they had rescued Lawler, she had tried to hold him off again by recalling that red coat. He had answered a second time, "Which I am not wearing." He had been about to tell her something when Mamie broke the spell.

And then that kiss. Such a kiss. In broad daylight. In the street. A kiss that might as well have been full possession. She had called him a redcoat then, too, and he had not been wearing one that time, either.

She realized, strangely, that tonight was the first time she had actually seen him wear his red coat. He had put it on to save her. She regarded him steadily, and he returned her gaze steadily. Tonight was the first time she would not wish to accuse him of being a redcoat.

She followed his eyes roaming her face, detailing the dishevelment of her hair, tracing her body, touching her breasts and waist and hips. His eyes were filled with desire for her, but that lust was layered and textured now by other, deeper emotions. She saw in his gaze that he desired her, but she read admiration for her there, too. She saw in his stance that he wanted her, but he needed her, too. She saw in his face that he demanded something of her, but his arrogance was gone, and a humble dignity accompanied his silent request for her comfort in this context of anguish and defeat.

She gave him that comfort through her eyes, and was comforted, in turn, by his stark acknowledgment of his desire and admiration and need for her—and the message that he would not let anything bad happen to her body this night.

The Capitol burned around them, and together they were aware of the dimension of the destruction. It was not just the fiery disappearance of the red morocco chairs of the Senate, the desks in the Hall of Representatives, the journals of the House, the law library and the Library of Congress, the handsome gilt eagle surmounting the clock above the speaker's chair, or the clock itself, those hands pointed to ten o'clock as the fire began. Together they knew that it was the end of the past as they had known it, that it was the end of the future as they had dreamed it, that it was the end of the grand American experiment. They shared that knowledge, and the accompanying pain.

Stewart was the first to break the gaze. His attention was claimed by one of his comrades who slapped him on the back with grand bonhomie and commented expansively on the magnificent blaze before them. Jane, too, became aware, again, of the hooting and hollering and merriment around them. Stewart was taking part in it, but Jane knew that his participation was perfunctory.

Stewart had stared too long at Jane, and now had to make up for lost time. He took the risk of turning away from her to engage in celebratory discussion with several lads from the Forty-fourth, but just then another kind of ruckus broke out.

Some American soldiers—those who had entered Washington to defend it and who had been captured by the British troops roaming the city and brought to Capitol Hill to have their noses rubbed in defeat—had begun to riot. The British quickly quelled this outburst by tying the soldiers' hands behind their backs, silencing them with gags, and then tying them to one another, as in a chain gang. Admiral Cochrane compounded the indignity when he gave the order that all civilian Americans, including women, should be so tied and gagged, to prevent further unrest.

Just when Stewart turned his back to Jane, she was grabbed by one of the redcoats assigned to task of subduing the Americans. Without a word of explanation, her hands were wrenched behind her, and a rope lashed firmly around her wrists.

She gasped loudly and uttered a stifled protest before a bandana bit into her mouth, and she was dragged away to be tied to some other unfortunate women. These lovelies would certainly be handed out to the conquering soldiers later, when the fire had died down, despite the commanding officers' pious orders against pillage and rape. Terror struck her anew.

Fortunately, Stewart was alert to the sound of Jane's gasp, and he turned in time to see what was happening to her and where she was being taken. Unfortunately, he could not follow her immediately without raising suspicion, for the comrade beside him said, with a suggestive leer, "That one was a sight too shy for you, my lad. There'll be others, bolder ones, mark my words, and you'll have your pick."

Stewart had to school himself to casual acceptance of this remark. For the next minute or two he bandied rude comments, remarked on the fire, rolled back on his heels, crossed his arms over his chest, smiled and wisecracked.

When he could stand it no longer, he took his leave of the group. He blended into the nearest roving band of soldiers, then melted away from them when he was out of sight of his cronies from the Forty-fourth. He anxiously scanned the crowd for signs of Jane.

It was easy enough to spot her, for she was being led in a line of women bound to one another at the waist. He saw them being herded toward the nearby park, where they would no doubt be ignominiously ravished, more than once. He saw, as well, the lines of subjugated American soldiers converging on the line of women.

Stewart first trotted up to one of the lines of American soldiers.

He hailed the officer in charge of the prisoners and asked, jovially, "What's this all about?", pointing first to the American men, then to the American women.

The redcoat's self-satisfied grin suggested that he and his comrades had hit on a truly brilliant notion. He nodded insolently at the American soldiers and explained, "Since the savages enjoyed so much the burning of the Capitol, we decided to let them watch this next fun, too."

Stewart was not so much shocked that the captured soldiers were to be made impotent witnesses to the defilement of their women as he was murderously angry. He had never been so close to exposing himself as an American, and it was all he could do to contain himself. In the event, he was saved from finding himself tied to the line of American men only because another man in that line effectively diverted his attention.

The captured soldiers had guessed what was going to happen to the women and had foreseen their role as unwilling audience. At the moment Stewart was speaking with the officer in command, the lines of the men had come close enough for one soldier to recognize one of the women in the line opposite.

This American choked on the gag in his mouth, but was able to emit a gut-wrenching cry, muffled but unmistakable. "Jane! Jane! Jane!"

Stewart's head whirled around. His eyes focused immediately on a young soldier with tousled red hair, a splash of freckles across his nose, his face contorted with helpless rage.

The epithet *The idiot!* flashed through Stewart's mind, and he knew it to be the moment for gutsy action. He held up his hand to the officer in command and, with an appropriately wolfish smile, said, "This one is mine."

Withdrawing his pocket knife, Stewart strode over to the furious American soldier and slashed the rope on either side of the man's waist, thereby releasing him from the line. He pushed the boy, so that he stumbled back about three feet, then stepped forward to grasp the lapels of the boy's jacket, thereby preventing him from falling. Stewart's back was to the line of men and to the British officer. He pulled the boy hard against his chest.

The boy looked up at him, angry, afraid, defiant, murderous, with brown, lustrous eyes so like Jane's.

Stewart said, low and harsh, into the boy's ear, "If you're wanting to see your sister violated by a dozen men here and now on the cobblestones in front of you and every other soldier, then keep it up."

Johnnie Shaw's eyes widened, groping desperately for comprehension.

Stewart jerked the boy up against him, tighter and closer. "Not another sign that you know her or any other woman over there. Do you understand?" he grated.

Johnnie Shaw nodded, slowly, with bewilderment.

"All right, then." Curtly: "Now double over with pain." The boy's eyes were glazing over.

"Now!" Stewart whispered harshly as he pulled back his fist and made as if to punch the American soldier in the stomach.

Johnnie Shaw pulled back, to flinch from the blow. When the man's fist did not make solid contact on his gut, he began, in a dazed sort of way, to understand that this redcoat, at least, meant him no harm.

Stewart proceeded to make motions as if roughing up the American, and in so doing he reached around behind the boy and loosened the knot of the rope at his wrists. When Stewart was satisfied that he had made a good enough show of gratuitous brutality, he turned the boy around and shoved him back to his original place in the line. Johnnie Shaw stumbled obligingly and looked as if he had been soundly beaten.

Stewart retied the rope ends on either side of the boy's waist, linking him to the line. Stewart pulled the rope ends down firmly, as if tightening the knots, but he deliberately failed to loop them over one another a second time, and Johnnie Shaw realized this. When Stewart was done, he ran his eye up and down the line and called out, with scathing irony, "Do any other of you brave savages take issue with our plans for your entertainment?"

Not one American attempted to test the limits of his gag.

To the boy, Stewart mouthed the words, "Don't break away yet. When I come to the end of the line of women, your sister will have been freed. Grab her, then run for your lives."

Stewart turned back to the man in command and nodded with satisfaction.

"Good work," the redcoat said, approvingly.

Stewart shrugged nonchalantly, as if he had only been doing his duty.

The next few minutes tested Stewart's steady nerves. He joined the British who had taken an interest in the line of women. Instead of approaching the women from the front, he chose to descend the line from behind. He reached out to one or the other of them, to touch and caress, as if at his leisure, and slowly made his way toward Jane. Along the way, he would loosen, here and there, the bonds at the women's wrists, tell them in a low voice, "Don't run yet." With his knife, he would unobtrusively slice halfway through the ropes holding them together, making their separation possible with a few firm tugs when it came time for the women to scatter.

He came to Jane. He cut into the ropes that bound her on either side. He loosened the bond at her wrists. Then he reached out and touched her, boldly and possessively. His hand rested a moment against her breast. He felt her heart leap against his palm. He said, "Your brother is over there. Do you see him?"

She nodded infinitesimally.

"Count to sixty, then *run* to him," he urged softly.

She did not look around. "What about you?" she whispered.

He was only two-thirds of the way through freeing the line of women. His parting words were "Don't worry about me."

Chapter Seventeen

J ane did worry about him, though. All through that harrowing night. All the way to Riverdale the next morning. All the way back to Shaw Plantation the day after. And all the day after that.

When Stewart came up behind her as she stood in the line, she felt a thrill of pride in him, his wit, his resourcefulness, his heroism. His words and actions, and even that bold caress, so theatrically insulting, so privately reassuring, gave her courage and confidence. She knew his wild, risky plan was going to work.

And it did. Almost by purest luck. When Stewart finished releasing the line of women, he gestured away from the lines of Americans in the direction of imaginary escapees. He urged his British comrades to follow a false path by shouting, "By God! They're getting away! After them! Run! Run!" He began to run in that direction himself and, thereby, drew several redcoats into the diversionary feint.

At the same moment, the beautiful pillars of the Capitol cracked and broke, and the noble dome, painted and carved with such beauty and skill, fell to ashes in the cellars beneath the still-burning ruins of the building. The great collapse of the roof created a further distraction. Suddenly, the line of women fell apart, and Johnnie separated himself, thereby creating two lines of men where there had been one. There were not enough British soldiers in the immediate area to bring the suddenly free and violently angry American men and women back into order.

All was pandemonium, and it was only thanks to their fleet feet that the British officers who had engineered this humiliation of the Americans were not fatally injured by the unarmed savages suddenly swarming all over the area.

Jane and Johnnie, hands cemented, fled blindly away from Capitol Hill, not knowing where they were running, not knowing whether they were being pursued, and not much caring, either. They were looking only for a darkened street or corner or abandoned house in which to hide for an hour or two. Jane had tried to keep track of the direction Stewart had taken, but she had quickly lost sight of him in the utter confusion. She kept alive a tiny hope that she would run into him again, by chance or by the grace of God, as she had earlier in the evening. However, such luck was not to be hers twice in one night.

Within an hour after the collapse of the Capital dome, the sky changed from the peculiar leaden hue portending a windstorm to midnight blackness. Then came the crash and glare of incessant thunder and lightning, and the wild beating of a rain followed, the fury of which Washington had never before seen. Every last American interpreted the rain as the imposition of a belatedly benevolent Providence, for it damped the fires and kept them from spreading from the public buildings to the private neighborhoods. A tornado whirled through next, driving the enemy back to their ships and out of the city.

By that time, Jane and Johnnie had found their way out of the city, and were on the trail to the north and east. Johnnie would not release Jane before he had delivered her safely to Riverdale. It was the very least he could do before he returned to the tattered ranks of the Fifth Maryland. By sunrise, they had arrived at the McClelland property, and Jane knew enough not to attempt to enter by the main alley, in the event that General Ross was still there.

In fact, just after sunrise, the party of British soldiers was trotting down the tree-lined drive, away from the house. General Ross was astride his horse, feeling triumphant and satisfied, and calmly planning the destruction of Baltimore.

Johnnie stayed long enough to greet his aunt and uncle. Since, during the night, he had already scolded his sister for her disastrous impetuosity of the day before and heard what she had to tell him of the mysterious James Stewart, he had nothing more to do than kiss Jane goodbye. He availed himself of one of his uncle's horses and rode back toward George Town, where he expected to meet up with the reassembled remnants of Starrett's men.

Thereafter, for Jane, the day inched forward at a depressing pace. She changed into clean, dry clothes, but beyond that, there was little constructive action to take. Her aunt and uncle were nearly dumb with shock at the ruin of Washington and the invasion of their house. The only bright spot for them was the realization that Jane had done well to have been away from the house for the day and night, in company with her brother.

Barbara Johnson did not descend from her bed chamber until midafternoon, and when she did, her face was serene and her back was straight. However, her carriage was a little less proud, and her eyes were deeply shadowed. She said not one word on the subject of General Robert Ross, and no one chose to raise that painful subject, either. The destruction of Washington was mentioned, at times, but mostly there was mortified silence.

Jacob Shaw shattered that silence the next morning when he appeared on his sister's doorstep, angry, outraged, and ultimately happy to find his daughter unharmed. When he had heard the news of the burning of Washington at the meeting house, he had saddled up and ridden through the night to Riverdale. He expounded in blustery periods on how it was that he was taking Jane—and Mrs. Johnson, too, if she cared!—back to North Point. It was his considered opinion that Jane would be safer on her own property, even with the British camping out on it, than in any vicinity they might choose to set on fire.

Barbara Johnson accepted the escort. She spoke with uncustomary kindliness to Jacob Shaw during the entire return journey, and bid Jane and her father a pleasant goodbye when they arrived at her farm at nightfall.

Jane asked only, "Will you be all right?"

Barbara Johnson smiled, a little sadly, and said, "Why, yes, Jane. Quite all right." She paused and repeated, "Quite all right. I am sure of it. No matter what."

The no-matter-what was the return of the British to the area, and half of the Forty-fourth had already returned by land to Shaw Plantation when Jane and her father returned. The other half arrived the next day by ship.

Neither General Ross nor Lieutenant Richards spared Jane one look or one word beyond the barest civility. Nor did Corporal Thomas seem to recognize her when he passed her, once, in the yard, as she went about her chores. The British suspected her of nothing, and even if they had known she was still spying on them, they would have laughed scornfully and pointed out that her efforts before the attack on Washington had produced pitiful results. They would have invited her to continue her spying, for all the good it had done the Americans.

And she did.

That first night, she listened again, as Ross and his men planned the attack on Baltimore. Before the dawn, she scaled down the tree and ran in the swirling white mists, hoping against hope to find Michael Shiner alive and waiting to receive her message. She found no one. The second night, she listened again as the British plans developed. She learned, significantly, that the number one name on their list of wanted men was that of James Stewart.

Lieutenant Richards had ascertained that James Stewart was not among the casualties, nor had he returned to North Point by either land or ship. He had last been seen by Corporal Thomas.

General Ross had little to say on the subject beyond the chilling demand to "find him", and Lieutenant Richards correctly interpreted that order as his personal mission.

The next morning, before the dawn, Jane was again at the meeting spot in the woods, alone, disappointed, and worried about Michael Shiner, about his loyalties, his life, and his fate. After waiting half an hour, she returned, disconsolate, by way of the fields. On a dejected whim, she headed toward her private grassy spot at water's edge, where she could collect her thoughts and recruit her forces.

She crossed the fields and forests and the meadow and arrived, at last, on that delicate nub of land, facing east. She sighed, tired, but content to have come. The sun was rising, shredding the fog and promising another blaze-hot day, heavy with humidity. She dragged the kerchief off her hair and combed what she could of her tangles. Then she unbuttoned her blouse and shrugged out of it. She untied the shoulder ribbons of her chemise and pushed it down to her waist. She closed her eyes and let the dawn of day kiss the skin of her face and throat and breasts, drying the sheen of perspiration that was beading up through every pore. She stepped over to the water that was rhythmically lapping the tiny sward of land and dipped the tips of her fingers in the bay. Then she flicked her face and breasts with water, causing her nipples to peak.

She had often lain fully naked on this spot, and she intended to do so this morning, as well. She unhooked her skirts, and when they fell in a swirl at her feet, she stepped out of them. Then she stopped short and listened.

Her ears pricked up. She was familiar with every slightest noise associated with this spot. Just now she had heard the unaccustomed soft breaking of a branch underfoot, the sigh of a limb being lifted, the brush of a body against a bush.

She turned and saw a man step out onto her woman-sized spit of land.

She felt her heart contract, then blossom, at the sight of him. She breathed in, once, in wonderment, and caught a lungful of the bold, fecund air of her most favored spot in high summer. It was an aroma, exquisite and sensual, of tidewater brine lacing low-country marshes. It was a smell like warm milk and male sweat and spilled wine. It was the tang of the earth in heat.

He was looking tired and scruffy and very pleased with himself. "Jane Shaw," he said.

"James Stewart," she said. She cocked her head and looked at him. "That *is* your real name, isn't it?"

He smiled at her directness and understood the nature of her doubts. "Yes."

"I wasn't sure, you see." Only then did she remember her undress. She plucked at her chemise and pulled it up over her breasts. She was not embarrassed. She simply did not want to give away too much too soon.

He took several steps toward her, shaking his head, denying her need to cover herself, silently stating his desire to see her naked beauty.

He stood before her, gazing into her brown eyes, eyes that were warm and shining and showed unmistakably that she was happy to see him.

Arms still crossed across her breasts, she ran her eye over him. His cotton shirt was torn and open, his trousers were bedraggled, and he was barefoot. She asked, "How did you get here?"

"Last night I stole a rowboat on the other side of the Patapsco and crossed to Old Roads Bay, by the Johnson farm. Then I camped out in your forest along the trail I thought you took in the mornings. I didn't see you leave the house, but I did happen to see you on your return, across the meadow." With his head, he gestured behind him. "I followed you here."

She was smiling and letting herself be pulled, unresisting, into his lazy, seductive green gaze. "They're looking for you, you know."

He shrugged and placed his hands, lightly on her shoulders. "Let 'em look."

"You aren't worried?"

"Not at the moment." His hands caressed her shoulders, causing a shiver down to her toes, then slid down her forearms and moved to her hands lodged at her breasts. His fingers stroked hers. "Does anyone know about this spot?"

She shook her head, her eyes never leaving his.

"Are you sure?"

She nodded. "I'm the only one who's ever been here." She paused. "It's my private spot."

He lifted a brow, suggestively, then looked around him, taking in the beauty of the setting. He cast his eyes across the wide bay to the bluff of rocks on the shadowy shore opposite, still veiled in virginal fog. He glanced down both sandy legs of the coastline spreading away from the little grassy spot where he stood holding her, touching her, wanting her, but not quite ready to end this initial moment of tender talk and fragile intimacy.

"No one's ever been here with you before?" he repeated. "I'm glad." He took her hands and placed them on his shoulders. The chemise she was holding fell, leaving her breasts open for his touch. He cupped them with his palms.

She swayed toward him, peaking her fingers on his shoulders so that she was touching him fingertip to shoulder, breast to chest. She lifted up slightly so that only her toes touched the damp grass. She raised her lips to his, but she stopped short of kissing him. Sensing the rhythm of his desires and feeling comfortable with the mounting of her own, she, like him, was not yet ready to end the mutual tantalization or the soft electrification of this touching.

"Did you make it out of Washington with much difficulty?" she asked.

He nodded his head, both as a response to her question and as an agreement to take it slow. "Some. It was not a pretty escape I made, but it was an escape. And you?"

She smiled her gratitude. "You got me out. With my brother. We made it back to Riverdale the next morning."

"Young fool," he said affectionately, in reference to Jane's brother. "He almost got you raped. I couldn't let that happen."

She shivered again, and a complex of emotions coursed through her, part remembered fear at having been tied and readied for violation, part relief at his rescue of her and all the other women, part anticipation of the reward that he was seeking now and she would joyfully give.

"You didn't let that happen," she said simply.

"No," he said. His caress became bolder, more possessive. His hands moved from her breasts, down her sides, to her hips, to her thighs. He bunched up her petticoat so that he held the thin cloth in handfuls. He slipped his hands under her petticoat and frowned in mock disappointment.

"You're wearing your drawers," he chided, then added provocatively, "I much prefer speaking to you when you're not."

With that, he pushed the dainty white cotton drawers down over her hips. Kneeling as he did so, he pushed them farther, gliding his hands down the back of her thighs and calves, pushing them to the ground, where she still stood, in anticipation and readiness, on tiptoe.

"There, now," he said, satisfied, standing up. Her fingertips had never left his shoulders. With his action of slipping off her drawers, she grasped his shoulders tighter, sliding the whole of her fingers against his flesh. He worked his shoulders, liking the feeling of her touch. He brought his hands up to the small of her back and pressed her hips into his. "Much better."

He was ready to bend and kiss her, but she was wanting to string him along, just a little longer. "Since when do you prefer speaking to me without my drawers?"

His lazy green eyes had lost their laziness. They glinted now. "Since the day I caught you washing your hair at the well." One of his hands moved down her thigh, lifting her petticoat again as it descended. When he touched her knee, he slid his hand under the cloth and trailed light fingers up the inside of her bare thigh, stopping, swirling a pattern on tender skin, then moving higher. "Or, in fact," he continued, "from the first day I saw you, without your drawers or anything else to cover you." He bent his head to her neck. "In your bath." He placed his lips on her skin. "In the clearing."

She arched her head and back to enjoy his touch at her neck and at her thigh. She said, a little dreamily, "I thought it was only my shoes you preferred me not to wear."

The memory of that episode at the tree outside her bedroom window, when she had fallen on top of him, when he had had her stretched out beneath him, caused a line of fire to course through his body. He hung on to his control. His fingers under her petticoat were nearing their goal. He moved his lips from her shoulder, up her neck, to her face.

"I've had you dozens of times since then," he admitted, "in my thoughts. But never like this. Never like this." His lips sought hers.

She laughed—it was a low, delighted laugh—and shifted her lips and her hips away from him, still not ready to concede, for she knew his kiss and his touch would mean the end of her dominion over him. Now that her surrender was so near, she realized that she had not yet asked the most basic question, the one that needed to be asked before all others.

She brought her hands down from his shoulders, slid them inside his open shirt, parting it, allowing her body's skin to more fully cover his. She stopped her hands at the fastening to his trousers. She shifted back so that her lips and her thighs were open to him.

She said, against his lips, nibbling them as she spoke, "You told me once that you were from the south. Exactly where in the south are you from?"

He smiled and said, "Savannah." Then he tasted her with his tongue and finger. She was warm and delicious.

"I should have known," she said, trembling and laughing and lustful.

"You should have," he agreed. He was through with her teasing now, and he began to force the pace. He eased her down to the ground, working off her petticoat and his shirt and trousers and explored her at will.

She stretched out luxuriously, as she had so many times alone on this grassy spot. This time she was happy to be no longer alone, happy to be with him, happy to be alive and in his arms, kissing him, touching him, inspiring him. They nestled together, down on the damp, salty ground. An errant thought crossed her mind. She uttered it between kisses. "Mamie will be pleased to know where you're from."

He kissed her, caressed her, cherished her, and finally brought her beneath him. "I doubt she'll be surprised."

"Maybe not," she said idly, loving this talking and touching, sinking into her desire for him, sinking into the moss jelly, but this time with no fear or guilt. "Do you think the zombies are here?"

"Their magic falls far short of this," he said thickly.

He was right. There was nothing ghostly or ethereal about the way she was wanting him, or about the thick, moist cloud of heat and desire that muffled them and bound them together.

She remembered that strange night of zombie mischief. "You were cruel to me."

"I wanted you."

"You insulted me."

"You teased me."

"You deceived me."

"You misread me."

He knew what he was doing to make her ready for him. He was at once slow and sensual, impatient and hot. She had never before experienced what she was on the verge of experiencing, but she sensed that it would transform their relationship and her life. "Are all those mistakes and insults behind us?" she whispered.

He had her—at the exact place, at the exact moment—where he wanted her, where he had wanted her for days now. Nevertheless, he paused in his kissing and touching. He propped on an elbow. "Not all of them," he said, laughter and desire lighting his irresistible eyes. "I still expect that you're a savage American." He lay down again and touched her, with pressure and love and urgency.

She smiled and gasped. "You hope!" she breathed.

"Oh, I do," he assured her.

That was the last he allowed her to speak. He took her then, fully, giving her all the promise and passion that was his to give. He kissed her, everywhere, traveling deep into a garden, surprised and enchanted by that lovely experience, which was a doubling and a deepening of the first time he had kissed her on the street in the city. This time, however, the experience was far more satisfactory. He was already in a wild garden, her garden, holding her, surrounded by her, mounted on her tiny sward of land. From there he passed into the garden of his youth, through the thick hanging fringes of Spanish moss, to arrive at the center, a lush orchard, where he could feast, forever, on ripe peaches.

It was a blending of her to him, of wild Maryland country to cultivated Georgia garden, of marshes where land and sea, fresh water and salt, wet and dry, met and mingled. It was a blending where the tidal ebbs and floods continuously reorchestrated the seams between their bodies, negotiated the spaces, created new ones, filled others. During those infinite moments their shapes altered and adapted with the coursing of their desire, and their blending was thorough. Like the crisscrossing of channel creeks and coves, this love was produced by a rich flowing of stroking, kissing, sighing, gasping, spending, loving, being.

He had had one goal in mind since being with her in Washington, since experiencing the burning of the Capitol through her eyes. One goal. It had driven him. It had kept him alive when he was being pursued by the red-coated men who had suddenly realized he was not one of them. It had maintained his focus when he had had to dodge a conquering army on the alert for a traitor. It had smoothed his tongue enough that he could talk himself past a series of guards. It had kept him running through the thunderstorm to safety. It had helped him find a horse, row across the Patapsco, and spend a night in the forest of the Shaw Plantation.

When he had accomplished that goal—when he had fulfilled his desire and need for her—he had thought he would be at rest with her. He found that he was not. He had finished completing himself with her, comforting himself, comforting her, and he was holding her, but he was not through with her.

He raised his head and framed hers with his hands. He looked into her eyes, eyes that were still shining, though dreamier and more satisfied now, and he felt happy and weak. He bent his head into her fragrant neck and drank in her taste and smell. He looked up again and settled his elbows into the moist ground on either side of her. He saw a family of canvasbacks waddle out of the water, to shake and shiver the water off their red-and-brown bodies. He saw them walk, unconcerned, over the spit of land. He saw them disappear beyond the growth obscuring the marsh beyond.

The sight of these web-footed amphibians, beautiful and slick, replaced his weakness with strength and renewed his desire for the woman in his arms. Perhaps it was the way these marsh-nurtured creatures moved so easily between wet and dry that inspired him. Perhaps it was the way they represented the happy defiance of the usual demarcations between land and sea, male and female, love and need, comfort and desire, that he himself had just experienced.

Or perhaps it was because his woman moved just then, rearranged her limbs to meet his at just the right junctures. Perhaps it was because she made her continuing desire for him readable in her eyes.

He looked down at his hands, his fingers spread and framing her face, and contemplated the tiny webs between his fingers at his knuckles. His separate, articulated fingers were no good for swimming efficiently, but they were good for touching and sensing. He moved his hands down her arms so that his fingers intertwined with hers, their tiny webs interlocked. The gesture was, at once, sweet and sensual.

He moved with a purpose and saw her eyes widen with surprise.

"James!" she chided gently.

"Jane!" he mocked lovingly.

"No, I mean it," she said.

"So do I."

He freed his fingers, then smoothed the tangles of hair away from her face. He kissed her. "You asked for it."

"I did not."

"How little you know yourself," he commented. "And how glad I am that you do not."

She attempted to shift away from him. "I'm tired."

He drew her more fully to him. "Not nearly as tired as you will be."

Chapter Eighteen

Awakening from a drowsy doze, Jane's eyes fluttered open to perceive a world suddenly luminous, as if it had taken on the lustrous pearl of tortoiseshell or was being seen through the filter of stained glass.

She nestled into James and smiled. James. Loving, patient, passionate James. From Savannah. She should have known.

But she could not have known. She shifted to look at his face. His eyes were open, and she saw that his gaze had sailed high into the limitless blue sky. At her movement, he brought his eyes down and reeled in his thoughts. His eyes focused on her. Then they narrowed, meaningfully.

The sight of his eyes stained with satisfaction and desire nearly melted her. She shook her head clear of the temptation to make love again, for she had many questions to ask. She came straight to the first one. "Why didn't you simply *tell* me?"

He did not pretend to misunderstand. "What, and spoil all the fun?"

"No, I'm serious," she said. "You deceived me."

He rolled over on his side, so that he could look at her directly. With his arm bent on the ground at his elbow, he propped his head in his hand. Jane moved likewise. "It's hard to say which one of us deceived the other first," he said.

"I'm not so sure," she countered. "That one morning when I was returning to my room and you caught me on the trail..."

"You mean, the second time I saw you?" he interpolated. "The next morning, after the bath?"

"Yes, that's the time," she answered. "Well, you could have just said, simply, 'I'm American. I'm spying on the British. Is that what you're doing, too? Let's work together.'"

He shook his head. "Too risky, from my point of view. Don't you see?"

"Only partially," she conceded.

"In addition to which, you convinced me that you were actively engaged in *other* activities."

"Yes, but if you had wished to give me the benefit of the doubt, you could have guessed that I had to make up a story about those other activities because I thought you were British."

He laughed, once, in acknowledgment of the fact that he had *not* wished to give her the benefit of the doubt. "How was I supposed to know where your sympathies lay?"

Jane smiled pleasantly. "You seem to be a pretty clever fellow. One conversation with me should have been sufficient to figure out how I felt about redcoats."

"True," he acknowledged, "but that would still not tell me what you were doing, running barefoot through the fields before dawn every morning."

"No? It seems pretty obvious to *me* what a redcoat-hating woman would be doing, running barefoot through the fields before dawn every morning!"

"Ah! But that's precisely the point of contention. It did not seem similarly obvious to me, you see!"

"And why not?" she demanded. "Here you were an *American* all this time, for heaven's sake! Knowing your own motives, you should have guessed mine."

"You forget that the first time I saw you, you were naked."

She blinked. "What does that have to do with it?"

He looked at her, as if surprised by the question. "Why, everything."

She blushed at the look he gave her. "Men!" It was an invective. "Is that all you ever think about?"

He considered the question. "Mostly," he admitted. "That is, when we're not thinking about eating." He reflected. "No, even then, too."

She frowned at him disapprovingly. "So you were incapable of thinking of me as doing something useful—or even, say, brave—because you could only think of me as...as..."

"Fair game?" he suggested helpfully.

Her pretty mouth fell open. "*Fair game!*" she echoed, indignant.

His eyes swept down the lines of her beautiful, relaxed nakedness, then returned to her face. His smile was rakish. "My dear Jane, you are very fair, and *very* game!"

"It's an insult, an *insult!*" she said. "Especially when you consider what I really *was* doing all those mornings!" She was torn between anger and amusement. Amusement won. So did pleasure, for she felt protected and contented and well loved under his gaze. A thought occurred to her. Her eyes narrowed in triumph. "Now is the time to make good on your boast."

His hand reached out to fondle the places his eyes had just touched. "Which one?"

She moved luxuriously with his hand on her skin, and the feeling was as warm as the touch of the buttery early-morning sun. "How many have you made?"

"Never bothered to count."

She waved this secondary boast away. "I am referring to the one that you never have difficulty admitting when you are wrong."

"Ah, that one."

"Yes, *that* one, and now you can admit it."

"Admit what?"

"That you were wrong. About me."

He shook his head.

She flicked his hand away from her.

"I won't," he said, still shaking his head, unrepentant.

"You can't admit it?"

"No, I *won't* admit it, because I wasn't wrong," he stated. His eyes were very green when he added, wickedly, "The story you told about your lover was most convincing—and, I am nearly happy to say, true!"

He knew many things about her, of course, including the fact that she had not been a virgin. He did not give a damn that she lacked traditional feminine virtue. In fact, he had come to appreciate her honesty on the subject, as well as her honest acknowledgment of her own desires—an appreciation he felt keenly in the present situation. So, when he saw her eyes shadow at his comment, he did not imagine that she was playing coy. Rather, he realized that he had inadvertantly teased a sore spot.

"Jane, I'm sorry," he said. He reached out to touch her again. This time the gesture was meant to be not arousing but comforting.

She smiled at his understanding. She shrugged a little and gave her head a tiny shake. He pulled her into his arms, so that she settled across his chest, her legs laced lovingly around his. She was strongly aware that her feelings for Bobby Harlan had fallen far short of the intensity she was feeling now, in James Stewart's arms.

She said, after a moment, "He's dead."

He nodded. "I might have guessed as much. I remember your slip the night of the rain and the zombies, when you mentioned that he 'had known' you most of your life."

"He was from the farm beyond Mrs. Johnson's."

"I see." He stroked her nape and back, kneading her muscles. "What happened to him?"

"He died in the first engagement of the war. In Detroit. Isn't that absurd?"

He breathed deeply. He began to feel the sadness of this waste of a war, a sadness he had been holding off for almost two years. He said, softly, "Damn."

"It's a grief I no longer feel actively," she said. "But I remember it."

Her voice held enough of the remembered anguish of loss for him to ask, "Were you going to marry him?"

"Yes," she said.

"I admit to mixed feelings about his death, then. But," he said, moving on, "why was it you were not already married to him before he left?" He lifted her chin off his chest and asked, "How old are you?"

"Twenty-two," she replied. "How old are you?"

"Thirty," he said. "So why weren't you married? Two years ago, before he died, you were already of a highly marriageable age."

"My father didn't like Bobby," she said.

"Bobby, was it?"

"Bobby Harlan," she said, not finding it at all odd to be speaking of her dead love in another man's warm arms.

"An objectionable lad? Too cocky? Too sure of himself?"

Jane shook her head. "No, that's you. Let's just say that my father liked Bobby well enough as a person, but not as a potential son-in-law. His farm was indebted. He was poor." She sighed. "He was, as they say, beneath me, and Father forbade the marriage."

Stewart's eyes drifted lazily back up into the limitless blue sky. He said, merely, "The oldest of old stories." Then his eyes dropped and came to focused points on Jane's face. "But I can't believe that you submitted, as it were, to your father's opinions." He added softly, a little slyly, "Not my impulsive, headstrong Jane."

She smiled, mischievously. "Well . . . you're right," she said. "I would not have held him off as long as I did if I had been truly *determined* to marry him. But it was a hard decision, whether or not to run off and marry him, and I had not yet quite made up my mind when he decided to join the army. Actually, he joined because of me."

He grunted. "Yet another old story. He wanted to become something of a hero, I suppose? Restore the family name and honor?"

Jane sighed. "So he thought. And he was probably right in thinking that if he were to return a hero, his credit in the region would be restored, and he could once again work to make a profit off his land." She pulled a face. "It seems a wild folly now, of course! But, two years ago... Anyway, on his last night before enlisting, he had me promise him that I would marry him when he returned. Although I *still* didn't know my own heart, he insisted...and I thought...that is, one thing led to another, and we decided..."

She did not continue.

After a pause, he said, "So that's how it was."

"That's how it was."

He thought, in spite of himself, *She's generous*. To a maybe-love on the eve of his uncertain future. Generous Jane. Should he admire her for her generosity? Or fault her for her recklessness? He knew that some men would deem her ineligible for marriage, hold her experience against her—no matter what the circumstances under which she had given away her virginity. Some men, anyway.

She knew it, too. She felt a cold shadow cross her happiness as she regarded the play of thoughts on her love's face. She wished to recoup some of the ground she thought she had just, indefinably, uncomfortably, lost. She tried for a playful note. "So now that you know absolutely all, admit it! Admit that you were wrong about me!"

He smiled affectionately, dispelling the shadow across her heart, and took her face in his hands. "You are brave and resourceful, and you take the most ungodly risks," he said. "Sure, I know now what you were doing all those mornings. You were at the source of a chain of communication which passed along information from British headquarters at North Point to the American leaders in Washington."

She smiled. "How did you figure that out?"

His superior smile matched hers. "Because, as you have pointed out, I'm a pretty clever fellow."

"Clever," she murmured, "but not quick."

A brow raised. "Are you complaining?"

She did not respond to his warm look, but kept to the topic at hand. "And just how long did it take you to figure out?"

"I became sure of it within an hour of having seen you in the capital," he replied. "That is, within an hour of having been kissed as I'd never been kissed before."

She smiled at the pretty compliment and kissed him lightly on the lips. However, since she was not ready to lose herself again in his ready desire, she drew back and resisted his attempt to prolong the kiss and make it go deeper. "The knowledge came to you in a vision, perhaps?"

"No, in Brigadier General Stansbury's tent at the Navy Yard," he answered. "The information he already had on the British operation was precise, and could only have come from someone who had heard the British develop their plans." The desire he felt for her was mixed with admiration when he said, simply, "The information could only have been you, and my best guess is that Mrs. Johnson is involved, as well."

Jane nodded. "Along with everyone else between here and Washington."

He commented, with an edge in his voice, "The only regret being that our leaders did not know what to do with the fine information their resourceful citizens culled for them."

Happy with his smile and touch and admiration and obvious desire for her, Jane did not notice that he had not quite disavowed his assessment of her as "fair game," or admitted that he was wrong in his initial opinion of her. Instead, her thoughts followed the turn in conversation he had introduced and snagged on the ineffectiveness of all those nights listening through the floorboards and all those mornings running through the mists.

Shaking her head sadly, she looked away from his face. Her eye fell on the ugly gash on his upper arm, which he had received the night of the burning of Washington. She saw that it was healing imperfectly. She placed a light finger in the center of the crusting blood and skin. He winced. She moved her finger to the skin around the wound. She traced around the jagged outline, smoothing the skin as she went, and soothing it.

"Which brings us, I suppose," she said, looking up and at him levelly, "to your role in these affairs."

"My role?"

"We were doubly ineffective, you and I," she said. "You must have been sent here to spy, too, I imagine. How did you manage to become part of the Forty-fourth? Did you go to England to enlist?"

He shook his head. "No, I had a forged letter from Admiral Cochrane, which I presented to Ross on this side of the Atlantic. At Benedict, in fact. It was amazingly simple. As good luck would have it, other transfers were being made there between Cochrane and Ross, and I became merely one of a list."

Jane glanced back to her finger, which was still tracing the wound on his arm. She was trying to piece together what she knew about him. There was a tiny crease between her brows when she said, "I thought you might be some kind of trader."

He laughed and said, offhandedly, "My father's a merchant."

"Are you in the army, then? A soldier?"

"Army Corps of Engineers," he said.

Her frown disappeared, and she said the first thing that came to her mind. Her eyes gleamed fondly. "You never outgrew your love of playing in the dirt."

He nodded, an answering gleam in his eyes. "That's right."

"But how does one get to be in the Corps of Engineers? I mean, you can't exactly enlist, can you?"

"No. I trained at West Point."

She searched her memory. "That's in New York, is it not?"

He nodded again.

"But why you, an engineer, infiltrating the Forty-fourth?"

He shrugged minimally. His answer was truthful, but incomplete. "Because the accent in Savannah is nearly indistinguishable from the general run of southern British accents—you know, Georgia being a former royal province and all—and there were so few other southerners at West Point."

"Did it work, then, your infiltration? Did you get the information you wanted?"

His smile was wry. "It was almost as good as yours."

Her answering smile was tinged with sadness. "But what happened? Why was our information, finally, so ineffective?"

He laid his head back, and his gaze traveled high into the sky again. He caressed her shoulders, absently. "God, Jane, I don't know. Stupidity, mostly, I suppose, in the highest places. Plain, brutal stupidity."

They fell silent, absorbing the awful weight and truth of his statement. After a moment, he took her hand in his. He spread her fingers and nodded to the tiny webs at the knuckles. "Spandrels," he said.

She looked down at her fingers, then up at him. "Hmm?"

He touched the spaces between her fingers with his fingertips. He explained, "Those are called spandrels, the triangular curves that result from joining two walls to make an arch. It's an engineering term." He shrugged. "An architectural term, really."

She smiled. "What do you like to build? Dams?"

His eyes drifted back up at the sky. Just now, after they had made love the second time, he had mentally built a structure, as he often did in his idle time. He had laid its foundation, put the frame up three stories high, then encircled it with a wide porch. He had built a house. Interesting. This was the first time he had built a house.

"Bridges, mostly," he replied. "Long, graceful, sturdy bridges." He thought of the first bridge he had ever built. It was of wood and arched perfectly, like a miniature rainbow, over a meandering crick, deep in a lush Savannah garden.

"How many have you built?"

He laughed a little. "Never counted. A dozen, maybe. The first was when I was nine."

"That's sort of like me and my experimental herb garden. Ever since I can remember, I wanted to make strange-smelling and strange-tasting things grow." She toyed with his fingers, which still caressed hers. "Well, you'll be able to rebuild a dozen more bridges in Washington alone. What will you do now that—"

He cut her off. "You ask too many questions," he chided gently.

He did not know the answer to whatever question she was going to ask. He did not know what he was going to do now that it seemed likely the United States would no longer remain independent. He did not know what he would do after the war, a West Point engineer who had spied, to no good effect, on the British. Some vague notion, at the back of his mind, assured him that his family could buy him out of any trouble—if he lived long enough. However, all that was too distant to contemplate, and at the moment, he did not even know what would happen on the morrow.

He knew only that he was alive now, today, and that he was happy to be alive, happy to be with Jane—*very* happy to be with Jane.

His hands moved down her back, then up her sides. He shifted his legs and hips so that she was on top of him. He pulled her forward so that he could kiss her. Her breasts felt warm and soft and sensual, pressed to him. Her legs felt like silk, interwined with his, and a fire spread through him.

She drew back when she felt the immediate response in him. She shook her head. "You really must be going. It's full day by now."

He squinted at the rising sun. "It can't be past seven o'clock."

"But it is," she insisted, trying not to feel the heat in her body as it pressed intimately to his, as he moved, slowly, to increase her heat.

"Seven-thirty, then," he said. He kissed her, at length. "I'll be gone in an hour."

She shook her head again and said against his lips, "Too long. Too risky."

"So you've become cautious?"

"Only for you."

"Make it half an hour, then."

She closed her eyes, her senses swimming with his touch and breath and taste and gentle movements. Still, she managed to shake her head. "Too long," she repeated. "Too risky."

With a firm grasp of her hips and a clear positioning of her legs around him, he said, low and rough and challenging and teasing, "I can be gone in two minutes."

She opened her eyes and saw the flare of laughter and desire deep in his. Then, a touch, a melting, a soft gasp, and a joining. "No need for *so* much efficiency," she breathed.

"No need at all," he agreed.

She gave herself to him then, generously. He accepted her generosity and gave himself to her, generously, slowly, easily. Whereas his answers to her questions this morning had been incomplete, his lovemaking was not. It was not that he had been consciously selective in his answers, hiding parts of himself from her, holding her off, not letting her near him. It was rather that, with the crumbling of their world around them, in a world with no clear future, he was responding to her and her alone, and to her courageous, impulsive, ever-present ability to live honestly in the moment.

He loved her, then, demandingly, thoroughly, in the heat of the summer morning, as if he were a man with no expectations. As if he were not the heir to the greatest fortune in Savannah and all of Georgia. As if he had not lived a life of luxury and privilege. As if he were not courted by the most well-born, eligible women to cross his path. As if he were not desired by the most beautiful ineligible women to cross his path. As if he had no name, no lineage, no fortune, no future, no responsibility. He gave himself to her, carrying nothing, expecting nothing, responding only to her generosity and to the sheer physicality he felt when he was with her.

And he had never before experienced the like, the being in himself, the being in his body, the being inside her body. It was solid and weightless and wonderful, all at once—and it was over far too quickly.

When they were spent and content, she opened her eyes a crack and quipped, "Two minutes, braggart? One, at most."

"But such a minute!" he said, unabashed. Then, lightly: "What you do to me!"

She whispered, seductively, in his ear, "And what I am going to do to you now is send you away. It's late."

They disentangled themselves reluctantly and dressed silently. Words were unnecessary, for they were both of them still bathing in the warmth of affection and comfort and satisfaction.

Before she had finished buttoning her blouse, he took her in his arms and smoothed the curls back from her brow. He stroked her hair gently.

She breathed in deeply. "And so?" she asked.

He closed his eyes and leaned his chin against her forehead. He inhaled the beautiful scent of her hair. He caressed a breast that was still open to his touch. He moaned, part in satisfaction with what he had just had, part in frustration that he could not have it again any time soon.

He shook his head. "I don't know." He straightened and held her away from him so he could look at her. "I've got to get back to the capital—or what's left of it—and Stansbury."

"Tell him that Baltimore is next on the British list. They plan to strike in about two weeks."

He nodded, gravely, but a gleam of appreciation lit and lightened the depths of his eyes. "Any other messages to relay?"

She smiled. "Yes. On your way out, stop by the Skinner farm and tell Ben Skinner to get someone to meet me tomorrow morning at the assigned place."

"You're continuing your morning adventures, then?"

"I don't have a choice," she said. "So long as the redcoats are under my roof, and there's even the smallest possibility I can help to defeat them, I'll do it."

He regarded her then, saying nothing, though many conflicting thoughts churned in his mind. As he looked at this beautiful, spirited, sensual woman, he was dimly aware that some structure inside him was crumbling. It was an old, useless structure that had dictated his ideas of what women were and how they should behave. However, his experiences with the woman who was Jane Shaw were too fresh and immediate to have yielded a clear new vision of womanhood, unclouded by breeding and prejudice.

He was sure of only one thing. "When and where can we meet again?"

She said, on a note of alarm, "Don't risk coming back here. Please!" She continued, anxiously, "And I don't even know that we have time now to figure... to figure *us* out." She bit her lips and said, almost at random, "You can send me news of your whereabouts through Ben Skinner, I suppose, since I can't think of anything better at the moment!"

"You'll meet me somewhere if I can get you the message?"

"I'll try," she agreed, "if it will be no risk to you."

"Or yourself."

She shrugged off his concern. She gently pushed him away. "Go, now, do! You've tarried far too long."

He glanced up at the sun, which was climbing higher in the sky, and nodded. He kissed her, once, and caressed her, memorizing with his hands her rich and generous curves. Then he left by the way he had come. Before slipping through the bush, he glanced back and fixed his image of her.

She stood watching his departure. Her clothing was askew, and her blouse unbuttoned, revealing the firm swelling of warm, peach-smooth skin. Her back was straight and proud, and she seemed unmindful of her undress, or, rather, comfortable with it. Her hair was tangled from their lovemaking, her lips were swollen from his kisses, her cheeks were flushed with the satisfaction of his body in hers. Her eyes, brown and lustrous, remained on him avidly, filled with concern, with love, silently bidding him Godspeed.

He had said, lightly, too lightly, *What you do to me!* as if he deserved the love and physical satisfaction she had so generously given him. As he disappeared, thinking only of arranging the occasion for her to do it to him again, he could not have guessed the full extent of what she would do to him. He could not have foreseen the consequences that the effect of Miss Jane Shaw, poor plantation owner's daughter and fair game, would have on his life of aristocratic education, monied security and male privilege.

Chapter Nineteen

General Robert Ross swung onto his black stallion and called peremptorily to the three men who were to accompany him off the Shaw Plantation. He did not like waiting, ever, and particularly not now. The three men fell quickly into line behind him. The general nodded, turned his horse, and began to trot off down the main drive.

The early evening was mild and pleasant. Ross looked up at a sky less hazy than usual and streaked with soft pinks and lavenders. In the past weeks, he had ignored the discomforts of the savage American summer in the Maryland low country. Even so, he felt a twinge of relief that the heat and humidity of August had broken and had not survived into this first week in September. The relief he felt was not for himself, but for his men and the effect of the weather on them. In the relative cool, they would have more starch in them for the next operation, and they would perform even more efficiently than they had in their magnificent performance at Bladensburg.

It was an inspiring thought.

He decided to storm Baltimore, that bustling seaport brimming with wares, within the next week.

He and his men trotted leisurely down the now-familiar Long Log Lane, past the Skinner Farm. The Forty-fourth was in firm possession of this entire tract of land, and although they feared no ambush, they still made no errors of judgment, and they did not relax their guard. They came to a particular crossroads and took the turning to the left. They arrived at a dusty, dual-rutted trail and came to a stop.

General Ross turned to his men. "Richards," he said calmly, "I shall continue on alone. Make yourselves invisible."

"Yes, sir," Richards said promptly, looking about for cover for three men and their horses. "Shall we each of us take a lookout point?"

"Of course."

"One for the drive, one for the front of the house, and one for the back of the house, sir?"

"My thoughts exactly."

General Ross did not deign to give his lieutenant further instructions. This was an amorous operation, not a military one, although the only distinction between the two in his mind concerned the different amount of cavalry and artillery he thought necessary for the success and safety of each.

As he walked his horse along the trail to the Johnson Farm, his thoughts touched briefly on the mystery of James Stewart. If there was a tiny blot on his satisfaction of the last days, it was his puzzlement over Stewart's defection and his inability to put his hands on the slow, efficient soldier with the sharp look in his eye. Although Ross hardly thought this soldier's whereabouts ultimately pertinent to the achievement of his goals, he might have counted his liking for the infantryman a mistake—that is, if General Robert Ross had ever made a mistake.

So far in his American campaign, he had not, nor had he any reason to think otherwise. He was recently victorious and very nearly triumphant, and he wore his recent victory, and his near triumph, as naturally and as easily as he wore his scarlet coat. At the end of the trail, he swung down from his horse and tethered it, arrogantly, in full view of Mrs. Johnson's front door. He strode across her front porch, his fine British boots announcing his arrival, and knocked at the door.

When he received no answer, he kicked the door in. It ceded easily and swung, crazily for a moment, on ancient hinges. He entered Mrs. Johnson's sitting room and felt that the house was empty of her. He looked around at its spare furnishings, its lack of real comforts, it orderliness, its cleanliness. He had a tiny, appetizing sense of seeing what he was not supposed to see, of visually violating Mrs. Johnson's personal space.

He stood a moment longer, to fill the room with his presence, to make it his. He saw three stringed instruments hanging on one wall, the room's only decoration. He felt a primitive urge to carve a Union Jack over the mantel of the large stone hearth. He dismissed the urge as more typical of one of his infantrymen. In its place surged the desire, equally primitive, to brand her in a very different way.

Which was, of course, why he had come.

He crossed the sitting room and peered behind one of the two half-closed doors on either side of the fireplace opposite. Satisfied by what he found, he entered. It was her bedroom, as spare and clean as her sitting room, but with feminine touches here and there: a doily on an old, polished chest of drawers, and sheers at the two open windows, surmounted by lace valances, fringing a view that looked west and filtered the sunset into dappling pastel lights cast across a white candlewick bedspread. At the head of the bed were plumped two extra pillows, for comfort.

He crossed to a chair with its back to one of the windows and unbuckled the sword hanging at his thigh. He unsheathed it and laid it across the night table between the chair and the bed. Then he sat down to wait.

At that moment, Barbara Johnson was turning her buggy off the main road and onto the trail to her house. She, like every other citizen on the North Point—and, perhaps, more than most—was on the alert for redcoats. She saw nothing as she moved onto her own property. Soon enough, however, came into view a lone horse tethered to her front porch, and her heart began to beat a little faster.

By the time she had arrived at the house, she had calmed herself with long, slow breaths. She drew in the reins, set the brake, and climbed down from her porch in a leisurely, unruffled fashion. She eyed the black stallion critically as she passed by it, but did not hesitate, even when she saw the front door, which had been opened by violence. Her step was at all times light, but even so, she knew that the sound of her arrival could be heard throughout the tiny house. Her hand went automatically to the cameo brooch at her throat. Its touch gave her reassurance. She straightened her back and entered her sitting room.

Nothing was out of place. The violence had, apparently, begun and ended at the front door. Yet she felt him. His presence. His clean scent. Vivid memories of that night in Riverdale, with Washington ablaze in the background, leapt to her mind's eye. She pushed aside those feelings in order to face the present occasion. She dismissed, as well, the normal sense of vanity at the thought that he had sought her out upon his return to North Point.

She untied her bonnet, removed it and dangled it in one hand as she crossed to her bedroom, whose door was ajar. To gather her courage and her resolution, she dug back to older, deeper memories. She remembered tales told by her black mammy and her father. She recalled that her earliest childhood memories were of graves and cemeteries. In her mind's eye, she fashioned those cold headstones with names and dates that the little girl within her was incapable of reading, but whose significance did not escape her.

These memories made her bones feel solid and good, her blood thick and strong, her resolve unwavering. She came to her bedroom, pushed open the door with the flat of her hand, and stood in the doorway.

Her face betrayed nothing when her eyes fell on General Robert Ross, seated at his ease, one leg crossed elegantly over the other, his hands resting comfortably on the arms of the chair, his eyes level and focused on her, as if no other woman had ever existed in the world. His handsome face registered no emotion other than calm knowledge of the inevitability of what would happen in this room. The nuances of whether he was happy to see her, or merely lustful, were lost on her, for the evening sun was behind him. His face was bathed in shadows, and the sun created a warm nimbus of fire around his head and shoulders, silhouetted against the window.

His eyes seemed to pull her into the room. She took a step in. It was her room, after all. Her house. Her private property. He had not moved a muscle in his body or his face. He had not even blinked. His eyes lingered on her, a caress, an insult.

"That red coat offends my eyes," she said coolly.

He smiled then. He stood and shrugged out of the coat. "For you," he said, "Mrs. Johnson," as he laid the hateful red coat on the night table next to his sword. He shook out the lace at his wrists and sat down again. He resumed his relaxed pose, looking precise and formal, even without his coat. He regarded her, steadily, saying nothing. She looked very beautiful and wise to him, standing in the doorway, calm and collected, thick gold hair framing her classical face, and blue, blue eyes challenging him, hating him, exciting him. The next word he uttered was low and forceful: "Undress."

At the command, the bonnet fluttered to the floor. She did not look down at the cloth at her feet, the only evidence of her nervousness. She remained dignified and proud, breathing steadily, standing straight. He loved her dignity and her pride and felt his own rise within him to meet hers. He saw her eyes narrow as they remained on him. A slow smile spread across his face. He said again, pleasantly, "You are to undress for me, Mrs. Johnson."

His voice was devoid of menace, but she heard the threat nevertheless. She would do nothing so undignified and pointless as attempting to run away. She thought of the front door, which had been so easily forced and broken. Her hand went to her throat and touched the warm coral cameo. She slid her fingers behind the stone and felt the delicate catch. She imagined him rising from his chair, taking three strides across the room and breaking the catch with two fingers. She imagined the cameo falling from her throat and splintering on the floor.

She slid open the catch and withdrew the cameo from the high collar of her blouse. She walked to the bed on the side opposite him and put the cameo in its accustomed place, atop the doily on her chest of drawers. She stood next to the chest, not moving, not speaking, not removing her eyes from his face. His smile had frozen, and she saw something in the depths of his fine eyes that told her it would go better for her if he was not forced to rise and undress her himself.

With an authoritative gesture, he motioned for her to step to the end of the bed, so that she would be in front of him, only a few feet away from his chair. She hesitated a moment, then obeyed. She stepped into an elongated rectangle of light from the setting sun.

She decided not to let him get the better of her, even in this most disadvantageous of situations. She began to unbutton her blouse. At the same time, she began to speak. "I am alive," she stated, "because of you."

He watched her long, work-roughened fingers as they undid the tiny buttons on her white cotton blouse.

Her fingers paused. When he did not respond to her, she let her hands drop to her sides. The weight of the unbuttoned collar caused the blouse to sag provocatively at the swell of her breasts. "Did you hear what I said?" she asked.

Her tone was as commanding as his. She was a womanly woman, one who demanded attention and respect, even from him. He liked that. Very much. "Yes, I heard you," he said. "You are alive because I saved you in Washington?"

She shook her head. "I was not in any danger there," she said quietly, "until you showed up."

He nodded his head, politely, as if at a compliment.

"No," she said, beginning again to unbutton her blouse. "I am alive because you killed my five older brothers."

He looked puzzled.

"Before I was even born, of course," she continued. "Almost forty years ago, it was."

"You are speaking of the American rebellion, I take it."

"It was a revolution," she corrected, "and it worked."

"For a little less than forty years," he countered, as if the present war were already won for the British.

Her anger at him, at his violation of her personal space, at her vulnerability, flared out into rage. She attempted to master it. She saw, by the hateful smile on his lips, that he had seen the quick flush of anger in her face. She had finished the unbuttoning. She had no choice but to lift the ends of the blouse out of her skirt and to remove it. She felt hot with anger, and her gesture of taking off her blouse and dropping it on the end of the bed reflected her emotion.

She concentrated on the older anger and hatred that had knotted her heart for so long. She decided not to remove yet her chemise, which was thin and opaquely provocative. Instead, she bent to unlace first one half boot, then the other. By the time she had stepped out of her boots, she had regained a measure of her control. She knew what was going to happen, and since she could do nothing to prevent it, she thought her wisest course was to resist as little as possible, to give in to the ultimate violation, and to unman him as much as possible.

She placed a foot on the end of the bed, pushing her skirt over her knee so that he had a good view of her calf and part of her thigh. She began to unroll the stocking, and, as she did so, she resumed her story. She slanted him a glance and said, "Yes, you killed my five older brothers, one at Trenton during the first year of the war, one at Princeton the next, and three at Charleston during the third year." She dangled the stocking across two fingers.

He did not bother pointing out that he, personally, had been but a young man at the time, not even in the army.

She dropped the stocking, almost flirtatiously, on the floor. She brought her one leg down and placed the other foot on the end of the bed. "My parents were understandably distraught by the loss of all their sons, and tried to begin their family again. I was the child born of their grief and misery. My mother died in childbirth. My father was left with no sons and a baby girl." The other stocking was off. She dropped it on the floor. She held the pose a moment, her one leg raised and bent, with the foot on the end of the bed. She drew her skirts up, provocatively, almost but not quite to the apex of her thighs. Then she bent forward across her thigh, propped an elbow on her bent knee, and regarded him from under thick gold-tipped lashes.

"And that is why I owe you my existence," she said, "for if you had not come and killed my brothers, I would not have been born."

"For that, you hate me?" he asked, his eyes dilated with lust from her display and from anticipation.

"With a passion," she said, her voice throbbing with her hatred.

"It seems rather that you should thank me," he said.

She shook her head.

He gestured for her to continue. He pointed a finger at her skirts. When she did not immediately move at his command, he tensed the muscles of his arms and legs, making as if to rise from the chair.

She stood straight again and brought her foot down to the floor. She unhooked her skirts at the back, and they fell to crumple at her ankles. Her anger and hatred were welling up inside her. Her eyes strove with his. He won. She felt her resolve breaking. She felt like the little girl she had been, whose heart had never had a chance to grow and bloom. She felt like the mature woman she was as her own heat rose, with her disrobing, with her own needs, so long deferred. She lifted her petticoat and tugged at the white cotton drawers that covered her modesty. They came down around her knees, then her ankles. She looked down at her skirts and drawers. She looked up at him.

His eyes were blazing. His breathing was coming more rapidly now. He crooked his finger for her to step out of the pool of cloth. He wanted her closer to him, so that he could bathe in the warmth of her heat and hatred. He saw the gauzy outline of everything he wished through the thin cotton chemise and petticoat that still covered her. He wanted to see more, of course. When she stepped toward him, he wondered aloud, "Why do you tell me this?"

"To give you fair warning," she answered.

He smiled, indulgently. "We should not have had our success in the past weeks if more Americans had memories like yours, Mrs. Johnson." He was a superb strategist, never impatient. He would not attack too soon, but he would unnerve and demoralize when he could. "You are a young woman. Many of your fellow countrymen are older than you, and remember the war, firsthand. Why have they not done a better job of letting their hatred for us show?"

He did not want her to answer the question. Instead, he wished for her to remove her chemise. He nodded at it, meaningfully.

She felt betrayed, as he had expected her to, by her countrymen, who had not defended her, who had left her open to violation by British conquerors. In a defiant gesture, she untied the drawstring of her chemise and stood before him, breasts naked and proud. She felt the warmth of the pale evening sunlight streaming across her skin.

His eyes devoured her. He saw the subtle beauty of her age and imperfections, and was even more aroused by her resistance this evening than the night when Washington had burned. He was seeing the end of the battle, and was already savoring the victory. He could now demand capitulation.

"The petticoat," he said. It was a command.

She defied him. She shook her head.

Casually, still seated, he reached over to the night table and grasped his sword. He handled the grip expertly, quickly balancing the steel, then arced the blade across the two feet separating them so that its tip almost touched the waistband of her petticoat. It was an arrogant, insulting gesture. It asserted his domination and his superiority; it underscored her subjugation and her weakness.

The steel had flashed in the light, momentarily blinding her. She gasped in disbelief and renewed anger.

"The petticoat, Mrs. Johnson," he stated again.

She shook her head again and felt the wonderful, cleansing surge of her resolve return. He could possess her and soil her, but he could not rout her hatred of him. She turned her emotions deep inside her, and they fled magnetically, like chips of iron, to the metallic core of her heart.

His blade twitched and cut the drawstring of her petticoat, without marring her skin. His lust and arrogance had taken him one step too far. For this humiliation she would never forgive him. The petticoat fell in a *whoosh*.

He rose from his chair and came toward her, lowering his blade so that the tip stuck into the floorboards. His eyes and mouth hungered for her. He reached out with one hand and grasped the back of her neck. With the other hand, he dug his fingers into her hair, causing the pins to scatter and the heavy fall of old gold to unfurl around her shoulder and down her back.

"And now, Mrs. Johnson," he said, as he bent his lips to her ear, "you may undress me."

He pressed her nakedness to him. He placed his lips on the warm skin of her neck. He trailed his lips up her throat to her cheek. He looked into her fathomless blue eyes. Not believing himself capable of error, he allowed himself to sink into her gaze. He saw there her defiance and her capitulation. He saw that she would do as he said. He saw that she might even be persuaded, with strategic kisses and caresses, to enjoy him as he would enjoy her.

But he did not see that she would live to see him dead.

At the Shaw Plantation, Jane was experiencing a similar attempt at violation and humiliation at the hands of a British soldier, but the outcome was to be for her, fortunately, very different.

With General Ross and Lieutenant Richards otherwise occupied for the evening, Dick Lawler decided to approach the house, which had been forbidden him during the week of the return of the Forty-fourth to North Point.

Taking his chances that the Black Juno would not be around to spook him, and counting on Master Shaw's distraction in the front yard by some soldiers, Lawler had dared to invade Miss Shaw's kitchen garden. He considered himself a smart enough fellow, and so was pleased when he hid himself behind the stone well at the edge of the garden, where she was weeding in the cool of the evening. When she crossed to the well for a bucket of water, he came around the side and startled her.

He caught her off guard, but only for a second. In that second, he took her chin in his hand and pulled her close. "So, missy... Pining away that you haven't heard from Dick Lawler lately?"

Jane wrenched out of his grip and took a quick step away. She was repulsed by this large man, with his swarthy skin and his coarse stubble of a beard and his unwashed odor. She was not afraid of him, because she knew him for the cowardly bully that he was. Her scorn for him shone in her eyes.

He was stupid, but not that stupid. He knew how to recognize scorn, since he had received so much of it in his life. "So you think you're too good for me, little American?"

"You don't really want me to answer that, do you?" she replied, throwing caution to the wind.

He did not like scorn, and he did not like sarcasm. He reached out and grasped the top of her bodice so that his large, beefy hand touched her breasts. He felt her reaction, but he was too desperate to know that he had made her skin crawl. He knew only that he had affected her, and he felt a surge of anticipatory triumph. He could violate her in broad daylight, right now, if he wanted. No doubt he would be punished for his bad manners, but the punishment might be worth the satisfaction of proving his manliness to this little American who had so often eluded him.

A thought occurred to him. She had so often eluded him in the presence of James Stewart, now vanished from the Forty-fourth. Lawler's brain moved slowly. His eyes narrowed to black slits. "Did you think you were too good for the other one?"

Jane felt a reasonable fear. "What other one?" she asked flippantly, trying to hold him off.

"Stewart," he said, adding slyly. "The traitor."

She held his hot, horrid gaze, the depths of her eyes closed to him. She would not be so foolish to betray any emotion regarding James Stewart.

He made an obscene reference to her body and her behavior with James Stewart as he pulled her closer.

She felt faint from his foul odor. She denied involvement with James Stewart indirectly by saying, "I hate all redcoats," and her voice rang with the honest force of conviction.

"But I don't think he's a redcoat," Lawler pursued, "and I know he doesn't have what I have." When he pulled her hips to his to prove his statement, Jane realized, with a sickening lurch of her stomach, that he was ready to rape her, here and now.

That realization, and her fear, must have shown in her eyes. His eyes flamed. Just as she felt the first tug of his hand that would strip her of her blouse, just as she was about to shout for help, there was a distraction.

"Jane!" her father's voice boomed from inside the house. "Jane!"

Lawler's head jerked up. His attention was diverted just long enough for Jane to raise her knee, hard, into Lawler's most tender organ. She was promptly released, and Lawler crumpled where he stood, wounded and whining, as Jane dashed away.

"Yes, Father!" she called. "I'm in my garden!" She ran, panting, into the kitchen, which her father had just entered from the hallway.

He frowned when he saw the state she was in. "You've been working too hard outside, child!" he reprimanded her. "It's too hot for all the gardening. You'll stay inside tomorrow."

"Yes, Father," she said obediently, her heart recovering its normal pace. "Is that what you wanted to tell me?"

"Huh? Well, no, it isn't," he said, fishing around in his pocket. "It was that I had forgotten to give you this!" He handed over a plain envelope. "Ben Skinner brought it by a little earlier today, when he delivered the grain he had promised me. He said it was a list or something."

With a happy leap of her heart, she imagined that it was from James Stewart. Still, she managed to accept the envelope without regarding it with any particular interest. "Oh, yes," she said, offhand, "I wanted Mr. Skinner to give me an entire list of herbs he has so as to see if he has any I am missing, so that I can tell him whether he should let any go to seed in the next few weeks." She sighed and covered a tiny, artificial yawn. "You were right! It *is* too hot for gardening. I think I'll go upstairs to my room and rest for a bit."

Master Shaw thought that sounded reasonable, and he went back to his business.

With the letter in her hand, itching to be opened, she made haste slowly through the hall, up the stairs, and into her bedroom. Leaning her back against the door to close it, she turned the letter over eagerly and opened it.

She was surprised to see from the handwriting that the letter came not from James Stewart, but from Johnnie. She wondered what news could have been so important that Johnnie had not wished for her to wait until the next morning to hear it through the chain of communication that had been reestablished. As her eyes scanned the letter, she felt a more intense, more sickening feeling grip her stomach than the one she had just experienced in Dick Lawler's presence. But Johnnie's scrawl was jumbling in her brain, and she had to start over to grasp the full implications of his cheerful, breezy news:

Dearest Jane,
You'll never believe what I just learned about our savior that night in Washington, James Stewart. He is from *the* Stewart family in Savannah, owns half the city and most of the county, and is heir to the Savannah Trading Company fortune. He was educated at Eton College, Cambridge University, and West Point Military Academy...

Chapter Twenty

Jane accomplished more in the next few days than she normally did in a week. Her garden was beautifully weeded. The chicken coop was immaculate. The porch and the yard were swept with precision. The mending basket in the parlor was empty. All rips and rents had been repaired, all buttons replaced. The kitchen was clean enough to receive guests. The only reason Jane was not scolded by Mamie for being underfoot in the dark priestess's domain was that Jane worked too quickly, scouring pots and polishing working surfaces, to get in Mamie's way.

During these same days, she worked absolutely undisturbed by any of the men in the Forty-forth. If a soldier or an underofficer was unwise enough to wish her good-day, or to smile at her, or to wink at her, or to have a gleam in his eye that held the tiniest trace of warmth, he was frozen by one of her stares and sent away with his ears buzzing. Dick Lawler made the supreme mistake of approaching her, and he received a look so fierce from Miss Jane Shaw that he actually felt a sizzle of fear. He had some hazy notion that she might be possessed by the zombies, or by some other, unnameable spirit that was out to do him harm. He crept away from her, his tail between his legs.

Jane felt a puny satisfaction in slaying Lawler with a mere glance. She would have liked to wring Lawler's neck. With her bare hands. She would like to wring any redcoat's neck. With her bare hands. Come to think of it, she would have liked to wring any *American* soldier's neck. With her bare hands. That would have felt good but not nearly as good as having one man's neck in her hands. One man on his knees before her. At her mercy. One man. James Stewart.

Being honest and uncompromising in her self-assessment, she could not get around the fact that she had been *had*. She felt foolish. She felt shabby. She felt humiliated. When her thoughts touched on James Stewart—which they did not do more than two or three dozen times a day—she inevitably recalled two moments, not juxtaposed in time, but highly significant when considered together. First, she remembered when she had been naked, stretched out next to him, and he had labeled her "fair game." At the time, thinking him an ordinary military man endearingly from Savannah, she had been perversely pleased.

Foolish woman!

Second, she remembered what he had said to her on the street that day in Washington, when she had thought him an enemy redcoat and he had kissed her senseless. She had asked him the question "Are you who you say you are?" He had answered, "More or less," and he had added, "But nothing I could tell you now about myself would improve your opinion of my manners." She had agreed with the statement at the time, but had not understood the implications.

For she had not known then, of course, that he was an American. And she had not known, when she had given herself to him so thoroughly, so wantonly, so whorishly, the other morning, that he was a fine southern gentleman who would never treat a fine southern lady the way he had treated her. During the episode of that steamy kiss on the streets of Washington, he had been right. Nothing he could have told her about himself would have improved her opinion of his manners. Knowing who he was now, she could not interpret his frank desire for her as anything but disrespectful.

No gentleman of manners and breeding would have accosted a lady of his social class so openly and sensually. No gentleman of manners and breeding with honest intentions would have so intimately kissed a lady of his social class or so ardently seduced her. No gentleman of manners and breeding would have kept his manners and breeding hidden from the notice of a lady of his social class.

It would almost have been better if James Stewart *had* been a common redcoat. She could have dismissed what there was between them as the lust of a soldier far from home and the aberration of a young woman caught in the web of enemy occupation.

Instead, James Stewart was rich and educated and had been bred a fine southern gentleman. He had assessed the run-down condition of her plantation and deemed her "fair game."

He had wanted one thing from her, and he had gotten it.

And he had gotten it in her most private and wondrous place on the bay, a place she had never shared with anyone before.

She thought back to how she had felt after the night she had spent with Bobby Harlan. She had not felt the shame she was feeling now. Instead, she had felt nothing but regret for having resisted the poor boy for so long—and she had also determined to marry him upon his return. What had she felt when she heard the news of his death? She had grieved, of course, but she had still not regretted her last night with him. As for no longer being a virgin, she had known that some men might reject her out of hand as unmarriageable. However, she had never felt that any man who truly wanted to marry her would care.

For what she had had with Bobby Harlan had been sweet and true, and it remained so. She and Bobby had been equals. They had understood one another. They had known what they could expect from each other. They had played no games. She had given him love and affection and honesty, and he had given her constancy and good faith and respect.

What had James Stewart given her? Respect? Hardly. Good faith? Not a trace. Constancy? Oh, he'd be back.

She felt violated.

She felt besmirched.

She felt strong with righteous indignation.

Her energies whirled her through the chores in the house and garden and yard. They propelled her through her days.

They kept her awake, to listen through the floorboards every night for details of the British attack on Baltimore. They propelled her through the fields every morning before the dawn, they fuelled her return, they kept her going throughout the day. She funneled her feelings into her chores, so that she would be too tired to lie awake in bed at night, when anger and humiliation could sweep through her bones and curl around her innards.

Still, all this exhausting expenditure of energy did not quite buy her the emotional oblivion she craved. It was simply that she was filled to overflowing with so many strong, conflicting, unpleasant emotions that no amount of work could absorb them all, and a part of her desired to protect herself from the whole truth. She had only to relax her guard, at any moment during the day or night, for her ever-vigilant, honest, uncompromising self to rise up and remind her, *Yes, you've been had, but you wanted him, too!*

In those moments when she was being brutally honest and uncompromising with herself, she could admit to wanting him still, and she began to understand what it was to be a fallen woman. She had made love with a man of her own free will, and once she had known this passion outside of marriage, it was impossible to deny or to turn off.

Had James Stewart truly deceived her? Not exactly, for the terms of their relationship had been clear from the beginning, and she had been a willing participant in bringing those terms to their natural conclusion. And had James Stewart's intentions been dishonest? Well, here was the delicate point. A man with honest intentions was one like Bobby Harlan, who urged marriage and assumed fidelity. James Stewart had not uttered a word about marrying her, and so was not "honest" in one sense, but that did not mean that he had been dishonest, either. He had not promised her anything he was not going to give her.

He had made some comments on the subject of marriage and Bobby Harlan. It was difficult for Jane to remember his exact words, for she had been stretched out naked next to him, entwined with him, and her senses had been awash in a hazy, happy, sated pleasure. She had told him that her father had been against her marriage to Bobby Harlan because the young farmer was beneath her socially. And what had James Stewart, the wealthiest man in all of Georgia, replied? She could not rightly remember, but he had accepted without objection the explanation of social disparity as a legitimate bar to marriage. "An old story," he had said, or something to that effect. Of course, he would know all about *that* old story!

Jane burned with shame in recalling that particular exchange.

He had not let her ask very many questions about him that morning, either. She had thought at the time it was because there was nothing special about his background that she needed to know. She had a vivid image of him as he had stood before her on the tiny sward of land, when her heart had stopped, then flowered, at the mere sight of him. He had come to her that morning tired and unshaven, his clothes unkempt, but infinitely attractive. He had even been barefoot. She would never have guessed that he was the finest of fine southern gentlemen.

Or could she have guessed?

And if she *had* guessed, would she have behaved differently?

She knew the answer to that with an unshakable confidence. She was impulsive. She was a risk-taker. She was mightily attracted to James Stewart, to his sexy hazel eyes, the set of his shoulders, the way he walked. But she had pride. She had a sense of herself and her place in the world. She hated to be held cheap, even more than she hated admitting a mistake. She would never, *never* have given herself to him if she had guessed that she was not his equal in every respect.

Had she made a mistake? Yes, she had made a grave error in judgment, and how she *hated* to admit it!

It was a strange few days for Jane, when the whirlwind of her activity made everything hurtle toward an unknown future, while, at the same time, time seemed to have ground to a painful halt. Finally, by the time the first frenzied, interminable week in September had dragged fleetingly by, it was clear to everyone alive who was not an infant or an idiot that Baltimore was soon to be attacked. The precise dates and the particular points of attack still seemed important to Jane, although from the information she was receiving back through the chain of communication, the citizens of Baltimore did not feel similarly. Baltimore, a brawling, bellicose town during the past two years, had become anything but warlike in the past two weeks.

Jane understood, but she passionately refused to share in Baltimore's apathy.

One morning, in the dark, gauzy dawn, at the third water oak in the forest beyond the Shaw property, she was telling Michael Shiner that the citizens of Baltimore were wrong to have given up before the fight. To one of Michael Shiner's replies, Jane said, "Oh, I know that the shattered remnants of Stansbury's and Starrett's militia tumbling into Baltimore from Bladensburg are not the most... *inspiring* sight, but to predict defeat—!"

"Yes'm, Missy Shaw," Michael Shiner said. "There's talk in town that they'll surrender before the attack."

Jane sighed. "As the only way to save the town, I suppose."

"And the state," Michael Shiner added.

"Are *any* preparations being made?" she asked, plaintively. "Is any of my information proving helpful?"

"The regulars have not yet abandoned Fort McHenry," Michael Shiner told her.

"That means they're still guarding the entrance to Baltimore harbor, then," she said, although she was not particularly cheered by what should have counted as good news.

"With five eighteen-pound guns," Michael Shiner offered.

Jane fired back, "Five guns—I don't care *how* big!—against the whole of the British Navy?" She halted, midsentence, what could have easily become a tirade. She drew a deep breath. "I hardly need repeat to you the number of enemy forces now massing just a few miles down the bay. The prize-conscious British want Baltimore. They know it has more to offer them in the way of booty, really, than the capital." Her spirits sank, then rose when a thought occurred to her. "But what about that crew of men you worked with in Washington? You said they were a good group. Could you muster them again?"

"They scattered, missy," he said, "after we was sent away from the trenches."

"Well, at least you were sent away from Washington and not into it," Jane said, "as I had feared."

"Yes'm, and I'm sorry you and Massa Johnnie risked what you did to find me," Michael Shiner said. His tone was even and direct and had to serve as the thanks of a man who did not know the way of it.

Jane was about to smile and say, "No harm done," but her smile went awry, and she said instead, "So am I." They had been over the subject of the Washington disaster before, she and Michael Shiner. She did not want to belabor it, for it only underscored her bad judgment and the impulses that had led her, in more ways than one, into the arms of James Stewart. To turn the subject, she looked out through the forest into the lightening day. She nodded over her shoulder in the general direction of the plantation. "It's getting late. I'd best be going. We've done our business. Until tomorrow, Michael."

Michael Shiner nodded. "Until tomorrow, then, Missy Shaw." He turned away to go, to head deeper into the forest. He vanished into the ghostly darkness, his tread noiseless.

She moved in the opposite direction, toward the field and daylight. She was at the fringe of the dawning shadows of the forest when she stopped short.

A branch broke underfoot ahead of her, and a shadowy male figure materialized before her. Her heart sank, and she felt a calm born of the knowledge that it had been inevitable that she would finally be caught.

Then she saw who it was.

"Miss Shaw," he said, slowly, lovingly, taking another step toward her.

She moved in a circle around him so that she could see him better in the barely perceptible daylight. She faced him. "Mr. Stewart," she said, coolly, politely.

They had moved so that their faces were in profile to the dawning day. Half his face was visible, the other half obscured by the forest shadows. Thus were the clean features of his face—the straight nose, the well-shaped mouth, the lean jaw—set in high relief. He was freshly shaven, too, and his hair was neat and tied back at the nape. His trousers and shirt looked as if he had spent the night in the woods in them, and he was barefoot. She had never seen him look more appealing.

He made as if to move toward her. At her minimal, unwelcoming reaction, he remained where he was. "What's wrong, Jane?" His tone was wary, his expression concerned.

"What are you doing here?" she asked.

"I came to see you, of course," he said. "I waited the past several mornings for you at your spot on the bay."

She nearly winced at the reference.

"But you didn't come."

"No," she said. She did not know whether she would ever be able to return there again.

"Why not?" When she did not answer, he continued, "I realized yesterday morning that you wouldn't be going back there—for whatever reason—so I decided to follow you to your morning meeting." His mouth sketched a slight smile. "I should have done this a long time ago."

She opened her mouth to reply, then closed it. There was no easy response to make to his comment. If he had followed her a long time ago, he would have known that she was not coming to meet a lover. They would have been working together, instead of at odds with one another. Either they would have become lovers sooner, or they might not have become lovers at all.

"What would that have changed, in your opinion?" she asked.

His eyes had narrowed. "It might have altered," he said, "the way you feel this morning, perhaps." He took a cautious step toward her.

Jane knew she had only to smile at him and to say, "No, I'm fine, really. It was the surprise at seeing you that has caused me to react like this." She knew she could take the next step toward him, put her arms around him and kiss him—as he might have expected she would do—and things would be as they had been when he last left her, when she had been a happy, satisfied woman. He would kiss her in return and satisfy her again, right here on the forest floor. She would revel in the hot currents that flowed between them. She could blend with him and blend with the moist earth.

It was a temptation. To kiss him, to caress him, to feel him within her again, would not change anything. He had not deceived her; she had deceived herself. Everything about him should have told her that he was a man of confidence and fortune, the way he held himself, the way he spoke, the way he treated the British officers and her father and Mamie, the way he always got what he wanted, the way he had made love to her, with no apologies and no cheap talk. He had risked much to seek her out this morning. Why should she deny herself the pleasure of his touch, of his taste, of his eyes on her? Something in the way he was looking at her now, something in the way he always looked at her, gave her great pleasure in her body.

Until this moment, she had been hot and tired and feeling generally unlovely. Now, however, she had the impulse to drag her kerchief off her head and let her hair tumble free. She wished to unbutton her blouse for him and to step out of her skirts for him. She had the wanton, unashamed desire to stand naked before him, so that he could see her where she wished to be seen, so that he could touch her where she wished to be touched. She did not understand the intensity of these powerful desires. Neither did she try to deny them.

Nor could she have explained why it was this man who made her feel this way. Why this man with the hazel-green eyes, the blond-brown hair and the compact, muscular build? Why this man who had teased her and flirted with her and insulted her? Why this man who was heir to the richest fortune in all of Georgia? Why this man who had only to look at her to make her melt?

Certain sensitive nerves whispered seductively, *He already knows you for what you are. One more time won't change anything!*

He had completed his step toward her, and his statement demanded a response. However, she did not smile, nor did she say "I'm fine, really. You just surprised me, is all." She did not step toward him, as he had stepped toward her, or put her arms around him.

Instead, her honest, uncompromising self rose up inside her and took control. She said, "The way I feel this morning has to do with a message I received."

Stewart was puzzled by the strong barrier she had thrown up between them. He would never have attributed to her such banal evasions as feminine pique or sarcasm, but he thought it worth a try to discover whether she was angry that he had not sent her a message this week, as he had promised.

"If you're interested to know why I was unable to contact you, I can explain that I was—" he began, but she cut him off.

"No, not a message I did *not* receive," she said, shaking her head, "but one I *did* receive. From my brother."

Stewart's puzzlement was hardly dispelled, but at least he knew he had been right that neither feminine pique nor sarcasm was driving her. He slanted her a glance. "And the message?"

At that moment, he perceived a large, shadowy figure looming up behind Jane. He started forward, to protect her, but the large figure moved around in front of her and stopped.

Jane gasped. The two men looked at each other first in the antagonism of natural adversaries, then in recognition and surprise. Stewart spoke first. "Michael Shiner," he said. His voice was cool and composed.

"It's all right, Michael," Jane said quickly, mechanically registering the fact that Stewart knew his name.

"I heard a man's voice and so came around back behind you, to make sure you were all right, ma'am," Michael Shiner said to her, without taking his eyes off James Stewart. "You were scared just now, Missy Shaw."

"You surprised me, Michael, because I didn't hear you come up behind me," Jane said. She repeated, "It's all right. I know the man. He means me no harm. He's not a redcoat."

"That's right," Stewart said. "You know me."

Michael Shiner's face was characteristically shuttered. He blinked his eyes once. He said slowly, "Yassir, I know you."

Stewart looked up at the black, implacable face and knew enough to admire the man for coming to Jane Shaw's defense. He knew enough to fear him, too, both his power and his restraint. This was no Dick Lawler standing large in front of him, hardly distinguishable from the shadows. Michael Shiner meant business.

Stewart could not have guessed from Michael Shiner's still face and motionless body the conflict within him. From experience, however, he knew a piece of a freed Negro's problems. That same experience counseled him to keep his voice composed. "I'm glad you remember me."

"He's been working with me, almost from the beginning," Jane said, in an attempt to ease the taut strings in the atmosphere.

"Good work," Stewart said.

Michael Shiner's eyes betrayed a flicker of emotion then. He relaxed, slowly.

Stewart asked, "Do you have anything else to say to Miss Shaw?" He nodded briefly at Jane.

"No, sir," Michael Shiner replied. He began to back away, one step, then another.

"And if I'd been a redcoat?" Stewart asked, when he thought the worst of the danger had passed.

With no change of expression, Michael Shiner replied, "That would be up to Missy Shaw."

Stewart quirked a brow. "You're honest, in all events."

"Yassir," he said, melting deeper into the shadows.

Jane looked at her large, mysterious friend. "Thank you, Michael."

Michael Shiner lowered his lids, then raised them to acknowledge her thanks.

When Michael Shiner was one with the shadows, Stewart turned to Jane. He demanded, "And the message?"

Jane drew a deep breath. "It concerned you."

"So I had supposed. Was it interesting?"

"Very."

Suddenly, he felt that the brief, strange incident with Michael Shiner had made his background as real and as present as the cloud of desire that vaporized so quickly between them. "Does it concern my family?" he asked.

"Yes."

He was still a little puzzled by her attitude. "You seem displeased by it," he said. "My family background is not usually held against me."

She looked sad. "It made me realize how little I know about you, to have heard so much from my brother," she said, "and not from you."

He had not thought any of that important. In fact, he had grown to like the heightened sense of living with Jane Shaw in the moment, apart from his past. "What would you like to know?" he asked.

Without thinking, she said, "Well, for one, are you married?"

His face darkened.

Her heart stopped.

Chapter Twenty-one

"Does it make any difference?" he demanded coolly.

"Y-yes," she said, her voice faltering, her heart withering from weakness.

"I'm glad to hear it," he said with a slight nod of his head. "And the answer is no. Anything else you want to know?"

Her heart regained a beat. "Nothing I can think of. At the moment, that is."

"You could have assumed I wasn't," he pursued.

"Wasn't what?"

"Married."

"But I *assumed* at first that you were a redcoat," she said, "just as, until recently, I *assumed* that you were an ordinary soldier. Engineer, that is," she amended.

"Which I am," he pointed out. "So give me credit for having told you what is important about myself."

She was not listening closely enough, and she shot back, "But you aren't ordinary!"

He kept his composure at the price of warmth. "What, exactly, did your brother write you about me?" he asked, his voice chilling.

"That you are one of the richest men in all of Georgia."

He paused. "That's true." His green gaze was focused on her in a startling new way. "Are you angry that I did not tell you that myself?"

She had to consider the question. "Not quite," she said, honestly enough, "but it seems unfair, given everything, that I did not know it...before, when you knew so much about me."

"Unfair?" he echoed. "Given everything?"

"Yes, unfair," she insisted. She never cried, but if she had been of that nature, her eyes would have been filling with tears. "You've met my father, you've slept in our barn, you've gutted fish in our kitchen, you've heard my Mamie's stories, and you've eaten off our dishes." She dashed away a sparkle of moisture in her eyes that was not a tear. "You even know the name of my dead lover and the circumstances under which I gave myself to him!"

"And it was unfair that you did not know anything similar about me...before?" he said. "Before what?"

Jane flushed and could not answer.

His face took on a knowing look. "Well, now, what's done is done, and it's too late to undo our lovemaking—which, as I recall, was rather thorough. Or are you of another opinion?" He did not expect her to answer that, and he continued, forcefully, "Since I cannot tell you anything about myself *before*, I can certainly tell all now. What is it you want to know?"

"I don't know! Whatever you want to tell me, I suppose."

"I told you what I wanted."

"And to have left out so much was unfair!"

The look he gave her was hot and hard, but held a trace of the puzzlement he was still feeling. "Many a woman has come to my bed because of my wealth, Jane. Is that what you would have wanted to know? The extent of my wealth?"

She set her chin pugnaciously. "No."

"But surely you can see the advantage. I have only to say my name and where I'm from. It works like a charm. Are you suggesting that I should have wooed you in the same way?"

"Are *you* suggesting that you didn't need to with me?" she replied, not minding her tongue but lashing out blindly in her hurt and humiliation.

"Yes," he said, "and you may take that however you like."

At his bald response, Jane was speechless. This exchange was not going the way she would have expected. He was not embarrassed or apologetic or conciliatory. He was being as harsh and hurtful as she was, and his behavior proved only that she had ignored a fundamental of human nature: people often behaved according to others' expectations. She was expecting the worst from James Stewart, and he was giving it to her.

When she remained silent, James pressed, angrily. "What else do you still desire to know about me? Your brother must have told you that I am a Stewart of the Savannah Trading Company. Do you want to know how many ships the company sails? Or how great the losses have been during the war? Or, even better, how much of the fortune remains in spite of these losses? Do you want to know how many plantations my father owns? How many acres? How many slaves, perhaps?"

Jane had paled. "How many slaves?" she asked quietly.

"Two hundred and thirteen," he said, without hesitation.

"Good God!" she breathed, the number signifying a fair index of his wealth.

"It's a nice life for those that have it," he commented. "Anything else?"

She frowned. "Is that how you know Michael Shiner?"

"No, I met him in Washington, digging trenches, only a few days ago."

Her frown vanished. "So *you* were the one in charge of that operation!"

"I was the one."

"I went into Washington that night to look for Michael, you see," Jane disclosed, "because I felt responsible for having sent him to those trenches. I didn't find him, naturally..."

"The risks you take!" he chided, roughly. "I had sent the men, black and white, toward Bladensburg."

"I know," she said, glumly. "Michael told me. You sent them in the opposite direction from the danger."

"I have my measure of humanity."

She was not going to respond to that. Moisture seemed to have gathered in the corners of the eyes. She was determined that not a drop of it would fall. She choked it back. "Do you have brothers or sisters?"

"Three sisters," he replied, "all younger."

She looked surprised by this.

The smile he favored her with was both charming and hard. "I grew up around women. I like them and know how to please them."

"Your sisters are like you?" she ventured.

"Not one of them ever liked to play in the dirt," he said. "They're southern ladies, none more refined, all married to planters. My youngest sister lives in South Carolina, my middle sister lives in south Georgia, and the husband of my eldest sister oversees the important Savannah properties."

"Not you?"

"I like to build things, remember?"

She remembered. "And your mother?"

He regarded Jane with a fine scrutiny. His eyes rested blatantly on her hair, bundled away in a kerchief. They took in her old clothes, and the bodice sticking immodestly to her breasts. They fell on the bare toes peeping out from under her ragged hem.

He said, "She is the most genteel woman I have ever met."

Jane took it as an insult to her evident lack of gentility. He had not meant it as an insult to her, but he had meant to emphasize the differences. "I see," she said.

"Do you? I wonder."

"What is that supposed to mean?" she challenged.

He was angry, very angry. "That is supposed to mean that I am still puzzled by your attack."

"My attack?"

His brows quirked. "This is not the greeting from you that I expected."

"In your arrogance, you thought I would fall at your feet again?"

With his eyes, he stripped her naked and took her again, right then and there. "In my arrogance, I know when I've satisfied a woman. And, Jane Shaw, you were *mine*."

She gasped in indignation and in a thrill of pure arousal. She stepped forward and brandished her fist in his face. "I was 'fair game' for you once, but I won't be twice!"

He grasped her wrist in a hurting grip and pulled her to him. His eyes were blazing. "I won't apologize for that a second time."

Pressed to his chest, she felt many wild emotions, but fear of what he might do was not among them. "Oh, did you apologize a *first* time yet?"

"So I had thought," he enunciated.

"I missed it."

"You've missed a lot."

She shook her head and stamped a foot. She tried to pull her hand out of his grip, but was unsuccessful. "Let me go," she said through clenched teeth. "Let me go!" she cried a second time, and was released so suddenly that she stumbled back a pace. "That's right! Keeping insulting me! Tell me how much I've missed! Almost everything, in fact! But not by my own stupidity!"

"And what would your knowledge of my background have changed, in your opinion?" he asked. "To repeat the question you asked of me a moment ago."

Jane knew the answer to that. "Everything."

Derision touched his features. "What, you only give yourself to farmers?"

Furious, her hand came up on the instant to slap him, hard. His hand came up quicker and blocked hers. When he had imprisoned that wrist, he caught her other wrist in a rough grip, as well, bringing both hands up between them. They were locked arm to arm, chest to chest, nose to nose.

"I've never raised a hand against a woman," he growled, low, "and I don't intend to start." His glittering green gaze pierced her. "I've never raped one, either."

"You've probably never been that desperate."

There was a fractional gleam of humor in the depths of his eyes. "A handsome admission, that."

"Like Michael Shiner, I'm honest," she said.

He thought she was many things just then, with desirable heading the list. "Then you will admit that I had reason to think you might receive me differently this morning."

"Had it not been for the message."

They had come full circle, or almost. They were not standing apart, as they had at the beginning. They were standing together, in an embrace that was not yet loverlike but could become so with the barest change of mood and the slightest, sweetest provocation. A swamp of moist heat had risen up around them as they stood together, but both were so drenched in other emotions that they were not responding yet, consciously, to each other's body, or to the scent of pleasure.

He relaxed, fractionally, the severity of his grip on her wrists. He turned her hands so that, if she unclenched her fists, her palms would be against his chest. He shifted his weight on his legs and bent more receptively into her curves. He lowered his head toward her cheek so that his lips almost brushed her ear. His eye fell on a damp auburn curl that had escaped her kerchief. It teased him, like a crooked finger, beckoning him to come closer, to touch his lips to the peach of her skin and to taste it.

This sight, her smell and her touch affected him unconsciously, for his conscious mind was intent on discovering what it was that she was holding back from him. He asked, with a real desire to know the answer, "And what did that message change?"

She had nearly given in to him, to the feel of his body so achingly close to hers, the promise of received pleasure, the desire to give it herself. He felt so right that she had to force herself to remember who he was and what her principles were. They seemed flimsy now, and further tattered by his prolonged closeness, but the feelings of damaged pride she had nursed during the past few days had not yet been drowned in the strong tide of her passion.

She looked up into his eyes and said against his lips, "It made me see that this between us—" here she looked down, referring to their intimacy "—has no future."

He nuzzled her chin up again so that she would look at him, so that he could see the desire shining in her dark, lustrous eyes. "An excellent future," he contradicted. "Right now, for instance."

Her eyes, velvet brown pools, did not disguise their desire. But she shook her head, slowly.

"What is it you want?" he asked lazily, moving into her again, causing her to moan slightly.

She allowed her breasts to press into him more fully. "I told you once," she said, with a sultry lift to her brow, "that I want constancy, good faith, and respect."

"All three are yours," he granted on the instant.

"I do not think so."

His lips fell to her neck and tasted her peaches. "Do you doubt me?"

"No. Only the situation."

"Which is?"

"This." She moved slightly away from him.

He looked up quickly and focused on her, his narrowed eyes stained black with desire. She had brought him to the point of great desire and was now pulling away from the precipice. "Are you a tease, Miss Shaw?"

"Not intentionally," she said. "But I'd rather be a tease, in your opinion, than hold myself cheap."

"Is that what this is about?"

She drew farther away. She pulled her hands out of his light grip. She nodded. "Mostly."

"I can afford you," he said. "We've established that."

The desire in her eyes widened to include the sadness that had been there from the beginning. "No," she said. "You cannot."

He knew that the word *marriage* hovered unspoken between them. A distinct part of his body told him to offer marriage on the spot so that it might be instantly satisfied. However, his brain was not yet ready to concede the point, not in this fashion. She had not asked for it, anyway. He had come to her this morning with another plan in mind, and it had not included marriage.

He breathed in, deeply. The rush of air in his lungs cooled his burning senses, but did not quite quell the violence of his passion, or the burning of his anger.

"What are you saying?" he said, as calmly as he was able, though there were rough edges to his tone.

"That we've gone as far as we can go."

"Any particular reason?"

"Because you are the son of a rich Savannah trader, and I am the daughter of a poor Maryland tobacco farmer."

He shook his head. "Not good enough."

"For me, it is. On my terms, it is."

"And your terms are what, exactly?"

She still would not utter the word *marriage*. She would not make herself ridiculous. She would not underscore the disparities in their backgrounds. "No terms," she said. "Let's just say that I know your type as well as you know mine."

He was unpleasantly jolted. "Type?" he repeated.

"I had thought on several occasions that you needed a lesson in manners," she said. "I imagine now that your gentlemanly manners are perfect. It is only my ladylike manners that are lacking." She stood before him, her stance and expression brazen. "And I proved the other morning that your opinion of me wasn't wrong."

He was having difficulty sorting through the strong surges of emotion that were flowing through him. The hot passion he felt for her was being transmuted into something else, but he had never before experienced it, and so could not put a name to it. Nor did he have the words to change the course of this disastrous conversation.

When she took a further step away from him, he saw that he had lost a battle he had not started, one whose territorial boundaries were not very clear to him. He was an engineer, not a military man. He knew how to move earth, not defend it. He built bridges, but he did not know how to repair the delicate span of intimacy that stretched between them, for it followed no rules of the physical world, no rules that he had ever before tested. Something good between them was breaking, and he did not know what it was. He felt something inside of him crumble and fall from damaged foundations. He was disoriented and confused and angry that she should treat him so shallowly. He felt violent and helpless in the face of all this destruction.

She looked over her shoulder, to the lightening of day and the lifting of the fog. She wanted to get away from him quickly. If he continued to look at her that way, she just might reverse her intentions and indulge her most unladylike desires.

"I'm going," she said, turning away.

He had hardly had half a minute to absorb the jolt and the unsettling of his emotions that she had caused. She said she was going, so he must respond. Because the encounter had gone so differently from what he had expected, because he had had so little time to adjust, because he knew the desire coursing through his body would be frustrated, he fell back on familiar patterns of behavior to get him through the rest of it.

He was one of the richest men in all of Georgia, and he could have any woman he wanted. He was not going to beg for her. He could leave her now, without a backward glance. He was good at ending relationships, for he had had much experience with the art, and it would cost him nothing to be a gentleman about it.

"All right, Jane Shaw," he said, "I won't keep you." He smiled, lazily, a little carelessly. "I confess that I've enjoyed you."

She glowered at his charming ease, and he was pleased. He was emboldened to say, "A kiss, then, in parting." He would let her know what she was missing. Before she had a chance to protest, he closed the space between them with two strides, took her in his arms, and kissed her so that she would remember him. He made it fond. He brought it from the heart. He even had it mean something. But he did not lose control.

He broke the kiss and looked down at her. He smiled. "Goodbye, Jane," and kissed her again, on her nose. He released her, turned, and walked off into the woods, disliking himself immensely.

Jane stood immobile for one full minute. When she recovered her senses, she was of a mind to call him back and demand—really *demand*—that *she* be the one to have the satisfaction of leaving! He had done it. He had turned the tables on her, and he had done it so effortlessly!

She was seething.

She might have felt better had she known exactly how angry James Stewart was feeling when he walked off into the woods. Out of the collapsed structure of his birth, breeding, and education, only anger had emerged intact. An anger he had never before felt. An anger he did not yet understand. But it was there, hard and hot, in his gut and chest. Confusion, too. And an abiding, inbred pride. She had touched a nerve. No, she *had* a nerve, the Maryland tobacco farmer's daughter! She had a nerve, to string him along so prettily and then to draw back when he was panting after her! And to throw *his* background in his face! His fortune!

Type? She dared label him a *type?* His father was a type. His brothers-in-law were types. A type would not have left the plantation to become an engineer. A type would not have engaged in the rather quixotic adventure of enlisting in the Forty-fourth to spy on the British. A type would not have appreciated the unusual qualities of a woman like Jane Shaw. A type would have long ago married his Savannah sweetheart.

What was her name? What *was* her name, dammit! Now, *she* was a type, if there ever was one: sweet and dainty and china-doll beautiful. Melanie. That was it. Melanie Archer. The most perfect southern belle to have been born. Ladylike. Properly resistant to all his advances. Until, of course, the moment she had succumbed to his lovemaking. At the proper time. With the proper amount of reluctant passion. But she had bored him. Really bored him. Heartlessly, he had bedded her and abandoned her. He remembered her tears. He remembered his mother's initial shock. He remembered every Savannah matron throwing her eligible daughter in his way. He could have done the same thing to every one of those proper young ladies, and done it with impunity.

It was a nice life for those that had it!

Melanie Archer was properly married now, and he felt deep relief at the thought. He thought back on all his past loves, his affairs with married women, the mistresses he had kept. Lately, he had noticed that he had lost his taste for married women and mistresses. Their passion had become too... too what? Too selfish? No. He realized that it had become too much unlike Jane's. And he hadn't even met her then.

Anger blazed through him like lightning, and a flash of pure possession, too. She was *his,* Jane Shaw, in a way that Melanie Archer had never been.

Melanie Archer. His equivalent of Bobby Harlan.

Through the anger and the confusion and the pride, he had the oddest thoughts about a man named Bobby Harlan. It was the first time he could remember envying a farmer. A dead farmer, no less.

Chapter Twenty-two

What, you only give yourself to farmers?

Jane had turned that phrase upside down and inside out a hundred times, and it still rankled.

Of all the insulting things he had said to her, this was truly the worst. It did not matter that she might have provoked him into uttering something so hateful. It merely proved that she had been right about him, just as he had, ultimately, been right about her. She had proven to be "fair game" and an easy target for his charm and sexuality. And he had proven to be a rich and arrogant southern boy who got what he wanted, with no apologies.

I confess that I've enjoyed you.

Yes! She knew all about rich and arrogant planters' sons. She was not the daughter of a poor tobacco farmer for nothing, and sweet and kind Bobby Harlan had not been her first beau, not by any means! She remembered the one who owned all those beautiful acres outside of Annapolis. He was handsome, but above all, he had liked her. In particular, he had liked her kisses, and he had liked her breasts. She had even liked his kisses and his hands—at first. Thank God she had seen through him before it was too late! He had wanted to marry her so that he could get his hands into her skirts, as well as her blouse. She might have married him, too, if he had not been so full of himself! Blasted rich boy!

So who did James Stewart think he was, except for the richest man in all of Georgia? Just who did he think he was, this man who had seen her naked in her bath, talked to her without her drawers, pinned her to the ground by the tree outside her bedroom window, provoked her into recounting her lovemaking with Bobby Harlan, seen through her night shift to the desire she carried so evidently on her body, kissed her senseless on the street in Washington, saved her virtue in the light of the burning Capitol, made exquisite love to her in her most precious, most private spot in the world, violated her with his eyes in the forest, insulted her violently.... Just who did this James Stewart think he was, anyway? Did he think that, just because his family would be insulated from the financial ruin that would surely follow the collapse of the United States, he could *have* her, just like that? Again and again? At will?

And why did knowing his most hateful qualities not diminish the desire she felt for him?

She decided that she needed to talk to Barbara Johnson.

The next morning, Barbara Johnson surfaced from a deep but unrestful sleep. She had dreamt of death and dying, as she often did, but this time it had not been her own death. Still, she felt unrested. She stirred slightly and moaned. When she flopped a hand above her head to yawn and stretch, she felt him next to her.

She was startled, and gave a tiny cry.

He, too, awakened from a light but restful sleep, and he quickly rolled over to defend himself. When he saw who lay next to him, he relaxed, knowing that he stood in no danger from her. She was beautiful in the morning, too. Beautiful and wise and naked, with a full treasure of gold flowing around her head and spilling across her pillow, her blue eyes blinking back her surprise. She inspired in him a mature passion. It struck him, even, as an elegant passion. Refined. He had certainly never before experienced anything quite this elegant and refined, not even in the most elegant and refined boudoirs of London. He had not experienced as mature or as inspiring a passion with his wife.

Her blue gaze focused in recognition, then shuttered against him. She noticed now, for the first time, in the soft morning light, that his eyes were a quiet, steady gray. She had not regarded him so closely before. She saw the dark hair graying with distinction at the temples. She turned away, to look up at the whitewashed planks of her bedroom ceiling. "It's you," she said.

"Of course, Mrs. Johnson," General Ross said, pulling the sheet that was covering her down below her navel. His eyes swept down her body. "Could it have been anyone else?"

She shook her head, minimally. "No." She was still looking at the ceiling, but she was aware that his eyes were on her. She felt a tightening within her. "I had forgotten, since, when I went to bed, you had not yet arrived."

He placed his hand on her. She did not move a muscle or blink. His hand was warm to her. Her skin was warm to his touch. There was pleasure on both sides, but of a very different kind for each of them. "I arrived after midnight," he said, "when we had done with the plans."

"The plans?" She rolled her eyes, lazily, over to him.

The quiet, steady light left his gray eyes. It was replaced by a gleam, hard and proud. "For today, Mrs. Johnson."

She did not ask for further explanation.

"When we had done last night," he continued, "I came. It was late. You were asleep. I woke you." He paused. His hand moved on her body. "Do you remember?"

She shivered then. That movement, too, was pleasurable to both. For different reasons. She looked at the ceiling again. "I remember you telling me about the plans," she said. "I don't think you told me what time it was, though, when you came."

"I didn't. What else do you remember about last night?"

"That you were angry that I had tried to lock the door."

"I wasn't angry," he said quietly.

"No, not angry. You were . . . dismissive of my efforts."

"They did not work."

She smiled slightly. "That is true. The door is broken, I am afraid."

His hand moved across her breasts to her throat, which he caressed possessively. His hand came back down, rippled over her breasts, stopped at her stomach, which was free of the lines and stresses of childbirth. "I am afraid it is," he agreed. "What else do you remember?"

"Not much. I was tired, only half-awake."

"Really?"

"Really."

"You are lying, Mrs. Johnson." His hand traveled lower, under the sheet.

She shook her head. "I never lie to you."

"Then tell me that you do not remember what we did last night."

She nodded, once. "I remember now."

"Ah," he said. "Now tell me that you did not enjoy what we did last night."

"I did not enjoy what we did last night."

His hand found his goal and felt her reaction. He felt her resistance, too, and knew that she would always resist him. With dignity and pride. He felt his body striving for hers. He knew that pleasure was a complicated experience, and so did not deny her denial. As long as his pleasure was keen and complete, he knew something of her pleasure, and was happy. He was happy, too, with her resistance. He wanted her this way. A woman who was beautiful, resistant, but easy to overpower. A woman who would provide him with what he wanted, when he wanted it. A woman to serve his needs. A woman to inspire his fantasies. A woman with no legal rights. A woman to colonize.

He pulled the sheet away from her and rolled over, half on top of her, pinning her legs with one of his and planting a strong arm on either side of her. He bent over her and said into her ear, "Then you will not enjoy what we are going to do this morning."

She looked at him with a fathomless blue gaze, half avid, half shuttered. "Oh? And what is that?"

He whispered his fantasy into her ear. Her eyes widened. He rolled back, bringing her with him, so that she was lying half-across him.

"No," she said as she tried to pull away.

"Yes," he said, using only a fraction of his strength to keep her next to him.

"You are right," she said, "I won't enjoy it." She shook her head. "I won't do it."

He looked ruthless, then, his handsome features hard and uncompromising. "You don't have a choice, Mrs. Johnson," he said, and began to prove himself right. "And by tonight, every inch of your body, every foot of your land, and every mile from here to Baltimore to Washington, shall be mine."

She gave in, a little. "By tonight?" she prodded.

He had never before found the woman with whom he wanted to indulge his most basic fantasy. "I'll dine in Baltimore tonight, or in hell," he boasted. "Think of me, this afternoon, when I travel down Long Log Lane and cross before the meeting house."

She felt a rich mixture of fear and desire and resistance and resolution. She moved against him, following his orders. "And when will that be?"

"Two-thirty."

She gave in, a little more. "I will think of you."

He nodded. "And know that I am your master."

A September breeze slipped over the sill of the open window, cooling the desperate heat of the room. She looked up and over at the window. She found the sight of the sheer curtain being lifted over the hip of the sill both indecent and tantalizing.

That afternoon, when General Robert Ross had already pulled out from the Shaw Plantation, with the Forty-fourth, in all its well-disciplined glory, behind him, Jane had traveled along the backwaters to the Johnson farm. She was pacing in Barbara Johnson's living room, venting her emotions on a rather amused audience of one.

"And what, Barbara, do you find so funny?" Jane demanded at one point in her energetic tirade.

"Do you see me laughing, my dear?" Barbara asked, mildly surprised.

"You are not laughing," Jane conceded. "In fact, I have never seen you laugh. And, if I may interject at this point, you would feel better if you *did* laugh at some time in your life!"

Barbara Johnson was seated in a rocking chair, her hands folded calmly in her lap. She smiled placidly. "You may interject anything you like. It is your discourse, after all. If you have never seen me laugh, that is because, my dear Jane, I have never had anything to laugh about in my life. But, as for my reactions to your very charming observations on a remarkably interesting young man, I find them rather more entertaining than laughable."

Jane glowered. "A remarkably interesting young man?"

"Well, what would *you* call him, my dear?"

Jane opened her mouth, then closed it. "The precise words are not fit to be uttered."

Barbara said with a perfectly straight face, "Oh, you're having a belated attack of ladylike manners?"

Jane rounded on her and drew a sharp, angry breath. When she saw Barbara's too-composed face, the wind sputtered out of her mouth. "That's right! Tease me!" She struck a dramatic pose of woe and ill use. "James Stewart insults me! Barbara Johnson teases me! And *she* is supposed to be my friend!"

Barbara bit her lip, then held up a finger as if trying to balance a precise point. "But, now, I thought that it was your unladylike— How shall I say? Passion? Passion, then—that prompted you to assume that he would judge you as a wanton woman, unfit for a fine southern gentleman who has the audacity to be one of the richest men in Georgia. Which is why I mentioned that your concern for ladylike behavior was belated." She refined her point. "Assuming, of course, that you care for his opinion, which you quite strongly claim you do not!"

Jane was not about to defend herself from this gross misrepresentation of everything she had said. She shot back, hotly, "Well, if *you* like him so much, *you* can have him!"

"I admit that he is a little young for me. However..." Barbara mused thoughtfully.

"And what difference should that make to him?" Jane wondered. "He is out to seduce any woman he can get!"

"You cannot raise *all* of our hopes, Jane," Barbara reprimanded, "for that would be irresponsible. My age may make no difference to him, and why should it? He does not seem to have as many prejudices as you may think."

Jane snorted.

"It's just that I have rather a taste for older gentlemen, I think. Ones with a touch of maturity. Some life experience." She paused. "Call it a quirk."

Jane looked at her friend. "For instance?"

"Well, no one in particular, my dear. It's just a fantasy, I suppose."

"If you're thinking of General Ross..." Jane began.

"I do not think of him, my dear," Barbara said. "Or, rather, I should be thinking of him—" She broke off. "What time do you suppose it to be?"

Jane looked out the window at the blazing sun. "About three o'clock, at a guess. Maybe three-thirty."

"So late?" Barbara said lightly. "Then I should be thinking of him now." She closed her eyes. Unbidden, and to her complete surprise, a vivid, bloody picture flashed through her brain. A strange clattering of emotions rang down her spine. She drew a long, slow breath. She opened her eyes, looking grave and slightly transformed. "There," she said, with a touch of amazement, even relief. "It is over. Now back to your story."

"It is not a story."

"It most certainly is, and I am wondering how you plan to get him back."

"I don't plan to get him back!" Jane protested indignantly.

"Remind me what he did to insult you so. I am not sure that I grasped the nuances in your account, although I think it had something to do with him being indecently rich and making mad, passionate love to you—without you knowing it. Without you knowing that he is indecently rich, that is."

Jane flushed. "I did not say mad, passionate love," she said, a little feebly.

Barbara cocked her head. "True, and now that I think of it, you did not say anything about the nature of the experience you two shared the other morning at water's edge. No doubt *there* lies the problem. Your James Stewart is perhaps not a considerate lover?"

Jane flushed deeper. "No, it's not— That is, he is... I felt— Don't you see that—?" She stopped.

Barbara nodded appreciatively. "I do see, my dear, and lucky you," she murmured. "Now, tell me. How do you propose to get him back?"

Jane opened her mouth to utter some further foolishness, but just then Ben Skinner could be heard yelling in the yard.

"Widow Johnson! Widow Johnson!" came the old farmer's wheezing voice. "It's the news you were waiting for!"

The two women left the sitting room for the front porch, where they encountered the gaunt, wizened farmer, who was puffing badly from having ridden in haste from the meeting house to the Johnson farm. He doffed his old straw hat.

"He's dead! Shot!" Ben Skinner announced, almost overcome by the heat, the excitement, and the phlegm choking him. "Thanks to you!"

Barbara put her hand on Jane's arm to steady herself. Jane hardly noticed, for she was absorbed by the news. "Who's dead, Mr. Skinner?" Jane asked.

"General Ross!" he said gleefully, then coughed, deep in his throat. He withdrew the red rag from the back packet of his overalls and coughed again, disgustingly, into the cloth.

Jane gasped in horror, in happiness. General Ross dead? General Ross dead! With great concern, she turned to Barbara and did not mistake the meaning of her friend's pale face. She said, quietly, "Barbara?"

Barbara's hand was still posed, lightly, on Jane's arm. She was steady, though her face was white. "You see, Jane," she said, looking directly at her, "I did not lose my resolve."

Jane turned to the farmer for details, "How did it happen?"

Ben Skinner nodded. "It's to the widow Johnson's credit," he said. "We all knew at the meeting house that the general had taken a liking to Mrs. Johnson, and was planning on bothering her in a way that wouldn't be right for a man to bother an unprotected woman. But Mrs. Johnson here—" Ben Skinner nodded to the statuesque figure standing immobile next to Jane "—assured us men that we did not have to defend her honor—yet! Which was a relief, I can say! So when she told us this morning—before noon, it was—that she had heard the general would pass by the meeting house at two-thirty this afternoon on his way to Baltimore, why, we called up some of the sharpshooters on the North Point, and one of them did the job! Picked him right off!"

"Were a lot of redcoats killed?" Jane asked, glancing every now and then at Barbara Johnson's blank face.

"No, just the general! He was riding out in front. A bullet got him in the arm, and then in the chest. He was staggered by the blows and toppled off his horse. Naturally, there was immediate replying fire from the redcoats, harrying our good American men in the bushes. But they got out of there fast! Anyway, I was one of those who were watching the redcoats march by, and so I saw the whole event! But if it wasn't the durnedest thing—the British soldiers marched past the fallen general, without saying a word, pretending not to notice! Of course, the first of the soldiers that reached him pulled him out of the lane and called for the medic. But, otherwise, you would have never known from what anyone said or did that they had just lost their leader!"

"I suppose it would be demoralizing to acknowledge his loss," Jane said.

"No doubt!" was Ben Skinner's considered opinion.

"And then?" Jane prompted.

"And then they covered him with a blanket. Dead!" Ben Skinner pronounced with satisfaction. "I waited awhile to see if anything else was going to happen. But it seemed only that they were looking for a Union Jack to wrap him in. The details didn't interest me, so finally I left to come here and tell you the news! It's the best thing that could have happened, and we may just have turned the corner in this war!''

Barbara Johnson removed her hand from Jane's arm. Her face was perfectly composed, although it was still pale, and her voice was steady. "Thank you for the news, Mr. Skinner," she said.

"No, thank *you*, Widow Johnson! It's an act of heroism and patriotism to have passed that information along so promptly. Well, I guess that I should be thanking Jane Shaw, as well," he said, "for having set up the chain of communication. It's from you, Miss Jane, that the information must have originated, I reckon!"

"Yes," Jane said quickly. "That's right. I heard it last night, when they finalized their plans for the attack on Baltimore."

"Well, then, it's congratulations to you—to the both of you—on a job well done!" Ben Skinner said heartily. "And now I'm wanting to move on. To spread the word, don't you know!"

There were a few more things to say, some parting remarks, general commendations on the cheerful tidings, and finally he was gone.

Jane said, cautiously, "Do you want me to stay with you?"

Barbara shook her head. "You're a resourceful young woman, and you're needed to help get information to Baltimore. Go," she said. "Go home and tell your father the news. You and he together can figure out what to do next."

"I didn't hear a word of their plans last night, you know," Jane said. "I listened all night. I know they were in the dining room, and I know they broke up before midnight. But Ross never uttered a word, out loud, about the details of his plan. How could you have known them?"

Barbara held Jane's eyes. "Well, my dear, do I need to spell it out for you? I've done what I can." She looked away from Jane, into the house. She smiled, serenely. "I wish to lie down. Alone. Thank you, my dear."

Jane left her, and Barbara went to the bed where she had lain not too many hours before with General Robert Ross.

She stretched out, fully clothed, on the bed, and laid one arm above her head, the other across her eyes. The room was warm, with the westering sun streaming in. She was surprised at the amount of grief she felt. She was surprised that the sleeves of the blouse on the arm covering her eyes became damp. She drew her arm away and dabbed at her eyes with her fingers. Her fingers came away wet. With some disbelief, she realized that she had been crying.

She was not crying for General Robert Ross, however. Nor was she crying over the extraordinary love and passion that could have existed between them under other circumstances, in another time and place. She was crying for the little girl inside her, whose brothers all had died, whose mother had died, whose father had finally died from the weight of his unbearable grief. She was crying for the little girl who had grown up to marry a cold man, a widower, Jonas Johnson, who was grieving for his first wife. She was crying for the young woman inside her who had not carried the children she should have conceived. She was crying for the woman she now was, and for the children she did not have. Jonas had entered his second marriage with no children from his first. And it had been Jonas, to whom she had been married, faithfully, for ten years, who was not capable of making children. She was sure of it.

So she cried for herself for the first time in her life, and it felt good, wonderfully good. The sun set, leaving her room warm and comfortable, and still her tears came. Then came laughter. Tentative at first, then welling up inside her. Jane would be proud of her, she thought, and she laughed some more. When the stars came out to sequin the sky, she laughed and cried and felt ancient weights lift off her heart.

Once released of its iron weights, the hard knot that beat under her left breast began to loosen. She felt a kind of wonderment. Her laughter and her tears were slipping in and around that dense knot, catching at its tangles, poking fingers in its snarls, untangling it. The unknotting was frightening at first, because she thought she might die from it. At the same time, it felt glorious, and there was nothing she could do to stop it anyway. So the tears and laughter continued on until the moon was riding high in the sky, and she thought again of General Robert Ross.

She felt a kind of shuddering, delicious, childish happiness to discover that she had not loved him. The reason was simple: She had not been capable of love before his death. She felt capable of love now, for his death had wiped her heart clean. She sent his spirit a silent prayer of thanks, but she added no apologies. She felt too good, too clean, too pure, now, to excuse herself for anything.

At two-thirty in the afternoon, General Robert Ross had ridden out ahead of his men, feeling full and satisfied with love, with life, and with the competent exercise of his profession. Knowing Long Log Lane and the meeting house and every other landmark in the eight remaining miles to Baltimore, he had realized that his advance guard was drawing too far ahead of the light companies. That was not the way it had been done going to Washington from Bladensburg, but he could allow the irregularity.

No, he decided, he could not allow the irregularity. Not even when meeting the insignificant Americans. He reined in his black stallion, intending to return to the first of his advance guard and call a brief halt.

He never completed the action, for just then, gunfire opened up from the woods. In disbelief, he felt a bullet enter his arm. The pain was so pure that he could not feel it. Then he received a bullet in the chest. He felt a magnificent rage, stronger even than the pain exploding around his heart.

He felt himself falling off his horse. He attempted to remain upright, but could not, for the world was tumbling, topsy-turvy, around his head. Or was it his head that was turning around the world? After a black moment, he realized that he was looking up at the sky. He must be lying on the ground on his back. With his good arm, he felt for blood on his chest and arm. It was everywhere, his blood, spilling out of his body.

After another black moment, he was looking into the face of Lieutenant Richards. *Poor boy,* Ross thought, without compassion, *he's in a panic.*

"From what direction did the fire come?" Richards asked, as he pulled his beloved general out of the dirt of the lane. Richards cradled Ross's head with one arm. With the other, he attempted to stanch the flowing wounds.

"From the brush on the right," Ross managed.

"How could anyone have known our course today?" Richards demanded, indignation electrifying every nerve in his body.

Ross felt the great dimension of betrayal, like a rent in the earth, opening to swallow him. "Could it . . . have been . . . James Stewart?" he ventured, thinking first of that efficient infantryman who had won his affection. The mysterious James Stewart who had, unaccountably, disappeared before Bladensburg, then surfaced briefly in Washington, then disappeared again.

"I will find him, sir, and bring him to account for this— this outrage!" Richards ground out. He looked down, horrified at the suffering he saw on his commanding officer's ashen face. "But could it have been evil luck that anyone would have known the precise time of our march?"

The flash of a more brilliant idea momentarily dazzled Ross's fading senses. He felt a betrayal more immediate than James Stewart's defection. He had a vision of tarnished gold and ancient blue. He felt anger at her for this theft of his life. He felt the strangest emotion turn in on himself. He had little time, and less energy, to find what that emotion might be, but he managed to catch just the hint of a realization that he might have made a fatal mistake.

Ross looked up at Richards, who was looking down at him pitifully. Ross opened his mouth to say something, but it was at that moment that the light of life left his gray eyes.

Chapter Twenty-three

The breezes that blew on the thirteenth of September were cooler and more congenial to the efficient performance of the British-born troops. However, the well-drilled machine that was the invading army had lost its brains, and so there was some consternation among the remaining British leaders about how the operation at Baltimore would go. Admiral Cochrane looked forward to "a second edition of the Bladensburg Races," but Colonel Brooke, who now commanded the beautiful scarlet army, was anything but sure of himself.

Brooke was leaving it to Cochrane to negotiate the shallow, shoaled waters of the Patapsco. He would let Cochrane ring Fort McHenry—that little tinderbox—and choke off Baltimore's lifeline at the jugular. He would let Cochrane's numerous gigs, cutters and barges wipe the smiles off the faces of the sniping, sniveling ruffians who were rejoicing at the death of General Ross. The problem was that Brooke had not been able to penetrate Baltimore by land and had lost three hundred men during his unsuccessful assault that day. He had been halted a good mile to the east of the city by some hastily rigged earthworks. These had withstood assault, and from all reports the citizens of Baltimore had found a renewed fighting spirit.

James Stewart was among the citizens who were rejoicing at the miraculous repulse of the British. The cooler afternoon breezes that wafted around the earthworks reminded him that it was good to be alive. It was a grand surprise to be alive, as well. When the hundreds-strong American garrison assigned to the earthworks to the east of Hampstead Hill had had nothing left to do but trust in luck, their luck had held. They had been pounded the afternoon long with shells and shrapnel, and yet there had been almost no loss of life. They were tired and scared and fighting for their lives—and exceptionally lucky. Suddenly, toward the end of the afternoon, a rooster had appeared from nowhere, mounted the highest crest of the earthworks and begun to crow. The exhausted men in the trenches had laughed and cheered and hailed it as an omen.

Stewart wished only that he might have shared the moment with Jane.

Stewart was on the verge of formulating a thought about her and their relationship when his attention was claimed by reports that the British bombardment of Fort McHenry was going badly. Now that it was clear that the British army was in retreat, a jaunty spirit had seeped into the tired bodies of the Americans defending Hampstead Hill, and great cries could be heard all over the eastern part of the city. The Americans had routed the red uniforms. They wanted now to chase the fancy blue uniforms of the Royal Navy back to their insignificant island across the Atlantic.

One hundred men of the militia were encouraged to volunteer to stay behind at Hampstead Hill in case of another attack by the British. For this task, they were left with a good quantity of rum, and little fear that the British would return. With a cavalier abandon, they assured their departing cohorts that they could hold off the whole of the Forty-fourth—that is, if the redcoats dared to poke their noses in the east end of Baltimore a second time this day.

Stewart lead a group of men to the red-bricked harbor on Baltimore's waterfront. The soft evening light was spreading its wings over the city, and along with it came the relatively good news that Admiral Cochrane's daylong bombardment of Fort McHenry had so far proved futile. In the subsiding daylight, the growing dark sky showed the occasional distant red glare of Cochrane's rockets as they arced and whistled toward the fort.

Although Fort McHenry was two miles from the harbor, Stewart was not surprised to find the waterfront packed with the good citizens of Baltimore. Everyone was there, shoulder to shoulder, fashionably dressed women, neat in bonnets and carrying prim parasols, next to black-visaged sailors, their grimy hair pulled back into pigtails.

Stewart, along with everyone else at the waterfront, knew that there was little point in Cochrane taking Baltimore unless he could lay his hands on the immense wealth of the city. Cochrane—and everyone else—knew that there was no way to take the city without taking Fort McHenry. And unless the fort surrendered, there was no way for Cochrane to take the fort without risking high losses—the sort of losses that might ruin the admiral's brilliant plans for the south, and the even greater wealth of New Orleans.

So Stewart stood with the citizens, rich and poor, who were ready to tear up the cobbles of the waterfront and defend their city with their bare hands should the British penetrate beyond the fort. A chain of communication was established to report on the action around Fort McHenry. Each rocket that went up caused a shudder to go through the citizenry. The boom of return fire from the fort reassured Baltimore that the fort was still holding out. How much longer the punishment could continue, no one knew, but everyone there was prepared to wait as long as necessary.

Then Stewart saw her.

Since she was never very far from his thoughts, he wondered at first if his eyes were playing tricks on him in the twilight. He blinked.

No. No tricks. It was Jane Shaw he saw. She was standing a good two hundred feet away, around the curve of the harbor, on her father's arm. She wore one of her outmoded frocks, and her bonnet had even fewer claims to fashion. A shadowy Michael Shiner stood behind them. They were in a throng, but somehow she stood out from the rest.

Perhaps it was the way she was standing, so proud and comfortable in her body, that made him notice her, and when he did notice her, he was of a mind to get her out of the crowd, quickly, before she started a riot among the men. To his way of seeing her, she looked so infinitely desirable that she might as well have not been wearing clothes—which was, of course, the way he liked best to see her.

He shook his head clear. She was causing no riot. No men were inappropriately accosting her. She was with her father. She was properly dressed. She was still a very desirable woman, any way a man wanted to look at her, but Stewart began to imagine that other men might look at her differently from the way he had become used to seeing her.

How did Michael Shiner see Jane Shaw, for instance? Or Ben Skinner? Or her brother? They could not help but see the pretty face and curvaceous body, but they probably also saw a courageous woman with an impulsive nature, who took ungodly risks, who hated to be wrong, who was generous, who lived her life in the moment, and according to what she thought was right. How had Bobby Harlan seen her?

Stewart blinked again and suddenly saw a warm, loving woman with some faults and many qualities.

He shook his head clear again and tried to make sense of what was between them. He looked away from her to collect his thoughts, and his eye intersected with the regard of a bold beauty near him. This woman was smartly dressed, and wore a pretty bonnet with a bow tied at a coquettish angle under her chin. She was fair and buxom, and if ever a woman was trying to catch the attention of a man, it was she.

How many times had James Stewart received such a look from a woman? A hundred times? A thousand? He had followed through on dozens of such looks, and had initiated many dozens more. At his scrutiny, the beauty shifted her hip, tipped her parasol, and shot him a smoldering come-hither signal from under lowered lashes. He smiled, but shook his head, and shifted his gaze back to Jane.

Across the two hundred yards separating them, he could see, indistinctly, that Jane's face was serious. She was exchanging desultory remarks with her father, but otherwise she was silent and worried and brave and ready to do whatever would be needed of her next to help her country. At one moment, she bent down, fiddled a moment at the hem of her skirt, and then put something into the reticule hanging from her arm. A moment later, she bent down, did the same thing, and then slipped something else into the reticule. Then she stood upright, and her serious face looked a little less serious and a little more relieved.

His Jane had taken off her shoes! Stewart blinked a third time. When his eyes opened and focused on Miss Jane Shaw, he felt some wonderful new structure rise up within him on the old broken foundations. It was a lovely, lacy structure, like a web, delicate and durable. It was love, true and unprejudiced. Transfixed by the realization, he stood, rooted where he was. He did not know how long he stood thus before his wits surfaced and he came back to himself.

With the returning of his senses, he suddenly understood two things. First, he had been wrong, and second, he knew why Jane had so unsettled him the other morning in the forest.

He had been wrong about her. He had *wronged* her. He had thought her a type, an easy type, "fair game." He had wanted her, and in order to have her, he had summed up her worth and treated her accordingly. He had taken unfair advantage of the attraction between them. He had teased her. He had hooked her in every way he knew. He had even saved her virtue in Washington. He had wanted his reward for his efforts and his patience and his rescue, and she had given her love to him generously, with no questions asked.

And then . . . and then . . . and then, when she had discovered who he was, she had summed *him* up. She had the nerve to think that she knew *his* type. She had the nerve to think that he owed her some kind of explanation. She had the nerve to want nothing more to do with him. She had the nerve to be right!

For all his self-evaluation to the contrary, he had behaved toward her, not as a man behaved toward a woman he had grown to love, but according to type. The type he had been with Melanie Archer. The type he had thought he had left behind in Savannah. The type who behaved as if all women owed him their submission.

But he was not concerned with all women. He was concerned with only one, and in the case of Miss Jane Shaw, she did, in a sense—now that he came to think of it—owe him her submission. For as revelatory as this moment had been, he was not a man to exaggerate his faults or magnify his failings. He had been wrong in his dealings with the desirous, delicious Miss Jane Shaw—but only up to a point.

He came to a decision. A plan of action, really. A simple, honest plan of action. One that could not fail. One that he could implement on the instant. One that he owed her. And himself. It was similar to the one he had had in mind to present to her the other morning in the forest, when he was going to ask her to run off with him. However, this plan had the advantage of being right and good and respectable.

He looked over to the spot where Jane had been standing, and discovered that she was gone. His gaze darted restlessly around the crowd ringing the harbor, but he could see neither her nor her father. Nor even the large figure of Michael Shiner.

Then the whole harbor shook with a roar. Suddenly, the difficulties of finding her increased, given the ensuing pandemonium, and Stewart was lost in a scattering of bodies that impeded his progress toward the other end of the waterfront. Conflicting reports spread through the crowd. The British had destroyed Fort McHenry, and the whole of the British navy would soon be sailing around the point of land protecting Baltimore, which was defended by the fort; no, the great roar had been produced by the Americans, who had let go with everything they had, once the British had become impatient with their long-range shelling and come within firing distance.

Soon enough it was reported that the tremor that shook the harbor had come from the fire of both sides, signaling that the battle had been engaged in earnest. It was now eight o'clock.

At no moment was Stewart particularly concerned about the hostilities in the harbor, except in the tangential consideration that, knowing Jane as he did, he feared she would persuade her father to take her into the heat of the action. Other than that, however, he was not preoccupied with discovering what the British were doing or how the Americans were responding. His entire being was given over to his reunion with Jane, and all his actions were devoted to that end, too.

He proceeded with the enthusiasms of his youngest manhood, when he had thought that nothing could ever go wrong. He would find Jane. He would tell her what he had to tell her. He would take her in his arms. He would kiss her. He would lay her down on the ground....

This plan was not merely right and good. This plan was inspired and *great*. And what, after all, could go wrong now? To be sure, there was a war raging, but the outcome seemed less important to his personal future than setting things right with Jane.

These enthusiasms carried him through the crowds and the confusion, and around the harbor in the direction in which he thought Jane had gone. These enthusiasms carried him on into the night, his energy fueled by the elixir surging through his veins, the elixir of first love, when all was possible and even a fierce naval battle being waged just offshore, with the fate of his country hanging in the balance, did not seem a serious bar to success.

Eight hours later, in densest night, although tired and unsuccessful, Stewart still believed in the inevitable good outcome of his plans—providing, of course, he could *find* Jane first. Along with the crowd on the waterfront, he had followed a path out of the town that would lead to the thumb of land that opposed the tip of the index finger of land occupied by Fort McHenry. It was not so much that

Stewart wished to observe the naval battle firsthand. It was rather that he thought he would find Jane on the spot.

However, he did not. Finding any particular person on that thumb of land, populated by the vigilant citizens of Baltimore, would have been a matter of purest luck. He pressed his luck and searched for her diligently in the crowd for several hours, while keeping one eye on the extraordinary exchange of fire between British ships and Fort McHenry that lit the night sky.

It was transfixing to watch the fuses of great two-hundred-pound bombshells trace fiery arcs across the sky, while the flights of the rockets gave a weirdly festive look to this deadly serious night. In the light from the fire, Stewart saw in the channel below British boats blown in half and blown from the water. He heard balls from the American guns strike the British barges. He heard the shrieks of the wounded. He smelled an improbable American victory, but that sensation might have been due to the enthusiasms still coursing through his body at his discovery of his love for Jane Shaw.

Between three o'clock in the morning and the sunrise at 5:45, the heavens flared red and bloody—and Stewart did not find Jane. However, many British sailors, some badly injured, some unscathed, did swim ashore from their damaged vessels, to the delight of the gathered crowd. Some bodies washed ashore, as well, and although there was general happiness at any British casualties, death is always a grim affair, and the crowd that waited to learn the fate of its nation was not, in truth, bloodthirsty. Besides, there was more satisfaction to be had taunting a live British soldier than shaking a head over a dead one.

Then the sun peeked over the horizon, and the fog tattered enough to expose the outline of Fort McHenry. There could be seen, still flying, the flag of a small, young and not always wise country that had taken a stand against the strongest nation in the world. With an immediate acceptance of the amazing outcome of this night's brave stand,

Stewart saw the fifteen white stars, the eight red stripes and the seven white, fluttering defiantly.

Instead of rejoicing in the miracle of the American victory, he had the inspirational flash of an idea that, with the survival of Fort McHenry and the retiring of the enemy down the Patapsco, Jane would probably already be on her way back home. Other people in the crowd were moving east, scrambling around the coast, following the retreat of Admiral Cochrane and the enemy. He knew with certainty that Jane would wish to have the pleasure of waving the enemy farewell from North Point.

Fired now with new purpose, and finding no horse to bargain for, Stewart set out to cover the remaining few miles to the Shaw Plantation on foot. Daylight was breaking, helping him to find the way. What he did not know was that daylight was helping the cause of a man he had thought he would never see again.

Dick Lawler was one of the soldiers who had had his ship blown out from under him and made it to shore, ending up not too far from the Bear Creek inlet. After the repulse of the British army at Hampstead Hill, Colonel Brooke had sent half his men north to safety, and had put the other half on transports waiting in the main British anchorage off Old Roads Bay. These transports had gone in an ill-fated attempt to meet Cochrane's fleet. Lawler was one of the lucky ones. He had escaped virtually unharmed and had found the perfect piece of floating wood from the wreckage of the ship to carry him ashore.

Once safe on dry ground, Lawler had moved inland, not knowing quite what else to do, except to try to find the other half of the army, in retreat to the north. With the lightening of day, he got his bearings and reckoned himself not far from North Point. With the dissolution of the pearly Chesapeake fog, he was able to perceive a lone figure making its way through the marshland, perhaps one hundred yards ahead of him. Lawler stepped up the pace. Yes, there was something about the way that figure was moving that gave Lawler the idea of his life.

While Stewart moved through the countryside with the continued energies of love and enthusiasm, Lawler moved behind him, tired and spent, but moving forward with an animal's unthinking desire for revenge. It did not take Lawler too long to figure out where James Stewart, spy or deserter or both, was headed, and Lawler grinned doggedly when he thought of settling the score with both Stewart and the pretty little Jane Shaw. He imagined holding a dagger in his hand, and tasted the satisfaction of sinking it into Stewart's chest. He imagined a different kind of satisfaction when he thought of where he would stab the fleshly dagger in his trousers.

Lawler decided not to trail Stewart too closely, and fell back. Since he knew where Stewart was headed, he need not expose himself to possible discovery. He also wanted to savor this moment of knowing that complete revenge was soon to be his. He nursed all the slights that Stewart had inflicted on his existence. He had never liked the man, his way of talking, his way of walking, so efficient and confident. He had not liked the way Stewart always seemed to outsmart him, whether it was at the table in the dining room or in the kitchens with the black giantess or in the army camp.

If he had been a man capable of expressing his thoughts in words, Lawler would have said that he did not like Stewart's calm assumption of superiority, his breeding, his refinement, his confidence, his contempt for brutish men. By all rights, Stewart should have been cowering and running to Lawler's bidding. That was how Lawler measured men, by the respect they owed him due to his size and strength. Stewart had never respected Lawler, and Lawler hated him for it.

Then an even brighter idea lit Lawler's dull brain. He realized that he would be a hero if he could truss Stewart up and take him, alive, to Lieutenant Richards. New thoughts began to churn. He would hold off stabbing the little man. Better that Stewart be taken alive and delivered to Richards for a proper execution. Better that Stewart be alive, to witness Lawler's possession of his little American piece. Better that Stewart be alive, so that Lawler could scorn him, the way Stewart had always scorned Lawler.

Much better.

These thoughts kept him on the trail to the Shaw Plantation. As the sun rose to kiss an earth rendered more comfortable by the cooler westerly late-summer breezes, Lawler kept to his purpose. Still, he was sweating with the effort of crossing this land, tired from the battle the day before, but fired by thoughts of revenge and heroism. He imagined curling his large hands around Stewart's neck. Then, upon consideration, he decided he would confront Stewart with a weapon—not that he would not be able to subdue the lighter man with sheer force. Nevertheless, Lawler hoped Stewart's path would take them by the Shaw barn, so that Lawler could slip in and look for a pick or a hoe or some kind of a knife.

Lawler's best weapon, of course, was Stewart's complete lack of awareness that anyone was following him. By early morning, Stewart reached the Shaw property, his heart still pumping with steady purpose. He approached the house from the back, skirting the hedged clearing where he had first seen Jane in her bath, making his way around her kitchen garden, then arriving at the tree that stood outside her bedroom window. Only at the moment of thinking he would climb the tree and enter her bedroom did it occur to him to discover whether Jane and her father had returned. To that end, he circled to the front of the house, where he saw both the remains of the ruined porch and the Shaw buggy hitched in the yard. Satisfied, but unwilling to enter the house by so ordinary a means as the front door, he returned to the tree at the back of the house.

Stewart reached his arms up to grasp the lowest branch of the tree, and was about to raise his leg to hoist himself up when he heard, from behind, the words "Now, I have you, Stewart, and you're a dead man."

Stewart dropped his hands, whirled, and kept his balance. He was looking into the twisted, tired, angry face of Dick Lawler, who was standing five feet away, an axe raised over his head.

Chapter Twenty-four

Stewart rapidly adjusted to this unexpected situation. He nodded his head in reference to the axe. "Where did you get that thing?" he asked, surprised but unruffled.

"From the chicken coop," Lawler answered, his voice rough and gruff.

"That's what I thought. You should be careful with it, because the handle looks weak," Stewart commented.

"I'm not as stupid as you think," Lawler growled, taking a step forward. "You want me to look away from you to inspect the handle? What do I care about the handle?"

"That depends on what you intend to do with the axe," Stewart replied. "The handle wouldn't hold for chopping wood, by my reckoning." Unobtrusively, he felt for the dagger that was thrust into his trousers at his waist. At the same time, he stepped away from the tree, as Lawler came toward him.

"But I don't want to chop wood with the axe," Lawler said, with an animal grin. "I want to hurt you with it. Real bad."

Stewart had guessed that much. His movement out and away from the tree drew Lawler's steps around, so that the two men circled one another for a few paces.

"Not kill me?" Stewart inquired, conversationally, gaining precious time as he mentally worked out his own plan of attack. He continued to circle, so that Lawler was standing under the tree. Stewart wanted his back to the open yard, in the event that all else failed and he needed to run.

"Not yet," Lawler answered. "I'll be delivering you, alive, to Lieutenant Richards. He'll know what to do with you, deserter."

"I never deserted, because I never was in the British army," Stewart explained.

"Then he'll execute you for being a spy, and for the death of General Ross."

"I see," Stewart said. "You wish merely to capture me now, is that it?"

Lawler had liked Stewart little enough when he had thought him British; he liked him far less as an American. A superior, upstart American. With a little more provocation, he would be happy to chop the superior, upstart American in half, Lieutenant Richards be damned.

"Don't push it, Stewart," Lawler warned.

Stewart shrugged. "No? I'd like to know what you think I have to lose by pushing it."

Stewart's comment seemed too complicated for Lawler to sort through. It confused him, and his brain was tired. The axe felt heavy and wobbly in his hands. "Your head," Lawler said.

Stewart laughed a little, derisively. "You'll never be able to chop my head off with that thing," he said. "And why should I let you, anyway?"

Stewart had calculated his scorn. He knew to a nicety just how much his calm superiority grated on Lawler. The bigger, beefier man's judgments were muddling, along with his ability to act and react, and the axe was drooping in his arms. However, just when Stewart thought he had things well in hand, he became aware of a new danger in the situation.

"You won't have a choice," Lawler returned, with some of his old swagger. He raised the axe threateningly, although his gesture wavered.

Stewart did not dare look up, but out of the corner of his eye, he was aware that Jane was shinnying across a branch over Lawler's head. She must have been in her bedroom and heard them talking. He had no idea what Jane intended to do, but he imagined that it would be unutterably risky. He felt a trickle of real fear skim down his back.

"I would tell you to look up now and watch out, Lawler," Stewart said calmly, hoping to convince Jane that she should stay out of this, "but I don't think you'll do it." And in so saying, he whipped his dagger out of his trousers and prepared to go on the attack.

He was too late to prevent Jane from seriously endangering herself. She had positioned herself perfectly over Lawler's head, and he knew she would not think twice about dropping down from the tree and onto Lawler's head. Stewart saw Jane's movement and, at the same time, saw Lawler raise the axe ominously. Stewart lunged forward with his knife in order to draw Lawler into combat. Fortunately, Lawler lowered the axe to run at Stewart at the moment that Jane's body tumbled around his shoulders. Her skirts fell over his head, blocking his vision and confusing his senses. They fell together on the ground in a heap, with Jane's upper body on top of him, as if she were seated on his shoulders, and her legs pinned beneath his chest.

"Good God, Jane!" Stewart called, coming forward and attempting to pull Jane off Lawler.

Jane resisted. "No, I've got him now!" she cried, batting his hands away. "Don't spoil it!"

"Don't spoil it?" Stewart echoed. He pulled on her arms, without effect. "Good God, you could have really, *really* hurt yourself! Didn't you see the axe?"

"Of course I saw the axe!" she retorted hotly, seated upon Lawler's shoulders, still resisting Stewart's attempts to pull her off. "That's why I jumped on him. To save you!" She looked up at her love, fiercely. She saw him looking down at her, every bit as fiercely, his eyes snapping green fire. She felt a bolt of emotion course through her, but she was not about to submit to that emotion—yet. She said, angrily, "You might say 'Thank you, Miss Shaw'."

"And I might strangle you for your stupidity," Stewart returned hotly. "I was more than able to take care of myself!" He was angry now, too, really angry that she had taken such a foolish, *foolish* risk. He gestured with the dagger in his hand. "I had *this!*"

"A dagger against an *axe?*" she said dismissively.

"The axe handle was defective," he said.

"Oh, I know you told *him* that," she said. She nodded down at the 'him.' "But I am no stupider than this lout, and I think I can recognize a diversionary tactic when I hear one."

Lawler's head was still under her skirts. With one hand, Jane was pushing the side of his face in the dirt. With the other, she was leaning into his shoulder, holding him down. Lawler's body was further constrained from moving by Stewart's boot in the middle of his back. Both Jane and Stewart apparently thought the more immediate need was to fight it out between them before deciding what to do with this lump of vanquished redcoat.

"A diversionary tactic, Miss Shaw?" Stewart repeated. He laughed, without humor. "What I said happened to have the ironic merit of being true. After all, the axe is one of your father's fine tools."

"And what is that supposed to mean, Mr. Stewart?"

"That he doesn't take good care of his equipment," Stewart returned without hesitation.

"Oh, is this about the management of my father's property?"

"Yes, for if he took better care of his property, then the axe *would* have been in good order and your help *would* have been necessary! As it was, you risked yourself—body and limb—needlessly. *I was able to take care of myself!*"

She was firing up to deliver a crushing retort, when he gestured dramatically at the axe lying on the ground not far from Lawler's hand, where it had fallen. "And, Miss Shaw, if you are having difficulty understanding what I am saying, just *look!*"

Jane did look. She saw an axe head that had fallen from a rotten handle that had broken in two, like a toothpick, with the fall. It was perfect evidence that what he said was true. "Well, he still could have hurt you with it!" she said. "It's an *axe*, after all!"

"Providing he could have touched me with it," he shot back, "for I saw the head wobble once he had raised it. And what's more, it was obvious that he hardly knows how to wield the thing. With the head wobbling the way it was, he was more likely to hurt himself with it, or *you*, falling on it!"

Jane's angry outrage was transmuted into an anger of a very different sort. "I just hate it when you're right!" she said in disgust. "I just *hate* it!"

The first currents of fear and anger had surged through him, and the implications of the realization that she had risked her life for him were beginning to dawn on him. He was looking down at her, and the awe of his love for her was replacing his fear for her and his anger at the risk she had taken. She was unceremoniously plopped atop Dick Lawler, her hair was askew, and her old dress awry. She was barefoot. And he had never seen a woman so desirable.

"I'm not always right, Jane," he said slowly.

Her expression changed at the new note in her love's voice. She glanced away from the axe and up at him. She could not grasp the nuances of the new emotion she felt when their eyes intersected, but the outline of her love and desire for James Stewart was clear to her in the look she read deep in his hazel-green eyes.

"You're not always right?" she asked, breathlessly and in wonderment.

He was smiling down at her, fondly, repentantly, with love. "No," he stated simply. "And that's why I'm here—"

He was interrupted by the blustering voice of Master Jacob Shaw, bounding through the kitchen door and coming around to the tree outside his daughter's bedroom window. "What is all this racket I hear, Jane? And what," he said, his eyes bulging when he took in the complexities of this extraordinary scene, "are you doing here, sir? And *who,* may I ask, is this?"

Jacob Shaw was pointing a blunt finger at the inert figure beneath Jane, whose head was hidden from view by her skirts.

Stewart reached down to help Jane up, and this time she did not resist. A frightened Dick Lawler was revealed.

"I'd thought we'd said goodbye to the redcoats," Master Shaw stated with deep disapproval, still pointing his finger at the man in the dirt, who was making a vague attempt to rise. "In fact," he continued, looking up at Stewart, "my Jane and I returned just now from Baltimore, in order to freshen up before going down to the Point to wave the lot of you a hearty good riddance! So what could you be doing here now?"

"Well, you see, sir, Lawler here threatened me with your axe," Stewart explained, nodding toward the tool lying benignly in the dirt.

"My axe!" Jacob Shaw exclaimed, his thoughts rapidly diverted. "That good axe will cost me two good dollars to replace!"

"It wasn't worth two bits," was Stewart's caustic reply.

"Oh, and what do you know about it?" Shaw challenged.

Stewart's anger had returned. "That you don't take care of you and yours," he said, not mincing words. "The handle hadn't been oiled in years, and it was rotten. The blade was blunt and rusty, suggesting that it had been left out in the rain a few too many times!"

"If you were as shorthanded as I am," Shaw returned irascibly, immediately on the defensive, "you'd sing a different tune—"

Stewart cut him off. "You've taken no care of your axe, or your house—" he gestured toward the peeling paint "—or," he added, coming to the heart of the matter, "your daughter!"

Jacob Shaw's expression had changed comically from incomprehension to surprise to anger. "My daughter? What about my daughter?"

"Only that you've left her unprotected from the desires of any passing man!"

"Oh, and just what do you know about it?" Shaw challenged again, unable to find any other formula to suit the occasion.

"That I'm one of the men you should have been protecting her against!"

Jacob Shaw was understandably taken aback by that admission. He managed, "And so, sir, what are your intentions?"

"Entirely honest, I assure you!"

"I'll have no daughter of mine marry a redcoat," he mumbled.

"We're agreed on that point!" Stewart retorted. "I'm from Savannah."

"From Savannah?" Jacob Shaw echoed, astonished by all these revelations. "From Savannah?" he repeated. He frowned. "James Stewart from Savannah?"

While her father was attempting to discover why the name Stewart, associated with Savannah, should operate so powerfully upon him, Jane was looking rather dreamily at James. "What did you mean by that?" she asked him.

James Stewart looked at her with all the confidence of the richest and most sought-after man in Georgia. "It's clear enough that I want to marry you," he stated, "which is what I should have told you the other morning in the forest."

His Jane waved this irrelevance away. "No, I mean the part about you not being always right," she said.

His expression softened considerably, and he fell in love with her all over again. He smiled, almost in reminiscence. "I was wrong about you from the start—" he began, but he was interrupted a second time.

Mamie had heard the noise below and had descended from her third-floor bedroom. She was swathed in a voluminous white dressing gown, giving her the appearance of a charcoal angel. "Massa James!" she exclaimed, with evident delight, upon seeing her long-lost white son. Her expression transformed to one of lively curiosity upon seeing Dick Lawler, now standing unsteadily on his feet. "And the soldier fella, he here, too. Oh. A brave one, he is. Or a foolish one. What you want, soldier fella?" she addressed Lawler directly. "Another visit from the zombie womans?"

That did it for Dick Lawler. When Jane had first fallen on him from the tree, he had had the brief thought that the zombies had returned. He had understood soon enough that it was Jane Shaw who had felled him, but the entire event was so disorienting that he was having trouble assimilating it. Now with black Mamie's appearance on the scene, Dick Lawler was sure that zombie magic was playing tricks on him again, and he knew a good time to make an exit when it was presented to him.

He looked at the three white people, who had suddenly been reminded of his presence. He began backing away. He held his hands up in front of him as if holding off some threat. Still backing away, he shook his head and said, a little incoherently, "No, no zombies. No zombies. No harm. It was just a little axe. The handle was rotten. I knew that. No zombies. No harm. No zombies. I didn't mean a thing. Not a thing. I don't know who these people are. Or what I am doing here, really. I'm going, though. Maybe I can catch a ship that's leaving. No harm. No zombies."

Then Dick Lawler turned tail and ran as far as he could from the Shaw property. Later that day, he was found, muttering deliriously, by a kindly couple some miles to the north, and was restored to Colonel Brooke's retreating Forty-fourth.

Mamie turned to Master Shaw and said, "Well, now, you wanting breakfast? I got me eggs and bacon," she told him temptingly. She raised a finger to the air and felt the fresh breezes swirling through. "And it's a perfec' morning for biscuits. I declare! A perfec' morning!"

Without another word about Dick Lawler or the circumstances that had brought him and their other visitor to Shaw Plantation this morning, Mamie went to the kitchen, saying, "Now Massa Shaw, you come with me. Missy Jane and Masser James they follow us later. You want you' breakfast now. Oh, I can almost smell those biscuits cooking!"

Before obeying Mamie's orders, Master Shaw eyed Stewart at length. "From Savannah?" he said.

"Yes, sir," Stewart said, moving closer to Jane so that he could put his arm around her.

"And your intentions are honorable?" Master Shaw pursued.

James Stewart drew Jane to him, possessively. He smiled an arrogant smile to indicate that Jacob Shaw would not fare well if he doubted Stewart's word.

Jacob Shaw turned to his daughter. "And you, Jane?" he asked, rather bewildered by this amazing turn of events, but unable to do much beyond entering into the flow of them. "Are you willing to marry him?"

"I don't know," she replied. She glanced up at James, enjoying his nearness and the feeling of contentment she had at his side. Nevertheless, she was not going to make this an easy conquest. "That depends on the admission that he has to make."

"It's a proposal, surely, that he will be making, Jane," her father pointed out.

"First an admission," Stewart said, "then a proposal." His smile of affection in his eyes when he looked down at her subtly deepened into something warmer. "And you really don't have a choice, you know. You'll be accepting my proposal, whether you think you want to or not."

Returning the warm look in his eyes with a sultry one of her own, Jane shook her head slowly. "Tsk, tsk, Mr. Stewart," she said provocatively. "I think your arrogance is incompatible with the humble admission you seem prepared to make."

He turned her so that she faced him. The look on his face was cool and commanding. "I never said it would be a humble admission, Jane," he said, "and remember that I do not count arrogance among my faults."

"And what *do* you count among your faults?" Jane wanted to know.

"Quick prejudice," he answered, "which is counterbalanced by my ability to admit a mistake."

"Which admission I am still waiting for," she said.

He raised his hands to her bodice, which was agape. He drew her toward him, so that they were standing intimately though not yet in an embrace. His hands nestled between her breasts. He bent his head down and said, quietly, suggestively, "This is not quite the setting I had in mind for my admission."

She responded powerfully to his light touch. She placed her hands delicately on his shoulders. She raised her face to tantalize him with the promise of a kiss, the way he was tantalizing her. "And what setting did you have in mind?"

His hands left her bodice to grasp her by the hips. He glanced up the tree and nodded minimally toward her bedroom window.

Jacob Shaw was watching this steamy byplay with a stunned expression on his face when he was summoned by Mamie. He was momentarily torn between calling a halt to this indecent display of physical and verbal affection and responding to the lovely aromas of breakfast emanating from the kitchen. When Mamie called him a second time, he hesitated, then reluctantly left the scene under the tree, looking back over his shoulder only two or three times before entering the house.

Completely absorbed in each other, Jane and James had forgotten about Jacob Shaw. "My bedroom?" she asked lazily.

"Mmm-hmm," he answered, against her lips. He pressed her to his length. "We'll have to be climbing the tree soon— that is, if you don't want me making my admission here, under the tree, in the broad daylight."

Her lips curved up against his, in a smile. "We're going to climb the tree to my bedroom?"

He nodded. "You can't imagine how long I've wanted to climb that thing to your bedroom." His lips left hers to explore her neck.

Her eyes narrowed with passion, and she leaned back slightly to give him more room for his exploration. "How long?" she breathed.

"Since the early morning of the day I saw you in your bath."

Her eyes opened, and she drew away slightly. "*Before* you saw me in the bath? How is that possible?"

He moved closer to her, grasping her tighter. She was all heat and love in his arms. He kissed her with purpose. "Now that I think of it," he said after a moment, "my first sight of you was a young man's fantasy. I was looking up your petticoats as you climbed the tree and slid into your bedroom."

Her eyes widened. She struggled against him. "You're even worse than I thought! Looking up my petticoats? Where were you?"

He nodded back at the bush behind them. "Lurking in the shrubbery." He kissed her again. "Strange to think that from that moment I have wanted you as I've never wanted a woman before."

She was shaking her head. "How is that possible?"

He looked down at her, his eyes stained with desire. "I think it had something to do with seeing the way you moved across the branch, with your legs wrapped around the thick limb."

Her mouth opened. She would have delivered herself of her low opinion of him, if he had not pushed her mouth closed with a firm finger under her chin. "I know. I know," he said, turning her around and propelling her toward the tree. "If we don't get upstairs soon, we'll disgrace ourselves under the tree. Although," he added, "disgracing ourselves here is not a bad idea."

"That was not what I was going to say," Jane said indignantly, as he lifted her so that she could grasp the first branch.

"I am aware of that," he said, climbing up after her "But my interpretation of your outraged expression was fa more interesting, and much more to the point."

They were clambering through the tree now, and they fi nally made it to the branch that stretched itself to Jane' open bedroom window. Jane settled on it and wrapped he legs around it. She bunched up her skirts at her waist an began inching herself forward. James was immediately be hind her.

Jane paused in the middle of the branch and turned t look at him. "I think you're right," she said, feeling the ef fects of the action of sliding along the branch with him jus behind her.

"About what?"

"About your thoughts when you saw me moving across this branch."

James laughed, making his hazel eyes dance green. A mobile brow rose. He reached forward and grasped one o her full breasts. "Of course I am right."

Jane felt a tingle all over her body. "Good Lord, Mr Stewart! Do you want to make me fall?"

"I'd catch you," he said confidently.

"Would you?"

He nodded. "I can provide what you need, Jane."

She continued to look at him. "What I need?" she re peated. She gestured to the branch beneath her, aroun which her legs were wrapped, and to him, so close behin her that heat had sprung up between them. "This?"

He smiled, lovingly. "This, yes," he acknowledged. "Bu I can also provide you what you really want and need."

"Which is?" she asked, a little breathlessly.

"My constancy, good faith, and respect," he said sim ply, smiling still. "That's what's important to you, isn't it?"

She nodded. "And for you?"

"I want your love, affection, and honesty," he said, "bu I think you've given them to me, generously, long since."

She nodded again. They were balanced provocatively or a tree branch some fifteen feet above the ground, making love to each other with their eyes. After that morning in the forest, she had decided that their physical desire for one another had created a barrier to their establishing a deeper emotional attachment. Now she realized that desire was in their relationship the way salt was in the ocean, giving it a taste. Yes, desire with James Stewart was sweet, but it was salty, too, and Jane was glad.

She said the first thing that came into her mind. "You know, James, I won't last a day in respectable company in Savannah."

"Not even an hour," he agreed. "But I don't want to return to Savannah, anyway. I've already applied in Washington to build bridges for the government. I want to go west, and I want you to go with me. As my wife." He paused and said into her ear, tickling her lobe with his tongue, "And this is a *very* dangerous position to be in, my love. If you continue to look at me like this, and we don't get inside—quickly!—I can no longer assure you that I will be able to catch you, if we fall off this branch engaged in an activity *not* designed for tree branches."

Jane scrambled the rest of the way into the room and turned to be enfolded in James's arm when he climbed in after her.

He kissed her and looked at her, inquiringly. "So, Jane? What's your answer?"

She looked at him, mischievously.

"Are you thinking that I am worthy husband material?"

She shook her head slowly. "No, James Stewart, I'm thinking that you're fair game," she said, and put her hands at the fastening of his trousers.

They made it to her bed before tangling together, happily and lustily, while the fresh smells of frying bacon and eggs and the new day curled up and around them, carried in on soft westerly breezes.

* * * * *

AUTHOR'S NOTE

Every effort has been made to portray accurately the major figures and the closing sequence of events in the Second War of Independence, known to history as the War of 1812. However, some liberties have been taken with the details of the British operation at North Point, Maryland, and the characters of Jane Shaw and James Stewart are purely fictional.

New York Times Bestselling Author

Sandra Brown

Tomorrow's Promise

**She cherished the memory
of love but was consumed
by a new passion too
fierce to ignore.**

For Keely Preston, the memory of her husband
Mark has been frozen in time since the day he was
listed as missing in action. And now, twelve years
later, twenty-six men listed as MIA have been
found.

Keely's torn between hope for Mark and despair
for herself. Because now, after all the years of
waiting, she has met another man!

**Don't miss TOMORROW'S PROMISE by
SANDRA BROWN.**

**Available in June wherever Harlequin
books are sold.**